The Complete Tales Most Strange

Jeremy Hayes

This book is for all you people out there that enjoy a wonderfully-weird, tale most strange.

Other Books By Jeremy Hayes

The Stonewood Trilogy

Book I: The Thieves of Stonewood

Book II: The Demon of Stonewood

Book III: The King of Stonewood

Evonne and Vrawg: Bounty Hunters

The Goblin Squad

Tales Most Strange

Even More Tales Most Strange

Northlord Publishing

Visit us at: www.northlordpublishing.com for news about
upcoming releases or to contact the author.

Interior Illustrations by Vince Rae: contents p3,2,9,10,29,47,82,
103,111,186,208,285,302,336,338,360,368,440,490,500,511,558,
564,578
Interior Illustrations by Taramarie Mitravich: 130,318,442,539
Website/Logo: Cody Kotsopoulos www.kotsysdesigns.com

CONTENTS

INTRODUCTION

I decided to combine my books, Tales Most Strange and Even More Tales Most Strange into one giant volume of delightful strangeness. This volume, however, contains three new stories that were not printed in the previous books. The Voiceless in Benshala is a tale of strange fantasy featuring the bounty hunters, Evonne and Vrawg. The bounty-hunting duo are beloved characters that appear in my Stonewood Trilogy as well as in their own spinoff novel. Zed's Traveling Puppet Show and All the Silver in Cloverton are two odd tales similar to the likes that make up the rest of this book.

Another added bonus to this volume are some wonderfully-creepy interior illustrations provided by two amazing artists. Vince Rae is an extremely-talented sixteen-year-old and you can see more of Vince's work on Instragram @preterthings. And Taramarie Mitravich is a graphic designer with an incredible eye for the eerie. You can check out Taramarie at www.tmillustrations.com or @tkmillustrations on Instagram.

For those of you who have read some of my other work, welcome back. And for those of you that are new, I certainly hope you enjoy.

- Jeremy Hayes

THE VAMPIRE PAPERS

Tendrils of lightning reached across the night sky as thunder rattled the shutters of my window. The wind howled like some otherworldly beast and the draft from under my apartment door caused the candles on my desk to dance about, threatening to wink out of existence at any moment. It was a dreadful night, but oddly, the most perfect atmosphere to begin my writing.

I felt that everything I had learned in the past eight years needed to be recorded, so that it may be of some use to others in the future. I know things, intimate details, that should not remain locked in the dark recesses of my mind. Would it not be a sin to hold such knowledge and never share? I thought so.

I only wish that more comprehensive writings had existed and were accessible to me eight years ago, so that I may have made better judgment and also saved myself so much trouble. But alas, everything I had learned, I had to learn myself, the hard way. To study the elusive creatures of the night, I needed to get close to one, befriend one, and that was no easy task. Vampires were not trusting by nature. My quest for knowledge was fraught with dangers that lesser men would shy from.

I first learned of vampires as a young lad from reading old books of folklore. They were mysterious villains, linked to the deaths and disappearances of many, though were seldom seen. The stories had hinted at their existence but provided no solid evidence. When strange things happened it seemed a simple thing to blame it on the doings of a vampire.

Folk feared the night and hung garlic and crosses on their doors, for no other reason than that someone else told them it was a good idea. Reading the stories when I was young frightened me and yet intrigued me all at the same time. I sought more books, more stories, I became obsessed with learning everything I could about these malevolent undead. I needed to know whether the tales were true or not. Did they exist, or were they just creations of our minds used to frighten children and adults alike?

As I got older, my curiosity led me away from the

pages of books and soon I was visiting the sites of these vampiric encounters. I began talking to locals, hearing their accounts and their take on the tales, gathering what information I could. The more people I spoke with, the more I believed these stories to be true. After a year and a half, my laborious investigations eventually led me to, Maximilian Decker.

My unwavering determination was rewarded, though for a time, I questioned whether a reward it truly was, for I saw horrors that no living being should have to bear witness to, and my mind, and even my very soul, still suffer to this day. They say time heals all wounds but those who say it, have never met Maximilian Decker. No, time can do nothing for me now; I shall carry my psychological wounds for eternity and beyond. I have been damaged beyond which there is any hope for repair.

Thunder boomed overhead and drew me out of my internal musings. I dipped my feathered quill into the inkwell and then placed the tip of my writing utensil upon the blank parchment that lay stretched out before me. I began to write.

Are Vampires evil incarnate? Devils born of darkness whose sole purpose in life is the destruction of mankind? To this I say, no. Are they capable of committing horrendous atrocities which any decent person would deem unimaginable? Most assuredly. But Vampires are not spawned in hell, then unknowingly unleashed upon us. They were human once, flesh and blood, born of this world. They lived, they breathed and they possessed a soul at one time. All this and more, I learned from Maximilian Decker.

I leaned back in my chair as I recalled our first

meeting. He was a most charming man, well-spoken and educated. Max could disarm you with a smile and then freeze you in terror with but a stare. His eyes could penetrate; peel away your skin until your very soul lay bare before his scrutiny. Try as you might, there is no secret you could withhold from this man, if he set his mind on extracting it.

I shudder still, when I think back to that night when he discovered my true purpose in seeking him out. Where by sheer force of will, he made me relate to him of my fascination with vampires and my quest to learn all that I could about their kind. He invited me to live with him in his mansion home, so that he might indulge my curiosities and show me things that no man had ever seen and lived to tell, or should ever see.

Max was terrible and kind, concurrently, and his mood could change with a moment's notice. The staff that lived with and served him knew this all too well. They lived their lives, day to day, in a perpetual state of nervousness. For the most part, Max treated them with respect and decency, but woe to those who angered him. Fear kept them from fleeing his home; fear of being brought back for punishment.

While I still walked about on eggshells, Max afforded me no reason to fear him. I was treated differently from all other humans who had dealings with the wealthy lord. Dare I say, he even enjoyed my company. I believe he truly relished the idea of recounting his life to someone for the first time. And I absorbed every word; every tidbit he chose to share with me, for this had been my lifelong dream.

Now, eight years after setting out on my quest, I felt

it was the right time to chronicle all that I had learned. I glanced around my smallish, one-room apartment, which was littered with books featuring stories or accounts of vampires. But these books, every one of them, would pale in comparison with my writings when I finished; mine would eclipse them all. I would expose the falsities contained within those yellowed pages and reveal the frightening truths that were made clear to me during my stay with Max.

I leaned forward again and continued to write.

Maximilian was not born evil; his mother and father had not been demons or devils. He was born into a normal, albeit wealthy family, and from his retelling, lived a most average life. But was he now a monster? Oh yes, indeed so, most undoubtedly. The insights I sought though, were, what made the man into a monster? Did the conversion from life to undeath alone cause madness? Did one lose one's soul after becoming undead? What made the Vampire capable of ghastly acts which would have been repugnant to the same person in life? The first and simplest answer to this, was of course the most basic, and not unique to the undead, hunger; the instinctual need to feed. Humans had been slaughtering animals for food in gruesome ways since the beginning of life itself, and yet we did not label ourselves as evil for doing so. Vampires too, needed to eat to survive; only, they required the blood of humans. Max made the point of stressing to me that he at first did not relish this new life. He was horrified by that which he was required to do in order to survive.

A door slammed shut down the hall giving me a start. My noisy neighbor to the right must have just arrived home for the evening. Nobody would have dared slam doors as such in the home of Maximilian Decker. At times I missed the peaceful silence that shrouded the mansion. Of course there were times when that silence was shattered, the times when Max fed. But for the most part, you could have long uninterrupted moments alone with your thoughts.

For the longest time during my stay, I could not readily adapt to Max's schedule and spent much time alone during the day while the undead master of the house slept. We would talk long into the night until I could no longer keep my eyes open and sleep would claim me. My time alone during the day allowed me to reflect on my nightly conversations with Max, to ponder everything that I had been learning.

Much of the things I had learned about vampires in my books were myths and I had to chuckle at the things which some people believed would keep them safe. When I inquired about their aversion to garlic, Max continued with a tale of his youth, while casually fidgeting with a garlic clove he retrieved from the kitchen. And what of crosses nailed to doors? I had asked him. He did admit to me a weakness to crosses and to many things holy. But a cross nailed to a door did nothing; the item needed to be held by someone of unwavering faith to have an effect. Of wooden stakes, he would not speak.

I shook my head; my thoughts were straying from my task at hand. I again placed quill to paper.

Was hunger alone, enough to make a man into an unconscionable monster? Max did relate to me that he was horrified at first by what his cravings had forced him to do. So then, what changed him? Max's uncomplicated reply to this was mankind. He blamed us. Whether one viewed it as a blessing or a curse, Vampires were immortal and could exist for an eternity. Max was already close to a thousand years old when I had met him. He told me that mankind was capable of far more terrifying things than any Vampire, and the longer he spent with people, he saw them for the monsters that they truly were. He said that I had not lived long enough to completely understand his meanings, but were I to spend hundreds of years among my own kind, I would soon learn the truth of our nature. He claimed that he had not just simply become desensitized to murder, but had eventually developed a love for punishing wicked humans. And a love for it he certainly possessed. Many a night I stood rooted in horror, as I was forced to watch the man feed; carnal pleasure clearly written all over his pale-white face. Max had used certain words when describing the feeling he got as he sunk his fangs into the neck of an unfortunate individual and drank the blood of his victim.

I was attempting to recall his exact description when a knock at my door interrupted my thoughts. The storm still raged outside and I had to wonder if it was the elderly woman who lived to my left, seeking company as storms generally unsettled her.

I didn't need to unlock my door as I never bothered to lock it in the first place. I opened it a crack to peer into the hall. To my surprise, it was the always-noisy neighbor to my right. He had a grubby appearance; his clothes invariably bore holes and stains. The man had an acute fondness for drink and my nostrils were assaulted with the distinct smell of cheap alcohol.

"Might I trouble you for a spare candle or two? It appears I have burnt my last to the very base," he asked with a slight slur to his speech.

"Very well," I replied and motioned him to enter,

closing the door behind him.

"You are writing, I see. Did I interrupt?"

"It is alright, I was momentarily paused, stuck on recalling the proper words to continue."

"What are you writing about? Perhaps I could help."

"Yes, perhaps you could."

His eyes went wide with horror, as I revealed razor-sharp fangs which were now visible as I smiled. I lunged forward with great speed and clamped down on his neck; his oh so warm and inviting neck. I drank his most delicious blood while spilling some onto my clothing and carpet. I devoured every drop until the man was quite dead and then allowed his lifeless body to slump to my dirtied floor.

Ah yes, I thought to myself, those were the words that Max had used to describe his feelings. I sat back down at my desk and continued to write.

WRITER'S BLOCK

I resisted the urge to yank out all of my hair. How could I, me of all people, suffer from writer's block? I have created possibly my greatest work, a thrilling tale that is sure to be loved by all, young and old, but I cannot think of a proper ending.

I was made famous with my classic yarns, *The Turning of Winter*, *The Grand Adventure*, and of course who could forget, *The Bird People*. Sales from my amazing tales bought this gigantic old mansion. This house was to inspire me to new heights in my writing, having such character and history.

Oh, but if these walls could speak, the stories they

would tell. Lavish parties, scandalous meetings, political back-room dealings. But that was in the past. Now all that these walls bore witness to was the tap-tap-tapping of a lonely man on his typewriter. A boring, middle-aged writer, who could not even finish the most fantastic story he had yet written.

How many times had I wrote, then rewrote, then rewrote again, my final chapter, before tearing it out and placing it in a most unpleasant manner into the waste paper basket? Countless! That's how many times. And here I still sit, staring at a blank page, save for the heading, which reads:

Chapter Twenty-Four

Abraham's Return

But what on earth did Abraham return to? The true worth of a good story rested solely on its ending, of this I firmly believed. I built my career on it, in fact. A twist, an unforeseen event, anything the reader did not see coming, left them with a sense of awe and ensured they would talk of the story for years to come. Twenty years after I wrote *The Panhandler's Will*, people still debated and discussed that heart-wrenching conclusion.

It had been nearly ten years, though, since my last great work. For a while there were rumors of my retirement, my demise even, and now, there were not even rumors at all. I was becoming forgotten, no longer in the spotlight.

My latest story, the thrilling adventures of an explorer named Abraham, was destined to be my best yet. Well, if I could only finish this damnable last chapter. Was it a month now, that I had been stuck? Longer? God only knew. Hours turned into days and days into weeks. I do not even recall my last meal. I do not even feel hungry, so consumed am I with finishing this book.

Bah! I stood up in frustration and paced around my small writing room, causing candles to flicker and create dancing shadows on the walls. Rain pelted the large window that dominated the north side of the room, providing a soundtrack for the dancing shadows with a steady rhythm.

It was well after midnight but the exact time I could not tell. The ancient clock that leaned against faded wallpaper had ceased working and I had been too distracted to bother having it repaired. I tended to write throughout the night and sleep throughout the day. I had maintained that pattern for years, living as a night owl. I did my best work while most everyone else was sound asleep. I preferred the mood, the atmosphere if you will, of the night.

I needed a break from Abraham's adventures and decided to place a record on the phonograph. The Dorchestian Orchestra could always chase away my stress and worries, for a short time at the least. I picked up a feathered quill and walked about the room waving my arm around as if I was the conductor leading the band.

Requiring more space for my mock performance, I wandered into the dimly-lit hallway, continuing with my tomfoolery and becoming lost in the music. Down the corridor I went with a skip in my step, passing by several chambers which I had not even entered into for years. My house was quite immense, especially for one lonely writer, with only two women employed as cleaning staff whose chambers rested on the main floor.

A younger version of myself had explored this house at great lengths, looking to unearth any vanished secrets. If there had been any, the house guarded them carefully, holding them in close, not willing to share with its new owner.

Reaching the end of the hall, I whirled about, working my arm in the air frantically as the phonograph spit out a grandiose crescendo. Then it went silent, spoiling my performance.

Most curious, I stalked back to my writing room to investigate this mystery. To my surprise, I found the plug resting on the floor, removed from the socket. I poked my head back out into the hallway but there had been nobody who had come and gone from the room. I had been in the corridor the entire time, albeit a little distracted, but still I would have noticed the presence of another.

I replaced the plug back into its socket when I heard a door slam shut, just nearby. Odd, how could a door slam shut if none on this floor of the house had been open in the first place? I raced back into the hallway with a candle in my hand.

"Hello? Who is there? Greselda? Gertrude? Hello?"

The sound had come from the right and could have been any of the five doors located on that end of the hall. They led to rooms seldom used or visited. Thunder cracked overhead and I wondered if it had been the work of the wind from the nasty storm that continued outside. Some draft from a window, I convinced myself. The cleaning staff did not work at night and would not venture up to this floor at this hour.

Sensing the sun was soon to rise, I decided to retire to

my bedchamber. My brain had overdosed on Abraham and I would continue my quest for a suitable ending later this evening.

As per usual, I slept the entire day through and awoke to a dark chamber, feeling quite refreshed. I quickly changed into my crimson smoking jacket, and foregoing a bite to eat, proceeded directly to my writing room, lighting candles upon arrival. I sat myself down in front of the typewriter and again stared hopelessly at the blank page that awaited my creative genius.

It seemed that it would have to wait awhile longer, as no thoughts came to my idea-depleted mind. As magnificent as the story of Abraham was, it was nothing without an equally astonishing ending.

Minutes became hours and then I stood with a growl, yes an actual growl, akin to an angry dog. I thought to relieve some of my rising stress levels with a little music and turned to my phonograph. Strangely, the record would not spin. I looked to the socket and again found the plug on the floor. The cleaning staff had been told years ago to never enter my writing room, that I would look after its care alone. And they had always obeyed that one and only house rule.

My attention was suddenly drawn to the sound of footsteps from the hall. Good, I thought, now I could speak with the staff and get this matter cleared up. I marched out of my writing room to find the corridor outside empty, devoid of anyone at all. Nobody could have walked that quickly, to reach the stairwell down before my entry into the hall. I had not heard any of the doors open or close.

"Hello? Who is up here?"

This was ridiculous, I thought, and stomped my way downstairs, past the living room, past the library, to find the guest quarters where my staff slept. I was about to knock on Gertrude's door when I stayed my hand. All was quiet and all was dark. It did not appear as either of the two women had been up and about. I decided it was too late to disturb them and most likely they would not be decent.

I sighed and strolled back to my library, particularly admiring the shelves that contained all my works. I was about to pick up *The Unremembered Soldier* when I heard those same footsteps above. I froze in place, listening.

Someone walked from one end of the hallway to the other, then back, as if patrolling.

"See here now! You stand still up there!" I shouted, as I ran with all haste back to the stairs and straight up.

To my surprise, I found the hallway once again to be deserted. This time my skin prickled as I scanned each of the doors to find them all closed. This silliness needed to stop.

Beginning with the first closest door, I opened it wide and stepped into the room, inspecting for occupants. I found the chamber with one lone window to be vacant, so I proceeded to the next room and entered. Also empty.

Two doors down I heard the sound of breaking glass, as if a vase had been thrust towards the floor. Ah ha! Caught you, I thought, and I rushed down the hall and forcibly threw the door open. I did indeed find a broken vase with pieces strewn about the floor. This had been a sitting room at one time and was occupied by several comfortable old chairs. I had decorated the mantle with several knick-knacks that I had acquired over the years.

The particular vase, which now lay in ruin, was a gift long ago from one of my aunts.

Again my skin prickled upon the realization that the room was empty of living beings. The window stood closed and the latch was firmly held in place. No storm, no wind, no thunder from outside. How then did the vase just suddenly fall? And who was the owner of those footsteps I had most assuredly heard and not imagined?

A door slammed shut and I swear I nearly jumped through the roof. If there was a mirror in front of me, I am positive my face would have been visibly paler.

I dashed into the hall to find it empty, of course. That was enough for me. I can admit to feeling thoroughly unnerved and retired to my bedroom. As unsettling as this evening had been, I found sleep came easily enough.

I awoke the next night to find that the vase had been cleaned up. All traces of its existence now gone. My staff had been instructed to leave written messages slid under my bedroom door with any questions or concerns that they might have. This way I would not be disturbed but I could still keep up with the goings-on of my house.

Curiously, I found no messages. I would have thought my staff might inquire about the fate of that vase at the very least. I thought to go downstairs, but again, it was late, perhaps I would leave them a message before I retired.

Instead, I turned on my phonograph and sat down at the typewriter, continuing with my nightly ritual of staring at a blank page. Why? Why? Why, could I not think of a proper ending? Abraham had been gone a long time, so what did he return home to? I was not known for endings where everyone lived happily ever after; it was not my style. So what sinister fate awaited Abraham upon his return?

While pondering that question quite deeply, I heard the sound of someone running up the stairs, loud enough to be heard over the phonograph. I leaped to my feet and ran to the doorway. I found nobody belonging to those footsteps in the hall, so continued on to the stairwell, which was also quite clear of human traffic.

Before I could storm down the stairs, my music ceased playing again. I sprinted with all speed back to my writing room, nearly sliding right past the door on the smooth hardwood floor. I grabbed the door frame to halt my progress. Breathless, I scanned the room for the culprit behind this misdeed. I found the plug removed from the socket but nobody occupied this room but me.

Hairs stood on end as I considered the possibility of spirits, rather than a human suspect, much like my story, *The People of the Attic*. That thought disturbed me and I returned to my bedroom and hid under the covers. I was not tired and I was admittedly frightened, so sleep did not come to me for several, painstakingly-long hours.

The next night when I awoke, I did not go to my writing room, instead I opted to remain in bed. I lay there, as quiet as a field mouse, listening. There were of course the customary "house noises" that all houses were wont to make. But as the hours passed, I heard those footsteps again from out in the hall. I held my breath as they went from one end of the hall to the other, then back again and down the stairs.

As they faded away, I exhaled and trembled. I was in no mood for writing and spent the remainder of the night in bed. Approximately two hours after hearing those first steps, they returned and patrolled the same route. Shortly thereafter, sleep must have claimed me and I awoke the next night.

This time, as I lay there pondering these ghostly events, an idea struck me like a brick to my skull.

"That's it!" I actually spoke aloud, sitting straight up.

The ending of my story came flooding into my mind, as if the dam that had been holding it back all this time had finally collapsed. Ghosts! That was it, ghosts! Abraham returned home to find his house occupied by ghosts.

Forgetting about my own ghostly problems, I flew out of bed and raced to my writing room. Not wishing to waste time with candles, I turned on the lamp that stood next my typewriter and typed away. That last chapter just flowed through me and onto the paper.

I spent several hours perfecting my ending then collapsed back in my chair, mentally exhausted. I did it; I finished my story, my greatest story of all. Just wait 'til my publisher gets ahold of this, I thought, with a childish grin. Satisfied, I went to bed and slept soundly with that same smile displayed on my face.

The moment my eyes opened, I quickly ran to the typewriter to proofread my marvelous conclusion. To my horror, a blank page stared back at me with no words upon it, save for the chapter number and title. In a crazed state, I turned that room upside down in search of the missing chapter. It was nowhere to be found, no trace of it at all.

I was about to go question my cleaning staff, when I sat down and began to type. I figured I had better write it again, while the ending was still fresh in my mind. After a handful of hours, I had finished and was positive it was as close to the version I had written the night before as I could get. This time, I locked the door to my writing room with the only key in the house before going to sleep.

The following night I was awakened by those same ghostly footsteps. I did not move until the patrol was finished and the steps faded back down the stairs. Then, despite the fear that gripped me, I ran to my writing room. I found the door locked just I had left it, so produced the key and proceeded in towards my typewriter.

My heart stopped beating for a moment. Blank! The page in the machine was again, blank! Desperately, I sat down, my fingers tapping away again at the keys, trying to recall exactly what I had written. Sweat dripped from my brow as I typed in a feverish panic. Tap-tap-tap-tap-tap-tap-tap-tap-tap-tap-tap-tap-tap-tap.

When I finished, I was certain that my words had not been exact, my original ideas having become hazy since last night. But I was still satisfied that it was a well-written ending, worthy of the story. Feeling drained, I wrapped my arms around my typewriter and decided to sleep right here, right on top of the machine. Let's see someone try and take my chapter now, I thought, victoriously.

I slept soundly throughout the day and I awoke to find myself in the exact same position I had been in when I fell asleep, draped across my typewriter. I smiled at my cleverness and sat up to inspect my page.

BLANK! The page was blank! I let out a maddening roar. Teary-eyed, I again began typing. Tap-tap-tap-tap-tap-tap-tap-tap-tap-tap-tap-tap-tap.

*   *   *   *

"Now if everyone will just follow me into this room, we can see where Francis did a lot of his writing," the female tour guide said. "There is the exact typewriter that he used. That stack of paper there beside it, is said to be the greatest story that he had ever written, though sadly, he never completed it. It is believed that his frustration at being unable to think of an ending is what drove him to take his own life. The staff that knew him at the time said he was deeply depressed at being afflicted with writer's block. Even today, the security guards that patrol the house, and the cleaning staff that work here, claim that sometimes they can hear music playing from that phonograph, and other nights, they hear the tap-tap-tapping of the typewriter."

THE DESERT OF DISAPPEARANCE

I was drenched in sweat when I awoke. My clothes clung to my body as if I had just stepped out of the shower. I spit out something...dirt? Why was my mouth full of dirt? No wait...sand! I must have been on a beach but how on earth did I get to a beach?

My mind was muddled. I felt disoriented, like the feeling of awakening from a long nap. I had no idea where I was or the time of day but I apparently lay face down in sand with something resting on my back.

A sharp spasm of pain shot through my right side as I sat up into a kneeling position, a cushioned chair sliding off my back. A chair?

In a panic, I looked about. Stretched out in front of me appeared to be miles and miles of sand dunes. My god, I was not on a beach, I was in a desert! Behind me lay the answer to the multitude of questions that had suddenly forced their way into my foggy mind. My heart sank to the most lowest of depths upon viewing the wreckage of the airplane, and then, I remembered.

Many hours ago, the plane had taken off from the Big City; its destination was the far eastern side of the globe. My boss and I were traveling to attend a business conference. I glanced down and noticed I still wore that silly tag on my buttoned shirt, *Hello my name is Julia.* My boss thought it would be a good idea to wear the name tags for when we landed at the airport and met those who would be waiting for our arrival.

I was struck with a sudden pang of sorrow, realizing my boss was most likely dead inside the wreckage of the plane. I never particularly liked him, or enjoyed putting on a fake smile and pretending to laugh at his stupid jokes, but he didn't deserve to die like this.

I realized I must have been ejected from the plane before impact, as I sat several yards from the wreckage, my seat in the sand next to me. I remembered the captain's voice over the speakers ordering everyone back to their seats as the seatbelt signal lit up. I had been returning from the restroom when the first of the turbulence began, sending me into the lap of an elderly gentleman. Under different circumstances he may have welcomed a young woman on his lap, arms draped around him, but the violently shaking plane only sent panic through the several hundred passengers.

I promptly returned to my own seat to find my boss pale and visibly shaken as he was not a fan of flying to begin with. I wasn't quite fond of it myself, though I was less nervous about the whole process than he.

The plane shook for several long, tense minutes, and

then stopped. There was a collective sigh of relief along with some cheering and clapping, but it was short-lived. The plane suddenly dipped and I left my stomach somewhere far above in the clouds. Oxygen masks dropped from a compartment in the ceiling and then I knew this was bad, real bad.

I secured my mask and turned to my boss whose fingers were dug deeply into the armrests of his seat. I smiled weakly, an admittedly poor attempt to downplay the seriousness of our current situation. The plane then rolled and my memories stopped there. Now I sat in the sand, blistering heat beating down upon my golden locks.

A quick inspection of my body miraculously revealed no major injuries. The right side of my body was sore and most likely bruised, but considering the state of the plane, I would gladly accept some bruising. How I survived was beyond my knowledge. I wasn't known for having an abundance of good luck. Though, looking around at my surroundings, I wasn't so sure if this was good luck or not.

We must have crashed somewhere in the Great Desert, since I was aware that our route to the east would have taken us over the vast ocean of sand. The desert was so immense that it was simply unavoidable.

How long had I been lying here unconscious? Was a rescue effort on the way? Would they even be able to find me in the middle of this wasteland? All these questions I could not answer but I hoped for the best.

The heat from the blazing sun was near unbearable but I could find no respite. I dared not enter what was left of the plane to seek shade, fearing its collapse, on top of what I would be certain to find inside.

I stood up to better assess my surroundings and

found I had lost one of my heels at some point, so kicked off the remaining shoe and propped up the seat that lay in the sand. With little else to do, I sat myself down and waited.

It took several long hours before the sun began to set and I felt awash with dread that no sign of rescue had come. I was almost certain that they would cease their efforts with the coming darkness, to renew in the light of the morning. That meant a long lonely night by myself.

With the dark came an uncomfortable chill that I would not have expected to feel within a desert. The sleeves of my shirt were fortunately long, though my legs grew cold as I wore a knee-length skirt. I was certainly not dressed for this drop in temperature. What a horrible place this was! It was too hot during the day and too cold during the night.

Between the biting cold and the despairing thoughts of my current predicament, sleep did not come easily. Try as I might, I managed only a few minutes here and there, nothing significant. The desert was unnervingly silent and the darkness played tricks on my eyes, spotting movement where there must have been none.

As the sun rose in the morning it could do nothing to chase away my foul mood. How long would I have to wait for a rescue to arrive? Surely the demise of our flight would be known by now. My parched throat cried out for a drop of water and if a rescue did not come soon, dehydration would be the end of me. Just my luck, I thought, to survive a plane crash only to die of thirst while waiting to be rescued.

I sat cooking in the baking sun that day and shivered all through the next night. By the following morning, I decided to take a walk around the entire wreckage to see if there was anything thrown from the plane to eat or drink, without having to venture into the nightmare within. My stomach was in pain, requiring nourishment soon.

On the opposite side of the plane I found myself vomiting into the sand. Someone else had been thrown from the plane, much like myself, but they were not whole. Debris was strewn about, but sadly, no food or drink.

Then I spotted something curious up ahead and approached for a closer look. There, in the sand, were footprints leading away from the wreckage into the vast wasteland. Several pairs of feet if I was not mistaken. I mean, I was no tracker, and was not the outdoorsy type, but the prints varied in size. It was most curious. The tracks led away for as far as I could see, disappearing over a distant dune.

There must have been other survivors, I came to realize. They must not have found me, or perhaps thought I was dead. But for some reason, they decided to trek further into the desert. To what purpose? I wondered. Surely a rescue party would be in search of the plane's wreckage, so staying near to the plane made the most sense to me. So why leave it?

Then the thought struck me. What if one of the other survivors was familiar with this part of the world? Maybe an outdoorsman. Or, what if one of the pilots survived? Perhaps they had known our general location before the plane crashed and they knew which direction to travel in order to find civilization. In that case, might it then be wise to follow the tracks?

I wouldn't dare to just venture into the desert, choosing a direction at random. The tales were many of people who had vanished in the Great Desert, never to be seen again, with no trace of them ever found. But I had a visible trail to follow and I would very much like to be in the company of others.

So my mind was made and I quickly took to following the footprints left in the sand. I figured I could always follow them back to the wreckage, if the need arose.

Within an hour, I found myself questioning the wisdom of my decision. The sun began to blister every inch of my exposed skin and the sand burned the bottoms of my feet. I had never in my life felt heat as brutal as this and soon felt dispirited. The desert appeared endless and each dune I passed brought me no closer to those I followed.

Several hours into my trek I was on the verge of collapse, when a sight up ahead gave me hope. With renewed vigor, I ran as quickly as I could in the burning sand towards a large pool of water. I had heard of oases before and counted myself lucky to have found one. Strangely, the quicker I ran, I could not get any closer to the oasis. As I moved closer, it moved farther away.

After an hour of chasing the phantom body of water, I did collapse in despair, realizing it had been a trick of the sun. As the sun disappeared, so too did the elusive oasis.

As chilly as the night was, I welcomed it this time, desperately needing a break from the heat. Though soon enough, I was shivering again. I could not follow the footprints in the dark, so pulled my knees to my chest and attempted to rock myself to sleep. Sleep did not come this night and I cried.

With the arrival of the sun in the morning, my body

resisted my attempts to stand and continue with my quest. I was sore and I was weak but I had to get up and move on. Somehow, I managed to find the strength and as the hours passed, my movements became more sluggish and I stumbled several times. Every direction I looked, water taunted and teased me off in the distance. I cried most of the day but still continued following the trail. The one good thing was that the footprints continued, so the others were still alive and had also made it farther than this. If they could do it then so could I.

As night fell, I was rocking myself to keep warm. I was completely exhausted and severely dehydrated. My stomach had given up complaining about food, thankfully, but I could not last much longer, this I knew. I found myself wondering if rescue parties had discovered the wreckage yet and contemplated turning back. No, it was too far to go back now. My fate would be decided by the footprints that I followed.

I was on the verge of crying again when I noticed something unusual in the blackness of the night. There was some sort of faint light source, emanating from over a distant sand dune. Of course I had to wonder if it was another trick played on my eyes but soon curiosity was winning out. If I risked following this strange light, it was possible I would lose the trail of footprints and find myself hopelessly lost come sun up. But the light could have been coming from a campfire or a city even, so my decision was made.

I forced myself to stand and fumbled about in the dark, making my way towards the dune and the strange source of light. The dune ended up being much farther away than I had anticipated but I drew hope from the fact that the light did get closer, instead of keeping its distance like the oasis had.

I was soon crawling up the sand dune on all fours to peer over the top. My heart skipped a beat and then I exhaled with elation. Before me lay a deep valley and a large bonfire burned somewhere near the center. Around the fire I could make out many dark forms milling about.

Forgetting my exhaustion, I half-stumbled and half-rolled down the opposite side of the dune into the valley, crying out for help with my parched throat. The dark figures stopped moving, frozen in place by my unexpected arrival. As I got closer, my skin prickled and the hairs on my neck rose. I was assaulted by a strange feeling, a feeling of dread. When the figures became visible by the light of the fire, I understood that feeling.

The figures were not human; of this I was most positive. Nor did I think they could have ever been human at one time. They stood like humans but their limbs were spindly and unnaturally elongated, with skin as black as coal. Their heads were bald with no hint of hair, and their eyes milky white, quite large and pupiless. I would have guessed them aliens, from some distant planet, but I got the feeling that this valley was their home; much like the Big City was mine.

Despite their nightmarish appearance, it was their voices that I have to say unnerved me the most. They gibbered to each other with indecipherable words, for gibbering was the best description I could assign.

After gibbering to one another for several moments, they turned on me, grabbing me roughly and forcing me closer to the fire. I was then thrown to the ground beside two others who were most definitely human, with my hands bound behind my back. My inhuman captors then walked away, leaving me alone with the two men, one of which wore the uniform of a pilot.

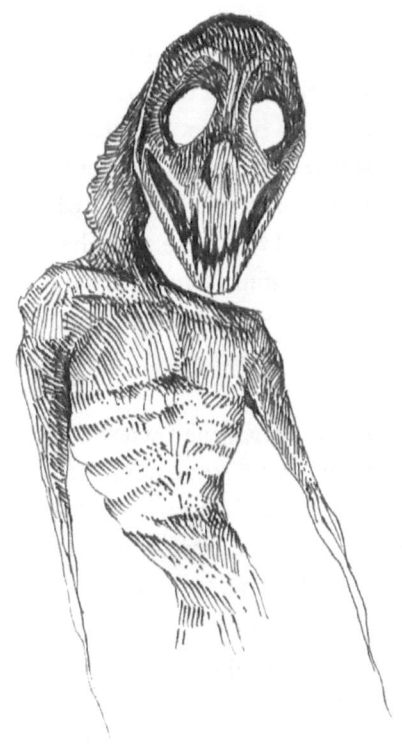

"You survived the plane crash too, huh?" the pilot asked me.

"Yes, I followed your footprints away from the wreckage. My god, what are those things??"

"Your guess is as good as mine," he said. "But I don't think they are friendly, whatever they are."

"You were the pilot of the plane?"

"Co-pilot, yes. I knew that being rescued in this vast

desert was no certain thing, so Winston here, and I, decided to take our chances on finding our way out. That didn't turn out so well, as you can see."

"What are they going to do to us?" I wondered aloud.

Neither man answered, but as it turned out, we didn't have to wait very long to find out. Two of the creatures soon approached, gibbering all the while, and grabbed Winston, hauling him to his feet. He struggled briefly and then was dragged towards the fire. To our shock and horror, he was thrown into the fire and I will never forget those screams. They will haunt me until the end of my days. Dozens of the creatures danced around the fire, whooping with delight.

I yelped out loud as something grabbed my bound hands.

"Sssh, be silent," the co-pilot whispered, as he began sawing at my restraints with something sharp.

"What are you doing?" I asked.

"I have been carrying a piece of metal from the wreckage, hoping to signal any passing planes by reflecting the sun. I think I can cut through these ropes."

And he soon did, freeing my hands.

"Give it to me, now. I will free you," I suggested.

"No point, we both cannot escape. I am going to attract their attention while you attempt to slip away."

"Nonsense! Let's both run, right now. I don't want to be alone again."

"We both cannot escape, they would be on us in no time. No, my dear, I will lead them away from here while you make a break for it. I will not argue with you. One of us needs to get out of here to hopefully tell the world what we have seen."

"I will die in the desert alone."

"Better to die out there, alone, than be burned and possibly eaten here by these things."

He had a good point there, so I nodded. I was about to ask his name, when he rose and ran, screaming for attention as he went. The horrendous creatures whirled about and gave chase. Fortunately, none of them paid me any attention, so taking advantage, I ran in the opposite direction and was soon scrambling up the side of the steep valley wall.

I cried out as something suddenly bit into the back of my right leg. Reaching back, it almost felt like the shaft of an arrow protruding from my skin. I felt warm blood begin to trickle down my leg. With a grunt, I managed to snap off the shaft, then ignored the pain and continued to climb.

I did not stop when I reached the top and I did not even hazard a glance back. I ran blindly into the night and did not stop until the sun had risen the next day. It's amazing what the body can do when fueled by absolute terror. But I eventually collapsed, my tank having run dry.

There was no sign of the valley I left behind and I was again surrounded by an endless sea of sand dunes, for as far as my eyes could see. My leg ached and continued to bleed. This was it, I thought, I could not continue any further. I was going to die here in this spot, or get dragged back to the valley come nightfall.

I gave into despair and lay in the sand, unmoving, until the sun began to set. Before the darkness could envelope the desert completely, I noticed some bobbing lights descending a large dune. I couldn't say for sure if what I saw was real. My eyes could have been deceiving me, or perhaps, it was the strange valley-creatures coming to bring me back.

Were it the latter, there was nothing I could do. I no longer possessed the strength to even sit up. As the bobbing lights drew closer, I thought I heard voices; human voices and not the mad gibbering of those otherworldly nightmares.

"Captain, look!" I heard someone say. "That must be one of the survivors."

"I believe you are right. Radio for the helicopter."

I was soon surrounded by several men in military fatigues. I smiled weakly and then blacked out.

The next time my eyes opened, the scenery had drastically changed. There was no longer a blazing sun overhead and there were no more dunes of sand in every direction I looked. I was in a bed, half sitting, propped up by several pillows. An IV line was attached to my left wrist.

As my eyes finally focused completely, I realized I was inside a hospital room. I could hear two voices speaking just outside in the hallway.

"Dr. Manning, how is our lone survivor doing?"

"She will be fine with plenty of rest and liquids."

"It's just incredible that she managed to survive not only the crash, but days in the desert."

"Incredible indeed. She was suffering from severe sunstroke when she was found and babbled constantly about a valley of dark creatures and that the co-pilot could be found there."

"Did they ever find the co-pilot's body?"

"Strangely, no. All bodies were accounted for except for the co-pilot and another passenger named Winston Bentt. There has been no trace of them at all."

"Well I would say she is quite lucky to walk away from a plane crash, suffering only from sunstroke."

"She was bleeding from an injury when she was found. I removed a foreign body from her leg."

"Debris from the plane?"

"Oddly enough, no. It was not metal, it was stone. And if I didn't know better, I would have said it was some kind of ancient arrowhead."

SCARECROWS

I received the call around noon on Friday. It looked like I would be spending the weekend in the country. Not that it mattered overly much; I do not have a family and had no real plans. Probably would have sat around my one room apartment with a bottle of whiskey, staring aimlessly at the picture tube.

I had nothing else on the go at work either, having successfully closed my last case the previous day. It had been fairly simple, took me all of a week. It's always the jealous husband. Were I to write a book about such things, that would be the shortest chapter. Chapter heading reads, *Murdered Wife*. Chapter text reads, *It's always the jealous husband*. End of chapter.

I had some papers to file away in the office before running home to pack a bag and make a quick corned beef sandwich. I grabbed a coffee from a corner shop and headed off for Bridgeway, an eighty mile drive south of the Big City.

I assumed the local sheriff's department was not used to handling such calls; it was most likely a rarity. Dealing with chicken thieves or the odd break and enter was probably the extent of the crimes in that rural area.

I wasn't sure if my boss gave the call to me because I had nothing else on my plate, or whether he thought I was best suited for the scene I would find there. I had been fairly successful in a few serial killer cases over the years and I had spent one year undercover, within *The Children of Darkness* cult. Boy, I had seen some things there that would give the hardest man goose bumps. Many details had to be left out of my formal report as they had no scientific explanation. I couldn't have my bosses thinking that I had gone mad.

Lord it was a hot summer day. The sun beat down on my car like a magnifying glass held over an ant. I was surrounded by cornfields and there were no trees to provide any shade to this lonely country road. At one point, I was forced to pull over and remove my jacket and loosen my tie. Even with all the windows rolled down, I could not get any relief from the sweltering heat.

Shortly before reaching my wits-end, I saw the police barricade up ahead. I turned down a narrow side road and was motioned to stop by a local deputy. I pulled up beside him and held my badge out the window. "Detective Edward Kane."

He nodded. "Is it just you, sir? Or is anyone else following?"

"Just me."

"You can park your car over there on the right with the others."

For now it was just me. My partner quit only a few

weeks ago. We were investigating a string of grisly murders. In one particular house we found the victim, well, maybe that's better left unsaid. My partner was deeply affected by the scene and quit shortly thereafter. He was a clever fellow but inexperienced. I worked better alone anyways, always had.

I decided to leave my jacket in the car. To hell with formalities, it was too damned hot. I didn't even bother to tighten my tie. My shirt was soaked underneath the straps of my shoulder holster.

I approached a group of grim-faced men that were standing amidst a cornfield and nodded to the sheriff. "Sheriff."

"Detective," he responded with a nod of his own.

The group of officers parted, leaving me with a clear view of the crime scene.

"Nobody has touched him or moved him in any way. We have been waiting for your arrival."

I stood and silently stared at the spectacle before me. When he noticed no reaction on my face, the sheriff spoke again. "I don't know if this kinda thing goes on all the time up there in the Big City, but around here, this just doesn't happen."

While I certainly had seen worse, this was still quite disturbing, and a new one for me. Before me was a middle-aged man with a slightly heavy-set build, tied to a t-shaped wooden post. His arms were stretched out to the side in some grim mockery of a scarecrow. Upon closer inspection I noticed his lips were sewn shut and his eyelids forced open. Straw was stuffed down his shirt and pants. He had probably been dead a day only.

"Do we have an ID?" I asked.

"Tom Willoby," the sheriff replied. "A farmer. Lives about three miles east of here. Good man, no enemies. Wife reported him missing about a week back."

"Why would someone kill him, then drag him out here to display him like this?" a deputy wondered aloud.

"He wasn't killed then dragged here," I answered.

"Huh?"

I got a little closer, squinting at some marks I noticed on the post and also on the man's skin. "I would say he was hung here while alive. See these marks on the post and the ones on his skin? It appears as though he had been struggling here for a time. He was possibly hung here while unconscious and then awoke to this nightmare."

"What killed him?"

"Dehydration would be my initial guess, as I do not see any wounds, aside from a little blood on his head. Probably knocked unconscious from a heavy blow," I figured. "Who found him?"

"Another farmer named Dan Burrows. While Tom does own his own cornfield, this one here belongs to Dan. Found him early this morning and called us immediately."

"I will need to speak with this Dan, then."

"Of course, Detective. He was told to remain on his farm for further questioning."

"You don't suspect this Dan?" I asked.

"He is an older man. Kind ole' fella. Doesn't have a violent bone in his body and certainly wouldn't be strong enough to do this," the sheriff assured me.

"This looks like something satanic, if you ask me. You think this could be a cult's doing?" inquired a deputy.

I thought on that a moment before answering. "Hard to tell at this stage if we are looking for a deranged lone killer or a cult acting together. But I mean to get to the bottom of it."

I followed a trail on the ground which indicated the farmer had been dragged to this spot before being hung on the post. The trail led out to the main road and stopped there. Further investigation of the immediate area revealed no other signs. I spent another hour widening my radius, and when nothing more could be found, I decided to pay a visit to farmer Dan.

I was not aware of any cults that operated in this region, but then, I admittedly was not too familiar with Bridgeway and the surrounding townships. My initial instinct was a lone killer. A dispute over farmland perhaps? An argument in a bar? There were several possible scenarios but I would need to speak with a few people that knew the man first.

I found Dan Burrows standing outside his house, wiping sweat from his brow with a dirty red handkerchief, and then returning it to his back pocket. As the sheriff had described him, Dan was a frail-looking, elderly man. His land looked overgrown and not well-tended at all. Dan had probably gotten too old for the upkeep, and as I soon learned, lived alone with his wife and had nobody around to help.

"So, you don't know anyone that had any recent altercations with Tom, for any reason at all? Anyone that didn't like him?"

Dan scratched the few wisps of white hair left on his otherwise bald head. "No, sir. Tom was a kind soul. Everybody gets along in these here parts."

Had to be about business or land, I figured. "I noticed everyone around here has a cornfield. They are everywhere. I imagine there is a lot of competition then, with selling corn, am I right?"

"No, no, I wouldn't say that. Selling corn to you folk in the Big City is big business. Plenty to go around for everyone."

Dan was ruled out as a suspect and when he offered nothing more of value, I decided to head back to the sheriff's office where Tom's distraught wife and sister were waiting. The two women were a mess and that was even with being spared the details of the crime. They were only told that his body had been found. The sheriff felt they didn't need to know any more at this point.

I got the same stories from them, kind soul, no enemies, no disputes over land. His wife said he had gone out in the evening to put away some tools and never returned. I figured I would visit their place first thing in the morning and take a look around.

It was getting late and I had not eaten anything, aside from that corned beef sandwich several hours ago. I thought to go check-in to a local motel a few blocks away from the sheriff's office, when a deputy called into the station sounding frantic.

"What is it?" I asked curiously, walking over to join a group of officers.

"Grab your coat," the sheriff replied. "Another body has been found, same as the other. Hung like a scarecrow."

I left my car at the station and rode with the sheriff in his squad car, sirens ablaze. We found the second *scarecrow*, approximately two miles away from the first, in a secluded part of a cornfield. The scene was exactly the same, the work of the same killer.

I found it amazing how frightening these fields could

be at night. The moon was high in the sky and the sounds of chirping crickets was nearly deafening. The darkness of the night chased away the heat from the day and I was glad I grabbed my coat before leaving the station.

The gruesome scene before me only added to the already eerie feel of the cornfield. The victim here was younger, possibly in his twenties. Slim athletic build. Not old enough to own his own farm. A farmer's son, or hired help, was my guess.

"Do we know the victim?" I wondered.

"The man who found him says the victim works two farms over. He is not from around here but works the fields for a summer job," a deputy replied.

"Where is this man?"

"Right over here, sir."

Indeed the man, with his dog, stood mere steps away but visibility was non-existent among the tall oppressive corn stalks. One could easily become lost within this living maze.

The man was older, forties, slim build. His dog was a shepherd mix of some sort. "How did you come to find the victim? We are a little far from your farmhouse, aren't we?" I asked.

"Yes, and I seldom make it out this way at all," he replied. "But something had Mindy here all agitated this evening. She kept running from window to window, barking. We couldn't rightly sleep with that racket, so I put on her leash and out we went, to see if I could find what was bothering her. She headed straight for the cornfield, so I grabbed a lantern and let her lead the way. Never seen her behave like this before. She led me right here to this spot. Mister, I ain't never seen a sight like that and I hope I never do again, for as long as I live. I am gonna be havin some nightmares you can bet on that."

"Did you hear anything at all? Did you see anyone in the area? Any cars perhaps, on the road?"

"Nary a thing. There is little traffic in this area after dark. Didn't see no one, didn't hear a thing."

"Thank you."

I walked back to the scarecrow and turned to the sheriff. "Have your men cordon off a large section of this cornfield. We will have to return in the morning to search for clues. It's too dark now, too easy to miss something. I would also like as many people as you can get to do a sweep of these fields. I have a feeling there may be more than just these two that we have found."

The sheriff shook his head in disgust but nodded in agreement.

"And before we head back to the station, we will need to visit the farm where this gentleman worked," I added.

The next day was just as hot as the previous. I sat in my car, which felt no different than an oven at this point, just off the main road and surrounded by cornfields. I was listening to police chatter over a radio. Officers from several of the surrounding townships were spread out and scouring the cornfields in search of more scarecrows.

Our second victim, Bill Clover, had also gone missing several days ago. The farmer he worked for said he was a drifter type, just doing seasonal work. He figured Bill had just decided to quit and leave and didn't think anything of his disappearance.

As with the first victim, Bill was dragged through the cornfield, most likely unconscious at the time. But even with the light of day, I could not follow the path to any particular destination of note and there were no other clues to be found.

I was fairly sure it was someone acting alone and not a cult. Probably someone living on their own, reclusive, even by Bridgeway standards. A large man most likely, strong enough to lift these victims in order to hang them in their macabre poses.

I was just about to pull away and start canvassing the closest farms when I heard over the radio, "We have another scarecrow."

By the end of the day, another was found, bringing our total to four. All men who worked in the fields, all displayed in the exact same way. The sheriff and his men were visibly shaken. They couldn't recall the last murder in Bridgeway and now they had four in the span of a couple days. They were looking to me for guidance and answers but I hadn't yet had anything solid to offer.

I spent the entire next day canvassing farms and speaking with people in town. News in these little towns spread fast and folk were spooked. Many would not readily answer their door to a stranger and I would need to hold my badge up when I could see movement behind curtains.

So far, there had been no signs of struggle in any of the victim's homes. They had to have been attacked outside.

I asked around about any particularly odd folk, someone maybe seldom seen in town. A common name thrown about was, David Borden.

"Gives me the creeps, he does," someone said.

"Don't often see him in town much and I tell you that is still too often for my liking," one store owner told me.

"Never looks you in the eyes, that one. Not right in the head," another said.

The descriptions I received of David, very large man, mid-forties, extremely reclusive. After enjoying a fantastic fried egg sandwich for lunch, I decided to pay David a visit.

I approached his farm which was set about two miles off the main road and I parked in front of a wooden gate. I could have easily unlocked it and drove further onto his property but elected to just climb the fence and continue on foot. I pulled out my revolver from its shoulder holster to double check that all six chambers were full, just in case, and then returned it.

The pathway leading up to the house was overgrown with grass and weeds. It was clear that it was seldom used. Folk did say that David was rarely seen, and in fact, nobody even knew if he had a family out here living with him. Not one person had ever visited his property.

I could see a large house, several sheds, and a barn. The entire property was surrounded by tall cornfields and chickens just wandered around everywhere, going about their business.

As I approached the front door to the house, I noticed its state of disrepair. Shutters hung at odd angles, a few windows were broken and it was desperately in need of a paint job.

I wiped sweat from my forehead and then knocked. When there was no response, I knocked again, more aggressively.

"Hello?" I shouted. "Hello, anyone here? I am Detective Kane, I just want to speak to the owner of the house. Hello?"

Nothing. I tried the door handle and it was locked. I walked the perimeter of the house but could not make out anything beyond the dark curtains that were draped across each of the windows.

I decided to check out the barn and found two horses inside, along with several more chickens. I spotted some fresh blood on the floor, but this was a farm, many farmers killed livestock for food, so I couldn't just jump to any conclusions. For all I knew, it was just animal blood.

Nothing appeared out of the ordinary, though this David was not an organized fellow. Tools were just haphazardly strewn about the property. He had clearly not cut his grass in a very long time and didn't seem to care much for keeping up appearances. While that alone was not enough to make the man guilty of these crimes, I did get a strange feel about the place. I felt I was being watched, though could find no evidence of it.

"Hello? Hello?" I called out a few more times.

I walked back to my car and figured that I would return later this evening. Perhaps David had made one of those rare visits into town this afternoon.

Back at the sheriff's station I learned that a fifth scarecrow had been found by officers. They were clearly on edge, panicked by these frequent discoveries. I got the feeling that if the killer were to be found, he would never make it to trial. These officers were hell-bent on dealing out their own kind of justice. I can't say as though I blame them. We were definitely dealing with a sick mind here and this man was not about to stop anytime soon.

After visiting the fifth crime scene, and finding it just like the previous four, there was no time to return to

David's house. It had gotten too late in the evening, so I went back first thing in the morning.

I parked my car in the same spot and hopped over the fence. Motion caught the corner of my eye as I trudged up the overgrown path. A large man emerged out of the cornfield and lumbered along towards the house. He must have stood about six-foot-four and easily weighed upwards of two-hundred and sixty pounds. He was heavy-set but not muscular, with unkempt brownish hair and a straggly beard. He wore dirty, disheveled clothing, with mud-caked rain boots.

"Hello? David Borden?" I called.

The man stopped and turned, regarding me with cold eyes, but did not answer. I held up my badge.

"I am Detective Kane. I am looking for a David Borden, just want to speak with him. Are you him?"

He slowly nodded, coolly scrutinizing every inch of me.

"Oh good. I have been talking with all the other farmers in the area. You were the next on my list but I must have missed you yesterday. I stopped by in the afternoon but I guess you were not home."

"I was sleeping," he said, looking away.

"Oh, during the middle of the day? I hope I didn't disturb you then?"

"I find it too hot to work in the middle of the day. I work mostly at night. And no, I did not even hear you," he replied in a monotone voice.

"That makes complete sense to me, this sun out here is deadly. And speaking of which, it's already getting uncomfortably warm, may we speak inside?"

"Is this about them scarecrows?" he asked, still

keeping his gaze elsewhere.

"Yes, as a matter of fact, it is."

There was a long moment of silence as he hesitated, I sensed an internal struggle waging inside of him. Then he nodded and proceeded to the house. I felt the hairs on my neck rise, so I adjusted my shoulder holster and followed the giant inside.

My nostrils were immediately assaulted by the smell of mold and sour milk, combined. We had entered into the kitchen and its state of disarray astounded me. The sink overflowed with filthy plates and glassware. Flies buzzed around everywhere, sampling crumbs and scraps of food that littered the countertops and tables. I did my best to maintain a composed face, not wishing to offend with my level of disgust.

"What have you heard about the scarecrows?" I finally asked.

"Just the whispered conversations of folk in the grocery store, is all," he replied, looking everywhere else but at me. He fidgeted with an egg whisker which he had picked up from the counter.

"Have you seen anyone strange in these parts of late? Maybe heard anything out of the ordinary at night?"

He slowly shook his head, no.

"Did you know any of these men at all, the ones that died?"

"Seen them in town from time to time, is all," he said with that same monotone voice.

I paced back and forth within the large kitchen area. I appeared to be deep in thought, thinking of my next question, but I was scanning every inch of the room, looking for something, anything, out of the ordinary.

"Do you keep any scarecrows yourself, out in your fields? The real ones, of course."

"Everybody does, you have to. Them damned crows will eat your crop to the last kernel of corn without them."

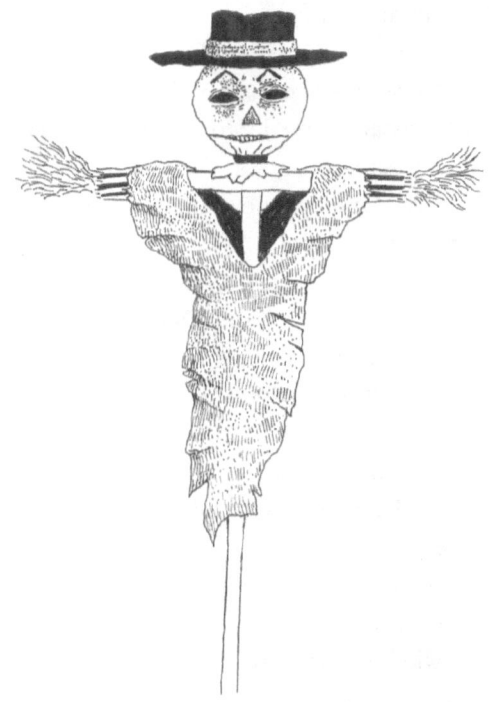

Then I spotted something on a table near a doorway. Several sewing needles with two spools of thin yellow yarn.

"Are you married at all, David?" I inquired. "Live here with your wife, maybe?"

"I am not married. I live alone."

"Parents?"

"My parents are gone. It was their farm, now it's mine."

"No siblings?"

"No."

Looking to the kitchen table I thought I noticed something etched into the top but it was obscured with a dirty plate.

"That's an interesting portrait," I said, diverting David's attention to the other end of the room.

As he glanced over to the wall I shifted the plate aside to reveal the message carved into the table beneath it. *God has forsaken us*, it said.

"That was Granny," he said in reference to the portrait. "She is also gone."

"Ah," I said in response. "Well I appreciate you taking the time to speak with me, David. I need to visit a few other farms this morning, so I won't take up any more of your time. I am sure you must be ready for bed."

David nodded and I excused myself. Before I made it outside he spoke again. "This town is cursed."

"Pardon?" I turned to face him again, and again his eyes were averted.

"The town is cursed," he repeated.

"Cursed? How so?"

"Them witches that were burned so long ago. They cursed the land within this town. God has forsaken Bridgeway. The people are doomed."

"Doomed in what way?"

Nothing further would he say, David stood as silent as a statue, staring off into oblivion. I nodded and left the house, walking back to my car.

Instead of driving back to the sheriff's office, I returned to my motel room and took a nap. I had been keeping late hours the last few nights and it had finally caught up to me. I was asleep the moment my head hit the pillow.

Several hours later, I was studying a map of the surrounding region which I had taped to the wall of my tiny, nondescript room. I began pinning thumbtacks to the map to represent the crime scenes. The five human scarecrows formed a circle around David Borden's farmland. The creepy giant had unnerved me with his demeanor and comments about a curse. So, David liked to work at night, did he? I planned to drop by later this evening to find out what he was up to.

I couldn't tell the sheriff about my suspicions. I couldn't risk him and his men rushing in to make a hasty arrest. He was under a lot of pressure from his superiors to find this killer as quickly as possible and they were all chomping at the bit to grab someone. This required a little more patience. I informed the sheriff I was following up on a lead tonight and to stand by and await my call.

After speaking with my boss over the phone, and assuring him I was getting closer to finding the killer, I got into my car and headed back to David's place. I turned off my headlights a half-mile away and parked about a ten minute walk from the gate to his property. I took a flashlight and a portable radio with me, in case I needed to call the sheriff for backup. Remembering I had one in my trunk, I stuck a flare gun in the back of my belt. Backup wouldn't do me any good if they could not find me.

Stealthily, I climbed the fence and used the full moon to navigate my way around the property. I had gotten a strange feel from this place in broad daylight; it only intensified as I crept about in the darkness. The only sounds were chirping crickets.

I noticed there were lights on within the house and I snuck up to one of the back windows. I could hear faint music playing, with the distinctive scratching and popping sounds of a record player.

I crouched down behind a wheelbarrow and watched as David came out a side door, whistling while he lumbered towards a large shed. He went inside and closed the door behind him. Taking advantage of the situation, I quietly entered his house through that same side door, taking care that it did not slam shut behind me and make any noise.

I found myself in a living room and it was no less disorganized than the kitchen had been. A musty smell hung in the air so thick I could taste it. Dirty dishes and glasses littered the room, and the stained furniture was on the verge of collapse.

My eyes shifted immediately to a message scrawled on the wall, *Where is God now?* Was it written in blood? No, maybe red paint. Must have been paint, it was too bright.

I found a similar message carved into the top of an end table, right next to a lamp. *Death awaits us all, in fields made of corn*, it read. I put down the flashlight and switched on the portable radio, I had seen enough. Static. All I got was static.

That was when I heard it. A blood-curdling scream from somewhere outside. A male voice. I drew my revolver and raced outside, goose bumps forming along the skin of my arms. Frantically, I looked about for the source but could find nobody. The door to the shed where David had entered was wide open. I raised my gun and cautiously approached the dark shed.

Rustling noises behind me caused me to whirl around

with a start. Something was moving in the cornfield, something large. I didn't have time to retrieve my flashlight, so decided to dash headlong into the foreboding maze of cornstalks.

Upon entering, the darkness closed all around me, tightening its eerie grip. I had to rely more on my ears, than I could with my eyes. Something was being dragged through the cornfield, or likely, someone. It was close, so I continued to fumble my way around in pursuit.

"David!" I shouted in the darkness. "David, this is Detective Kane! I need you to stop!"

The rustling sounds continued moving away from me into the depths of the cornfield. I attempted to use the radio one final time but still heard only static. Frustrated, I dropped the radio and followed the sounds, my gun held in front.

The chase lasted a few minutes more before the sounds ceased. I stood completely still, listening for any movement at all. My eyes had somewhat adjusted to the gloom and they darted back and forth, scanning for my target.

A soft moan to my right had me moving again. I burst into a small clearing somewhere within the vast cornfield. A short distance in front me stood a dark figure, its back towards me. It appeared to be tying someone to a t-shaped wooden post. My heart skipped a beat. I caught the killer red-handed.

"David! Turn around slowly with your hands in the air," I commanded.

No reply. He continued with the ropes.

"I will only say this one more time, turn around slowly and keep your hands where I can see them."

Nothing.

BLAM! A perfect shot behind his right knee.

No response.

BLAM! A perfect shot behind his left knee.

No response. Incredible.

"I said turn around! Turn around now!"

Nothing.

BLAM! A perfect shot to his right shoulder.

Then he turned. My god those eyes, those red eyes! Bright red eyes glowed in the darkness. The figure lurched towards me with jerky movements, like a newborn fawn testing out its legs for the first time. As it got closer, I realized it was a scarecrow. A scarecrow??

BLAM! BLAM! Two shots in the chest. It never even slowed.

BLAM! Click…click…click…click…oh damn.

It struck me in the head with a fist that felt like stone. My world went black.

* * * *

I awoke as my head was jostled to and fro. My eyes were open and yet I could not see. I was surrounded by blackness as dark as pitch. What happened? Where was I? Had I been dreaming? Wait…I was moving. I was being dragged. Someone held me by an ankle and was dragging me.

I attempted to lift my head and was rewarded with searing pain. Then I remembered it struck me. But what was *it*? A scarecrow? A real scarecrow with glowing red eyes? Is that what I had really seen?

Whatever it was let go of my leg and I stopped

moving. Clouds suddenly shifted aside and my vision returned with the arrival of moonlight. I propped myself up on an elbow and saw that dark figure in front of me dig a t-shaped post into the ground. I was still within a cornfield and it looked as though I was to be the next scarecrow.

It turned to face me and again those glowing red eyes sent chills down my spine. Something was digging uncomfortably into my back, when I remembered the flare gun.

I pulled the gun free of my belt as the monster walked towards me on unsteady legs. I had only one shot. I steadied my hand and pulled the trigger. My aim was true and the flare struck the scarecrow dead center in the chest. Its body exploded with an inhuman shriek that nothing born of this world could have possibly made. The scarecrow's head, arms, and legs, landed in a heap and caught fire. As the flames consumed what was left of the creature, the red eyes slowly faded and disappeared entirely.

I am not sure how long I sat there, attempting to digest all that I had seen this night, before finally getting to my feet. Was I really to believe that an actual scarecrow was the serial killer here? I know what I saw and it had not been some bizarre dream.

I attempted to orient myself by looking to the stars. I had to find David. I believed he must still be alive, tied to that post as a scarecrow. The man who was my suspect turned out to be the next target. To all appearances he was the craziest individual in this town but he may have actually been the wisest. The land was cursed indeed.

Well, I figured, as I set off, I could not explain this

night to the sheriff or my superiors. My boss would have my badge and recommend me for a psychiatric evaluation. I supposed *The Case of the Bridgeway Scarecrows* would be filed as unsolved.

THROWING VOICES

It is tough trying to make a living in the Big City. Without an education and without knowing the right people, your options are quite limited. The city is very unforgiving.

I am a struggling entertainer, a ventriloquist. For a time I had hit rock bottom and was near penniless. I didn't have the right chemistry with my last dummy and my performances suffered because of it. People were not filling the seats and club owners were becoming less interested in hiring us.

Recently, though, I found a new dummy and started a new act, *Sullivan and Micky*. I didn't mind allowing the dummy's name to be used first; my ego was not inflated enough to worry about such things as that. I was getting more gigs than before and that was all that mattered.

We went everywhere together, Sully and I. Parties, bars, restaurants, hell, even the picture show. People just always expected to see us both. Walking down the street we would get stopped by those that recognized us.

"Hello Sully," they would say.

Or, "Nice to see you, Sully."

The dummy always got the attention; everyone preferred to speak with the dummy. Club owners would even talk business with Sully. I supposed they found it remotely amusing to get the dummy's signature. As long as we made money, they could talk to Sully all they liked.

We lived in a tenth floor room at the Carville Hotel, two blocks from the theater district where we did most of our performances. It was a seedy part of town and the dilapidated hotel left much to be desired, but it was cheap, and we needed cheap.

"We have almost paid the hotel all the money we owe them but that still leaves us with quite a bit of debt. It gives us a roof over our heads, for a little while longer anyways," Sully said to me, as we stood in front of a mirror practicing one of our acts.

"We have three shows booked this week," I replied. "That should get us square with the hotel. We can worry about the others later."

"The others worry me more than the hotel, Micky," he said.

He had a point. We had borrowed money from the wrong sort of people, people who were not very forgiving about owed money and missed payments. Because of that, we were confined most nights to hiding out in the hotel. Our favorite pool hall was off-limits since it was a hangout for many of the gangsters and the malt shop was too close to the pool hall.

Anyhow, that gave us more time in front of the mirror to work on our act. People abhorred a ventriloquist who moved his lips. It was a disappearing art form that needed to be perfect.

A knock came at our door and Sully and I exchanged nervous glances.

"Who is it?" I finally risked asking.

"It's me, Dorothy, come on let me in."

Dorothy was a struggling actress who performed in a play at one of the theater's Sully and I occasionally worked for. She was a decent dame, one hell of a looker, just not so bright.

We unlocked the door and let her in.

"Aww, there's my Sully," even the women all loved the dummy. "Where have you been hiding, huh? I don't see you around the malt shop no more."

"Ah, you know, just working on our act and stuff. Micky and I got three gigs this week," Sully answered.

"Oh, hey Micky. That's good for you guys, I am happy."

"Hey Dorothy," I said.

"Look, me and a couple of other gals are going by Lana's tonight. It's that swanky new joint that opened at Royal Square. Why don't you come with us? I have told my friends about you two, they would love to meet you."

"Not sure we are up for that tonight, baby, but thanks for the offer. I think we are just gonna hang here tonight and work on our act," Sully replied.

Dorothy pouted and then pinched Sully's cheek in a ridiculous gesture. "Don't be such a wet blanket."

"I am serious, we are just not in the mood for crowds tonight, right Micky?"

"What he said," I replied.

"Alright, alright. Well if you change your mind you

know where to find me, ok?"

"Yeah, sure babe," Sully said as he locked the door behind her.

"She likes you," I told him.

Sully laughed.

"I am serious, she really likes you."

"It's you she really likes," Sully countered.

"Oh please, she never talks to me, she always talks to you. It's like I am not even in the room sometimes, unless she wants us to do an act for her."

Sully put on his best smile. "Well, what can I say? The ladies find me charming. I am bushed. Why don't we just turn in early tonight, eh?"

"Sounds good to me," I said. "We gotta be fresh for our show tomorrow night."

The following night, Sully and I sat restlessly in one of the dressing rooms at the Golden Cabana nightclub. On stage, we could hear a barbershop quartet entertaining a sold out crowd. I tapped my leg nervously, as this would be the most people in attendance that we had performed for yet.

"I think we should start with the bus stop bit," Sully said, breaking the silence.

I shook my head. "That is a good closer. We need to open with the grocery store bit that we practiced last night."

"We need to grab this crowd's attention right from the start. Let's go with the bus stop," he insisted.

"We never start with the bus stop. We gotta lead up to that one!" I replied, raising my voice.

"What the hell is going on in here? Who are you arguing with?" asked Denny, the club's owner, who had just entered the room without notice.

"Just working on our act, is all," I replied.

The large man just shook his head. "Look, you are on in ten minutes, just be ready."

As promised, ten minutes later, Denny took the microphone on stage and announced, "Now, for the first time at the Golden Cabana, I present to you, Sullivan and Micky!"

We took to the stage with a deafening round of applause from the audience, who were mostly intoxicated by this point. We bowed to the crowd, then the dummy waved with his goofy grin and we took a seat.

I made the decisions here, not the dummy, so we opened with the grocery store bit to a mixed reaction. Luckily, more people were laughing than sitting silent. We picked up better momentum as we went along and soon we had much of the room in stitches. They were laughing hysterically, pointing their fingers and slapping their knees.

Some people did get up and leave in disgust; apparently our brand of humor did not sit well with their sensitive sensibilities. Oh well, we could not please everyone.

As planned, we closed with the bus stop bit and people could still be heard laughing as we left the stage and returned to the dressing room. Each of us smiled, that was a great performance.

Shortly after, Denny visited the room wearing a perplexed look upon his face. "Are you for real?"

"Pretty good, eh? They loved us," I said.

He stood for a moment in silence, struggling to find the right words to say in response. "Alright, I promised you guys three shows. You be sure you do better for the second show. You hear me?"

"Of course, Denny, you can count on us," I assured him.

He left the room shaking his head.

"I would say the crowd enjoyed themselves, aside from the few who left," Sully said to me.

"I agree. We certainly practiced enough. But you know these club owner types, they expect standing ovations from every single act. We'll show him on Friday."

Friday night came and again it was a sold out crowd at the club. This time we followed a dark-skinned woman who sang with the voice of an angel, Clara was her name. She left the stage with a roar of applause and whistles. The crowd called for her to come back and sing one last song but now it was our turn.

Tonight we opened with a bit about me taking Sully to the doctors for a checkup. This time we received a few chuckles but the majority of the audience was silent. Ok, whew, tough crowd. We moved on to the grocery store bit and now a few people began to get up and walk out. There were even a couple boo's!

We nervously fumbled through the third bit, even messing up the punchline.

"Get off the stage, you bum!" one drunkard shouted from a table near the back of the room.

I decided that we should jump straight into the bus stop bit, seeing as that was probably our best. But it was too late to salvage this performance, the people booed and hissed and we didn't even get to finish the bit before the curtains dropped in front of us. Thank god, I thought, I didn't wish to spend another moment in front of that unruly crowd.

Sully and I sat in silence within in the tiny dressing room, when the door burst open and a red-faced Denny stalked inside. He did not look happy.

"I thought we had an understanding? You were supposed to give a better performance tonight. I am lucky I booked the Four Imbeciles so they can go out there and appease that angry crowd," Denny said, referring to a slapstick comedy team of four brothers.

"I don't know what went wrong, those bits are good bits," Sully then said.

"No, they are not good bits! I thought you were going to try harder tonight?"

"Probably a picky crowd tonight, is all," I added. "We'll do better tomorrow night."

Denny pointed at both of us. "Stop that, alright? Just stop that. We are not on stage here, so I don't want to hear both of you talking to me, gives me the heebie-jeebies, it's creepy. You are not going to be performing tomorrow night."

"What?" I shouted, maybe a little too loud. "You promised us three nights."

Denny shook his head in disgust. "I am not letting you on stage for a Saturday night crowd. I will honor the three nights but lord knows I shouldn't. You can have Monday night, then I don't want to see you again, you hear me?"

He slammed the door so hard the giant mirror behind us nearly fell to the floor and now hung at an odd angle. I couldn't really understand what happened tonight. We used the same bits as the night before and those ones seemed to have gone over well enough. I glanced over to Sully but he just shrugged his shoulders.

We walked home that night in silence, giving the pool hall a wide berth. We went to bed fairly early, considering it was a Friday night. I lay in bed attempting to conjure up some new bits that we could try out for Monday night. We had one last chance to redeem ourselves. If we bombed again, no other club would have us and we would be back in dire straits, yet again.

I managed to think of some funny new bits and Sully and I spent Saturday and Sunday in front of the mirror practicing. We even ignored a message from the front desk that was left by Dorothy, wishing us to join her and some of her friends Saturday night.

"These are pretty funny, Micky," Sully said to me, in reference to the new additions to our act.

"Thank you, Sully. I hope these will bail us out of trouble tomorrow night."

"Yeah, without the money from Denny, we can't pay the hotel what we owe them, let alone the gangsters from the pool hall," he reminded me.

I nodded. I wasn't a godly person but I prayed for luck on Monday night.

Monday night came and Denny was on edge, pacing back and forth behind the stage. Monday was usually the slowest night of the week but it appeared there was even less of a crowd than expected. Denny had not booked Clara or the Four Imbeciles tonight. Tonight there was only two acts and we followed a magician who called himself, The Great Fazoo.

I took a deep breath and we walked onto the stage. The room was less than half full and only a few people clapped at our arrival. It was as if the rest sat on their hands. Alright, I thought, let's open with the bus stop bit then. The crowd remained silent.

Sully shifted uncomfortably next to me as we both could feel the distaste among the audience. It lingered in the air, thicker than the cigar smoke. Ok, I decided it was time for a new bit, the funniest one I had thought of the other night. It involved us visiting an army base so that Sully could enlist.

Now the silence was replaced with the odd boo and the sound of chairs scrapping against the floor as people got up and left. I stuttered and stammered, ruining the beginning of the next bit, anxiety getting the better of me. The curtains dropped and my heart sank. We were done.

This time Denny did not visit us in the dressing room and Sully and I found him sitting in his office. We shut the door behind us and took a seat opposite him at his cluttered desk. The club owner looked at us both and then snickered.

Sully was the first to speak. "So, ah, sorry tonight didn't quite work out as we intended."

"No kidding," Denny replied.

"We will just collect our pay then and be moving along," I added.

"What did I say about both of you talking to me at the same time? Huh? I will pay you half of what I owe you, and believe me, that is still being generous," Denny shouted.

"Half?" I risked shouting back. "That's not fair! We still did our three performances. That was our deal!"

"You will take half and be happy you got that much," he responded and tossed an envelope on the desk in front of us. "Now get the hell out of here. I don't want to see either of your faces again, especially yours," he pointed at

Sully.

"Denny, without the full amount you promised us, we will lose our room at the hotel. We will have no place to live," I said, my voice sounding frantic.

"Not my problem. Beat it."

"But Denny…"

"Scram! Now! Before I really lose my temper."

I closed my eyes and slowly exhaled. I could not return to a life of poverty, not again.

BLAM!

"Jesus Christ, Micky! What did you do?" shouted Sully.

Denny fell back in his chair, a bullet hole in his forehead, and slowly slumped lifelessly to the floor.

"We need that money, Sully. We are not leaving here without it."

"You can't just murder someone like that! Where the hell did you even get that gun??"

"That's of no concern at the moment. We need to grab whatever money this greedy bum has stashed in that desk and get out of here quickly."

We ransacked Denny's desk, finding enough loot to pay off the hotel, the gangsters, and still leave us with some extra cash. Then we dashed out of the office, passing several astonished-looking stagehands, and returned to our hotel room.

I placed the small revolver on the table next to me and considered my next move. My partnership with Sully had proven to be disastrous. He was a good dummy, people did like him and he was personable, but we didn't possess the chemistry that I had initially thought. I figured it was time for a new dummy.

"What the hell are we gonna do, Micky? Huh? People know it was us that killed Denny. Oh my god, I feel so sick. We are in a lot of trouble."

"I am afraid, I am just going to say that it was you who did it," I replied calmly.

"Me? You pulled the trigger! For the love of god, I didn't even know you owned a gun!"

"This is the way it has to be, Sully, I am sorry. I am not going back to a life of poverty on the streets, begging and borrowing money from violent gangsters."

"This isn't fair, Micky! We are partners! I thought we were friends! You killed Denny, not me!"

"Our friendship ends tonight, sorry Sully."

In desperation, the dummy grabbed the gun off the table and pointed it at me with trembling hands.

"If it's gonna end tonight, then it's gonna end with a bullet in your selfish head. I can't believe you would just toss me aside like this and then blame me for a murder you committed."

Suddenly, and without warning, the door to our hotel room flew open, kicked in by a large police officer. Four of them in total rushed into our room with guns drawn, all aimed at Sully.

"Drop the gun, now!" commanded one of the officers, as they all looked back and forth between Sully and myself, confused by the bizarre scene in front of them.

"He did it," Sully told them. "He shot Denny. I didn't even know he had a gun."

"Place the gun on the floor and nobody else needs to get shot this night. Got it? Drop the gun."

Now I am not sure if Sully had meant to drop the gun on the floor, or if he had decided to raise the gun at me once more and finish me off, but the police were not happy with his movements and all fired their weapons. In total, Sully was hit with six bullets and fell to the floor, never to move again. I sat in my chair, head slumped with sadness.

One of the officers chuckled. "Well, I have never seen anything like this before."

"It's Sullivan and Micky. You guys never heard of Sullivan and Micky?" another asked. When the other officers shook their heads, he continued. "They are a ventriloquist act. Terrible! I saw them not that long ago and it was the worst performance I ever seen. At first people found them funny, like a novelty. I mean a ventriloquist's lips are not supposed to move at all, right? It's supposed to look like the dummy is talking. Not this act, no, it was the other way around. Like I said, at first it's kinda funny, but when it continues for the whole act, I mean come on, that's awful."

One of the officers addressed another and pointed at me. "Grab the doll, it's evidence. I'll write the report."

Doll? Did he just call me a doll? I will show them what a doll is capable of!

CHANNELING
EVAN MUNROE

I wish now that I had never heard the name of Evan Munroe. As good a friend as he was, I would have been much better off never having known him. Could I manipulate time and erase him from my memory, I surely would.

I suppose I could begin this tale on that dreadful Saturday evening in August, when Evan and myself, along with our boorish friend, Willard Barnes, spent the evening in Willard's basement playing cards and throwing dice.

A more ill-mannered person than Willard, I swear I had never met. I did, however, grow up with him, and as a result, counted him as one of my closest friends. Evan moved into our neighborhood two years past and became the third member of our trio.

I felt bad for Willard at times and I supposed my intimate knowledge of his home life led me to better understand him than most. To everyone else, he was a wicked bully with a cruel streak, and each of those things was correctly attributed to the large teen.

His mother was a neglective gambler, spending most of her waking hours at the bingo hall, and his father was an abusive drunk, contributing to a most foul behavior in their only son. Willard was a normal child when we had first met at the age of six; his change was gradual over the passing of many years. By the time his personality had become insufferable, it was too late for me, and we had already spent much of our lives as best friends.

In becoming our friend, Evan had little choice in the matter, having moved into the house between ours on the outskirts of town. His options for friends were limited in the beginning, living a good bus ride from our college and the rest of the town.

College was out for the summer and we did what most boys do; stay up all night long and sleep away most of the day. Willard's parents were rarely home, and even when they were, they cared little for what their son and his friends got up to, so we spent most of our time in Willard's basement.

Most people had a strong distaste for Willard, so Evan and I were guilty by association, and therefore rarely ever received invites to parties and gatherings from fellow classmates.

Evan, though slightly smaller than Willard, was a bit of a tough guy with strong opinions, which led to his butting heads with Willard quite often. The two could argue ceaselessly at times, as I looked on with only a shake of my head. I dared not insert myself into their debates, even when solicited by each to side with one over the other. I found it best to remain neutral; it lessened the headaches.

Their disputes were always petty and nonsensical in nature, much like the one that was fast escalating that Saturday night in August. They were embroiled in a difference of opinions over the origins of the particular card game with which we had been playing. I was positive neither of them had been correct but each of them was quite adamant in their stand.

More than once they attempted to drag me into the middle of their quarrel but I was having none of it. As their incessant fighting increased in volume and reached a fever pitch, I had decided I needed to step outside for some air.

It was a beautiful summer night. There was a slight chill to the air but it was comfortable, especially considering the oppressive humidity that dominated much of the day. Willard's house backed onto a sizable field which was quite dark, given the absence of street lights in our neighborhood. Even the radiance from a full moon did not afford me much vision in the darkness of the field.

My hopes had been to clear my aching head and listen to the sound of crickets but that was not to be. Even from out here, the muffled voices of Willard and Evan continued to pursue me, and to top it off, their voices were now joined by Willard's parents, who began their own verbal disagreeance from upstairs in the house. It sounded as if some plates might have been hurled against a wall and then out stumbled a thoroughly intoxicated Mr. Barnes from a side door. He somehow managed to navigate his way down the driveway and out onto the street without falling.

I shook my head and concentrated on what I believed was a deer running through the field. I was not entirely sure if it was in fact a deer though, or merely a trick of the eyes in the darkness. In any event, imagined or not, it helped calm me down and I was finally able to enjoy the silence and the sound of crickets.

Wait a moment, I thought, silence? The fighting in the basement had finally come to an end and I truly was left with only the sound of crickets. How serene that felt indeed. With a sigh, I figured I should go find out who won, or if both just agreed to disagree, as was usually the case, with neither willing to give in to the other.

"So, what's the verdict?" I inquired, while descending the steps back to the basement.

Strangely, I was met with only silence.

"Don't tell me you both fell asleep? It's too early."

I then saw Willard rise up from behind a long, chocolate-colored sofa; his face as pale as a ghost. I knew immediately that something was amiss.

"H-he made me do it. He left me with no choice."

"What are you talking about, Willard?"

"You know how he is. He made me do it."

I remembered my skin began to prickle. "What did he make you do?"

Speechless, Willard backed up and then sat himself down in a comfy chair which matched the sofa. Tentatively, I approached the sofa and peered over the edge, my heart nearly stopping at the sight which had greeted me. There lay Evan on the floor, very still, red marks around his throat, his eyes wide open in one final look of horror.

I promptly determined that our friend was dead and

my legs almost gave out from under me. I am quite sure I turned a shade of pale to match that of Willard's now pallid appearance. I had never before seen a dead body and it is something that will haunt me until the end of my days.

"He made me do it," Willard repeated.

My mind reeled. I was always the rational thinker of our group, the logical one, the problem solver, but in this instance, I had no idea how to proceed. As my stomach twisted into knots, I came to the conclusion that I needed to call for the police.

I turned to leave but Willard must have somehow read the intentions on my face. "Where are you going?"

"Willard, I need to call for help."

"No point, he is beyond help now."

"Regardless, someone needs to know. It's the right thing to do."

"They will put me in jail or hang me."

Yes, they most assuredly would, I thought, but kept that sentiment to myself. I continued to the stairs and Willard's tone changed drastically, his words stopping me in my tracks.

"Maybe you didn't hear me? I said they will put me in jail or hang me."

"Yes, I heard you but this is not right. I need to call for help."

"I told you already he is beyond help. The only person you need to help now is me. I am your friend, remember?"

"Yes, I am your friend. But so was Evan."

"Evan had that coming. We have been friends longer, you and I. You cannot betray me now."

"Betray you? Willard, you just murdered Evan!"

"With your help."

"Pardon me??"

"You stood there and watched and allowed it to happen."

"I did no such…"

"I will tell them. I will tell them you helped me."

"Why you evil son of a…"

"Careful, friend. We need to calm down if we are to get ourselves out of this predicament."

"We??"

"Yes, we. You and I. I think we should bury him in the field and claim he was never here this evening."

I stood there, my mouth agape, unable to formulate a response. I was the only friend he ever had and he would think to treat me as such? The ungrateful bastard.

"They will never believe you," I said, after finding some courage amidst my rising anger. "Look at the size of you over me. How could I have possibly stopped you? I wasn't even down here when you did it."

Willard rose in a flash, his pale skin turning a shade of red. "You wanna join Evan?"

"Pardon me? You are threatening me now? Your only friend?"

"I am not going to jail and I am not going to hang, not for him. Do you hear me? But if that happens, you will pay for it."

"If the police arrest you, how do you plan on killing me from prison?"

"I will tell my Uncle George that you did it and framed me, his favorite nephew. He will kill you."

Willard's Uncle George was a dim-witted hillbilly with the mind capacity of a child. How he survived on his own living in a cabin in the woods, I will never know. But Uncle George would believe anything Willard told him and I had no doubt that the simpleton would come after me and kill me. George was a hunter and shooting things was one of the few tasks he was actually good at.

My conscience nagged at me but I believed Willard's threat. "We bury him in the field then and he was never here this evening."

Willard smiled that wicked smile and nodded. "Grab his legs."

As repulsed as I was, I did grab his legs, and the two of us struggled to carry Evan's body out into the pitch-black field behind his house. As I mentioned, I had never seen a dead body before this night and now I had seen more of one that I would have ever cared to. I never imagined Evan could be so heavy and sweat dripped from my forehead as we finally found a secluded spot a fair distance away from the house.

Willard returned to fetch a shovel, leaving me alone with Evan, his dead eyes still wide open. I turned my back and sat on a stone, facing the opposite direction. I could not believe what I had just been a party to. There was no going back now; I was indeed an accomplice. I felt ill.

Willard promptly began to dig upon his return. When he grew weary, he handed the tool to me to continue, and gave me a look that told me that it was not open for debate.

An hour and a half later, with the moon high in the sky, our grim deed was completed. We had done our best to cover the hole and indeed it looked as though nobody had been digging in the first place. Nothing appeared out of sorts, and with luck, Evan would never be found.

We spent the rest of the night in the basement corroborating our story, that Evan had other plans this evening and had gone someplace else.

Not twenty-four hours later, Evan's parents began to worry and made phone calls and visits all over the neighborhood. That night, police began canvassing the area, and of course, came to speak with Willard and I, seeing as how we were Evan's closest friends.

As nervous and as sick as I felt, we both stuck to our story that we had no clue where Evan had gone that evening. The neglectiveness of Willard's parents, for once, provided benefit. They were home that night in question, but cared little to check in on their son, and therefore had no idea that Evan was ever downstairs. They told police that Willard and I were indeed home the entire evening by ourselves.

Days turned into weeks and weeks into months. The heat was off and soon life returned to normal and Willard and I were back in school. Evan was treated as a runaway, despite the protests of his parents that he would never have done such a thing. I tried my best to occupy my mind with my studies and think about that night as little as possible. I even tried to avoid Willard as much as I could.

Despite my attempts to forget, Evan haunted my dreams and sleep did not come easily for me. Guilt feasted away at my conscience, but my fear of prison or the hangman's noose, kept my feelings to myself.

It was October 31st, Halloween night to be exact, when I was invited to a classmate's party. It was to be a grand event with about thirty other students invited. To my surprise, and regret, Willard was also invited. Try as I might to avoid him, he was not well liked, and thus he followed me everywhere.

As the night wore on, a pretty girl named Edna entered the living room carrying a game board of some type.

"Hey everyone, I have a nifty idea. It's Halloween night, the night when our world and the spirit world come together and spirits walk the earth. Let's try using the Ouija board to contact some spirits."

A few people groaned, jesting that the board was just a foolish toy. Some others grew pale, obviously frightened at the prospect of inviting spirits into the house. The majority thought it was a fun idea and the majority won over.

Edna excitedly set everything up on a dining room table. Walter, who was hosting the party, turned off all the lights so that the room was illuminated with only four candles.

"Ok, who should we try to contact?" Edna asked of the full room.

"Erika Blayne," someone suggested, referring to a woman who had been burned as a witch, a century gone by.

"Horace Pickleton," another blurted, who had been a serial killer and hung for his crimes.

"Evan Munroe," a third person shouted, and the room went silent.

Willard and I exchanged glances, and I hadn't even realized I was holding my breath, until I was forced to inhale a gulp of air, lest my face turn blue from holding out too long.

"Evan isn't dead, he just ran away," Willard said nervously.

"I never believed that for a second," replied the boy who had made the suggestion in the first place. "Someone killed Evan, I would bet everything on it."

"I think so too," another boy added. "How is it that the police never found him anywhere? I think he is buried somewhere."

Edna smiled. "Evan Munroe it is then. If he is dead, we can call upon his spirit and ask him what happened."

Edna explained that four people would be required to each place one of their hands on the Ouija board, in an attempt to channel the spirit of Evan Munroe. She would participate, along with Walter, then she invited over Willard and I.

"You and Willard knew Evan the best, so you both should be involved."

As you can imagine, the two of us were both quite hesitant, but everyone agreed that we two were the best choices and did not cease in goading us over to the table. Alas, we relented.

I never possessed much of an opinion on the Ouija board. I was undecided about the possibility of an afterlife and what became of a person's spirit after death. I questioned the validity of the board, which could be purchased in a toy store of all places, for a nominal amount of money.

Reluctantly, Willard and I took a seat at the table with the others and placed our right hands upon the Ouija board, joining hands with Edna and Walter. A nervous sweat began to form on my forehead and worst of all, I was forced to relive that horrible night in my mind.

Edna wasted no time. "We here at this table, call upon the spirit of Evan Munroe. Evan, if you have died, come join with us now. Guide our hands and share with us your fate. Help us find closure in your mysterious disappearance. Please, Evan Munroe, come to us now."

Willard snorted with contempt right before the loudest clap of thunder I had ever heard boomed outside, shaking the house. Everyone jumped and a few of the girls squealed out loud. There had not been any storms in the forecast.

As everyone calmed, the candles on the table began to violently flicker, threatening to extinguish, despite the fact that every person in the room, sat or stood, completely still. My heart began to race as a breeze tickled my cheek, as if someone had passed closely by.

Suddenly, Edna yelped, and indeed I nearly did as well, as a tingling sensation flooded into my hand which touched the Ouija board. It was evident by the others faces that we all felt the same sensation.

"Evan, is that you?" Edna asked, in a nervous squeaky voice.

The board under our hands felt as though it moved of its own accord, for surely I had no part in pushing it. The Ouija board circled the game board several times before stopping over the word, *Yes*.

"Evan, were you murdered?" she asked next.

Again, the board came to rest over the word, *Yes*.

"Do you know who murdered you?"

Willard and I both held our breaths, as the board once again stopped on, *Yes*. There was a collective gasp among the others who huddled around the table now. Even the skeptics were leaning in closely for a better view.

"Evan, can you tell us who murdered you?"

My jaw dropped open in a silent scream as the

tingling sensation from my hand began to creep its way up my arm. A moment later it overwhelmed my entire body and suddenly I felt a presence within my mind. I don't know how to explain it exactly, but without a doubt, Evan Munroe was inside my body.

Involuntarily, I let go of the board and lunged towards Willard. He shrieked in terror as my hands wrapped themselves around his throat. Willard was much bigger and stronger than I, though he was helpless to break my stranglehold. Somehow, I had been imbued with great strength. Strength from beyond the grave it would seem.

To the absolute horror of everyone present, I choked Willard to death right there at the dining table. His eyes bulged and stared at me with disbelief, as his life slowly slipped away. My actions had not been my own, and as death claimed Willard, I felt Evan leave my body and I was left in control once more. I slumped to the floor sobbing while others ran about in a panic.

I can't say for sure how long I actually sat there before police arrived and took me to their station in handcuffs. During my questioning, I broke down and told them of everything. Of course I tried to plead my case that I had not been the one who killed Willard; that Evan's spirit had inhabited my body, but of course, the authorities wouldn't believe such a thing.

After my display of strength in strangling Willard, the police were unsure of my story that Willard had been the one who killed Evan. To them, both deaths were the same, so therefore, I could have been responsible for both.

I somehow avoided the death penalty and wouldn't hang but now I sat in a cold dark cell where I would spend the rest of my life. Every day I curse the name of Willard

Barnes and I am forced to remember that horrendous
night, when we channeled the angry spirit of Evan
Munroe.

IN THE COURT OF
THE JESTER

The immense ballroom was filled nearly to capacity, as revelers milled about laughing and drinking and sampling a decadent array of foods. King Christophe II had only recently defeated his hated enemies to the north and took over their lands, effectively expanding his ever enlarging kingdom. So today was a day of celebration.

Every lord and lady and wealthy merchant in all the lands was invited to partake in a day of feasting and general debauchery in honor of the King's great victory. They traveled from near and they traveled from far, whether they cared for the usually quite arrogant and unpleasant King or not. And why wouldn't they? The King spared no expense to provide the most palatable of foods and the most potent of drinks. And of course, who could forget the entertainment?

"Where is my Fool?" the intoxicated King bellowed

over the raucous crowd and the sweet sounds of a lute being strummed in a corner. "Fool? Fool, where are you?"

"Over here, sire," I answered most dejectedly, as I was about to sample my first bite of the fine assortment of edibles.

"Drop that food instantly, it is time to perform, I am in the mood to laugh," he commanded. "Wouldn't everyone like to see the Fool perform for us now?"

There was a chorus of cheers and applause in agreeance from the throng of partiers. Folk cleared a path for me to shuffle my way towards the King's raised dinner table; the bells hanging from my fool's cap jingling all the way.

Shuffling is what I had to do, as my left knee was twisted inwards since birth, preventing me from walking normally. Life might not have been so harsh, were that my only abnormality, but alas, the gods had truly cursed me, and for what purpose, I know not. My right arm hung significantly longer than my left, I was hunched over from a lump that protruded from the back of my spine, and I suffered from a lazy eye; my left eye chose to roam around, rarely if ever in sync with my right.

Freak, some called me, and others referred to me as a goblin. In any case, I was a sideshow to be mocked and laughed at by those more blessed than I. The King utilized me for his personal amusement and to entertain his guests. I supposed I should feel fortunate, being afforded a chance to live in the court, instead of being cast aside or put to death like others who suffered from similar deformities.

The crowd quieted as I now stood in front of the King's dinner table, all eyes on me. I cleared my throat.

"Ah...yes...well have you heard the tale of the bard from Fallhaven? No? Neither have I, he no longer possesses as head...heh heh," I was referring to a city in the north, where the previous ruler was obsessed with beheadings.

I only received a mild reaction from the crowd on that joke, so jumped straight into my new material concerning the defeated northern King. Sweat was forming on my brow as King Christophe yawned.

I suddenly yelped out loud as a tomato struck my face and splattered its juices upon my gaudy shirt. That sight received a warm welcome from the partiers as they burst into laughter.

"Heh, heh, yes sire, your aim is remarkable," I complimented the King.

"Oh, Fool, what is that you dropped there?" the King asked, after tossing a copper coin onto the floor behind me.

I knew where this game was headed and had to play along. "Where, sire? I don't recall dropping anything."

"Turn around, Fool. There on the floor, behind you."

I turned around and bent over to pick up the coin, bracing myself for the kick in the behind that was surely to follow. I was not disappointed, as the King's spoiled nephew planted his boot forcibly into my buttocks, sending me sprawling to the floor with an explosion of hysterical laughter. One particular slovenly merchant nearly choked on a mouthful of quail at the apparently uproarious spectacle.

"Oh my, I am so clumsy," I said, as I attempted to rise.

A second kick to the same spot, which had now left a considerable bruise I was positive, sent me back to the floor face first. The guffaws continued and Lord Bently, a middle-aged man with an inflated stomach, actually fell from his chair.

I accepted two more kicks to my hindquarters before the King tired and ordered some minstrels to begin with a little music. I was given a reprieve and finally struggled back to my feet.

Much later, as dessert was served, I received a cream pie to the face and a bowl of pudding poured down my trousers; a most successful party.

The following morning I found myself in the empty throne room, sweeping up from the previous night's celebrations. I enjoyed my time spent alone but it was not to last. I frowned as an all too familiar voice entered the room and broke the silence.

"Fool, look at this mess. How long must I suffer the sight of it?" asked the King.

"Not much longer, sire, nearly finished in this room," I answered.

The King shook his head in disgust and took a seat upon his most luxurious throne. He was strikingly handsome, with a neatly trimmed golden beard and a full head of matching hair. His eyes were a sparkling blue and his chin chiseled. Women swooned over him, especially since he was still single; never taking a wife after the Queen died many years past.

Yes, the King was a fine specimen indeed, and from the portraits I had seen, the Queen was a beauty with no equal. So why then was their son so hideous?

"What are you brooding over, father?" I dared to ask.

"Do not call me that!" he barked in response.

"My apologies, I only thought that since we were alone…"

"Do not think! You are my fool, you are not here to think. Anyone could have walked in at any time. You will never call me that."

"Y-yes, sire."

"But to answer your question, I await news from Sir Brandolyn, who is on a most important mission for me.

He should have returned yesterday but he has not."

"What mission? I thought the northerners were all defeated?"

Sir Brandolyn was the King's greatest knight, the fiercest and bravest of all the kingdom's warriors. If he had been sent on a mission, then it was quite important indeed.

"This does not have anything to do with the north. For years I have consulted old tomes in search of an ancient buried treasure. At last, with the aid of that blind old hag from Sulphur Swamp, I believed I had determined the treasure's whereabouts. I dispatched Sir Brandolyn and five of his most loyal men into the Valley of Mists to retrieve it."

"What kind of treasure?" I wondered in fascination.

"Not for a fool to know, now finish cleaning up. I feel my mood turning sour and will need you to make me laugh shortly."

Two days passed and there had still been no word from the knight. The King was entertaining envoys from a southern kingdom, so as usual, I was present and once again receiving a boot to my arse from the spoiled nephew. The guests found it quite amusing and tears streamed down their bronzed faces from laughter.

Just before I was about to be poked with the blunt end of a spear, a messenger hurried into the throne room to whisper words into the King's ear. His face significantly brightened.

"Everyone out! Now! Leave immediately!" he ordered, leaving no room for debate. "Not you Fool, you may stay," he added as I had turned to quicken myself away.

The two of us sat in silence for what felt like an awful

long time. I dared not ask any questions. Then, Sir Brandolyn entered the room, his always-gleaming armor dirtied and dusty. Black smudges dominated the parts of his face that were not covered with his bushy brown beard. In his hands he carried a small black box, similar to a lady's jewelry box.

Sir Brandolyn knelt before the King and extended his arms, presenting him with the black box. "My King, we found the tomb as your map had been quite accurate. That witch had been right and we found guardians inside. Skeletons rose up and fought us as we attempted to access the crypt. Myself, and Sir Malek, are the only survivors, but we found that which you sought. I offer it to you now."

"Marvelous, marvelous indeed! You have done well!" the King glowed with excitement as he accepted the black box. "Did you open the box?"

"No, sire. You commanded me not to. It has remained sealed and always in my possession, 'til now. I know not what is inside."

"Excellent, excellent. Now go clean yourself up, there will be a dinner in your honor this evening. Once again, you have proven yourself to be the greatest of my men."

"Thank you, sire," the knight said, before taking his leave.

I watched the King stare at the box for several long moments. I was most anxious to see what important treasure was contained within. With shaking hands, he eventually opened the lid of the box to reveal a long, thin, purplish bottle, sealed with a cork. My mind swirled with possibilities. A magic potion, perhaps? A priceless liquor from some forgotten age?

The King wasted no time in removing the cork and I

jumped back in fright as a white mist streamed forth from the open end of the bottle. It snaked its way out and pooled near the foot of the throne. I was on the verge of shouting a warning, that it was possibly a poisonous cloud, when the words caught in my throat. My jaw hung open in awe and I had to wonder if what I saw was even real.

As the mist cleared, there now stood a large man with purplish skin, who was oddly clothed and wore a strange hat, similar to those worn by the desert nomads of the south. He bowed towards the King.

"Thank you for releasing me from the bottle. My name is Al-Zorashan, a genie, and I grant unto you three wishes."

The King nearly fell from his throne, so taken with feelings of ultimate joy. The priceless treasure he spent years trying to locate was now his. His mouth was dry and his palms were sweating as his mind raced through the list of all his grandest desires.

"Gold," he blurted. "I want my entire bedchamber filled to capacity with gold coins."

The King's bedchamber was the largest room in the castle, occupying the entire top floor.

The genie snapped his fingers. "It is done."

The King called for a page, whose eyes nearly popped out of their sockets at the sight of the purplish genie, and commanded him to run to his bedchamber and return with news of what he saw. The young boy ran from the room with great haste and soon returned, thoroughly breathless and eyes wide with wonder.

"My King, I could not even see into your chambers as my view was obscured by mountains of gold!"

When the King finally finished roaring with laughter,

he dismissed the page and sat back in his throne in silent contemplation. His eyes then lit up as he reached a conclusion.

"I am handsome, and strong, and in the peak of my life. I wish to be immortal. So genie, I wish that from this day forward, I shall never age another year."

The genie nodded his head and snapped his fingers. "It is done. You shall never age again."

The King beamed with delight, as a tingling sensation was felt all over his body. I looked on quietly, truly amazed by the entire scene. A genie! A real genie granting wishes! The King was surely blessed.

Then to my utter shock and astonishment, the King said something that at first, I thought I had only imagined. I was prone to vivid daydreams and assumed I was having one at that very moment.

"I am now wealthy beyond imagining, more so than before. I am also now immortal and shall remain my handsome self for an eternity," the King proclaimed. "So, my son, I will give the third and final wish to you, so that you may wish away your unsightly deformities and return to this court as my long lost son, sent away for tutoring, or some other such excuse."

"Sire?" I could not believe my ears.

"Yes, you heard true. At this moment you are the only child I have. So go ahead, wish yourself normal, so that I might now introduce you as my son and prince without embarrassment and shame."

I was rendered speechless. It wasn't a daydream at all. After a lifetime of humiliation, serving as the King's fool, I was now offered the opportunity to change my life and wish for a normal body. I was beside myself with glee.

The purplish genie turned to me and smiled. "Is that what you wish? Speak it and it will be done."

*   *   *   *

I sat uncomfortably in the large chair as hundreds of lords and ladies gathered for a celebratory dinner. Sir Brandolyn was to be the guest of honor for his bravery in completing his most important quest. Without the courageous knight, the incredible genie bottle would never have been recovered, and thus, our three wishes never granted.

As the crowd appeared restless, I felt it was time for the entertainment. "Where is my Fool? Fool? Fool, where are you?"

"I am here, sire," the Fool answered, emerging from behind some gathered guests to stand before me.

He was a strikingly handsome man with a neatly trimmed golden beard and sparkling blue eyes. His matching golden hair was mostly obscured by his ridiculous-looking fool's cap with the jingling bells. He had shuffled over awkwardly wearing shoes four sizes too large.

I shifted on my throne as the hunch in my back impeded my posture. Well, I figured, as King I would just have a new throne built that would better suit my unshapely body.

I tossed a copper coin to land on the floor behind the fool. "Fool, what is that you have dropped on the floor there behind you? Go on, pick it up."

MARS-FOUR, CAN YOU HEAR ME?

I awoke to another dreadful day on this desolate red planet; the excitement of actually living on another world had long ago worn off. Most days now just felt very long and quite monotonous. You don't realize how much you take walking outdoors and breathing fresh oxygen for granted, until you can no longer do simple things as that.

Suiting up to step outside our home base is a one hour process. And you do not wish to rush that, as one small misstep could mean your doom. Even then, you are viewing the world around through the glass of a fishbowl that you are constantly wearing on your head.

Not that there is much to see, aside from mountains and a wasteland of red dust. The landscape on Mars did not differ much from certain regions found on Earth. There was nothing uniquely alien about it. It reminded me of post-apocalyptic movies, where much of the Earth was now devoid of any types of life.

We were hoping to change that; it was our mission here on the red planet. I had come here to the fourth planet from the sun with five others to begin the colonization process. We were supposed to make a livable and sustainable base here, allowing for more people to eventually join us. So far, we had been quite successful in the eight months since our landing. We had our home base, which sat nestled in the valley between two mountains, Vesta and Maia, as well as three greenhouses, where we managed to grow fruits and vegetables with the aid of solar panels.

Our mission was given the green light once scientists developed a method for us to extract water from the Martian soil. It was not a simple process but it worked. Every few months we received supplies from Earth as well, which did include extra water. The fact that water crystals were found in the soil was a good sign. We had hopes of one day unearthing some underground lakes or springs, which we firmly believed must still exist.

The future of life on Earth was becoming ever uncertain. Mankind was running the planet into the ground, much as we always had been. The impact on the environment in the wake of World War III was catastrophic. Many of our natural resources were dwindling to dangerously low levels and most disheartening to me, was the extinction of many of our planet's more common species. It saddened me to think that future generations would never know the joy of hearing a bird sing; that they would have to learn about our feathered friends from history books alone.

Humans needed Mars if our species was to survive.

Not only was it our neighboring planet and the easiest to reach but it was the most hospitable for our kind. Scientists truly believed that Mars was going to be the new Earth. My team and I were here to pave the way for future colonists.

"Martin, you're finally awake, I see," said Captain Lewis Prawn, our mission's leader.

I nodded and shook the cobwebs from my befuddled mind. "I am. I had trouble sleeping again."

"Well grab yourself a coffee and ungrog yourself. I need you, Vivian, and Dmitry, to get out there and secure those loose solar panels on Green-Two this morning."

"Why this morning?" I asked. "We have all day to do that."

"We don't, actually. Samantha has detected a very large dust storm headed our way. It should arrive this afternoon and the high winds could actually rip those panels off the roof if we don't get them secured this morning."

Great, I get to spend my entire morning doing repair work, and then the rest of the day will be spent twiddling my thumbs as we hunker down for a dust storm. On Earth I was an explorer, or an Archaeologist, if you will. I had salivated at the thought of coming to Mars to explore a new world. So far, I hadn't had much of a chance for exploration; we were too busy growing food and endlessly repairing things in the wake of the hostile storms that raged across this planet. And storms here just didn't last a few hours; they could go on for days. The longest lasted a month, but thankfully, that was just prior to our arrival.

I grabbed a mug of awful coffee and sat down at a table with Vivian, a stunningly-attractive woman of Asian descent. She was a genius mathematician.

"Any news from Earth?" I asked her.

"Not since Tuesday," she replied. "But the captain is scheduled to make contact this afternoon, if that storm doesn't interfere."

Which it probably would, I figured.

"Doesn't sound good over there, though," she continued. "Tensions are rising again between countries. Central Control worries about another war."

I shook my head in disgust. Of all the amazing things that humans had achieved since the dawn of time, destroying each other is still what we excelled at the most. And there seemed to be no end to that in sight. Our hatred for our own kind has ruined much of our planet, which is why we are forced to turn to Mars and seek a new home. As dreary as life was here on Mars, at least I was far away from those war-mongering barbarians on Earth.

After an hour of suiting up, then double and triple checking that everything was in proper order, myself, along with Vivian and Dmitry, stepped outside our base and began the ten minute walk to our second greenhouse, or Green-Two as it was called.

"Mars-Three, check," I heard Vivian say from the speaker inside my fishbowl helmet.

"Mars-Seven, check," Dmitry followed suit.

"Mars-Four, check," I then said.

"This is Home-One, I can hear you all loud and clear. Proceed to Green-Two," Samantha prompted.

Green-Two sat in a flat expanse of land away from the shadows of the two mountains. It was important that it received as much sunlight as was possible. We reached the large structure, which was responsible for producing most of our vegetables, and hurriedly got to work. Three of the largest solar panels had come loose during the last violent dust storm and we would most likely lose them if they were not secured before the next.

Dmitry, who was a mechanical engineer, quickly climbed to the roof to begin the repair process. I handed him tools as needed, while Vivian walked the perimeter of Green-Two, inspecting for anything else that required our attention.

"How does it look, Mars-Three?" I asked Vivian.

"So far so good. No visible structural damage that I can see," she replied.

Good, I did not want to be out here longer than we had planned. Dmitry's work was tedious enough as it was. It was very difficult to perform precise repairs while wearing the bulky gloves that were a required part of our space suits. Something that might have only taken twenty minutes on Earth, became a two to three hour job on Mars.

As one hour became two, Dmitry was finally working on the last of the three panels. Vivian waited impatiently nearby, having completed her inspection long ago.

"Mars Team, this is Home-One, please hurry. That storm is blowing in much sooner than expected. You do not have much time," we heard over the speakers.

Vivian paced nervously behind me.

"Mars-Three, go on back to base, there is nothing left for you to do here," I suggested.

"You're sure?" she asked.

"Of course, go on. We'll be right behind you. How is it looking up there Mars-Seven?"

"Curse these gloves, I hate them," he replied.

"How much longer?" I wondered.

"Ten minutes."

About twelves minutes later, I watched Vivian enter the base off in the distance. "Alright Mars-Seven, it's been over ten minutes."

"Five more minutes."

I shifted nervously from foot to foot as the sky grew darker and a distant mountain vanished behind a haze of red dust.

"Mars-Four and Mars-Seven, this is Home-One, I need you both to return to base now. Abort mission. The storm is closing in fast. Do you copy?"

"We copy, Home-One," I responded. "Come on Dmitry, let's go. Losing one panel won't be so bad."

"Two minutes."

"Forget two minutes, let's go! We have a ten minute walk back!"

Dmitry relented and began to climb down, mumbling to himself. As I glanced around, the dust clouds had cut the distance in half from the last time I looked. We headed back towards the base as swiftly as we could walk in our cumbersome suits.

Four minutes into our trek back, I cursed, having forgot the bag of tools on the ground beside Green-Two.

"Dammit! Mars-Seven keep going, I forgot the tools. I gotta go back," I said, angry at myself.

"No time, buddy. Forget them."

"We can afford to lose one panel but we can't afford to lose those tools. I will be quick."

Before he could argue further, I turned around and marched determinedly back towards the greenhouse.

"Mars-Four, this is Home-One, what do you think

you are doing?"

"I forgot the tools, I have to go back."

"Turn back this instant, that's an order! That storm is almost upon us. We can always replace those tools, we can't replace you."

"I am almost back at Green-Two anyways, I can see the bag. Won't be long."

As I reached the greenhouse the winds were already whipping around me, raising the red sand into a blinding fog of particles. This was not a good situation at all and I soon gave in to panic.

"Mars-Four, this is Home-One, get inside Green-Two and wait out the storm there."

I dreaded the idea of spending the duration of the storm alone in that uncomfortable greenhouse. After all, it could last days or weeks. No, I was determined to make it back to base. I picked up the bag of tools and marched onwards.

"Mars-Four, get inside Green-Two!"

"Negative, Home-One. I have secured the tools and I can make it back. See you all shortly."

Stubbornly I strode through the blowing winds. Visibility was steadily decreasing and I soon figured that I should have just stayed at the greenhouse. My pace slowed as strong winds now worked against my efforts.

"Mars-Four, this is Home-One, how are you doing? We have lost visual on you. Are you close?"

"I believe so, Home-One, five minutes away."

Then to my dismay, a particularly strong gust of wind forcibly pushed me several feet back and my boot caught on a rock, sending me tumbling to the dusty ground.

Regrettably, I dropped the bag of tools and now

could no longer see it, as a cloud of rust-colored dust spun around me in a mini-tornado. In fact, to my horror, I could no longer see our base or the greenhouses. I could barely see my own white glove in front of my face. Worst of all, my tumble had disoriented me and now I was not even sure which direction I had been traveling in.

"Mars-Four? Mars-Four? *SZZZZRRTTTTT* your status?"

"Say again, Home-One?"

"*SZZRRRT SZRRRRT* copy?"

"Home-One, I cannot see the base. I am waving my arms in the air, can you see me at all? I need you to tell me which direction to travel."

"Mars-Four, *SZZRTTTTTT* can *SZZZRRRRT* me?"

"Please repeat, Home-One."

My breathing began to rapidly increase and my heart raced.

"Mars-Four, can you hear me?"

"Yes, Home-One, you are breaking up but I heard that last transmission. I need you to tell me which direction I need to go in, please."

"Mars-Four, *SZZZZRTT* can you hear me? Hello? Mars-Four?"

Frustrated, and in a state of panic, I picked a direction and plunged forward. I played the odds since I had a fifty-fifty chance. West would bring me to our base and east would bring me back to the greenhouse. North or south meant doom but I was doomed anyways if I just stood still.

"*SZZRRT* Four, can you hear me?"

"Hello? Home-One?"

"*SZZZZRTTT SZZZZZZZZZRTTTTTTTTT.*"

"Hello?"

"*SZZZZRT* you *SZZRT SZZZZZZZRTTTTT.*"

My heart sank as over ten minutes had passed and I had yet to touch the outside of either structure. The wind blasted me with constant force and again sent me tumbling to the ground. The Martian Mother Nature was looking to punish the foolish human who thought he could outrun the storm. Perhaps she did not like colonists and was testing my mettle to see if I was worthy to call this planet home.

I struggled to stand and then marched for another twenty minutes or so before walking headlong into something very solid. I was pushed along at a great speed with the wind behind me and was fortunate not to crack the glass of my helmet when I collided with this object.

Feeling the jagged surface in front of me, I determined that I had reached one of the mountains. Whether it was Vesta or Maia, I had no way of knowing. Either one meant I was way off course and there was no way for me to place the location of our base. My best bet now was to seek some form of shelter from the storm within the mountain. We knew that some caves did exist but Captain Prawn had not allowed me to explore them yet. His priority was the stabilization of the colony first, exploration had to wait.

I no longer heard static from my speaker as all transmissions had gone completely dead. They would have been unable to help me at this point anyway; my only chance now was to find a place to hide.

My visibility was still almost non-existent and I was forced to feel my way around the base of the mountain. To my elation, I soon found a deep crevice where the slope downwards was not too steep. I decided to descend and was rewarded with relief from the buffeting wind. I took a seat to rest my weary limbs and calm my frail nerves.

What a fool I had been. I lost the tools and quite nearly lost my life because I didn't wish to be uncomfortable, spending time alone at Green-Two. And I was still not out of this predicament. Who knew how long this storm would last and I only had so much oxygen in my suit.

I activated the two powerful flashlights that were mounted on the top of my helmet and peered downwards into the crevice. It appeared to go quite deep, beyond the reach of my lights, and the slope was manageable, if I wished to investigate deeper. The explorer in me won the internal struggle and down I went, albeit quite slowly and cautiously.

The angle of the slope told me that I was now traveling underneath the mountain, and soon I was surrounded by pitch-darkness, with only the lights from my helmet to guide me. It wasn't long before I could not even hear the winds of the storm from above.

Curiously, I pressed onwards, further underground. I was fortunate to be able to stand to my full height within the tunnel as it leveled out and continued on, and a tunnel it appeared to be. The rocky walls looked strangely smoother down here and even the floor was less jagged.

The fear of being lost in this storm was soon replaced with the excitement of exploring this most curious tunnel. This is what I had signed up for in the first place; I was no farmer.

Further and further I went, when I noticed some bizarre markings on one of the walls. I couldn't be sure if they were alien in origin or just caused by natural erosion, so I approached for a closer inspection.

So focused was I on the wall markings that I did not notice the immense gap in the tunnel's floor, and I soon felt the terrifying experience of falling, as the floor disappeared from under me.

I landed heavily with a crunch and a scream escaped my lips. I was no doctor but I was positive I had just broken my right leg. I cursed at my lack of awareness. Now I had really gone and done it. Even if the storm ended soon, I highly doubted my radio would work this far underground to send or receive any transmissions from Home-One. I also figured that the dust storm would erase any tracks I had made on the ground, therefore rendering the others useless in determining the direction I had traveled.

Despairingly, I looked about at my surroundings and found I had fallen into a large cavern; so large that my light could not reach the walls. Then my heart skipped a beat, as I noticed I was lying on…what? Papers? It appeared that I lay atop several dust-covered papers. Newsprint by the looks of it. Newsprint, with writing! And writing…in English!

My hands shook with excitement, momentarily forgetting about the agonizing pain in my leg. I fumbled about with my bulky gloves, attempting to pick up one of the papers several times before I was finally rewarded. I lifted a newspaper up in order to read the headline on the first page, for a newspaper it most assuredly was! My mind reeled at the implications that I clutched some ancient Martian newspaper.

I was stunned by the headline that I read aloud.

"Politicians scoff at the notion of colonizing Earth."

This particular article went on to discuss how mankind was destroying Mars at a rapid rate and would soon become extinct if they could not find a way to colonize the monster-infested blue planet, called Earth.

So we destroyed Mars and moved to Earth. Now we were destroying Earth and were looking to move to Mars. Good lord, we were destined to be caught in this vicious cycle for eternity.

THE INHERITANCE

The cab driver carefully navigated the narrow winding road as we ascended the dark hill in the pelting rain. Winds threatened to force the small vehicle off the road, and on more than one occasion, I found my stomach caught in my throat, as I gazed out the window to a steep drop below. It would have been a frightening drive on the best of days and this horrendous storm only made it worse.

Even when lightning lit up the sky, it did little to improve our view, as thick weeping trees leaned over the road, reaching with gnarled branches to brush the vehicle as it passed.

I breathed a sigh of relief when we eventually reached the hill's summit and the gravel road evened out. That relief was short-lived though as I beheld the sight of that most sinister-looking house which sat at the end of the road. To think that this house was my destination was enough to cause my skin to crawl. It was akin to those mansions that were most often portrayed in horror pictures.

Soon I stood in the driving rain, looking up at the front door which was shrouded in darkness. The cabbie graciously dropped my bags beside me and hastily returned to the vehicle.

"Thank you, my good man. Now what do I owe…"

I never even finished my sentence as the cab sped off and was soon out of sight. I stood momentarily dumbfounded, until the rain was soaking through to my undergarments, so I grabbed my bags and dashed for the cover of the porch.

The two-story house, while looking ancient by its architecture, was in fairly good shape, considering it had not been occupied in at least a year. The glass of the windows seemed to be all intact; untouched by vandals. Though I supposed, despite its spooky appearance, it was not the most accessible of places for trouble-makers or squatters. Why would my father have chosen to live here, in such a remote and forbidding location?

The wind picked up again and with it carried a biting chill. The rain began to blow sideways and soon the porch offered no protection whatsoever. I fumbled about in the pockets of my overcoat to locate the keys that were presented to me from the lawyer. The key to the main door was large and looked no less ancient than did the house. It added character, I figured.

With a rewarding, "click", the heavy front door unlocked, and I rushed inside, dragging my bags behind me as quickly as I could. My eyes could not readily adjust to the blackness of the lobby and I was soon rummaging blindly through one of my bags in search of my electric torch. Luckily I had thought to bring it, as I had been informed that the aged house possessed no electricity at all.

With a push of a button, my vision returned, revealing a grand, spiral staircase, leading upwards, with several doors dotting the large greeting room in which I now stood. An old coat rack hovered to my right, but the chill air from outside had followed me in, and I thought to keep my coat on for the time being. I did, however, do my best to shake off my rain covered coat, before proceeding further into my new house.

Or soon to be new house, I figured I should say. In an odd move, my father had stipulated in his will that his house would only become mine, after I spent at least one night inside of it. It had taken me nearly a year, after the news of his death, to eventually travel to our old town and meet with the lawyer. I was a busy man and had to see that my endeavors at home would be well looked after in my absence.

Regrettably, my hectic work schedule did not afford

me much family time and I had seen very little of my father over the years. He meant well, I am sure, but I found I could only handle him in small doses. Father was a veteran of the Great War, and if allowed, could prattle on with an endless supply of war stories and heroic tales of friends long gone. I might have found the stories more engaging to listen to, if it wasn't for my father's terrible stutter; it required great effort for him to finish a complete sentence. The stutter was the result of an old war injury that he suffered from an explosion of some kind and subsequently made conversations with the man quite painful.

I rarely visited the old fellow who lived alone since my mother died over thirty years past. Father did press the issue, from time to time, but I usually had one excuse or another for not being able to make the trek. He was a hard-working tradesman his entire life and I don't think he approved much of my becoming a writer. Not that he ever said so, but I am sure he thought a man's hands were put to better uses than tapping the keys of a typewriter for hours on end.

Though, looking back, I figured I should have visited more often. He was my father and my only immediate family member, as I was an only child. I guess I figured he would have lived much longer, so there was no pressing need. I mean a bomb in the Great War, along with a tumble from a third-story roof, couldn't kill him, I just thought the reaper would have had a more difficult time in claiming him. And by god, that horrible stutter effectively repelled me.

Affected now by a slight feeling of guilt, I decided to head upstairs and find the master bedroom, where I might set down my bags and make myself more comfortable. Each step I took on the grand stairwell creaked quite loudly, as if a small rodent was hidden beneath each one and squealed as I brought my weight down upon it. There would be no stealthy burglars taking me by surprise in this house, I chuckled, albeit nervously, to myself.

The house was fully furnished and the décor matched the ancient-look of the architecture. It was reminiscent of visiting an old museum or historical building of some importance. My father had a love of all things antique, from ages long past.

The house would require a good cleaning though, as dust and cobwebs covered much of the furniture and trinkets found on shelves. I stopped briefly to admire a portrait that hung on a wall at the top of the stairs. It was of an elderly gentleman whom I did not recognize as a family member. Just some anonymous piece of art father must have liked. Goosebumps rose on my arms as I felt the eyes of that portrait follow me down the long corridor.

Thunder cracked outside and I quite nearly jumped out of my shoes, seeing as how I was still frazzled by the disturbing eyes of the portrait. Navigating this dark house with only the light of my electric torch did nothing to help calm my nerves.

Spotting a set of double-doors at the end of the hall told me that I had most likely found the room I had sought. The doors creaked open to reveal the master bedroom as I had expected. Antique tables and chairs filled the room, and the king-sized, four-postered, canopied-bed, looked quite inviting. Like the other areas of the house, there was a layer of dust everywhere, accompanied by an old musty smell. Three tall windows would have provided sufficient light, were the sun shining outside.

Above the bed hung a portrait of my mother, exactly how she looked before she had died. As I walked about the room, I was assailed by that same creepy feeling that the eyes were following me. Thunder boomed again and I almost dropped my light.

A little while later, I had gotten comfortable and had a fire roaring within the bedroom's fireplace; a nice touch indeed. I had changed into something more suitable for sleeping but still kept me warm. I lay on the bed which I had thoroughly dusted and shaken and found it very soft.

I had decided to explore more of the house in the morning, when it would have a much less chilling atmosphere. The warming-heat of the fireplace was causing my eyelids to droop and soon I was beginning to nod off. A loud crash from somewhere down the hall forced my eyes wide open and I sat up straight in a panic.

Had I imagined it, perhaps? Some noise that only existed in my subconscious mind? But then I heard something else, the sound of some object rolling across the hardwood floor. I was surely awake now, so firmly believed that what I heard was real. The question now was, should I investigate? The storm could still be clearly heard outside, so it was possible that whatever may have fallen was just a result of the wind or the wall-rattling thunder.

Curiosity won and I reached for my electric torch which I had kept within close-quarters on an ornately-carved wooden end table. I slipped into some fuzzy slippers and crept to the double doors. Try as I might, there was no opening them without causing such a creaking-racket that could have awakened the dead.

Instantly regretting that last sentiment, I shook the thought away and crept down the hall, attempting to discern the direction the noise had come from.

Even tip-toeing as I was, the aged floorboards still creaked, revealing my approach to any ears that cared to listen. Being a writer, I had a healthy imagination as one might expect and my mind unwantingly conjured all sorts of spine-chilling images.

The eerie rolling sound continued anew from behind a closed door, directly to my right, and if someone had been looking at me, I was most certain my hair would have been standing on end.

I approached the door, as the eyes from the portrait down the hall followed my progress, and pressed my ear against it, listening intently. Of course the sound would cease upon my efforts of discerning its source and I found myself inching the door open to shine my light inside.

I was somewhat relieved to find a long candle holder resting on the floor, where it must have fallen from a nearby mantle. Further inspection of the somewhat small room, though, revealed a most curious décor. I entered the room after deciding it needed a closer examination.

I shone my light all over the four walls of the small den, which were almost completely covered with photos and paper clippings. A single window looked out over a fairly steep drop down the side of the hill that the house sat upon. Lightning from outside would periodically light up the room as bright as day.

To my surprise, every photo in the room was a photo of me; various shots taken during book tours and book signings. The paper clippings were from reviews or articles concerning the many books I had written. A wooden table sat next to a plush reading chair and the tabletop contained a copy of each of the books that I had written. The entire room appeared to be some kind of shrine dedicated to me and all my works. And all this time I never thought father cared.

I slid open the one drawer under the table and found several handwritten letters inside. I skimmed through the contents of a few letters and found them to be correspondences from a good friend of my father's. From the replies in the letters, it would seem that my father would incessantly brag about his famous author son.

My eyes teared up at that moment. All these years my father was my biggest fan and I had not the slightest clue. And I shied away from having contact with him and made excuses to never visit. What a fool I was. I wondered, if in the end, he had actually hated me.

As I stood there facing the window in my moment of self-loathing, a strange light seemed to be emanating from behind me; I caught the reflection in the glass. I spun about in a panic, thinking an intruder stood behind me, also carrying an electric torch.

My heart stopped beating altogether and I stood there with my jaw hanging low; hairs standing on end. Before me, hovering in the doorway, was a ghostly specter, glowing with a pale-white radiance. The most unsettling aspect of this scene, was that this spirit resembled my father, complete with his small round spectacles and beard. It was also dressed in a suit and tie; father was rarely seen without one on.

Was I dreaming? Surely this could not be an actual ghost hovering before me. Then it spoke, or rather, it attempted to, and I fell back in fright, sending copies of my books from the table to the floor.

"I-I-I-I-I-I…" it stuttered.

"Good Lord!" I cried out in horror.

The glowing spirit floated closer; its arms extended towards me. "I-I-I-I f-f-f-f-f…"

Without a second thought I darted around the ghost and raced from the room. It seemed that my father had returned to not only haunt me with his ghostly presence but with his horrendous stutter as well. I accidently dropped my light and sprinted straight back to the master bedroom, slamming the double doors shut and locking them with a latch.

I was panting to catch my breath and running the situation over in my mind. I wondered if my father had planned to haunt me all along. He left me his house in the will and specified that I would have to spend a night in it in order to own it. He wanted to lure me here, to what purpose? Perhaps to shame me for never visiting him, to express his unhappiness at my admittedly poor behavior? I figured he must have knocked over that candle holder so that I would discover the room-turned-shrine.

My heart pounded in my chest and it sounded like drums beating in my ears. What would I do? Where could I go in this storm? My thoughts were interrupted as my father drifted effortlessly through a bedroom wall to enter the chamber and stare at me.

"I-I-I-I f-f-f-f-f-fo…"

I screamed with dread as it reached for me once more. I bounced off the doors, forgetting in my panic that I had locked them. With trembling hands, I unlatched the doors and dashed away, eluding the spectral hands that were nearly upon me. I couldn't be sure what would happen if the ghost touched me but I had no desire to find out.

I had dropped my electric torch back in the other room and decided to retrieve it. I scooped it up and turned to find the doorway completely blocked with the frightening specter. He had me trapped, right in the very room he had planned.

"I-I-I-I-I-I-I-I-I f-f-f-f-f-f-for…"

Seeing no other option, I leaped through the glass of the room's window to plummet down the steep drop with a scream.

The ghost drifted over to peer down through the shattered glass.

"I-I-I-I-I-I-I-I f-f-f-f-f-forgive y-y-y-you."

BEFORE THE GATES OF ST. PETER

As my eyes opened, I felt an immediate sting from the brightness. It took the better part of a minute before I was able to open them fully. Wherever I was, it was foggy, and I couldn't quite pinpoint the source of the light; it came from everywhere and nowhere, all at once.

I could make out no details of my surroundings, just thick fog everywhere I looked. I was not even sure what I was lying on but it felt soft and feathery.

I stood and wavered dizzily on unsteady legs, my head felt as foggy as my surroundings. Curiously, I noticed I was wearing a white robe of sorts; I have never owned a white robe. Where the hell was I?

I must have been dreaming, that had to be it. But everything seemed so vivid, so real. I pinched myself but felt no pain. Was that the evidence then to prove my dream theory? Surely you could not feel pain in a dream.

I tried desperately to recall my last memories to aid in solving this unsettling mystery. I remembered being in the bank, we were holding it up. I was watching the door while Hank and Eugene were collecting the money from the tellers.

I remember an argument, there was shouting, Hank was yelling at one of the tellers. Then, **BLAM!** Hank's shotgun went off and all hell broke loose. People started running in every direction and Hank and Eugene began executing them. We had agreed beforehand; no killing. But our plans had gone awry.

The moment I heard the first siren, I was out the door and speeding down the street on foot. The first two police cruisers on site decided to pursue me. I figured I had just bought Hank and Eugene some precious time before other coppers would arrive.

I ducked down an alley and soon heard the sounds of coppers pursuing me on foot. **BLAM! BLAM!** Two bullets whizzed over my head and struck the brick wall of a building. I turned the corner…then nothing. I can remember nothing after that.

Scratching my head, I exerted much effort attempting to put the pieces together after leaving the alley but that's where my mind goes blank. What happened? Did the coppers catch me? Not that it would have done them any good if Hank and Eugene got away. I didn't kill anyone and I didn't have any of the money on me. I would just say I was coerced into being a lookout for my two overly-violent partners. I would never give up their names. Not that I cared much about either of them but that was just the code on the street; you didn't rat on others.

I began walking and the ground beneath me felt so

soft. What a vivid dream indeed. I still could not see very far in any direction due to the thick fog.

Again I looked down to my robe, inspecting it closer. What happened to all my clothes? I opened the front of my robe and my jaw dropped in surprise. There were three strange marks on my chest; scars? Three small round scars. They looked almost like...bullet wounds.

Suddenly a new theory crossed my mind and I began to panic; my breathing became rapid. Was I dead? What if I turned that corner and those rotten coppers shot me? Shot me dead! Was that why I couldn't remember anything after that? Is that why I was walking around in this foggy haze?

Again I looked to my chest. Three apparent bullet wounds and no pain; I felt nothing at all.

"Hello? Hello? Anyone here?"

Oh dear god, I must be dead. I felt too aware for this to be just a dream. My hands began trembling and I ran about in circles. Everywhere was fog and it felt as though I must have been running on clouds. I was too young to be dead. Damn those coppers! Damn them to...hell?

Wait a moment; I was not surrounded by pits of fire. There was no wails of the anguished; no devils cracking fiery whips. Despite my life as a criminal, I made it to heaven. Was this heaven? Sure seemed it. White fog, soft clouds, very bright. I supposed that if I did have to die, at the very least I had made it to heaven.

A sound from off in the distance grabbed my attention. I turned to my left but could make out nothing amid the swirl of white mist. Cautiously, I crept ahead, following the sound of...paper? Someone turning the pages of a book?

I only had to walk about fifteen feet before a sight stopped me dead in my tracks. My jaw probably touched my ankles as I stood rooted in place. The fog had cleared enough so that I could make out a man seated at a small golden table. He wore a pure white robe, similar to the one I now wore. He had snow-white hair and a long white beard. Before him on the table, sat a gigantic leather-bound book, and the man paid me no attention as he leafed through the book, glancing casually at each page.

When I was finally able to gather my wits about me, I approached the man and cleared my throat to announce my arrival. He looked up from the book and those blue eyes seemed to peer straight through me.

"Ah, Stanley Goode, I see you have finally made it."

"Y-you, know my name?"

"Of course I do, I know all about you, Stanley. You were born in 1921, your father's name was Floyd and your mother's name was Angela. You had one older brother named Frank, who died in the Great War."

"Y-you are really St. Peter? The keeper of the gates to heaven?"

"Did Jesus not say unto me, 'I will give you the keys of the kingdom of heaven?'"

"Well yeah, I suppose he did."

"Yes, Stanley, I am St. Peter."

"So, I am not actually in heaven yet?"

"No, not yet, not until I deem you fit for entry."

"I-I am fit for entry. I mean, I have not led the most decent of lives but I never killed anyone. Not even in that bank, I was just the lookout."

"What happened in that bank, Stanley?"

"I don't know exactly. I was only watching the street

for coppers when I heard some arguing and then a gunshot. The other two men did all the shooting, I swear it. I ran after that."

"Who were these other two men?"

"Just guys, you know, old partners from the hood. I didn't even like them. Two real toughs."

"Stanley, you stand here in judgment. Now is not the time to lie or hold back information. If I deny you entry into heaven, you realize where you will go, do you not?"

"P-please you can't send me down there! I beg you!"

"Well the decision is really yours. Do you want to be cooperative? If you didn't shoot anyone in that bank, who did?"

"It was Hank Smith and Eugene Hale, I swear it. Please don't send me to hell! They both have killed many people. They are very violent individuals."

I didn't mind ratting out those goons now. I was dead, after all, they couldn't hurt me anymore. If ratting them out ensured my entry into heaven, so be it.

"If these two were not friends of yours, how is it that you partnered up with them? Where do you meet with them to discuss business?"

"The pool hall on West Addams Street. They hang out there all the time."

"Thank you, Stanley. I believe you are telling me the truth."

"I am, I swear. I wouldn't be fool enough to lie to you. Besides I have nothing to fear from them now."

St. Peter rose from behind his desk, closed his book, and then began to walk away.

"So, what now? Where are the gates? You are granting me entry, right?

"I am granting you entry alright, but not into heaven, Stanley. Instead you will be granted entry into a maximum security prison."

"Huh? What's going on here? Hey, where are you going?"

"Guards, Mr. Goode is all yours now."

*   *   *   *

"So he cannot see us up here?"

"No, this window is concealed."

"Impressive show. You say this works every time?"

"So far the success rate is one hundred percent."

"Marvelous. Those bullet wounds...,"

"Courtesy of a makeup artist who works in this studio."

"And when he pinched himself when he awoke...,"

"The prisoners are injected with morphine to numb their senses. They almost always think they are dreaming at first. They pinch themselves or attempt to cause pain in some manner but they feel none."

"He gave up the names of his partners quite easily."

"Indeed. These criminals have a strict code about ratting out others. Without this deception, we might never have gotten the names of the two shooters who escaped that bank. I highly doubt Stanley would have given us anything useful."

"Incredible. Great work, Chief Williams."

SHOOTING BY THE LIGHT OF THE MOON

The night of October 31ˢᵗ, one year past, Halloween night to be exact, still haunts me to this very day. I still awaken some nights crying out in a cold sweat from my nightmare-plagued sleeps. You would think that I should be happy and content, as I have never been more sought after for the female lead in big pictures. I am famous and I am wealthy, but I am burdened with guilt over the horrific knowledge that I have buried away in my mind.

From the time I was quite young, I had always wanted to be an actress. I was in all the school plays and joined a theater group when I was a teen. By the time I was twenty-one, my dreams were coming to fruition, as I landed small roles in some feature films. I was mostly playing the waitress, or the bartender, or the attractive girlfriend to a fringe character, with only minor speaking parts. Sometimes I could display my long, natural, raven-colored hair, and other times I was required to wear blonde wigs.

I continued with those types of roles for several years, until that fateful day when I received a phone call from a casting agent in the employ of the famous director, Otto Friedhelm. That phone call changed my life.

I lived modestly until that point, in a small bachelor apartment on the south side of the Big City. The odd time someone would recognize me on the street. "Hey, you are that girl from that movie," though, they never remembered my name.

I always had enough money to cover my rent, and my bills, but there wasn't much left over for anything else. I can admit to having a weakness for flashy jewelry; diamonds in particular. When I hung up the phone that day from the casting agent, images of exquisite diamond rings and brilliant new dresses flashed through my mind.

By some sheer stroke of luck, Mr. Friedhelm wished to cast me as the leading woman in his latest picture. I was still required to do a reading first but by the sound of it, it was merely a formality. I was informed that Mr. Friedhelm was very impressed with my previous work and felt that I was that undiscovered star, just waiting for the right role to flourish.

I wasn't given many details of the film over the phone, only that it was going to be a dark drama, bordering on horror. A plane ticket was purchased for me and I was to fly to a small town in the Wallachia region of Romania. I could not contain my excitement. A leading role, my biggest paycheck, and a free, all-expense paid trip to Romania.

Immediately upon my arrival, I was given the star

treatment. A driver was waiting for me at the airport to take me to a lovely little town where I had my own room at a charming, picturesque hotel, near the base of a large mountain.

The hotel was owned and operated by the amiable and ever-accommodating, Ms. Verdi. The food was fantastic and my every need was seen to. I had a beautiful second-story view of a forest, where the autumn leaves were a variety of stunning reds, oranges and yellows. The room itself was furnished with wonderful hand-carved antique furniture. The hotel, and the town on a whole, looked as though it was stuck in time, a quiet little community, living much as it had in centuries gone by.

I wasn't in town for very long before I was finally introduced to Otto Friedhelm. He was a charismatic and talkative man, with salt-and-pepper hair and a greying beard. He bordered on eccentric and seemed to have an endless supply of energy. He continuously rambled on about one such thing or another without stopping to take a breath. Sometimes, he didn't even complete a thought before changing the topic to something entirely different.

I was relieved though, that he thought I would play the perfect Emily. He only had me read a few lines from my first scene before announcing that I was the perfect choice. I will never forget my feeling of joy at being treated like a star. I even had my own chair with my name on it that would get delivered to the site of each scene by one of the crew members.

Curious, I stopped to chat with the young crew member. "What is your name?"

"Thomas."

"Nice to meet you, Thomas. And what is it that you

do here, for Mr. Friedhelm?"

"I carry your chair from set to set."

"That's it?"

"Yes, that's it. You are the star. Someone has to be sure that your chair gets to where it needs to be."

I was indeed flattered that somebody's sole duty on set was to carry my chair around. I would be lying to say otherwise. I remember hoping that this was not going to go to my head.

I had now received the full script from Mr. Friedhelm and discovered that it was a movie about a tormented man who had been cursed to live as a werewolf. I played the love interest of the man who would become the werewolf but my character was not to learn of this terrible fact until the climax of the film.

On the first day we were to begin shooting, I met the male lead, Luther Miklos. He was a tall, handsome man, with dark hair and a thin beard. He had nice wide shoulders and spoke English with a thick accent. I had never seen Luther in anything before but I was informed that he was more of a local actor. Like me, this was going to be his first big break, thanks to Mr. Friedhelm.

A week of shooting went by and I was having the time of my life. Mr. Friedhelm was a perfectionist and most scenes we shot several times until it was just right. Though he was always a gentleman about it and would apologize constantly for wishing to try different angles, or adjusting stances and items in the background. He had an endless supply of energy and was a whirlwind around the set.

We had just wrapped up shooting the scene where my character, Emily, meets Luther for the first time. Emily travelled a lot as a photographer for a magazine and Luther was her guide through a fictional town in the Old Country. The scene was shot in a café and after Mr. Friedhelm yelled, "cut", and announced a break, I made my way back to my special chair. I noticed a different young man was standing nearby it.

"What is your name?"

"My name is Marko."

"Well hello, Marko. What happened to Thomas?"

"Thomas fell ill, so I was hired to replace him. And it's an honor to carry the chair of a famous movie star."

"I hope Thomas is alright. And thank you, but I am not really a famous movie star. Not yet anyways."

Weeks turned into a month and it was now nearing the end of October. We worked every day and we worked long days. The weather had been turning cooler, and as a result, was causing many crew members to fall ill. For example, I was now on my fifth chair carrier! They were all local young lads from the town who were more than eager to carry a chair around for whatever Mr. Friedhelm was paying them, which I had to imagine would not have been much at all.

Our work schedule had been intense and it was now time to film the final scene, in which Emily discovers that the man she has fallen in love with turns out to be a werewolf. This scene was to be shot in a forest under a full moon. I wondered how they were going to work the transformation scene, as I had been told the makeup process for Luther was painstakingly long.

As fun a time as I had been having, I was eager to shoot the last scene and get back home to see my family. I was informed we had to wait another four days until the moon was full before we could start filming. We could have just used some stock footage of a full moon but Mr. Friedhelm was always insistent that everything had to be authentic. As I said, he was a perfectionist.

After such a frenzied month, I have to say that I didn't mind relaxing for a few days. I didn't realize how exhausted I had been until I was given my first day with nothing planned. It gave me a little more time to explore the lovely little shops in town and pick up a few souvenirs of my visit.

As the sun set on the fourth day, a young man approached me as I was lounging near a large window in the hotel's lobby, enjoying the view.

"Pardon me, Miss. Mr. Friedhelm is ready to shoot the last scene and has asked me to fetch you."

"Thank you, I shall grab a few things from my room and join you shortly. I have not seen you around the sets before."

"Oh, I just started. I get to carry your chair to the next location."

I rubbed my chin. "Let me guess, the last young man fell ill?"

"Indeed so and lucky for me. It's very exciting to work on a movie set."

I paid the comment no further heed and grabbed a few things from my room before following Emilio, for that was the young man's name. I was fortunate that I had the foresight to bring my sweater as there was a biting chill in the air this evening.

I found my young escort appeared jittery and looked about nervously with every sound. I suddenly remembered that tonight was Halloween and found it strange that the town seemed deserted. The sun had not vanished very long ago and it was still early in the evening, so where were all the people?

"Do your people not celebrate Halloween at all, Emilio? I see some decorations around the town but no people."

"Oh yes, we love Halloween."

"Well, where is everyone then? Is tonight not Halloween?"

"It is Halloween but tonight there is a full moon."

"So?"

"Normally, nobody goes out on a full moon," he replied, his eyes shifting about skittishly.

I decided not to push the boy further and just followed in silence the rest of the way. We hiked a good twenty or so minutes into a dark forest and thankfully Emilio had brought a lantern with him or surely we would have become lost. I was becoming increasingly anxious before we finally found a clearing where the others were waiting on us.

I was a little surprised by the fact that there were not many people present. There was Mr. Friedhelm, of course, who was rambling a mile a minute, Luther, who was pacing back and forth near a large tree, no doubt going over his lines in his head, and two crew members, one to work the camera and another to hold a spotlight. My chair was already waiting for me as Emilio had been here earlier.

"There is my Emily," Mr. Friedhelm announced excitedly. "I hope you don't mind my dear but time is of the essence tonight and we must begin presently."

I was fine with that. I had the last four days to practice my lines and was fairly confident that I had everything down to memory.

Luther appeared agitated but was able to compose himself as Mr. Friedhelm yelled, "action." Luther was also the name of the character he played. Emily and Luther met in the middle of the clearing within the dark forest. The night was cloudy, and at the moment, the bright full moon was veiled behind a cluster of thick clouds.

Luther, the character, had been acting quite peculiar as of late, which had Emily concerned. He had been disappearing at night without a proper explanation as to his whereabouts. Sometimes, she even noticed strange wounds upon his body; cuts and bruises that Luther had no recollection as to their origin.

Luther had grown weary of living a lie, so out of his love for Emily, decided upon this late night meeting to reveal to her his nightmarish secret.

My character had yet to be involved with any scene concerning the werewolf, so I had not yet seen what Luther looked like in the makeup. I remember feeling somewhat excited by the prospect.

Luther was a fantastic actor. Real tears fell as he began to tell Emily of a dark secret that he had so far kept hidden from her. Normally, Mr. Friedhelm stopped us to shoot many different takes of the same scene. It was not so this time. He stood silent behind the cameraman, riveted by our performance, or Luther's, more specifically. The camera kept rolling as we continued uninterrupted.

"Luther, my love, what is this dark secret you speak of? I know you to be a good man and I cannot imagine that there is anything that you could say to bend my mind."

"Emily, I am not a good man, I am in fact, a

monster."

"A monster? Oh please. By whose definition?"

"By mine. By the townsfolk. And by yours soon enough, I do not doubt. I have been cursed, my dear. I am truly a monster."

"Stop this nonsense, Luther, I…"

My words were halted in midsentence as the clouds overhead opened up and the light of the full moon filled the clearing. Luther suddenly doubled over and groaned as if in immense pain. According to the script, our conversation was to continue on awhile longer but it seemed that Luther had jumped ahead. Mr. Friedhelm had not yelled "cut" so I decided to stay in character and finish the scene.

"Luther, what is wrong with you?" I cried with concern, my hands pressed against both of my cheeks.

He stood up straight, his arms reaching towards the sky and let out a hideous, feral growl. It was then, and I remember it oh so clearly, that I witnessed something that defied logic. I had often pondered how this scene would play out in terms of Luther's makeup. I had imagined a long pause while a team of people worked feverishly to effect his transformation. I had been wrong, quite wrong indeed.

A scream, a real scream and not play-acting, got caught in my throat. So horrified was I by the scene unfolding before me that I could not even expel a single sound. My mouth hung open in silent terror.

My body trembled as I watched hair, no wait, thick fur, sprout from all over Luther's body. His fingers elongated and ended with razor-sharp claws. His shoes split open and his feet enlarged and resembled large paws.

There was a blood-curdling howl as a snout replaced his otherwise handsome face and as he howled, he revealed two rows of menacing fangs. His ears had become pointed and in mere moments, Luther resembled more beast than man.

I knew immediately that this was no act and that I had just borne witness to something so utterly terrifying and most likely seldom seen and spoke about. I had no idea what to do at this point. The others were not shocked by this and continued to watch; in fact the camera kept rolling!

Luther, or whatever he was now, a real werewolf I supposed, returned his gaze to me and growled hungrily. I am not embarrassed to admit that my legs turned to jelly and I collapsed to the ground. I was paralyzed with fear and lacked the strength or courage to defend myself. I lay there an easy victim for the hideous beast.

Unfortunately for me, the horror was not to end just yet. Suddenly from out of the forest, ran Emilio, the chair carrier, dressed in one of the police costumes and carrying one of the prop guns. He waved it bravely at Luther before the werewolf turned on him.

What Luther did to that poor young man, I dare not speak of. The images of what I saw haunt my dreams and the mere thought of it brings tears to my eyes. It probably lasted mere moments only but felt an eternity to me at the time.

When Luther finished with Emilio, he turned his attention back to me. If the actor I knew was still somewhere behind those cold eyes, there was no trace of it now. As he advanced towards me, a deafening gunshot startled us both, echoing off the trees around the clearing.

Mr. Friedhelm finally stepped out from behind the cameraman and approached cautiously with a large pistol aimed at Luther.

"That's a cut, Luther. Our filming is at an end now. Our contract has been fulfilled and you have been provided the agreed-upon meals. You may leave now."

The werewolf cocked his head and growled, before taking another step closer towards me.

"No, Luther, she was not part of our deal. I know you can understand me. You know what kind of bullets are in my pistol. Each is coated in solid silver. Do not make me use it."

Somehow, in that bestial head, Luther understood those words. He howled one last time then lopped into the darkness of the forest and vanished from sight.

Mr. Friedhelm exhaled and lowered his pistol. "That's a wrap. Excellent performance my dear," he said, turning to address me. "Worthy of an award to be sure. You have to know, this was all necessary to capture the most realistic werewolf picture ever made. Sacrifices were needed. I had to…"

He rambled on and on and I heard nothing more, so traumatized was I. I was put on the first flight home the next day and spent weeks recovering from the shock, unable to even speak with my family. I couldn't be sure who was more the monster, Luther, or Otto Friedhelm. It would seem I solved the case of the mystery illness which inflicted certain crew members and led to their eventual disappearance. All bargaining chips used to entice the werewolf into appearing in the film.

Many times I thought of running to the police to inform them of Mr. Friedhelm's crimes but who would believe me? What would they say when I confessed to witnessing a werewolf murder a young man? People would think me mad.

Not surprisingly, the picture was an instant success. Word spread quickly and theaters were packed the world over. My phone rang daily with agents looking to hire me for upcoming films. I did not return any calls as my feelings of distress had yet to subside.

A year later, I read a somewhat satisfying article in the newspaper. Mr. Friedhelm was found dead of an apparent strangulation near a pyramid in the Great Desert. As it turned out, he was researching his next monster movie which involved a mummy. The authorities were seeking the murderer but so far had no leads.

Of Luther Miklos' fate, I know not. I never seen nor heard tell of him after that Halloween night. He was given several awards for his outstanding performance in the picture, though of course, never attended any of the events to claim his prize.

SHADOW ALLEY

I gulped down the last drop of my mediocre coffee, left a dime on the counter for the waitress, and then proceeded straight to my car. A half hour earlier, I heard the call come over the radio about a body found in an alley of the Junkie Jungle. The Junkie Jungle was one of the nastiest neighborhoods in the bowels of the Big City. It was largely populated with junkies, of course, along with drug dealers, gangsters, and ladies of the night. All the undesirable types enjoyed congregating in that one area.

Normally I would not respond to a call in the Jungle, that was for the regular coppers. But I was in the area following up some leads on another case and the description of the body found in the alley piqued my curiosity. The average murder in the Jungle was carried out with your usual knives or guns. This one…sounded different. So I decided to drop by for a peek.

I parked my car as close as I could get to the police

cordon and locked my doors as I got out. I didn't need some junkie ransacking my car looking for nickels and dimes. A couple officers approached to intercept me so I flashed my badge. "Detective Edward Kane."

"Oh sorry, Detective, go on past."

"Thank you."

I continued on into an alley and nearly gagged from the smell of urine and feces. Graffiti dominated the brick walls and used needles crunched underfoot as I walked along. The alley was quite dark and about six people wide. I pulled out my hanky and held it over my nose to keep from vomiting. How did people live in these alleys?

"Stay awhile and you will get used to the smell," said Detective Banks, when he noticed my approach.

"No thanks, I don't think I want to be here that long," I replied.

"To what do we owe this honor? A visit from Detective Kane," asked Banks' partner, Detective Green.

"I was in the area," I said. "Heard the call on the radio and was curious to see what you got here."

"Well then, come and take a look. Bet you haven't seen this before."

I followed my two colleagues down towards the end of the alleyway where a police photographer was taking photos of the crime scene. That giant flash bulb blinded us with every photo taken. We kindly asked the man to return in ten minutes time.

Green was right; I hadn't seen anything like this before. "Death by a thousand needles, eh?"

"At least that. We haven't had them counted yet, but he was stabbed at least a thousand times with a needle."

"You have an ID on the victim?"

Banks nodded. "Harry Willis. Small-time gangster with The Jungle Cats gang. Needless to say, not a very nice individual."

"Wouldn't be such a travesty if the killer wasn't found," Green added.

"Any suspects?"

"Hmm, let's see here. Someone stabbed to death with a needle in the Junkie Jungle, so yeah, I'd say we have a few hundred suspects."

I didn't appreciate the sarcasm. I had known Banks for years; lazy detective. If the suspect was not standing a few feet away holding the smoking gun, there was a good chance that Banks wasn't solving the crime. He wasn't dim-witted, just lazy.

"No witnesses then?"

"None, or none that will talk anyways. Most folk down here tend not to speak out against the gangs. But you can be sure The Jungle Cats will also be looking for the killer. Street justice."

He had a point. Criminals like these usually dished out their own justice and were quicker at finding killers than the police. Perhaps some junkie got a bad batch of smack and took his frustration out on the dealer. In any event, it wasn't my case and what went on in the Jungle wasn't my concern.

I bid my colleagues a good evening and headed back to my car. It had been a long day and it was time to get home for some rest.

It was about a week later, I was at my desk in the office typing up a report, when I was approached by Detective Banks. He tossed a large envelope onto my desk.

"Take a look at these."

I opened the envelope to find a series of disturbing photos. Three different bodies in total; all appeared to have been stabbed to death by a thousand needle points. Just like the body I had seen for myself.

"These were all this week?" I wondered.

"Yes, each one about a day apart. The same alley for each murder."

"The same alley? Talk about brave. These all members of the same gang?"

"Yes, all Jungle Cats. This has to be some turf war between gangs."

"Since when did gangs resort to using needles as weapons? What happened to guns and knives? Those make a statement."

"Maybe the gang is trying to throw us off their trail? Make us believe it was someone else?"

"Since when did the gangs of this city begin to care whether we knew a murder was caused by them or not?"

"Maybe it's a smaller gang and they are not ready for an all-out war with the Cats just yet. So they are picking them off one by one."

"I doubt that. I think you have a serial killer here, Banks."

"Shhh, keep your voice down. I don't want the Chief to hear that. When it's gang members killing gang members, he doesn't particularly care. He starts thinking serial killer and he will be on my rear and fast!"

And there it was, lazy Banks didn't want to put much effort into tracking down a serial killer. All along he was hoping the gangs would sort this mess out amongst themselves. These were definitely not gang killings, in my opinion. I would be looking for a junkie turned murderer.

"If it's the same alley each time, have you staked out the alley?"

"I have had officers patrol the alley several times a night, for the last two nights. There has been no activity."

Of course there hasn't been any activity, I thought to myself, uniformed officers will keep the gangs and the killer lying low and out of sight. Banks left, taking his photos with him, and no doubt was going to stick to his gang war theory. Oh well, it was not my case.

The following afternoon, I was leaving my favorite sandwich shop, when I heard the call over the radio about another body found in the Junkie Jungle. Curious, I decided to stop by.

I was not surprised at all to find out that the body was that of a gang member, stabbed to death with a needle and found in the same alley. This time though, it appeared the victim put up a fight.

I approached one of the officers on scene and flashed my badge. "Question for you. Are you familiar with all the murders in this alley?"

"Yes, sir. Seen each one."

"Have the victims all been armed?"

"Yes, each one was packing a gun, but this guy here was the only one who got his out before he was killed."

"No signs that he wounded anyone?"

"Nope. Fired all six shots from his revolver and hit nothing. We recovered all the bullets and there were no traces of blood on any of them, nor any blood anywhere else in the alley."

The alley was not too large. Even if this guy was a terrible shot, I would think that one of the six bullets would have hit something. I also found it extremely odd that someone armed with only a needle, would risk attacking men armed with guns. Generally, that doesn't work out so well for the individual without a gun.

The first four men were killed before pulling their weapons. That told me that either they knew the killer, or they felt the killer was not a threat, such as some skeletally-thin junkie. Now the last guy emptied his gun before being killed. By this point the gang members would be jumpy and suspicious of everyone. He probably pulled his weapon upon first seeing someone in the alley. Not that it did him any good. He missed all six shots and was still murdered.

I stood there scratching my head in thought, watching the crowd that had gathered at the far end of the alley, just beyond the police tape. I locked eyes with a frightfully-thin man in a tattered grey coat, before he ducked out of sight.

I excused myself from the officer and quickly made my way down the alley and under the tape. I pushed my way through the gathered crowd and came out onto a street with a spacious park on the other side. A rusted old playground was in the middle next to a sandbox.

Frantically, I looked about for the man who wished to avoid my gaze and I caught a glimpse of a grey coat entering a building beside the park. I raced across the park and was disgusted as needles crunched underfoot. What kind of place was this for children to play? The city needed to do something about this and soon.

I used the sleeve of my coat to open the building door and found it led to a stairwell. I nearly gagged from the stench as I stood there contemplating whether to go up or down. A door slammed shut from below so I quickly descended the foul-smelling stairs. Another door led me to an underground garage. The garage, of course, was virtually empty; as people in this neighborhood could either not afford a car, or were not fit to drive one.

Fortunately for me, the man I sought sat cowering in a corner and the chase was over. He had short, salt-and-pepper hair, with facial stubble of the same color. His cheek-bones protruded from his face and I could tell most of his teeth had rotted and fallen out. He looked like a skeleton with skin, wearing a filthy grey overcoat.

"I would just like a word with you," I said after catching my breath. "Why were you in such a hurry to get away?"

"I don't like your kind," he lisped through missing teeth.

"My kind? What is my kind?"

"Lazy, good-for-nothing coppers."

"Good-for-nothing? What state do you think this city would be in without the police?"

"Ya do a lot of good here in the Jungle, don't ya? It's as lawless here as it was in the Wild West."

I supposed I could not argue his point there. Guys like Banks did tend to let the Jungle sort out its own problems.

"What do you know about these killings in that alley back there?"

The man spat on the ground. "Good riddance to all those vile gang members. Got what they deserved, they did."

"Who has been killing them?"

"Who cares, who? They are dead and that's all that matters."

"I thought the Jungle Cats controlled things for the

most part down here?"

"They do."

"So who would be brave enough to oppose them, using only a needle for a weapon?"

"Perhaps someone is sick of their evil ways. Perhaps someone didn't like what they did to poor Albert."

Ahhh, now we were getting somewhere.

"Albert? Who is Albert?"

"Albert Lockridge. And don't ya pretend like ya never heard of him."

"I am sorry, but I don't normally work the Jungle, I am not too familiar with the area. I have only popped in out of curiosity over these latest murders."

"Albert was my best friend," he replied, as his eyes became glossy.

"Albert was a junkie?"

"Albert was an unfortunate young man who ran into tough times."

So Albert was a junkie, I figured.

"What happened to Albert, then?"

"Those Jungle Cats, those animals, they killed him! Burned him alive, they did!" the man shook with rage.

"Why?"

"One of them stepped on a needle one day, got stuck in his shoe. He blamed Albert for throwing it there. A couple of them beat him near to death and then set him on fire."

"You witnessed this?"

"I sure did. Haunts me still, it does."

"Why didn't you tell the police who did this?"

"To what good? None of ya's ever listen to us down here. Ya never believe the words of a junkie."

"This happened in that same alley?"

"Sure did."

Ok, so we have revenge killings. Some upset individual, quite possibly the man sitting before me, is getting back at the Cats for killing this Albert fellow. My initial fear was that a serial killer could eventually leave the Jungle and continue his killings elsewhere in the city, becoming my problem. It did not appear that this would be the case here but I was thoroughly intrigued as to how this person killed five armed gang members thus far. The man sitting in front of me surely had the motive but hardly the strength. A single stab with a needle was not enough to take a man down. The moment a skinny junkie struck with the first attack, they could be easily subdued. As far as I knew, none of the victims had been poisoned.

"What is your name, sir?" I asked.

"Go to hell."

I took my leave and headed back to my car, avoiding the alley where Detectives Banks and Green were most likely present, inspecting the latest victim. I didn't care to speak with either of them; there really wasn't any point. Banks was determined to let the gangs sort it out and not entertain the idea of a serial killer. I had not been informed about Albert's death before, which of course, explained the recent killings to me perfectly.

Although it was not my case, curiosity did get the better of me, and I returned to the Jungle later that night. I replaced my normal overcoat with a ragged one I picked up from a thrift shop only hours before. I pulled the hood of a sweater I wore underneath over my head and carried an empty bottle in a brown paper bag.

I found two uniformed officers walking the beat

nearby the alley and flashed my badge. I told them I was working a special assignment and needed all uniformed officers out of the immediate vicinity. I needed the gang members and the killer to feel comfortable about walking the alley tonight.

The officers agreed and said they wouldn't be too far away. I entered the foul-smelling, shadow-haunted alley, and took a seat on the ground, resting my back onto a graffitied wall. I pretended to take sips from my empty bottle and just sat there, waiting.

After nearly two hours, my patience was rewarded, as three men entered from the far end of the alley. They spotted me and drew guns, then cautiously approached. I immediately regretted my poorly thought-out decision. Initially, my plan was to blend into the environment and appear as just another homeless man, to see what might unfold. But I suddenly realized the members of the Jungle Cat gang would not know who they were after, so they would target anyone found within this alley.

I cursed inwardly and my hand crept inside my coat to grip the handle of my revolver. I knew I was fast, just not sure if I was fast enough to take out three armed men before one of them got to me.

"You are one stupid junkie, you know that?" one of the three men shouted, as they cut the distance in half.

My suspicions were correct; they thought I was the killer. Even if I could convince them otherwise, they would kill me anyways. I made an amateur mistake in coming here alone.

"Stand up, junkie. Now!" another commanded, pointing his pistol at me.

"We ain't gonna make the mistake of getting close

enough for you to stab us with those needles. So you just stand against that wall there so we can fill ya full of lead," the biggest of the three said.

"You are making a big mistake," I said, and considered flashing my badge, for all the good it might do.

I did stand though, with my one hand still on my gun, quickly weighing my options.

"The mistake is all yours, coming back to this same alley," the biggest one continued. "Did you just think you were gonna keep killing our members and get away with it?"

"Let's torture him first," suggested one of the men with a red mohawk. "Killing him quickly is too good for him."

"You might be right," the biggest agreed, and he appeared to be the leader, of these three anyway. "Alright junkie, take that coat off, and slowly. No funny business or I will shoot you."

I figured the time to act was now at hand. I was about to drop my coat when a most curious sight caught my attention. The shadows behind the three gang members began to swirl about until they took on the shape of a man. I blinked several times thinking it was some trick of the eyes but there it stood. It was the form of a thin man but a man none-the-less.

Noticing the curious expression I wore upon my face, the three men hazarded a glance behind them. The man with the red mohawk didn't even bother to speak first and fired two shots into the shadowy form. It didn't surprise me that the bullets passed right through to strike the wall behind.

The shadow then rose up, elongating its body beyond

the size of a normal person, so that it towered over the men. It lifted its dark arms to reveal shadowy-hands, which ended not with black fingers, but with the shapes of needles. Indeed, ten needles sat where ten fingers should have been.

The shadow lunged forward and plunged all ten needle points into the chest of the mohawked gang member. The man fell and howled with a mixture of pain and terror. The creature, for I did not know what else it could be, raised its arms and drove them down again, repeatedly stabbing the man.

The two remaining gang members emptied both their pistols into the horrendous shadow-creature without consequence. Its needles apparently were real enough to cause actual harm, but otherwise, it was just an insubstantial shadow, spawned of the darkness itself.

As the screams of the mohawked man ceased, the shadow turned on the other two men and made living pincushions out of them before my eyes. They punched and kicked to no avail. They were better off attempting an escape, though, I imagine there was nowhere to run at night, when the shadows themselves were pursuing you.

Once all three of the men were lying still on the filthy ground of the alley, I instinctively drew my own weapon. I just witnessed how useless bullets were to this strange creature but force of habit had me pointing my gun at it regardless. I don't mind admitting that my hand trembled.

The thing before me made an odd motion, almost as if it saluted me, then it melted back into the darkness of the alley and vanished from sight. I am not sure how I knew this but I just knew; the shadow of Albert Lockridge had just claimed three more lives.

The alley soon flooded with uniformed officers, after having heard the gunshots and screams from nearby. I was forced to relate that the mysterious killer fled the alley and that it was simply too dark to get a description. What else could I say? That I witnessed the shadows themselves murder these three men? That it was the spirit of Albert Lockridge returned for revenge?

Nearly a half hour later, I finally extracted myself from the alley and was headed back to my car. I noticed Detectives Banks and Green headed my way.

"Kane, you saw the killer?"

"Your first instinct was correct, Banks, just let the Jungle sort itself out. You won't be solving these murders."

THE STEEP PRICE OF MAGIC

As time passed me by, people were becoming less and less interested in an aging magician and escape artist. There was a time when I was a much sought after act; filling some of the best theaters in the Big City. The last several years though, I was reduced to performing at children's birthday parties, where the name, The Great Fazoo, was no longer recognized, nor respected.

Where did it all go wrong? I supposed it might have begun with the arrival of Vlad Wasili, a young and cocky magician who started out by performing on the streets, dazzling crowds in the theater district. He was known for some revolting acts that thrilled and terrified at the same time. He could spend days trapped in various things, such as a block of ice, or a tank of water, in front of fascinated onlookers.

Somehow Vlad turned his street performances into a

successful stage show, and for the last decade, was a permanent fixture at The Four Aces Casino. As a result, he lived in a penthouse suite in one of the city's most affluent neighborhoods.

I could break out of a straitjacket in thirty seconds but that didn't seem to impress people any longer. I would need to appear to chew my own arm off during the escape, showering the front rows with blood, in order get people's attention nowadays. That was Vlad's style, not my own.

Being a magician was all I had known. As a child I had watched a live performance by Gary Ghostly and knew right then that I wanted to do what he did. Gary Ghostly, or the Ghost, as he was more commonly called, was the greatest escape artist of our time. He could seemingly break out of anything, as if he was indeed some ghost.

I studied magic books and learned tricks from the owner of a local magic shop. I started by performing for just my friends and then for schools. People began to pay me to perform and I dropped out of school as a teen to pursue my dream of becoming a career magician and escape artist.

This is the only job I have ever held. For much of my life it paid my bills and afforded me some small luxuries and level of fame. Now, I struggled to pay bills and make the rent for my decrepit, one room apartment, in what would be considered the slums of the city.

Granted, I had turned to alcohol many years back, which led to my steady decline and depleted bank account. I became a recluse, a mere shell of my former, charismatic self. I was unable to perform properly after several drinks, but without them, my hands would tremble, hindering my card tricks which made up the bulk of my act. I was required to find the right level of alcohol, which would cease my shaking hands but not impede the rest of my act.

These were dark times for me and if I didn't find more work soon, I would lose my apartment and be cast out onto the street, perhaps having to live in the Junkie Jungle with the other lost souls of the city.

I cleaned myself up to the best of my ability and spent the next week visiting each of the theaters and casinos in the city, all but begging for another chance to perform. Nobody was interested.

"The Great Fazoo? I thought you died forty years ago? Didn't you die?"

"Sorry, we all are booked old man."

"We don't put on magic shows here anymore, just concerts. People don't care about card tricks anymore."

"What was your name again? A Great Baboon?"

"Sorry, Fazoo, your tricks just don't impress this younger crowd."

It was Saturday night and I sat on the edge of my bed, staring at the exposed brick wall within my room. A storm raged outside and water leaked from several spots, thoroughly soaking my torn and stained carpet. Next door on my right, a husband and wife shouted at one another, and to my left, a baby cried ceaselessly. I lifted the bottle of whiskey that I had purchased earlier that day, using the last of my money, to the very penny, and took a mouthful.

Despite my poor living conditions, and my lack of funds, I found that the one thing that distressed me the most about my life was that I wouldn't be remembered as a great magician. To this day, people still spoke of Gary Ghostly. There was books written about him and even a movie was made. Even Vlad Wasili was featured on the covers of some popular magazines and tabloids. But everywhere I went, I heard the same things over and over. Who are you again? I thought The Great Fazoo was dead? Who cares about The Great Fazoo?

All my life, my one dream was to be considered in the same class as Gary Ghostly. That our names would be spoken in concert together, with the same level of respect. I never really cared about the money, just as long as I made a living. Being remembered was the most important thing to me and in that, I failed miserably.

I gulped another mouthful of the whiskey and relished the way it burned my throat on the way down. I closed my eyes and placed my forehead on my knees, listening to the rhythm of the rain, along with the occasional clap of thunder.

"I would do anything, so that my name would be remembered," I spoke aloud, despairingly. "Anything at all."

"Anything, you say?" a voice from within my room said.

I jumped to my feet and quite nearly dropped my whiskey bottle. I had not heard my door open so I was most surprised to find a man standing next to my window; a well-dressed man in an exquisite black suit and matching tie. Outside, the rain came down in buckets and yet this man's clothes were bone dry. He did not live in the building as I was sure I had never seen his face before.

His black hair was slicked back and shiny, most likely having used more than just a dab of Brylcreem. He had a thin dark moustache and a curious-looking triangular tuft of hair on his chin. His skin was a shade of pale and he had sharp features like protruding cheek bones. There was a calmness about him that I found immediately unnerving. He stood familiarly in my room as if he belonged here. In fact, I got the impression that he would probably feel as though he belonged anywhere he wished.

"Who the hell are you?" I demanded.

"I am just a friend that you haven't yet met."

"How did you get in here? I never heard that door open."

"The storm is loud outside and it appears you were distracted. In any case, that's not too important. That I am here now is the main thing."

"You speak in riddles."

I took another drink and sat back down on the edge of my bed. I felt if this man was a threat, he would have done something by now. Anyways, I had nothing to steal and nothing left to lose.

"You seem…down, my friend. What ails you?"

"What do you care?"

"I care about my friends."

"So, we are friends now? I don't even know your name."

"My friends call me, Dee."

"You have a last name, *friend?*"

"But of course, who doesn't? My last name is Eville."

"Well Mr. Eville, I don't need any friends. I can barely look after my own self."

"Then that is exactly why you need a friend. Friends help each other."

"And you just wander around looking for random people to help? What's your game, Mr. Eville?"

"No game. And yes, I like to help people, to our

mutual benefit of course."

"I am afraid that the help I require is far beyond anyone's ability. I have run out of time to achieve what I desire most. I will die poor, alone, and unremembered."

"Very little is beyond my ability. Name your desire and I will see it come to fruition."

"What business are you in?"

"I am an agent, of sorts. I can make dreams come true."

The strange man placed a cigarette into his mouth. He snapped his fingers and flames erupted from the tips to light the cigarette. Once lit, he blew on his fingers and extinguished the flames.

"You are a magician too?" I wondered.

"I am many things. But foremost, I am your friend, and I wish to help you."

"I have always wanted to be remembered as a great magician and escape artist, much like Gary Ghostly. But I am an old man who cannot find work. The Great Fazoo is no longer relevant. The drink has stolen years of my life and now it is too late."

"It is never too late, my friend. I can see to it that you will always be remembered."

I chuckled. "And just how would you pull that off?"

"I happen to know the secret to performing the greatest escape trick the world has ever seen. Were you to perform this particular escape, they would speak your name for centuries to come."

"Why haven't you done it then?"

"Because being remembered as the greatest escape artist is not my dream, it's yours. But I would be willing to share my knowledge with my new friend. Seeing your dream come true is what I desire."

"What do you get out of this?"

"The satisfaction of helping you."

"And that's it? Nothing else?"

"Well no, I would require something of you, but 'tis a small matter."

"Even with the secret of your great escape trick, I can't get anyone to hire me. Nobody is interested in me."

"Leave that to me. As I said, I am an agent of sorts."

"This isn't a joke is it? You can really help?"

"That all depends on you. How badly do you wish to be remembered? What is that worth to you?"

"It's worth everything to me. It's all I have ever wanted."

"Excellent, then we are in business."

Suddenly, Mr. Eville produced some documents from behind his back and handed them to me. That was quite a trick itself, hiding that amount of paper. I glanced through them to find diagrams of the escape trick he had described to me.

"This is all fine and dandy, Mr.Eville, but this seems impossible to escape from. I cannot imagine how that could be achieved and I am familiar with all the tricks of the trade."

"It can be done and I possess the secret. You will be forever remembered after performing this stunt."

"Tell me the secret."

He then produced another sheet of paper. This time it was just one but it was quite a long sheet with plenty of fine print that my aged eyes had trouble reading.

"What is this?"

"This is our contract. It outlines everything that we

have just discussed. That, as your agent, I will secure you with an appropriate venue and share with you the secret of the escape. The contract also states that I am guaranteeing that you will be forever remembered for this."

"You really are going to make my dream come true?"

"Yes, it's what I do."

"Then please tell me, how can I repay you for this?"

He smiled. "Just sign the contract and everything is written there below. We can go over it all together, in detail."

I supposed it didn't matter much what he wanted as I had nothing really to offer him. Most agents took a percentage of the money earned from the show. I didn't care how much of a percentage he wanted, just as long as I pulled this off and people would remember, The Great Fazoo.

"I don't have a pen."

He had one already in his hand, where one didn't exist a moment before. "Here, use mine. Sign by the X, right next to my name."

D. Eville   X _____

*   *   *   *

Butterflies danced about in my stomach as I stood on the empty stage and stared out at all the empty seats that would soon be filled to capacity. Mr. Eville was true to his word and managed to strike a deal with the owner of the Red Jester Hotel and Casino. They were the direct rival of The Four Aces, where Vlad performed. The owner was quite reluctant at first but changed his mind when we mentioned he would owe me nothing if he didn't agree at the end of the show that it was the best performance he had ever seen. Even if I bombed, he stood to make a pretty penny by not paying me.

For the next week the casino carried out an aggressive ad campaign; the last performance of The Great Fazoo, and the greatest escape you will ever witness.

There was a buzz in the city and I felt important again; a feeling I had long forgotten. I had shaved, cut my hair, and put on my best suit. I fidgeted with a deck of cards while peeking through a curtain as people began to fill the theater. To my surprise, even a few reporters had shown up.

I opened the show with some card tricks. I used a few oldies and a few that Mr. Eville had shown me. I was met with applause. I moved onto some sleight-of-hand, making flowers appear, as well as three live doves. I reveled in the looks of astonishment throughout the crowd, from the young and the old. I was truly The Great Fazoo again and I loved every minute.

After an hour of performing, the audience was given a fifteen minute intermission before the grand finale. As the last of the seats were full again, a long box, quite similar to a coffin really, was lowered from the ceiling. Every member of the audience was invited up to inspect the box and inspect the stage, to be sure that they could detect nothing out of the ordinary, that there were no hidden doors. Once thoroughly satisfied, they each returned to their seats.

Now, it was time. Everything I had always wanted depended on the outcome of this stunt. If Mr. Eville had spoken true, this would truly amaze everyone present.

Two lovely assistants helped me into a straitjacket and tied it tight. Then they wrapped me in chains, across my chest, further pinning my arms to my body, as well as around my legs. The chains were padlocked in place.

I took one final look out at the audience and smiled; basking in my moment of glory. I then stepped into the box and lay down. My assistants secured the lid of the box in place and wrapped it in thick heavy chains. Cables lifted the box into the air, suspending it a good twenty-feet above the stage, in full view of the entire audience. I knew the question on everyone's mind was, how could anyone ever escape from this?

$$* \quad * \quad * \quad *$$

80 Years Later

"Go on, Billy, open up that big one next. It is from your mother and me."

Billy, who had just turned nine, tore at the wrapping paper with wild abandon. His eyes lit up at the sight of the gift. "Wow, thanks! A Great Fazoo Magic Kit!"

"Interesting gift," Adam's father commented. "I didn't think kids nowadays knew who The Great Fazoo was."

"How could they not? He was the greatest escape artist that ever lived," Billy's father replied.

"But how do nine year olds know about him?"

"Billy loves magic. He has three books written about The Great Fazoo. And just recently, someone found some old 8mm footage of his last performance and restored it as best they could. It was uploaded online and everyone has been watching it."

"I can't believe that eighty years later, nobody can explain how he escaped. And to top it off, he just vanished? That box was really empty when they lowered it to the stage?"

"It was empty, alright. My grandfather was there at that show. Gramps said they lowered the box to the stage and when it was opened, all that was inside were the chains and straitjacket he was wrapped in. Nobody has ever solved that mystery and The Great Fazoo was never seen again."

"Creepy."

"You are telling me. They said he never even collected his pay. The casino had always said that his money was still there for him to collect, but nobody had ever shown up."

THE TRAGEDY OF
KING FINEAS

Everyone knew the tragic tale of King Fineas the world over. It was taught in schools, mostly through reading the version written by the amazing, and long-dead playwright, Samson Schmitt. Schmitt penned a wide variety of plays but seemed to focus on tragic tales from our storied past. Teachers would have their students read the play aloud and act out portions of it. Stage versions were performed in many different countries, but it was not until recently, that a particular reenactment had been grabbing notable attention.

I was a writer for the renowned magazine, *Millennia*. My focus was on reviews. Movies and plays mostly, and with all the recent buzz about the new play, *The Tragedy of King Fineas*, my magazine had taken notice. Surely there had been many other interpretations of the famous Schmitt play but the latest was quite unique indeed.

King Fineas ruled the kingdom of Hallandar a very long time ago. That region of the world, which was located north and east of the Great Desert, was riddled with volcanoes. Ironically, it was the eruption of Mount Fineas which buried the cities and towns of Hallandar. It wasn't until two years ago, that archaeologists unearthed the remains of the capital. Many buildings were still intact, including a good portion of the castle, where King Fineas dwelt.

Some extremely clever entrepreneurs, decided it would be most interesting, and indeed quite profitable, to stage a rendition of the play, *The Tragedy of King Fineas*, right amidst an excavated portion of the old King's castle. Folk had been flocking to the site to watch the play from every corner of the world. The atmosphere was said to be eerie and yet truly magnificent. An awe-inspiring, three-tiered theater, had been built in what was the original throne room. To just imagine, that you are watching the story of King Fineas, right in the exact location where this tragic tale played out.

Now let me be clear, in case you are unfamiliar with the tale, the eruption of the volcano was not the tragedy spoken of, though admittedly, it was an unfortunate event. No, the tragedy that had so enthralled the playwright, Schmitt, took place months before the region was buried under lava and ash.

The kingdom of Hallandar was under threat from the neighboring kingdom of Wakala, and more specifically, King Rudolf, ruler of Wakala. King Rudolf was a cruel dictator, ever wishing to expand his borders. And after swallowing other smaller kingdoms, King Rudolf soon set his sights on Hallandar.

King Fineas was Rudolf's polar opposite. He was a kind and gentle man, loved and respected by his entire kingdom. Hallandar prospered under his rule and never a negative word was spoken about him. Fineas adored his people and strove to make their lives enjoyable, even down to the poorest of citizens. But the love for his subjects would be his undoing.

King Rudolf amassed his armies along the walled-border of Hallandar, calling for the surrender of King Fineas. The evil invader promised that all of the people of Hallandar would be spared, if only the King would give himself up as a willing prisoner.

It was said that Hallandar possessed an impressive army, with more soldiers than that of Wakala's army. The generals of Hallander were supremely confident that they could repel these invaders; they had no doubts. But King Fineas, ever the peace-loving man, had other plans.

Fineas loathed the idea of going to war and having his loyal subjects die senselessly. Even if they were to win, and he had been advised that they surely would, he knew that they could not win without a cost. People were going to die, regardless of their impending victory, and that thought sickened him to the core.

In a most surprising move, and against the protest of his council, Fineas elected to surrender himself to the enemy, in order to save the lives of everyone in his kingdom. He was willing to sacrifice himself, so that not one person would lose their life in defending Hallandar.

King Fineas could not be dissuaded from his decision. He surrendered himself and King Rudolf's men flooded the kingdom and soon occupied the castle. The soldiers of Hallandar lost the advantage of defense, behind the city's walls, and were ordered to lay down their arms.

In a despicable move, and revealing his true colors, the evil King Rudolf forced the foolish and naïve King Fineas, to sit in the throne room and watch as all the members of his council and generals, were executed in front of him. King Rudolf claimed they could not be trusted and were too dangerous to be kept alive. When they had been dealt with, he moved on to prominent and influential citizens, beheading each one as the horrified King Fineas was made to look on.

One particular woman, adept with black magic, was dragged into the throne room for execution. In one last desperate act, before losing her head, she channeled her anger not towards King Rudolf, but towards King Fineas, blaming him for this slaughter. She cursed Fineas to live with the guilt of what he had done to their kingdom for an eternity. She prayed to dark gods that even death would not provide respite to the man who doomed them all.

Fineas was then shackled in a dungeon, unable to even take his own life, which he wished that he could have done. He was to remain there for the rest of his miserable existence to dwell on his foolishness. Then perhaps the gods took pity on the poor King, and Mount Fineas erupted mere months later, burying Hallandar and all the horrors contained therein.

Some folk escaped the cataclysm to spread the tales of King Fineas and what had taken place before the eruption. Hundreds of years later, those tales would spark the imagination of Samson Schmitt. Then another few hundred years after the play was written, would come the very performance from the excavated castle, where this tragedy unfolded.

As I mentioned earlier, this new play caught the attention of my magazine and I was quickly dispatched to the airport, so that I might fly to this destination and review the play myself. Several years ago, I had reviewed one such version of the play that was performed right here in the theater district of the Big City. While I had thought it was quite good, giving it four out of five stars, I was told that no version performed on the planet compared with this latest. I was quite intrigued.

The flight was long but uneventful. I had lunch in a rather bland café and then caught a few hours nap in the afternoon. As the sun set in what was once the kingdom of Hallandar, I readied myself for a night out. Dressed in formal attire, I made sure to grab my notebook and made the twenty minute walk from the recently erected hotel to the castle-turned-theater.

The walk was something of a treat in and of itself. I strolled through streets that were nearly a thousand years old. Construction crews had done a marvelous job at painstakingly excavating the buried capital of Hallandar. I passed buildings that used to house shops and families alike, so very long ago. Every direction I turned, I found tourists taking photographs of these astounding historical structures.

But all of these sights paled in comparison to the restored castle I soon beheld. It was impossible to tell which part of the castle was the original architecture and which was new. No expense was spared in seeing that the castle looked very much like it did in its glory days.

I joined the lineup of people waiting to enter, listening to excited conversations from those around me. For the most part, people were here for the first time and could barely contain their exhilaration. One fellow, about five people in front of me in the line, boasted that this was his third time attending the play, and was just as excited this time, as he was the first. He claimed that words could not describe the performance as it was unlike anything he had ever seen before. He also attested that the lead man that played King Fineas had to be the greatest actor to ever set foot on a stage.

I fed off the emotions of the crowd and was soon growing impatient as the line was not moving at all. I couldn't wait to get inside and witness this event with my own eyes. It wasn't too long though, before I was rewarded, and people began to enter and take their seats.

After showing my ticket at the front gate, I entered a long corridor which was illuminated with rows of torches along both sides. Between the torches hung exquisite paintings, or stood full suits of armor, all original pieces that had been found within the castle, which really added to the atmosphere.

Regrettably, the majority of the castle was off-limits to the public, as they were still doing restoration work. I should like to return one day to tour the rest. So as it turned out, the corridor led straight to the theater itself.

I must say the theater was magnificent. There were three tiers of seats sloping upwards, seating approximately a thousand people at a time, by my guess. Much like the corridor, original works of art dotted the walls, but the real attention-grabber was below. The stage portion of the theater was the castle's actual throne room, and there, in the middle of the stage, sat the real throne of King Fineas.

My jaw dropped at its undeniable beauty. Upholstered with red velvet and inlaid with solid gold and precious gems, the throne was absolutely priceless.

My skin suddenly prickled at the thought that this was the location of all those horrible executions. King Rudolf sat in that very throne, while Fineas stood nearby, forced to watch the ghastly spectacle unfold.

I hadn't even seen the play yet and I was already thinking that five stars would not be enough. The atmosphere alone was worth the price of admission and the plane ticket to get here. Fortunately for me, *Millennia Magazine,* picked up the tab for everything. And speaking of which, my media-status afforded me a front row seat. I would have preferred to be more in the center, as I had the last seat on the right-hand side, though I still had a decent view of the stage. There wasn't really an unfavorable seat in the house.

I was, however, situated close to the stage door, where the actors would come and go, so I could get a close-up look as they passed by. Not much was known of the actors and they had not granted any media outlets any interviews as of yet. By all accounts their performances were outstanding, which was not bad at all for a group of unknowns.

I sat impatiently for nearly three-quarters of an hour, tapping my leg out of habit, waiting for the play to begin. I realized we were waiting until every seat of the sold-out theater was filled, before beginning. As the last person found their seat, the torches lighting the theater were extinguished, casting us into total darkness. There we sat, in unnerving silence, for several long moments. I found I was holding my breath, afraid to even breathe.

I heard the stage door to my right open, though I could still see nothing; my vision had yet to adjust to the gloom. Then suddenly, a spotlight that hung from the rafters, came to life and illuminated the section of the stage where the throne rested. Folk gasped as there was now a figure seated in the throne, draped in a dark robe. The play had finally begun.

THE TRAGEDY OF KING FINEAS
ACT 1, SCENE 1

KING FINEAS: (Discards robe and leans forward in the throne, chin resting on palm) Welcome all, to my home. I am King Fineas, ruler of Hallandar, and this is my tale. Do not weep for me, or pity me, as my fate was brought on by my own foolishness. My compassion for my people was their ultimate undoing. Sit back and journey with us to a time long lost, and bear witness to a story that I am cursed to relive for an eternity.

(Stage goes dark. Enter council members for a meeting with the King. Lights back on.)

I was in awe of the costumes and makeup. Their skin was painted pale white, and with the use of special spotlights, caused it to take on an eerie glow. By the time we were midway through Act Two, I wholeheartedly agreed with the critics thus far, everyone's performance was superb, especially the King's.

Fineas played the part perfectly, his facial expressions were incredible. Even when acting out the portion of the story before the arrival of King Rudolf and his army, Fineas always wore a face of sadness, never breaking character and foreshadowing the doom that was to come. I really felt for the man and hung on his every word. Whatever this actor was being paid, I felt it would not have been enough.

By the end of Act Three, I found myself on the edge of my seat and nearly falling to the floor. I was forced to adjust myself and attempt to lean back and relax, but so enthralling was the play, I was soon back to the edge of my seat.

GENERAL LUKAS: My King, your armies are assembled and awaiting your orders. Let us go forth and crush these vile invaders and send them back to the holes from whence they came.

KING FINEAS: No, my friend. I have given this much mindful deliberation. The thought of even one of my loyal subjects losing their life, tears my heart asunder. I have decided to surrender myself, as this King Rudolf has requested.

(There is a collective gasp from all those assembled in the throne room)

COUNCILLOR ZIMAS: My Lord, you cannot be serious??

KING FINEAS: I most assuredly am. What kind of King would I be, if I was not willing to do everything within my power to keep my people safe? By surrendering myself, I will be ensuring the safety of everyone in Hallandar.

GENERAL LUKAS: But we can defeat them!

KING FINEAS: My mind is set. I will not sacrifice lives needlessly when I have the power to prevent it.

With the arrival of Act Five, the final Act, I noticed the entire theater was on the edge of their seats. Even the odd child, who had been dragged to the play by their parents, had stopped fidgeting and squirming in their seats, and brought their full attention to the play's finale.

Out walked Olga, shackled and being dragged by an armored soldier. The evil King Rudolf sat in the throne, a smug look worn upon his pale face. Beside him, stood King Fineas, rooted in place with horror, as he was forced to watch a procession of executions. No mere crocodile tears streamed down his ghostly cheeks, as was evident by the anguished expression he wore.

This actor was good. All great actors were able to channel some tragic event from their past, to bring it forth from their memories and relive it in that moment, adding such realism to a scene in which they were required to appear sorrowful and heartbroken. This man had mastered that and convinced the entire audience of the horror he was experiencing.

Hands down, this was the most marvelous play I had ever had the privilege of beholding. Even I was moved to tears as Olga cursed King Fineas and he fell to his knees and wept. Curtains dropped and the stage faded from sight.

The theater went dark again as there was a rumbling sound from overhead. The seats rattled and vibrated, in an interesting added effect, signifying the eruption of the volcano, as we all knew was the real ending to this tragic tale. This continued for about a minute until torches flared back to life, illuminating the theater; the play had ended.

Every man, woman and child, got to their feet and applauded the performance, expressions of adoration and wonder plastered upon their faces. I too, stood in amazement, and actually felt a pang of sorrow that it was over; so thoroughly had I enjoyed myself. I had been so lost in the play that I had forgotten to take any notes, but I did not worry, as I was sure I had plenty to say for my review.

Keeping with my initial thoughts of the atmosphere, I felt five stars was not nearly enough and would not do the play any justice. I found myself suddenly wishing I could speak with the actors and get an exclusive interview, especially with King Fineas. Before I even realized what I was doing, I took advantage of a distracted theater employee, and dashed through the stage door.

I had no idea what the penalty might be if I was to be caught. Permanently banned from the theater? A trespassing fine? I felt it was worth the risk to be the first person to secure an interview with the cast. I could even demand a raise, I was sure of it.

I was descending down a flight of ancient stone stairs, where sparsely placed torches afforded minimal light. There was a deep chill in the air and I was soon shivering. It was quite evident that this stairwell, and the underground room it led me to, was the original architecture of the castle, and not restored in the slightest.

I worried momentarily about the structural integrity, but figured that if it was safe enough for the actors, then I should be fine. The barren room I now stood in possessed only one wooden door. Luck was with me as none of the theater employees were posted down here and the door did not appear locked.

I was beside myself with excitement and my mind was assailed with a flood of questions that I had for the cast. I pulled the heavy door open slightly to peer into the room beyond.

The scene before me froze me in place. My jaw hung somewhere down to my chest and I had stopped breathing altogether. In the chamber I now faced, stood the entire cast of the play. This room no longer contained the special lighting of the theater; in fact there was no source of light at all! And yet, the cast still glowed eerily. Costumes were hung on hooks along one wall and I could see that the actor's skin was still a pale white, and upon closer scrutiny, I found I could see right through them!

"Good heavens!" I gasped involuntarily.

Ghosts! The cast members were all ghosts! The curse of King Fineas was true, and here he still dwelt, to relive his tragic tale for an eternity!

BABYSITTING TIMOTHY

Being a teenaged girl living in the suburbs of the Big City, after school employment opportunities were not many. A few of my friends worked at the local grocery store and another at the pharmacy. While looking after other people's children wasn't always so easy, I elected to take up babysitting. At least then I could sit them by the radio to listen to programs, or send them off to bed, affording me time to study or do homework, which was something my friends could not do at their jobs.

I was the primary sitter for John and Jessica, who were brother and sister, and very well-behaved, along with Alice, who lived next door to me. After spending a few evenings with Lester, whose family lived a block away, I had to politely decline further work. I blamed it on an increased workload from school, but in reality, Lester was too much of a handful. He had endless energy and couldn't sit still for more than five minutes at a time. He also hated to go to bed which made for a constant battle that I was no longer interested in waging.

I felt terrible for his parents, who were finding it difficult to find sitters, as word of Lester spread through the world of sitters. I simply wasn't paid enough for the headaches of looking after Lester; it wasn't worth it.

One Thursday evening, my mother called me over to the phone, which had me quite curious as I had never received a call after eight. It turned out to be Mrs. Harrison from two streets over on Oakley Drive. They were going out Saturday evening and their regular sitter was away camping for the weekend.

I hadn't planned to work on Saturday but I could use the extra money that I wasn't counting on. Her son, Timothy, was eight years old and from what I had heard, was a quiet boy. People said he was a little odd but generally kept to himself and certainly didn't cause any trouble. Odd I could deal with, so I agreed.

Saturday evening came and I packed a bag with a few things to help keep me occupied for the night and walked over to the Harrison's house. I was greeted by Mr. and Mrs. Harrison, who I had never actually met in person before, but were quite pleasant. They lived in a typical, cookie-cutter, two-story house, with a long driveway and a perfectly manicured lawn. They had a spacious backyard with several large trees.

They had left some cookies and cake on the kitchen counter so Timothy and I could have a fun snack later on. Since it was Saturday night, I was told that Timothy could stay up later than usual, eleven at the latest. They said Timothy was shy, and indeed, it wasn't until the Harrison's were about to leave, that they managed to coax their son downstairs to meet me.

Timothy was a small boy, small for even his age. He had short brown hair and eyes to match. Indeed he was shy, half-hiding behind his mother's leg, peeking around at me curiously.

"Now Timothy, I don't look so scary, do I?"

He paused and then slowly shook his head, no.

"That's right, Timothy, she is just a normal young girl and there is nothing to be worried about," his mother said. "Now you behave yourself and don't make any trouble for her. You can have some cake and cookies later, but not too late or you won't sleep. You can stay up until eleven." Then Mrs. Harrison turned to address me. "We should be home by midnight. We are going to a dinner party at the Thomas' and I have left their number on the refrigerator in case you need us. You are welcome to use the radio and the record player. Timothy's favorite radio program is on this evening."

"Don't let the aliens get ya, squirt," Mr. Harrison said, messing up his son's hair.

Mr. and Mrs. Harrison then took their leave and I locked the door behind them. People generally didn't need to lock their doors in this neighborhood but I always did out of habit, when at someone else's house.

"So, Timothy, what would you like to do?"

He leaned against the arm of a sofa, shyly averting his eyes and didn't answer.

"Oh come on now, there is no need to be shy with me. Let's turn on the radio then and listen to some music, shall we?"

Timothy shrugged his shoulders and I took that as close to a 'yes' as I was going to get. I walked over to the large mahogany radio and switched it on. I turned the dial until finding a station that was playing some big band music and stopped there. I plopped myself down onto the sofa to enjoy the music. I motioned for Timothy to join me but he continued to lean against the arm of the sofa, not wishing to get too close to this stranger just yet.

I found most children were shy at first and it wasn't always easy to entice them out of their shell. I did, however, learn that talking about their favorite subjects generally helped.

"Your mother said your favorite radio program is on tonight, which one is that? I wonder because I also have a favorite on Saturday nights."

Timothy looked up and I knew I now had his attention. "Invaders from Space," he softly answered.

"Wow, imagine that, that is also my favorite program," I replied, stretching the truth a little.

I had listened to the program a few times before; I just wasn't as interested in aliens from outer space as I was with the adventures of the orphan, Beatrice, or the explorer, Jungle Johnny. But to help break the ice here, Invaders from Space was my new favorite.

I had not heard any of the recent episodes, but fortunately for me, I recalled a conversation between two of my classmates during a lunch break only a few days ago.

"I wonder what Commander Foxx is going to do tonight? I don't think the other military leaders believe him about the alien threat," I cleverly asked.

Timothy's face brightened and he stood up straight. "Commander Foxx's men believe him. I think they will secretly take some planes and intercept the aliens all by themselves."

"Ooooh, I hadn't thought of that. But will that be enough?"

"Commander Foxx is the best fighter pilot in the whole world!"

I nodded. "Yes, he sure is. I guess no alien ship could stand up to him, eh?"

"Do you think Commander Foxx is real?" Timothy asked.

"Well no. It's just a radio program. Commander Foxx is just an actor doing the voice." Timothy seemed saddened by that so I quickly added, "But sometimes these characters are based on real people. They probably got the idea for Commander Foxx from a real pilot."

"I hope so."

"Why is that?"

"Can I have a cookie now, please?"

"Of course you can. Come on, let's go to the kitchen for a snack before our program starts."

I breathed a sigh of relief as Timothy seemed to have come out of his shell, which made my job much easier. We sat at the kitchen table and each had one homemade chocolate chip cookie, along with a small sliver of carrot cake. We washed it down with a tall glass of milk, then returned to the living room and prepared for the program that was soon to start.

Timothy and I sat on the carpeted floor, directly in front of the radio, and I was pleased that he did not try and sit as far away as possible; he was becoming comfortable around me. He didn't seem very odd to me, just a typical shy boy.

We listened intently to this week's episode of Invaders from Space. Just as Timothy had predicted,

Commander Foxx was unable to sway the minds of his superiors that a threat from outer space was imminent, so secretly gathered his loyal men to his side and took off with borrowed fighter planes. The episode, as was typical of these programs, ended with a cliffhanger; an alien attack was nearly upon us and Commander Foxx and his men were the only ones who knew.

"Aliens aren't really from Mars, like in this program," Timothy finally spoke, once the episode was over.

"Oh no? I thought scientists figured Mars was the most habitable of all the other planets? Where do they come from, then? Jupiter? Saturn?"

"Xaalox-9."

"Xaalox-9?" I chuckled. "And just where is that?"

"It's the third planet from the star, Syrealius."

"Oh it is, is it? How do you know that?"

"Do you wanna see my telescope? It arrived in the mail last week but I don't think it works very well."

"Sure, why don't you show me? Maybe we can find Xaalox-9 with it?"

"I doubt it, it's too far."

Timothy ran upstairs to his bedroom and promptly returned with a small telescope, no larger than a soda bottle. I felt sorry for the boy in that moment. He ordered the telescope from an ad in the back of a funny book, where it claimed you could view the planets with it. In a cruel joke, small stickers of planets were placed on the lens so that you saw planets anywhere you looked. I can only imagine how many budding young astronomers had their hearts broken when this piece of junk arrived in the post.

I tried to hide my amusement. "Well I don't think you need this thing anyways, it sounds like you are very familiar with the planets out there."

"What do you think would happen, if General Zasslar attacked Earth?"

"Who is that?" I had to wonder.

"General Zasslar is the military leader of Xaalox-9. He commands a great fleet of ships."

"Oh he does, does he? Well then, I guess we would need Commander Foxx to save us."

That sad expression returned to his face once more. "I thought you said Commander Foxx wasn't real?"

"Well Foxx might not be real, but I said he is most likely based on a real person."

"I really hope so. Xaalox-9 is a dying planet and the aliens there need a new home to conquer."

Timothy sure did have a fantastic imagination, thanks to programs like Invaders from Space. For the next little while I listened to music as Timothy sat on the floor and drew pictures of flying saucers with his crayons.

It was soon eleven o'clock and I reminded Timothy it was time for bed. He didn't complain at all and gathered his drawings, along with his telescope, and ran up the stairs to his room. The Harrison's should only be another hour at most, so I retrieved a book from my bag and settled in on the sofa to pass the hour reading.

I soon realized I had left the radio on and should turn it off, so as not to keep Timothy awake. I switched it off and returned to the sofa, when I heard something from upstairs. It sounded like someone was talking. I first wondered if maybe Timothy had also turned on a radio upstairs but as I moved to the base of the stairs to listen more closely, I found that it was Timothy's voice I heard.

Perhaps he was playing with his army men, as I knew

that was also something he enjoyed. He really needed to get to bed though; I didn't want the Harrison's to think I was allowing him to stay up too late.

I ascended the stairs and found his room was the first door on the right. It was an easy guess, from the drawings of space ships and green aliens that were taped to the door. From inside I could hear his voice clearly and it sounded like he was having a conversation with someone.

I knocked first and then entered. "Now Timothy, you are supposed to be in bed already, not playing."

Timothy was standing near his window, which was slightly open. He hadn't yet dressed for bed and was holding a tin can to his ear. Attached to the closed end of the can was a string that stretched from the can all the way out the window. I imagined another can at the other end of that string, as I had seen other boys create these devices in an attempt to communicate with each other, usually linked between tree-forts.

"This is much too late to be chatting to your friend next door, your parents wouldn't want you up this late. Now run along and change and brush your teeth before they get home and you get me in trouble."

"Alright," he said, placing the can on the floor and running off to the washroom to brush his teeth.

I approached the window and my eyes followed the string up the side of the house where it was indeed attached to another can which sat on the edge of the roof. The open end of this can was strangely attached to the lid of a garbage can, giving it the appearance of a homemade satellite dish, like those I had seen photos of.

I was a bit surprised, expecting the string would stretch over to a neighbor's window, or perhaps to a tree-fort in the backyard. I was about to close the window when I thought I heard a sound from the can resting on the floor.

Curiously, I picked up the can and placed it to my ear. A voice from inside the can caused me to squeal in fright; I threw it to the floor and ran from the room.

"Commander Timothy? *ZZZZRT.* Commander Timothy, are you *ZZZZRRRT* still there? I hope you are ready for our arrival tomorrow. *ZZZZRRRRT.* For the *ZZZZRRRT* glory of Xaalox-9, I look forward to testing our army against yours. General Zasslar, out."

THE UNREMEMBERED
SOLDIER

My eyes shot open at the sound of a loud explosion and I grabbed my Thompson machine gun which rested across my lap. I tried to orient myself in the darkness of the forest and there was just enough light from the moon for me to realize there was no immediate threat. The shelling was taking place somewhere to the north. It wasn't our concern; not yet anyways.

I looked about and noticed several of the other soldiers sound asleep and completely oblivious to the sounds of the distant battle. A few men snored away. Those are the ones I envied, as I cannot remember the last time I had a decent sleep. The ground was uncomfortable and there was always the constant threat of the enemy creeping up on us in the dark.

We were deep in enemy occupied territory and they knew this terrain well. They also knew we were coming as we had routed several of their companies three days previous. I couldn't tell if the shelling from the north was from us or them but prayed for the well-being of my comrades-in-arms.

I noticed a few other men nearby were as wide awake as I was. At first I thought to strike up conversation but then abandoned the notion; these men had not been so keen to make friends with me. It wasn't that these men were not friendly, quite the opposite in fact, they treated each other like blood, like brothers. I understood they were only being cautious; attempting to minimize the chance for heartache.

I was the newest member of this platoon, having joined up with them only a week ago. These men had seen plenty of action already, and as a result, had seen many good friends die. A bloody battle loomed before us, so I knew the other soldiers did not wish to get close to me before the coming fight, in the event that I did not survive. Then I would just be some random dead solider, a tragedy still, but not a beloved brother. So I understood their coldness and took it in stride.

I am a demolitions expert and was appointed to this platoon for a mission of great importance. There was a bridge about a day's march away from where we were currently camped. It was a key location that was held by the enemy and used to move their tanks and troops across. We needed to hold this side of their territory until more of our reinforcements could arrive. In order to achieve this, we were required to destroy that bridge. Without those damnable enemy tanks, we could most likely hold the land we had thus far taken.

I jumped as another distant explosion echoed

through the trees of the forest. One might think that a demolitions expert would not be so unnerved by the sounds of explosions but I was always unsettled when I was not the cause of it.

This was the closest I had been so far to actual combat and I can admit to feeling frightened by it. I had voluntarily enlisted, for it was the right thing to do, but I was unprepared for the feeling of dread one felt in the field of war. The grief these other men carried around with them was worn in plain view, as plain as their uniforms. I couldn't even begin to imagine the horrors they had seen. But I would be a party to the further horrors they would soon see, of that I had no doubt.

The next morning we were up and moving. We marched single file and spread out, keeping distance between each soldier so that one grenade, or one mine, could not cause several casualties.

I managed to keep pace with the others despite being more heavily laden. Like the others, I carried my gun, along with adequate ammunition and several grenades. On top of the backpack we carried with extra clothes and supplies, I carried two other heavy satchels filled with explosives; the tools of my trade.

Before joining the army, I worked for a large construction company in the Big City. There, I was trained in explosives in order to demolish old buildings to make room for new ones. When the military caught wind of that, I immediately began training with a demolitions unit. I trained for only six months before being given my current mission; to destroy that bridge.

Later that afternoon, my platoon stopped for a rest near the burned ruin of a barn and sent three scouts out to be sure the area was secure. I pulled an apple from my pack and decided I could use a snack to replenish some of my depleted energy.

"How long 'til we reach the bridge, ya think?" I asked one of the other men.

He glared at me and then walked away to join two others. Their voices were hushed but I could hear every word.

"What's his name anyways?"

"Who knows, I don't care to know it."

"Seems like a nice enough guy."

"You wanna know his name, you go ask him then. You really want another name to haunt you when he dies taking that bridge tomorrow?"

"Good point. I don't need to know his name."

I sighed and crunched away at my apple.

An hour or so later, our platoon leader announced the area was safe, or as safe as it could be, given where we were, and that we would camp at this farm for the night. The bridge was not too far away now and we would reach it tomorrow by mid-morning. He wanted us all to get a good rest in preparation for a tough fight.

Sleep did not come to me when the sun finally fled the sky. With the darkness of the night came renewed shelling to the north, and this time, it was it much closer. We were informed that our Delta Company was attempting to soften up the enemies defenses near the bridge before our morning arrival.

The sounds of mortar shells exploding soon mixed again with the snores of the men around me who somehow managed to find deep sleep. I would find no rest here in the ruined remains of the barn, so I picked up all my gear and headed out into the fields of the farm, looking for a quiet place to lie down out of earshot of the slumbering soldiers.

The sounds of their snoring traveled far and I soon found myself at the very edge of a field where the farm met the thick forest. I dropped my bedroll, when a curious sight caught my attention from the corner of my eye. A few feet away, I noticed some sort of mist rising up from the ground.

Cautiously, I approached. I risked pulling out my flashlight and still held my gun at the ready in my other hand. With the aid of my light, I noticed a small fissure in the ground where smoke trickled out. It was definitely a fire that produced this smoke, but from underground? How was that possible?

I leaned in for a closer look when the ground suddenly gave way beneath me. I cannot tell how far I fell exactly but I landed with a crunch and screamed out from the intense pain in my right leg. The shaft was not wide, nor smooth, and the rocky sides tore at my skin during my descent. I must have bled from several wounds but none compared to the pain I felt in my leg; I was sure it was broken.

Luckily for me, my flashlight landed within reach and I grabbed it to assess my situation; it was not good. The surface was too high up and I knew I could never climb back, especially in my current condition. Worse still, nobody knew I had come out this way and would have no idea where to look for me.

I cursed myself for wandering away then inspected my current location. I was now lying in a tunnel that was just tall enough to sit up in. The tunnel branched off into two directions and that curious smoke still emanated from somewhere down the eastern tunnel, to trickle up the shaft and out into the open air above.

I was fortunate, in a sense, that I had only dropped my bedroll when investigating the smoke. When I fell I was still carrying my equipment pack and weapons. I tied a bandana around my nose and mouth, since much of the eastern tunnel was filled with smoke, and began to crawl in search of its source.

I gritted my teeth as every movement I made sent sharp waves of pain throughout my leg. I came to the horrible realization that even if I managed to find my way out of this mess, I would be of no use to my platoon in tomorrow's battle.

The tunnel was certainly not smooth and did not seem to be made for travel, but it did appear to have been dug out by someone for a reason. Some chimney of sorts, I figured. Once I noticed a strange light ahead, I turned off my flashlight and approached more cautiously, trying to make as little sound as possible.

After crawling another twenty feet, I found this tunnel led straight to a strange chamber, and at first, I had to wonder if perhaps the fall rendered me unconscious and I was simply dreaming. My eyes stung and watered from the smoke that billowed up from a fireplace directly below my position. This tunnel looked out over the chamber from near to the ceiling, about twenty-five feet up.

The large chamber was clearly manmade with smoothed-over walls, floor and ceiling. There was electricity in this room and it was illuminated by several lights that hung from the ceiling. The most curious thing was the large machines which dominated the walls of the chamber. They were all sorts of shapes and sizes with strange gauges, buttons, knobs and colorful lights.

Disturbingly, wires from these machines were connected to several long tables which were occupied by men. I then made the shocking realization that these men were all dead. They were soldiers, dressed in the uniforms of both allies and the enemy. What on earth was going on here in this morbid underground bunker?

I decided to crawl back to the other tunnel to see if it led to a similar chamber but found that it was a dead end. My heart sank as there was only one way for me to go; that ghastly laboratory.

I returned to the chamber and was thankful that the fire was nearly out and very little smoke filtered into the tunnel. I was considering how I was going to drop down to the floor when someone suddenly entered the room. I ducked down trying to remain out of sight.

It was an extremely tall man with a bald head. His skin was nearly as pale as the white lab coat that he wore. He moved about the room, turning dials on different machines and flicking switches. The machines hummed to life and he whistled to himself while he went about his work. He was so nonchalant, despite the dead bodies that occupied the room with him.

The man picked up a beaker, which was filled with a glowing green liquid, then poured it into a funnel that protruded from the top of a machine. He pulled a lever and tendrils of electricity ran down the wires from the machine to one of the tables that held a body. Wires and tubes had been inserted into the nearly naked body and it started to twitch as the electric currents ran through it.

My mouth hung open at the gruesome spectacle but

the odd man watched with excitement; his hands clenched with nervousness.

I could not fathom what he was hoping to achieve until a moan shot forth from the dead man's mouth and the body actually sat up. I could barely contain my yelp at the horrific sight. The tall man's face lit up with joy and he danced about the room laughing maniacally.

"I've done it! I've actually done it!" he said with an accent I couldn't quite place.

He walked over to the table to stare at the man that now sat up. The former soldier sat there silently with a blank expression, his eyes a milky white. Strangely, I noticed his chest did not move; the man did not draw breath and so was still very dead. But as the man in the white coat walked around the table, the dead soldier's head followed him. A chill ran down my spine.

"You are the first of my children," he said to the dead soldier, "the first of many. The lifetime I have spent in research has paid off. This war was exactly what I needed to provide me with the specimens to work on. As your two armies continue your senseless fighting, the bodies of the dead will pile high. Soon, very soon, my immortal children will number enough that neither army will be able to stop us and we will be the true victors. I will take over this pathetic world and all will bow down to me."

I wished right then that I was unconscious and dreaming but I was quite sure that I wasn't. This mad scientist had somehow raised that dead soldier to some mockery of his living self; a zombie of sorts. He planned on creating an army of zombies using dead soldiers and I could not imagine the havoc he could wreak with them. How could you kill something that was already dead?

"Come my child, walk with me. We shall return shortly and awaken your brothers."

The zombie somehow understood the words of the man and rose from the table. It shuffled slowly on stiff legs and followed the man that beamed with pride from the chamber.

As the shuffling sound faded and the room fell silent, I knew exactly what I needed to do. I was still in possession of all my explosives and figured my best course of action was to destroy this room. I was not sure how long I had before that man and his "child" returned, so I needed to act fast, or as fast as I could, given my current injury.

I knew once I dropped down from the tunnel there was no going back up, so I decided to first attach explosives to the ceiling while I was still up here and able to reach. I figured it best to collapse the room as well and bury anything that wasn't completely destroyed by the blasts.

Once finished, I dropped my packs and machine gun to the floor below, right next to the fireplace which had now burned itself out. I gave myself a shot of morphine from my med pack, then hang-dropped from the tunnel to the floor.

I still gasped with pain and rolled around for several moments, before regaining some measure of control and suppressed the pain as best I could. I quickly returned to my task at hand, planting explosives connected with a long wire on each of the machines. I could use my remote detonator to blow the room from the safety of the hallway the mad scientist had left from.

Satisfied that I had rigged the room to the best of my

ability, I limped over to the fireplace to retrieve my gun. A voice from behind had me spinning around, my heart racing.

"Where did you come from?" the mad scientist shrieked, the horrifying zombie stood to his left, staring at me with those dead white eyes.

"I know about your plans and I cannot allow you to proceed with them," I answered.

The man looked around the room and only then did he notice the explosives that I had planted. He took note of the detonator I held in my left hand and his eyes went wide with horror.

"You cannot destroy my life's work! Do you even understand the gravity of what I have accomplished here? I have done what no one else has ever achieved. I have brought the dead back to life."

"That thing there," I indicated to the zombie by pointing with my machine gun, "is not alive. That is some mockery of life. That is just a monster."

The man growled. "You are a fool. You know nothing. Get him, my child. Feast upon his flesh."

The former soldier shuffled towards me, its mouth open and moaning, causing my skin to shiver. I unloaded all thirty rounds from my gun, and despite the terror that gripped me, more than half of those bullets found their mark.

Many of the rounds found the zombie's chest and two found his face. I staggered back in shock as the zombie paused only a moment and then continued towards me. No blood flowed from the wounds and the monster showed no ill effects whatsoever.

Behind the zombie, the mad scientist laughed. "Did

you think you could stop my child with your weapon? What good are bullets on the flesh of the dead?"

What good indeed? I thought. My options had just run thin. I threw down my machine gun and quickly drew my sidearm. Instead of aiming for the zombie, I pointed my pistol at the mad scientist but he dove out of sight behind one of his many machines.

In one last futile attempt to stop the monster, I unloaded my pistol into its body but found the result the same. On it came, despite the multitude of wounds. It was intent on feasting, with my flesh on the menu.

I sighed aloud when I realized I had only one choice left to me. I would use the detonator and blow the room as planned. I would destroy the machines and hopefully the monster and scientist too. If the explosions didn't stop the zombie, perhaps the collapsing ceiling would.

My life was about to end in this room and nobody would ever know of the sacrifice I made to save the world from this man and his monsters. Nobody would hail me as a hero and nobody would remember my name.

KABOOM!!

TOMBS OF THE FALSE

I will never forget, it was in the morning of April 1ˢᵗ, when I received the phone call, and at first, I had to wonder if it was merely an April Fool's prank played by one of my chums. The call had been indeed legit, but now looking back, I almost wished that it had been only a joke.

At the time, I had been quite ecstatic to have been chosen to lead an expedition into some newly unearthed tombs located within the Great Desert. The entrances lay buried deep beneath the sands for god knows how long. By all accounts, the architecture and symbols found on the sealed doors were completely alien and unique, when compared to anything that had been previously discovered on Earth. To say that I was excited to visit this site was an understatement.

It seemed that the dedication to my studies had finally paid off. I had graduated from the most prestigious university in the Big City and prided myself on the knowledge I possessed of ancient civilizations and languages. Naturally, I was the perfect choice.

My only distress at that time was that I could not choose my own team. I was appointed a partner by my superiors, a shifty and shady individual, of whose background and education I knew nothing about. In fact, everyone I consulted with had no idea of his past either.

The skeletally thin, mustached man, claimed to be an experienced archaeologist, though through the use of subtle querying, I found his knowledge to be quite lacking. Though I certainly had my doubts about this dubious character, it was not my place to say anything further and question my superiors.

After months of planning, Sebastian and I touched down in a makeshift airstrip that lay just outside the southern tip of the Great Desert. It was such a relief to land without incident as it was only recently that a plane crashed in the desert, killing all on board except for one woman who had miraculously survived.

A camp had been erected where locals who would serve as our guides through the desert awaited our arrival. I remember well that stifling heat as I exited the plane. The Great Desert was always hot, but it was now July and the heat was near unbearable for a city-man like myself. If Sebastian found it distressing, he never complained about it. It seemed that his eagerness to get to these tombs eclipsed his feelings of discomfort.

We were both anxious to begin our journey, and after a quick bite to eat, we gathered our hired help and set off into that desolate wasteland. The tombs had been discovered about a day's walk from the encampment. So we pitched tents when night fell and then resumed our dreadful march as that unforgiving sun beat down upon our heads once again.

There came a point when even my excitement did little to lift my spirits; the oppressive heat had thoroughly sapped my endurance. Sebastian spoke little and of that I did not mind. I had still not taken to my traveling companion and the less we said to each other the better.

Right at the point when I was about to plead to our guides to take a momentary pause, we spotted the tips of white tents peeking over the top of a distant sand dune. I was about to chalk it up as a mirage, a trick of my delusional, sunbaked mind, when our guides began to talk excitedly amongst each other in their own language and urged us to pick up our pace.

Not long after, we arrived at the appropriate spot. A large section of earth had been excavated, leaving a deep pit which was accessible by ladders only. The sun was nearing its time to set but there was still enough light for us to make out two strange stone doors positioned near the floor of the pit.

My excitement and energy soon returned and Sebastian and I were not willing to wait for the arrival of morning. We found ourselves descending the ladders with lanterns in our hands.

Through my studies in university, I was quite familiar with all known languages and symbols that had so far been discovered, but the hieroglyphs that had been carved into these doors were completely foreign to me. My heart skipped a beat as I realized we had truly found something completely new to the world.

The Great Desert had been home to a marvelous, ancient civilization, that had built the famous pyramids.

They had used hieroglyphs that were somewhat similar to what I was now beholding, though these still appeared slightly alien to those others.

"Let us open these doors and explore, shall we?" Sebastian suggested.

"What of the rest of our team? Perhaps we should wait?"

We had arrived two days before the remaining members of our team who would be charged with the task of cataloguing and recording everything that could be found within the tombs.

"You really wish to wait two days now that we are here standing before these very doors?"

"Well…I,"

"We won't disturb anything or remove anything. Let's just peek inside, the suspense is killing me."

I had to admit the temptation weighed heavily on me as well and Sebastian's suggestion seemed sound; we would just peek around and not disturb anything. I nodded in agreement and we began the task of inspecting the doors more thoroughly to determine how they could be opened.

They were thick stone slabs and would have weighed a ton. Where these stones came from and how they were brought here was another mystery entirely, much like the construction of the great pyramids.

We required more lanterns to continue our work as the sun was now fully disappeared and the desert was engulfed with darkness. After the better part of two hours, our efforts were finally rewarded, and by sheer luck, I might add. I noticed something out of the ordinary with a hieroglyph which depicted a door. As I ran my finger over it, I noticed a faint rectangular border around it. Curious, I pressed the symbol, and to my surprise, it receded back into the door. It was a button of sorts and soon the entire door groaned as it shifted back into the earth.

The walls of the pit we stood in shook and we were soon showered with sand. I feared we might be buried in a terrible avalanche when it suddenly stopped. I shook my head, attempting to remove the bulk of the sand from my hair, then stood rooted in place, as I realized the door had fully opened and a dark passageway now greeted us.

Sebastian and I looked to each other in wonder, and without any need for further conversation, we each picked up a lantern and proceeded inside, albeit with the utmost caution.

I took the lead, but not without a healthy level of nervousness, as I was well aware that some tombs were booby-trapped. Needless to say, the going was slow while I inspected the floors and walls to the best of my ability, each step of the way.

Fortunately for us, the ceiling of the black passage stood six feet tall, and since each of us were a few inches shorter than that, we had little trouble navigating the tunnel. The air was cool and dry but there was a smell. I couldn't quite find the words to describe it but we could almost taste it. It was faint, not overpowering, though it was clearly present.

The tunnel continued without turning and stretched on beyond our limited vision by lantern-light. As we traveled at a snail's pace, I glanced to my pocket watch and found that it had nearly been an hour. The walls of the passage were quite smooth and featureless. We found no further markings or symbols as we went.

I should have been thoroughly exhausted after trekking through the hot desert the entire day, but I felt none of that in the tunnel as my excitement and curiosity had effectively chased away any feelings of weariness.

I was beginning to worry that this tunnel would stretch on without end, when at the very limits of our vision, we noticed the passage opened up into a dark chamber. We paused, and again, Sebastian and I looked wordlessly to each other. We nodded and then continued.

We descended four stone steps, and upon entering the chamber, I turned left and Sebastian turned right. We were attempting to getter a better feel for the size of what turned out to be an enormous room.

I should first mention the immediate sense of horror I felt after discovering the ghastly truth of the floor that we tread upon. It felt uneven and I quite nearly tripped before I crouched low for a closer inspection. I gasped out loud but it did not seem to startle Sebastian, as he had already made the same discovery as I. The entire floor, for as far as we could see, was made up of bones. Initially I had wondered what type of animal they had belonged to, until a grim sight just about stopped my heart from beating. I spotted a skull, a *human* skull. And not just one as I soon learned, but hundreds, if not thousands.

This was not simply the tomb of some long-dead king or queen; it appeared that it was a mass grave of some sort, unlike anything previously found in this region. I must say it was quite uncomfortable, walking about and feeling bones crunch underfoot, but there was no way around it.

This also explained the indescribable smell I had noticed upon our entry. I had not put the pieces together earlier but it was in fact the undeniable smell of death. Still though, even in this chamber of bones, the smell was not overpowering, but it did indeed linger, and was detected on my tongue along with my nostrils.

Praising my foresight, I attempted to wash the taste from my mouth using the water bottle I had brought with me. It helped, somewhat.

"Where is the treasure? All I see is bones?" Sebastian wondered aloud, untroubled by the mass grave.

I looked around as we had yet to determine the actual dimensions of this tomb and gasped a second time when I observed a curious sight in the gloom ahead.

"Look, what is that?" I pointed in the appropriate direction.

Something glowed faintly, roughly thirty feet away from the edge of our light source. It was an eerie, pale white, and was just far enough away that we could not make out any of the details.

"Perhaps there is a shaft nearby leading to the surface," Sebastian suggested.

I scoffed at the notion. "It is night time. There would be no light coming from the world outside and it could not be reflecting off our lanterns."

My curiosity for this new object momentarily made me forget about the grisly scene underneath us. The two of us crept forward for a better look. We soon ascertained that the object in question was an ivory pedestal, standing just over waist-height. It appeared to be carved out of stone and bore no other features, save for two odd imprints of hands, found on the smooth surface of the circular top. The imprints were just large enough that most any human could have placed their hands comfortably within them.

The pedestal glowed slightly, but as to its source, I could not even begin to speculate.

"What do you suppose is the purpose of this?" Sebastian inquired.

"I cannot even hazard a guess. I have never seen anything quite like it before."

"Where is that humming sound coming from?"

I cocked my head and listened intently, and then I heard it as well. It emanated from the pedestal. There was a very low humming sound, almost electrical in nature, as if the pedestal had been plugged into an energy source, which of course was sheer lunacy.

"It originates from the pedestal," I told my partner. "A river running underneath us, causing the vibrations? I have no other explanation."

We left the strange pedestal for the time being and once again spread out with the goal of mapping this particular chamber. We found that it was indeed massive and circular in design. The glowing pedestal was situated directly in the center and the entire floor of the macabre room was covered with human remains. I could not even guess at the number of people that were buried in here.

The chamber possessed a high, domed ceiling, and had no other exits except for the one from which we had entered. There were however, many more hieroglyphs etched into the walls, similar to those we found on the doors. If we had been smart, we would have left right then, and never returned.

I pointed out one particular group of hieroglyphs which depicted a person placing their hands into the pedestal's imprints. Sebastian wondered if one of us should try and do just that but I heartily disagreed. I suggested more study needed to be done to learn the purpose of the strange object.

Much later, as I stared ceaselessly at the alien symbols attempting to discern their meaning, I noticed that my partner had become oddly silent. I glanced around to find him standing directly in front of the pedestal. Before I had time to shout any form of protest, Sebastian placed his hands directly into the carved imprints.

His scream was like nothing I had ever heard in this world. It was not just simply a scream of agony, or sheer fright, but there was something else to it…understanding? It was almost as if placing his hands on the pedestal revealed some horrifying truth that resulted in instant madness.

Sebastian's torture was not to last for too long though, as his body was suddenly engulfed in flames so intense, I had to avert my gaze. When it was safe to look again, all that remained of Sebastian was a pile of bones, the jaw of his skull still open wide in a silent scream of horror.

It took me quite some time to pick myself up off the floor and make my way back to camp. I was shaken to the core by what I beheld. I did not leave my tent for two days until the rest of our team arrived. I sent a message immediately to my superiors that their presence was required as soon as was possible.

By the week's end, our tiny little camp was teeming with activity. Archaeologists, scientists, media and even soldiers to secure the site. Even after I had explained the demise of Sebastian many times over, it took one more fool to place his hands on the pedestal before I was believed. Thankfully, I was not present in the tomb to witness that spectacle a second time.

For six months, myself and a group of the world's leading experts in ancient languages, studied the hieroglyphs from the chamber of bones, as it was aptly named. We had finally begun to have an understanding of their meanings, and if we were correct, the pedestal was a form of punishment for liars. Nobody could say who built it or how it worked, but any false person placing their hands upon it, was instantly punished.

Further investigation into Sebastian's past, revealed that he was not who he had said he was, much as I had thought. He was selected by an unknown source to be one of the first to enter the tomb, with the plan of stealing priceless treasure before anyone else even knew it was missing. This was determined by correspondences that had been found between himself and another equally unscrupulous individual who had not yet been identified. Sebastian had been leading a false life, and thus, had been punished by the pedestal.

Soon, world leaders were beginning to take great interest in the pedestal and were now in discussions for using it in a court, to determine someone's guilt or innocence. A liar would be immediately found out and dealt with, eliminating the need for prisons.

When all others had given up studying the pedestal and hieroglyphs, and moved onto other projects, I continued on, convinced there was more to this than we first thought. There were a few symbols that had so far eluded our understanding.

Two years after the discovery of the tombs, and mere months before the pedestal was to be used for the first time in court, I made a startling discovery. I determined that one of the hieroglyphs depicted a dark god, or devil more like it; a strangely tentacled being. It would appear, by my understanding, that the pedestal was a tool of this devil to gather souls from which it fed on. I wondered now if Sebastian was granted that revelation the moment before he died, which had led to that inhuman scream that still sends shivers down my spine.

I attempted to share my discovery with my superiors and beyond, right up to world leaders, but they were not interested. The mysterious pedestal was going to save them much money and that was all they cared about.

What happened to the souls afterwards was not their concern. I shuddered to think of what we had just unleashed on the world.

MY HAUNTED CHAMBERS

A tribute to Robert W. Chambers and The King in Yellow

My eyes fluttered open, as beams of sunlight penetrated the gaps of my dark curtains to bathe my face with its heaven-sent warmth. It did little to wash away the grogginess that clouded my head and I sat up, momentarily disoriented.

My heart rate decreased as I soon realized I was in my bed, within my own chamber. How many hours had I slept this time? Two? Maybe three at the most?

The ghost visited my room again last night and I had been paralyzed with fear. I do not mind admitting that I cowered underneath the covers, praying that it would leave me alone. It stood at the foot of my bed, as it usually did, watching me. I cannot say how long it stood there, for it felt an eternity to me. Eventually though, when I had hazarded to peek, it was gone, but sleep did not come quickly.

I rose from my bed and stretched the stiffness from my limbs, before opening the curtains fully to light my chamber. It was amazing the effect a little light could have by chasing away the shadows and putting me at ease. Let it be known that I am no coward but what could one do with a ghost, a spirit of the netherworld, except to cower?

Shaking my head, I put thoughts of the ghost aside and gazed out my window. I had a wonderful view from the tenth floor of the keep's tower. Sparkling with the light of the sun was the waters of Lake Hali. Giant and dangerous birds-of-prey floated serenely on the momentarily calm surface of the lake, heads scanning ceaselessly for their next meal.

Directly below my window sat rows upon rows of armored chariots, awaiting the call to defend the keep from unwelcome adversaries. All seemed in order with the world outside, it continued on with little concern about the events within the keep. Those vicious birds cared little for ghosts roaming the halls; they were blissfully ignorant of such horrors.

My stomach grumbled and reminded me that I had not eaten much as of late. I turned my attention to my chamber door and noticed the maid had left my morning meal on the floor as she had been instructed. Due to recent events, my door was locked at all times, and until I was sure it was safe to do so, I never left my room. Only Cassilda possessed a key to get in and she only used it when dropping off my meals. She never stayed and we never spoke.

I picked up the tray of food to inspect what I had been left. Scrambled eggs again, it seemed, along with some overly cooked toast with a raspberry jam.

As was my routine, I sat on a stool next to my lazy dog, and fed him bits of my breakfast to ensure that it was not poisoned. He was an obedient dog and never barked or made any noise, keeping a silent watch over my chamber. He remained silent all through the night as well, which led me to believe that the ghost was invisible to his canine eyes. I felt bad about feeding him some of my food first, putting him at risk, but it was a necessary evil as I had many enemies.

The tyrannical lord over these lands was now dead by my hand, but I am positive that he has loyal followers that wish me ill. They hide amongst common folk, blending in and scheming away. But I am smarter than they are, I remain one step ahead.

After assassinating the cruel lord, I named myself the new ruler and took over residence of the tenth floor of this tower. For my own safety, I immediately locked myself within, fearing retaliation. The lord was known for his cruelty, banishing many folk from the realm, and he personally made rounds, violently demanding taxes from people. I had seen enough.

He was not so tough and not so brave, as he pleaded for his pathetic life. It did nothing to help him and I joyfully drove that knife into his black heart. I had liberated the people of this realm and put an end to his tyranny. As things settle down, I will prove to the people that I can be a just and good ruler. They will accept me and everyone will live happier for it.

The dog appeared to be his usual self, so I was satisfied the meal was safe and ate the rest and quieted my angry stomach. I washed it all down with some warm water, then remembered that I had a meeting with two of my advisors.

I found the two men already seated at the council table, as Cassilda had been instructed to allow them, and only them, into my chambers. I promptly took a seat and rested my elbows upon the table, linking my fingers together.

The heavy man to my right had reddish-brown hair, with a streak of white running through the center. His cheeks were always puffy and had the appearance of a chipmunk, which had filled his mouth to capacity in order to bring food home to store for a long winter.

The man to my left, I had to be wary about. There was something unsettling about him; he appeared almost reptilian, in a way. He had a cold silent demeanor, with a longish nose and pointed teeth, resembling fangs. He had yet to provide me with reason for alarm but I felt I needed to exercise caution within his presence.

"Gentlemen, thank you for coming," I said. "Last night, I was visited again by the ghost. I know not why it chooses to haunt me. Whether it's the spirit of that vile lord, or some long forgotten tenant of this ancient keep, I cannot say."

Both men remained silent as they usually did at the mention of the ghost. I was not sure if it was purely out of fright, or if they simply thought me mad and imagining the whole ordeal. I decided to change the topic and put them both at ease.

"Moving forward, I would like to lower taxes for the people of this realm, undoing the misery imposed by the last lord. I want the people to like me, to love me even. Perhaps a parade is in order, when I feel the threat against me to be over and I can venture forth among the people."

My two advisors offered nothing of value this day and I dismissed them, growing irritated by their silence. I spent the rest of the afternoon sitting alone by my window, hypnotized by the rolling waters of Lake Hali.

Minutes turned into hours and day became night. Before I even realized it, the moon was high in the sky. I trembled slightly at the darkness that now engulfed my chambers, knowing the ghost would soon arrive. I dove into my bed and drew the covers to my chin, my eyes darting around frantically, attempting to make out shapes in the shadows.

In a corner, my dog slept, sensing nothing amiss within the room. But I knew different. My chambers were haunted and I could not have been imagining it. The dread I felt was very real and I did not believe that my eyes were deceiving me. The ghost must have wanted something, but what? Why visit me? Did these chambers once belong to it, and each night it returned, only to find someone else sleeping in its bed? Or was it indeed the cruel lord who I had murdered, come back to make my life miserable in revenge for the deed I had done?

Whatever the reasons, I needed it to stop, somehow. I could not continue on living this way; fearful of the night and not getting my much needed sleep. It was taking its toll on my body and my health. Eventually I would be driven mad; of this I had no doubt.

Clouds passed in front of the moon, sending forth more shadows into my chamber. My imagination created horrible shapes, posing in the darkness. They leered at me, mocked me, fueled by my fear.

Then I heard it. At first a distant shuffling sound, the

source of which was out of sight. A shape formed in the darkness and grew larger as it approached the foot of my bed. I pulled the covers over my face and froze, fearful to even draw breath. Silly I know, to think that lying completely still would somehow make me invisible to the ghostly presence in the room.

Drawing some measure of courage, I decided to peek, nearly crying out with fright, as the ghost once again loomed over my bed, staring down at me with those empty black pits for eyes.

Like the ghosts from children's tales, it was dressed in a long white sheet. A break in the clouds allowed enough moonlight to trickle through my window, causing an eerie glow to the already frightening spirit.

"What do you want of me?" I said, finally finding my voice. "Leave me alone! I have done nothing to you!"

The ghost waved its arms in the air and it suddenly seemed to me that it was attempting to communicate, though I could not understand it.

"Go away!" I shouted. "Leave me be! I beg you!"

To my horror, the ghost moved around the side of my bed, coming closer. Frantic, I kicked my legs out, trying to keep it away from me. It reached for me with a ghostly hand and I recoiled, feeling a stinging sensation on my right arm. I cried out without even realizing that I had done so. My vision grew blurry and then I knew no more.

I bolted upright in my bed, my body covered in a cold sweat. My heart raced and I soon realized that night had turned into day. Midday too, by the position of the sun outside my window. I slept the night through and the morning it seemed, as well. It was not a restful sleep though; I had had a terrible dream.

I got out of bed in search of some water as my mouth felt horribly dry and my head felt incredibly cloudy. Thankfully, Cassilda had left a fresh pitcher of water for me, along with my breakfast that had long ago turned cold.

Feeling a little refreshed, I sat on the edge of my bed, trying to recall the night's events. I remembered the ghost had visited again. I remembered shouting at it before it touched my arm. Its touch stung me, and then I must have passed out, for I don't recall anything after that, aside from my disturbing dream.

I shuddered as I thought of that dream. The cruel lord had sought me out and found me, standing alone by the shores of Lake Hali. I just knew it was the lord, even though his face was hidden behind a pallid mask. He was draped in a tattered yellow robe and was laughing at me. A most sinister, skin-shivering laugh. As he approached, I awoke, though that laugh still haunts me, even knowing it was only a dream.

Thoughts of the ghost soon chased away my musings over the dream and my focus was back to the nightly problem that I was having. The ghost had touched me, actually touched me, and I felt it! I was beginning to wonder if maybe this spirit was more solid than I would have first believed. Tonight, I figured, I would attempt to put that theory to the test. Provided that fear did not get the better of me again. And of course, before it could touch me. Its touch had caused me to black out, fall asleep. I would need to be quicker this time to surprise it.

I spent the rest of the afternoon and most of the evening staring out my window in silent contemplation. I did not wish to speak with my advisors and I had even passed on eating, as I possessed no appetite this day. At some point, Cassilda had refilled my pitcher of water, though, I do not recall her coming and going. I appreciated that as my mouth had been extremely dry since awakening.

I watched the moon slowly ascend in the night sky before deciding it was time. I picked up my dagger, which I seemed to have left on my meal tray, next to a stale piece of bread, and then slid into bed, pulling the covers to my chin.

Try as I might, and I did indeed try, I could not prevent my heart from racing. I was awash with nervousness, as though I had bathed in the stuff, were it real and tangible. My skin had probably turned a shade of pale that matched even the ghost, while I lay there waiting.

I could not be sure if it was mere minutes, or whether it was hours, but the ghost predictably arrived. A faint shadow in the darkness at first, then enlarging into the ghostly specter I had come to recognize.

Involuntarily, I stopped breathing, staring into those black pits for eyes; frozen in fear I was. Again I got the feeling that it was trying to say something to me and communicate in some unholy manner.

When I did not respond, as I had done the previous night, it moved around the side of the bed, gliding towards me. Under the covers my right hand gripped the handle of the dagger, knuckles turning white as my hand trembled with terror. It loomed over me, looking me in the face. My god those eyes! They were empty voids, like I was staring into oblivion!

I could take it no longer. I steeled my courage and lunged forward, driving my dagger blade towards the chest of the ghost. And...nothing. I had accomplished nothing. I was such a fool to believe that cold steel could actually harm some spirit of the netherworld. It continued to look at me, completely unconcerned about the weapon that I held.

Like the night before, it reached for me and my arm instantly stung. Again I recoiled and my vision became blurry. I dizzily collapsed to my bed and my room, the bits of it that I could make out in the darkness, began to spin.

I closed my eyes and drifted off to sleep. And there in my dreams awaited the evil lord in the pallid mask, laughing at me once more.

*   *   *   *

Dr. Vassef left the room, locking the door behind him, and placed his syringe back onto his cart. Before proceeding to the next room, he straightened his white smock and walked over to a phone that was mounted on the wall. He dialed a familiar number, then waited.

"Hey, were you asleep yet?" he asked.

(pause)

"Ok, good. You won't believe what this patient just did."

(pause)

"He just threatened me with a banana of all things. Can you believe that? A banana!"

(pause)

"Yeah he was holding it like a knife," he chuckled.

(pause)

"I know, I know, I am always careful. He is actually a small man, kinda frail. He was an artist, I believe, a painter from Paris. He is the one I told you about, he murdered his landlord."

(pause)

"No, nobody still knows why. His apartment was a disgusting mess when the police went in to arrest him. Weird paintings all in yellow paint were all over the place."

(pause)

"He has had some family drop by and leave a few gifts. Just some stuffed animals. He tries to feed food to the stuffed dog and he has a chipmunk and a crocodile sitting at a table. He talks to those ones sometimes about his plans to rule some place called Carcosa."

(pause)

"Really he just spends most of his day sitting by his window, staring out at the duck pond and the parking lot."

(pause)

"Oh yeah, one curious thing they did find in his apartment was an old book, ancient in fact. Could have been written hundreds of years ago, with no credited author. It was actually a play, oddly enough, titled, *The King in Yellow*."

(pause)

"No, I never heard of it before either. The police turned the book over to Dr. Tannis, he was going to look through it for any possible clues. Strange thing is, nobody has seen or heard from him now in three days. His family has filed a missing person's report."

(pause)

"Crazy, I know!"

(pause)

"Hey I saw that book on Tannis' desk still when I started my shift tonight. I should bring it home and we can both take a look at it. Seems creepy, you'll love it."

(pause)

"Ok, you get to sleep now. Leave the chain off the door for me in the morning."

(pause)

"Love you too."

(pause)

"Yeah, yeah, don't worry, I won't forget the book."

(pause)

"Bye."

DINNER WITH ARTHUR VANDERFROST

For several years, it was my life's goal to receive a dinner invitation from the wealthy and influential, Arthur Vanderfrost. It was a gloomy Tuesday afternoon when a messenger found me having lunch alone and handed me that most glorious envelope, sealed with the unmistakable wax seal, of Mr. Vanderfrost. The symbol consisted of a scale, flanked by a crow to the left side and a downwards pointing dagger to the right; the Vanderfrost family insignia.

Everyone in Ravensbridge, along with the surrounding regions, knew that symbol well. Arthur Vanderfrost was the most powerful man in the city and was even rumored to be pulling the strings of Mayor Ableton. He came from a large family but was the last remaining member; never having married and never had any children.

He looked quite healthy and vibrant for a man rumored to be somewhere in his seventies. He was tall, standing a few inches over the six-foot mark, with a lean body. His hair, and he still had all of it, was of the purest white, along with his neatly-cropped thin beard. He had penetrating blue eyes with a deep, very recognizable and commanding, base voice.

Mr. Vanderfrost dressed in the finest clothes; the best that money could buy. He never left his colossal home without his trademark blue overcoat and black top hat. The man could walk perfectly fine but always carried a cane that was capped with the solid gold head of a cat, with genuine rubies for eyes. He was very fond of cats and the snobbish animals roamed all over his property and were said to live inside his home as well.

His fortunes were vast and it was believed he had amassed an endless store of coins. Indeed he no longer needed to work but it seemed that the more money one had, the more money one wanted. He continued to trade and import goods into the city with no sign of slowing in his advanced years.

Once a year, Mr. Vanderfrost hosted a grand dinner party within his home, inviting only the city's wealthiest, along with those he did business with. It was quite an honor for someone to receive an invite and made that someone the envy of all their peers, who did not. It was the only chance that most people had of ever getting that close to the man and spend an evening with him.

My hands trembled as I held that invitation; my goal having now become reality. I didn't even bother to finish my lunch. I dropped a handful of coins onto the table; much more than was actually required. I didn't care, though; I needed to rush home as I had much to do before the party which was to be held in two days' time.

I bought a new suit; something more worthy of being in the company of the city's highest class, along with a new hat. I spared no expense, even when considering that I would most likely only wear these on that one evening. I felt it was well worth the money.

The next two days passed in a blur and my excitement had reached a fever pitch. I was up at the crack of dawn and spent much of the day pacing back and forth, awaiting the setting of the sun. It seemed that Mr. Vanderfrost was interested in my proposal to import an exotic red wine from the Far East. I had learned that he was quite enamored with red wine and was rarely seen without a glass of it at his parties.

My research had paid off and my letter must have grabbed his attention. Whether he wished to actually speak business with me tonight or not, I could not tell, though I did not care; attending the party was all I had really wanted.

At the appointed time, I took a deep breath, slung a satchel over my shoulder, and left my home to enter the hired carriage that had just arrived to pick me up. Despite the speed in which the last two days had vanished, my carriage ride seemed to last an eternity. In reality, it was only a mere twenty-five minutes to arrive at the gates of Vanderfrost Manor, but to me, the horses felt as though they were moving at a snail's pace. I couldn't get there fast enough.

I could barely contain my rising impatience as I was forced to wait in a long line of carriages, each pulling up to the front gates in turn to drop off their privileged occupants.

I tipped the driver upon my eventual exit from the carriage and stood with awe in front of the open, wrought iron gates. There was a steady flow of magnificently dressed men and women passing me by to enter the majestic manor grounds. An elderly man, obviously a member of the house staff, checked invitations as people passed.

Here I was, about to step onto the property of Arthur Vanderfrost, after spending so many years looking for my way in. This was the one and only night these gates stood open to welcome those who were not normally granted access at any other time. Many were the tales of those who attempted to gain uninvited entry to the manor, no doubt for nefarious purposes, and were never seen again. Those who thought to relieve Mr. Vanderfrost from some of his considerable wealth seemed to shorten their life span quite significantly.

I had most certainly chosen the right course in securing a proper invitation, signed by Mr. Vanderfrost himself, no less. While the exquisite wine which I had used to attain his attention did not actually exist, my enthusiasm for meeting the great man was very real.

I limped into the manor grounds using my own cane for support. My cane was custom-made and intricately carved with eastern symbols. It had been in my family for centuries and passed down when the previous owner no longer had any use for it. I only brought it out for special occasions and tonight was most definitely one of those special occasions.

There was nothing at all wrong with my right leg but the limp helped add credence to my story that the journey east to obtain this rare wine had been fraught with many dangers. Some embellishment to my false tale only gave it more life.

The manor grounds were breathtakingly beautiful. The grass was impeccably manicured and bushes and hedges were meticulously trimmed into all kinds of fascinating shapes. A large stone fountain dominated the center of the front lawn and was known to be a favored gathering spot for all sorts of birds, who were currently absent from the fountain, due to the late hour and the unusual amount of guests milling about.

Statues also carved from the same smooth stone as the fountain populated the grounds as well. They depicted all kinds of mythical creatures and were made with such fabulous detail. My favorites, thus far, being the statue of the Sphinx, as well as one of a Hydra, a five-headed dragon.

The sun had retreated to the west and brilliant, ornate lanterns, provided the illumination needed to navigate your way around the manor grounds in order to admire its beauty. My mouth hung open as I perused the gardens, spotting several species of plants and rare flowers that I had never seen before in my life. That was quite a thing, considering the many remote places I had traveled to around the world. It was evident that Mr. Vanderfrost was a connoisseur of many fine things.

After marveling at the many wonderful sights displayed outside the home, I felt it was time to enter the immense manor itself and behold the treasures that must be contained within.

I followed a procession of guests through the impressive double-doored main entrance to stand in the spacious front foyer. My eyes were immediately drawn to the incredible chandelier that hung from the ceiling which consisted of at least one hundred candles. A middle-aged woman in a violet gown to my right was as equally impressed.

"My goodness, Herbert, have you ever seen anything as beautiful?" she asked of the man beside her.

"Aside from you, my dear, no I have not," he correctly answered.

I moved further into the home, inspecting various paintings that decorated the walls. There was family portraits as well as stunning scenery; all painted with astonishing artistry. I imagined that some you could not have even put a price on.

Similar to outside, extraordinary statues and sculptures could also be found displayed in the foyer and hallways branching off. A wondrous staircase led upwards to the second floor of the house but was roped off, indicating that it was off-limits to the dinner guests. I was hoping to see more of the enormous house but it appeared that we were contained to the main floor, which was still quite a large area indeed.

I stepped into a library where I noticed other guests mingling and sipping drinks served by the house staff. A pretty woman in the black and white garb of the staff approached me carrying a tray of drinks, red wine of course, and bid me to take a glass. I graciously accepted the offer and carefully lifted a frosted glass of superb quality.

I took a sip and did my best to hide my grimace. Despite playing the part of someone who imported exotic wines, I had no real love for the drink. For show, I continued to sip and pretended to enjoy it while disguising my distaste.

"Quite the collection of books, wouldn't you agree?" a voice directly behind me asked.

I turned to face a large man dressed in a costly black outfit. Hints of grey were visible in his dark hair and long beard. He wore a monocle in his right eye. In his left hand was also a glass of red wine, which he sipped with much pleasure.

"Why yes indeed, his collection is vast," I replied. "Most impressive. Must have taken the family a century to amass so many."

"Mr. Vanderfrost is quite taken with reading. A wealth of knowledge, he is. He is a scholar of ancient history but I have yet to find a topic that he is not familiar with."

I nodded and took another sip, forcing an expression of enjoyment.

"I don't believe I have seen you around before, good sir," the man commented. "I am Donovan Brouwer and I manage the bank here in Ravensbridge."

"A pleasure," I nodded. "I am Edgar de Jaager. I import rare and exotic wines. I have managed to procure a very special vintage that Mr. Vanderfrost may be interested in investing in. I am hoping to add him as a business partner so that we can begin importing this splendid wine to the good people of Ravensbridge."

"Wonderful, Mr. de Jaager. I always enjoy a good drink. I look forward to that."

I nodded again and Mr. Brouwer moved off to mingle with the next closest guest. I wanted to keep my conversations with others to a minimum; not wishing to explain my false credentials for being here to many.

Something brushed my leg and gave me a start. I glanced down to see one of the many cats that Mr. Vanderfrost was said to own. In fact, I noticed several in the room. They must have followed their owner, as there, standing at a far door to the library, stood the tall, and elegantly-dressed, Mr. Vanderfrost. I sucked in my breath.

A heavy-set man also noticed the arrival of the cats but not of the party's host.

"Such dreadful creatures," the man said, indicating to one of the cats. "Wicked little buggers, actually, and quite dumb. Can't train them like a good dog."

The man must have noticed the change in expressions of those around him and the blood drained from his face as he turned to regard our gracious host.

"Cats are quite intelligent, my dear, Mr. Voort. They are difficult to train because they simply choose not to listen. They are cunning, independent, and see themselves as superior to all other beings, not willing to submit to anyone. A quality I find most admirable."

"Ah, well, yes," Mr. Voort stammered. "My apologies for my rude remarks. I have simply had too much wine."

"I am sure."

Then to my surprise, Mr. Vanderfrost looked straight at me and strode across the room in my direction. My heart raced at his approach. For a split-second I had to wonder if he had come to realize the falseness of my story and was about to confront me, but my imagination was running wild and he could not have known.

"Mr. de Jaager, is it?" he inquired calmly, in his deep voice.

I paused momentarily, not believing that I was

standing this close to the man. "Yes, yes it is."

"One of the doormen told me you had arrived and provided me an ample description. Enjoying the wine?"

"Yes, yes indeed I am."

"I apologize that is most likely not as exotic a vintage as you are used to, but it's the best that Ravensbridge has to offer." Then he added, "Though we will have to change that, won't we?"

"Yes indeed, we shall."

"Excellent, I will look forward to talking business with you a little later." Then he raised his voice and addressed everyone in the room. "Dinner is about to be served, please, everyone, find your appropriate seats."

Mr. Vanderfrost turned and strolled from the room, breaking the trance that I felt I was under. I was finally given a chance to converse with the man and I couldn't spit out more than one sentence answers. I felt almost locked in his hypnotic gaze and struggled to find an appropriate reply. I shook my head and exhaled, then followed other guests to the dining hall.

In my mind, I had envisioned the lavish sprawl of food that someone of Mr. Vanderfrost's wealth could provide, and the layout before me exceeded my wildest expectations. First of all, the sheer enormity of the dining table was mind-blowing, as it must have sat eighty to a hundred people. Someone sitting at one end of the long rectangular table wouldn't even be able to see those seated at the other end.

The variety of food was simply amazing. There was everything one could think of, from seafood, to fruits and vegetables, to meat dishes and pastries, and the staff kept bringing more. There was also a frosted glass of red wine beside every plate.

The seats were numbered and I quickly checked my invitation to find that I was surprisingly close to Mr. Vanderfrost, a mere ten seats away from the host himself. I took my seat and attempted to refrain from gobbling my food like a savage, given that I was extremely hungry. I had refrained from eating all day, waiting for the dinner which I planned to thoroughly enjoy.

I was most curious to watch Mr. Vanderfrost throughout the dinner. He didn't touch an ounce of food, electing to watch, and to listen, to those seated closest to him. He did, however, sip on a frosted glass filled with red wine. He was a highly intelligent and calculating man, and it was evident to me that he was reading his guests, discerning their strengths and their weaknesses to further aid him in future business dealings.

"Ghastly thing, all those bodies being found. Appears Mr. Shletzborg is the newest addition to that growing and mysterious list," someone nearby commented.

I nearly choked on some pheasant. This was hardly the place or the time to speak of such gruesome things. The man could have waited until later, or at the very least, when dessert was served, but not during dinner. Murder was not a topic to be enjoyed with food.

The expression on Mr. Vanderfrost's face told me he also disapproved of such talk while others were eating. His penetrating eyes met mine again and he raised his glass.

"This time next year," he announced, "I hope we will all be enjoying a rare wine from the Far East, courtesy of Mr. de Jaager."

I cleared my throat before replying. "We need not wait until next year, for I have brought a bottle along with me for you to sample."

I attempted to gauge the reaction from our host but there was none. He sat there stone-faced; his expression never changing.

"Shall I pour you a glass?"

"I fear if I drink much more this evening, I will not be able to perform my duties as a proper host."

"Just a sip, then," I said, rising from my chair.

I opened the satchel which I had stored under my chair and pulled out a clear bottle, half-filled with an inexpensive red wine that I had purchased right here in Ravensbridge. I grabbed my cane and limped my way over to the head of the long table where our illustrious host was seated.

I poured some of the wine into an empty silver goblet and sat the bottle on the table in front of Mr. Vanderfrost. I took a step back and fixed my eyes onto the bottle.

"Perhaps our great mayor would like the first taste?" he said, motioning to Mayor Ableton, who sat directly to his right.

"I certainly would not mind that, pass it here, my friend," the mayor replied.

As Mr. Vanderfrost reached for the goblet, I pulled my cane in half, revealing a sharpened wooden tip that was concealed within. To the horror of those present, I drove my weapon into the left side of Mr. Vanderfrost's back with all my strength. The sharpened end slid right through the man to exit from his chest, perfectly piercing his heart.

Jaws hung open in shock. Terrified guests were rooted to their seats unable to react otherwise. Then, as if that spectacle was not enough to unsettle them, Mr. Vanderfrost let out an otherworldly shriek and melted right before their very eyes. In the blink of an eye, all that remained of our host was a puddle of disgusting goo, along with his clothing.

"I believe there will be no more missing people in Ravensbridge, with the…departure of Mr. Vanderfrost," I said, breaking the deathly silence that followed his destruction.

Arthur Vanderfrost had been very careful in keeping his identity a secret. I found no mirrors present anywhere within the main floor of his home. Even the glasses that were used to serve drinks were frosted and provided no reflection. I wasn't completely sure he was the monster I sought, until placing my own bottle in front of him and noticing he cast no reflection in the glass of the bottle.

I tipped over the glass he had been drinking from and immediately noticed the difference in texture from the liquid that poured forth. Our host had not been drinking wine like the rest of us, he had been drinking blood.

Mr. Brouwer was seated near the head of the table and was the first person to find his voice. "Quite a show. I get the impression that you are not, Edgar de Jaager, an importer of exotic wines."

"Indeed sir, you are correct. I am Sigmund Helgaard, Vampire Hunter."

THE WEEPING WILLOW

It was midafternoon on a Friday and I was in the office typing up a report. For the first time in quite a while, I had no pressing cases that required my attention over the weekend and I had planned to visit a cabin near Lake Everest. That was the plan anyways, until I was approached by Detective Milton.

"Hey, Kane. You got a minute?"

"I have several, but how many I have to spare depends on what for."

"Well…I am working on this missing person's case and…"

"Milton, it's Friday afternoon and I am going to the cabin this weekend. Gotta run to the supermarket and grab some food for the grill as soon as I am done with this report."

"Please, Kane, I am stumped. This rich woman has disappeared and I know the husband must be behind it but I've no evidence. It's been a month now and I've got nothing on the guy. His wife has just vanished."

"She has not run off with another man?"

"No, it would not seem so."

"You've searched his car for traces of blood, in the event that he moved a body?"

"Completely clean."

"The house?"

"No traces."

"The husband stood to gain much by her disappearance?"

"Much indeed. Her ailing father is the owner of The Four Aces Casino. She is an only child and heir to that fortune. The husband is a nobody with several fraud charges."

"Quite suspicious, I would have to agree with you. Why can't these criminals just make it easier on us and leave the smoking gun on the table, huh?"

"Yeah, you're telling me."

"So, she had no reason to run away? There were no prior signs of distress?"

"A note was left behind."

"You have this?"

"Yes."

"Let me see it."

The young detective searched through the papers of an overflowing folder until he found what he was looking for and handed it over.

You have never treated me like the adult that I am. How long did you think to continue with such behavior until you drove me away? I am more than capable of making decisions on how to govern my own life and I do not need you sticking your nose into all of my affairs. I love you and I always will, but you are smothering me to the point where I can no longer breathe. Of this latest matter, I shall not back down, and you have left me no other choice than to leave this house for good. Perhaps one day you shall see the error in your ways and regret your attempts of controlling every aspect of my life. I am sorry to say that this is good-bye.

Ethel

"It looks to be the handwriting of a woman, very neat and orderly. Have you confirmed that it is her writing?" I wondered.

Milton nodded. "Yes, I have compared it with several other letters she had written, along with grocery lists. I would say without a doubt that this was written by her."

I scratched my head. That ruled out my forged letter theory to cover a murderer's tracks. Maybe this Ethel did run away after all. There were plenty of places for someone to hide away in the Big City, especially someone with money.

"Where do they live?"

"A large house on Canadine Avenue, over in the Midwest section of the city."

"Yes, I know exactly where that is, I have to pass by there to get home." I sighed. "Alright, look, give me the address of the house and I will stop by there on my way home. I'll speak with the husband and see what I can find out."

"Thanks Kane, I appreciate it, really I do. I got no read on the guy. He is a fraudster with practice in the art of deception. I owe ya a coffee."

"Yeah, yeah."

Once I had finished my report about a half hour later, I decided it was time to leave. Milton had given me the address and the name of the husband. Questioning a man about his missing wife was not how I had planned to spend my Friday afternoon but I didn't mind lending a hand to Milton.

Detective Milton was only promoted from the police force last year. He was fairly young, as detectives go, and inexperienced. Previously he had worked in the bowels of the city, the Junkie Jungle and other such neighborhoods. He was used to dealing with a certain type of criminal; the drug dealers, the gangsters, not so much the clever and sophisticated kind. Gangsters weren't generally concerned with hiding bodies. Their murders were brazen and meant to send a message.

But the city was full of intelligent killers; those that went to great lengths to hide evidence and concoct the perfect stories. Those were the most dangerous ones. This Wallace Wells certainly seemed to have every motive to eliminate his wife. Nobody was perfect though; they all made mistakes.

I grabbed a hot coffee along the way, despite the summer heat, and was soon cruising down Canadine Avenue scanning for the correct house. Some of the houses on this street were virtual mansions, with some gated. There was a lot of money in this area. It was not generally the type of neighborhood you would find a two-bit hood, like Wallace Wells, living in.

I located the house and parked on the street directly in front. It certainly wasn't the biggest house in the area but neither was it the smallest. With the failing health of

Ethel's father, she had apparently already inherited most of his wealth. The land was well-kept and was most likely the result of hired help.

The long driveway was occupied with three expensive cars. I worked honestly and could never afford to drive any of them. Rubbed me the wrong way when someone like Wallace came by this dishonestly. Of course the man was innocent until proven guilty but my gut already told me the verdict. Now it was just a matter of finding out where he slipped up.

I tightened my tie but left my jacket in the car; it was just too hot. I approached the front door and knocked. I didn't think someone like Wallace would work and hoped that he would be home. After a minute I knocked again.

The door opened and I was greeted with a rather skinny man in a bright red smoking jacket. He had greasy black hair and a thin moustache; reminding me of someone who sold used cars. He appeared to be in his forties, which would make him about fifteen years younger than his wife.

"Whatever you are selling, I don't want or need any."

"I am not selling anything, I am looking for a Wallace Wells. Is that you?"

"Yes, that is me. Who are you?"

I pulled out my badge. "I am Detective Edward Kane and I just wanted a moment of your time to discuss your missing wife."

"I have already spoken to enough detectives, Mr. Kane. I don't know what else I can tell you. Unless you have any leads there isn't really anything further to discuss."

"Well that's just it, Mr. Wells, there has been a

possible sighting of your wife just outside the city. I am now helping with the investigation and wanted to ask you something about the letter she left behind."

His eyes narrowed. "Alright, do come in."

He led me to an extravagantly decorated sitting room where it appeared he had been reading the newspaper prior to my arrival. Next to the paper rested a still-smoking pipe which he promptly scooped up and took a puff.

"Do you smoke, Mr. Kane?"

"No. I have enough bad habits that I don't need to pick up any new ones."

"Well then, what is this you say about a possible sighting of my dear Ethel? I miss her terribly."

"I don't mean to raise your hopes just yet, but someone meeting her description was sighted yesterday in a train station outside the city."

"Interesting," he said, before puffing on the pipe again.

I pulled out the letter that Milton had given me. "I had a question about this letter, though."

"I would be happy to help."

"Ethel mentioned something to which she wouldn't back down from. What was that all about? You were arguing about something in particular?"

"Why, yes, 'tis a silly thing really, and one I do come to regret now. Ethel wished to take some courses at one of the universities. At first I thought it ridiculous, given her age and all. On top of that she is extremely wealthy already so it seemed like a dreadful waste of time."

"She became very upset by this, I take it?"

"Oh yes, much more than I had anticipated. I realize now that it wasn't my place to tell her what she can and cannot do. I fear my pigheadedness has driven her away for good. If I could only rewind time and apologize for my behavior."

"This makes sense, Mr. Wells. The sighting was at the Oakvale train station, and as we know, Oakvale is home to one of the top universities."

"Yes, yes indeed! She must have gone there to continue with her plans. Oh, Mr. Kane, you must find her."

"I will do my best," I said as I stood to leave. "I know you must be worried sick about her, along with her father. How is he doing by the way?"

His expression soured. "I wouldn't know. We do not speak, him and I."

"Oh, I am sorry to hear that. Well, try and enjoy the nice weather this weekend, Mr. Wells, and I will keep you informed of my progress."

"Thank you, and please do."

The supermarket would have to wait. I figured a trip to visit Ethel's father was now in order. If her father and Wallace Wells did not get along, then it was quite possible to learn some valuable information from her father, who would have nothing to hide.

Her father lived thirty minutes in the opposite direction of where I was headed but I had involved myself now and needed to see this through. I agreed with Milton, Wallace was involved with the disappearance in some way, but how? I didn't buy the whole university disagreement.

Heavier than usual traffic, due to being a Friday, made my trip to Ethel's father's place take longer than expected. Forty-five minutes later, I arrived at the apartment building and shortly thereafter was knocking on the door of a penthouse suite.

A young woman dressed as a maid answered the door.

"Good afternoon, Miss. My name is Detective Kane and I was wondering if I could speak with Samuel Davis for a moment."

"Mr. Davis is in poor health, Detective Kane, and he is resting."

"Please, I will not be long. It's concerning his daughter."

"My daughter did not run away, Detective!" Mr. Davis roared, after I was brought to his room and introduced by the housekeeper.

He was then wracked with a fit of coughing for his exertion. The frail elderly man lay in a bed and was hooked up to an oxygen tank. The sight reminded me of just how mortal we all are. Here was one of the richest men in the city, but that wealth could do nothing to help him now, as he was bed-ridden and wasting away.

"Tell me about Wallace Wells, if you may."

"He is a no-good scoundrel. A liar and a thief, pure and simple. I was against their getting married from the very beginning. But my Ethel couldn't be swayed. She threatened to run away and disown the family if I didn't allow her to make her own choice."

Hmm, very interesting, I thought. I pulled out Ethel's letter and showed it to her father. "Mr. Davis, have you ever seen this letter before?"

The housekeeper fetched his glasses upon his request and he glanced over the contents of the letter. "Of course I recognize that letter, she wrote that for me when I told her she could not marry that crook. I told her that he was only after our fortune but she wouldn't listen to me."

"So this letter, when was it written?"

"Nine years ago. Just before she ignored my protests and married him anyways."

"Thank you, Mr. Davis, you have been most helpful."

When Detective Milton first told me that Ethel had left a note behind prior to vanishing, my first thoughts were that it must have been a forgery. Milton was convinced that it was her handwriting and indeed it had been; only the context was all wrong. Wallace had somehow gotten ahold of the letter written years ago to her father and kept it handy. He cleverly informed police it was written only recently and referred to an argument between the two of them over her plan to continue her education. As I said earlier, everyone slips up.

I decided to call it a night and head home. Sadly the cabin would have to wait, as I now planned to visit Mr. Wells again in the morning with some developing leads. Milton was going to owe me more than a coffee for this.

"Detective Kane, you are back again so soon?" Mr. Wells said, as he answered his door at precisely eleven o'clock the following morning.

"Yes, I have received word that someone matching Ethel's description has now been seen on the campus of the Oakvale University. I was wondering, Mr. Wells, did Ethel have a study? Or any kind of room where she kept personal books and items?"

"Why, yes, she did have her own study with a library of books."

"Might I take a look around, if it's not a bother? Perhaps I might find some clues as to what program she might have enrolled in at the university, to aid in our locating her. Or perhaps you have an idea?"

"By all means, you can look around. I only know that she was interested in business, seeing as how she would be shortly taking over The Four Aces Casino."

We proceeded up the stairs and down a long hallway to a cozy little room with a large window facing the backyard. There was one tall bookcase against a wall filled with all kinds of books covering a wide variety of topics. There was a writing desk and a leather chair, facing the window, so Ethel could enjoy the lovely view while sitting there working away on whatever she might have been doing. The room smelled pleasantly of pot pourri.

"I am not sure what kind of clues you might find here, Detective. As you can see, she had a wide range of interests when it came to books."

"One never knows, Mr. Wells, sometimes we find the most helpful clues in the unlikeliest of places. That is a lovely photo of Ethel there on the wall. Was that fairly recent?"

"Yes, in fact that was taken only a week before she vanished. I thought it only appropriate to hang it here in her favorite room."

"Where was that photo taken?"

"Right here in our backyard. I took it myself."

The photo depicted Ethel in a long flowing dress, standing in the grass. Other houses could be seen in the distance behind her.

I walked over to the window to regard their sizable backyard. The grass was emerald green and the only things that occupied the large space was a patio table and chairs, near to the back door, and a weeping willow tree that was placed almost directly in the center of the yard. The tree was not yet very tall which told me that it was not too old.

I paused for a moment in thought and then turned back to the photo of Ethel. Curiously, the photo that was taken only recently, did not contain the weeping willow tree.

"I have always loved those weeping willows," I commented. "They are strangely beautiful, in a creepy sort of way."

"They were Ethel's favorite."

"Thank you for your time, Mr. Wells, I must be going."

"You didn't look at her books."

"Perhaps another day. I just remembered an appointment that I must get to. I can show myself out, good day."

When I arrived back at home I got on the phone and called Detective Milton. "If I were you, I would get over to the Wells' place with a team and dig up that willow tree in the backyard. I believe you might find what you are looking for. Yes, yes, you are going to owe me more than a coffee."

I was a little disappointed that I was not able to make it to the cabin this weekend. I tried to make up for it on Sunday by going for some ice cream and a walk with a lady friend.

After dropping her off, I took a minor detour on my way home and turned onto Canadine Avenue. I was not too surprised to find several police cruisers parked out front, with much activity in the driveway. I spotted Detective Milton speaking with a couple of officers so decided to park my car and head over.

"Kane! What a surprise. You won't believe what

happened."

Poor Ethel, I thought. I had a feeling she was buried beneath that tree. "Found her, did you?"

"Sadly, you were correct. But there has been a twist."

"Oh?"

"Come around back and see for yourself. A complete mystery, this is."

I followed Milton through the house and out the backdoor to the yard. There, around the willow tree, stood several officers gawking at a body that hung from the branches of the tree. I could see that a portion of the ground around the tree had been dug up.

As I got closer, I realized the body hanging from the tree was that of Wallace Wells, and he was quite dead. Strangely, several branches were wrapped around this throat in some bizarre death grip.

"We found what was left of her body beneath the tree," Milton informed me. "The roots had actually grown right through her. But now, who could have hung Mr. Wells up like that? We had an arborist come by this afternoon, you know, one of those tree experts? She said it was near impossible for anyone to wrap those branches around his neck without them snapping. She said it was almost as if the tree itself had grabbed him and is refusing to let go. It's the darndest thing."

Yes, I thought, the darndest thing indeed.

"What do you suppose happened here, Kane?"

"Justice."

APRIL SHOWERS

As storm clouds gathered in the dismal sky above, I thought it best to turn into the ramshackle gas bar that was fast approaching on my right side. I wasn't familiar with this backwoods road but I did know that there wasn't another service station for another eighty miles. In fact, there wasn't anything at all for another eighty miles.

My car was beginning to pull to the right as one of my tires was becoming dangerously low. I figured I had best have an attendant fill it with air before continuing on my trek. The sun would be setting shortly and I didn't want to have to make any more stops until I reached my destination.

I am a reporter for the *Heavensville Sun* paper, and I was rushing to be the first to interview a witness in one of the bizarre cult murders that happened only two days ago. Until now, nobody had caught any glimpses of the suspects involved with a string of abductions and murders which all pointed in the direction of some loathsome cult.

This witness, one, Gerard Stone, claimed to have seen four men wearing black masks and driving in a dark-colored pickup truck, only a half-mile from where the last person was abducted. He had been very cooperative with the police so far but had yet to speak to any of the media. One of my coworkers demonstrated his investigative skills and came up with Stone's home address, so now I was attempting to secure the first interview.

"What can I do for you, Miss? Shall I fill it up?" asked the white-haired gas bar attendant.

"Yes please. Fill it up and also check my tires if you would, I believe one of them is dreadfully low."

"It would be my pleasure."

I figured I would arrive in Tanners Run too late this evening to call on Mr. Stone, so I would just check into a motel, visit Mr. Stone in the morning, and hopefully make it back in time for a family gathering tomorrow night. It was my Aunt Matilda's birthday and my Uncle Gus was a professional chef, which meant it was going to be a meal that I did not want to miss out on.

"You are right, Miss, your front right tire has a nail in it. So far it would seem the nail has plugged the hole and you are only losing air slowly. To be on the safe side, I could change the tire for you, if you like?"

"I am afraid my spare is flat."

"I could call over to the next station and see if they have the right tire, I don't believe I have the one you need here. I am sure they would."

"How long would that take?"

"Oh, maybe about an hour at most, to get the tire brought over here and put on for you."

"Hmmm, no thanks, I don't want to wait that long but I appreciate the offer."

"Well as I said, it's a slow leak, it could be fine for another day or two."

I smiled and nodded, then grabbed my purse to pay the man and clumsily dropped my wallet, spilling cards onto the ground. The man was kind enough to gather them all up for me and hand them back. He did, however, notice my name on my driver's license and smiled.

"Interesting name."

"Yes, my parents had a sense of humor it would seem."

"Much obliged for the tip and you drive carefully now, Miss Showers."

"Thank you for your help and yes I shall."

Oh wonderful, I thought, as I attempted to adjust the radio dial after pulling back onto the road. It appeared the reception out here in the middle of nowhere wasn't very good at all. I tried all my favorite channels, along with a few not so favorite, and all I got was static. I did not relish the idea of a long, lonely drive, without music, or at the very least some news.

I decided to hum and whistle to myself, listening to imaginary tunes in my head. I wondered what my cat was doing at this very moment without me around to supervise. I had a sneaking suspicion that she got into much hijinks when I was not around and just played the innocent sleepy-head when I was around. Plants and ornaments had a tendency to be in different positions each time I returned home from a short trip. Of course, Mayla always wore that innocent face.

I found my grip on the steering wheel was getting

tighter, the darker it got. The clouds blotted out all the light from the moon and the stars, and of course, there were no street lights along this lonely road. My headlights did not afford me much distance and I was forced to decrease my speed as the road took many sharp twists and turns.

A thick forest, as black as pitch, lined both sides of the road, and according to the map, stretched on for the better part of my trip. Deer darting across the road suddenly became a concern of mine. I had heard tales of the tremendous damage they could cause to your vehicle if struck, and I would be absolutely mortified, to top it off, if I had ever ran into an animal.

I began going over the questions I had planned to ask Mr. Stone, to distract myself from the unsettling drive. I was curious to know if he had gotten the license plate number of the truck he had seen. So far none of those details had been released by the police.

Suddenly, and without warning, my car pulled violently to the right and I swerved off the road. Fortunately for me, I was able to apply the brakes in time to prevent myself from running headlong into a large tree. My heart was beating so fast it felt as though it were about to burst through my chest.

With my hands still trembling, I fumbled to open the car door and step outside to assess any damage. I cursed myself for not putting fresh batteries in the flashlight I kept in the glove box; the others had died months previous.

My headlights offered the only source of light, making it difficult to properly inspect all angles of my car in the gloom of the night. It appeared to be alright, well, aside from the flat tire. Of course I would be made to pay for my impatience at not wanting to wait for a new tire. The evil nail had done its worst, effectively ruining my tire and making it undriveable.

I cursed myself for the second time at not waiting until morning to make this trip. In my haste to get to Mr. Stone before anyone else in the media, I made a rash decision. I dreaded the thought of having to walk back to the service station in this frightening darkness. I had been driving for nearly thirty minutes, which would translate into a two hour walk, I figured, at the least. But I didn't know what else I could do; I certainly couldn't just sit around and hope that someone would drive by on this isolated road. Who knew how long that wait could be?

Despairingly, I turned my car off, locked the doors, and trudged off in the direction I had come. All I could hear was the sound of chirping crickets all around, until the hoot of an owl gave me quite a start.

"Whooooooooooo," I heard it call.

"Me, that's who," I answered. "Just a foolish woman who didn't heed the advice of the gas bar attendant."

After roughly twenty minutes into my miserable trek, my heart skipped a beat at a glorious sight up ahead. Two headlights off in the distance joyfully announced the approach of a vehicle. With luck, perhaps I could convince this person to take me back to Heavensville. I would certainly be willing to pay them if that's what it took.

As the vehicle got closer, I felt a knot form in my stomach and a sudden nervousness overtook me. I had no idea who this person could be. I decided it might be wise to step off the road and not draw attention to myself.

I scampered off the road and ducked behind the first

tree I found. It was too late though, I soon realized. The driver must have spotted me as the vehicle began to slow. Several voices could be heard telling me it was not a lone driver. The engine made a deep rumbling noise, which to me, sounded like a truck. My suspicions were soon confirmed as I noticed it was a pickup truck, with two people inside the vehicle, and two others sitting in the back. The license plate read, DRKNSS.

The vehicle crawled past my position and now I could hear their voices quite clearly.

"I coulda swore I saw someone on the road."

"You're right, I saw it too."

"Looked like a woman."

"What would a woman be doing walking this road at this time of night?"

"Who knows, but I mean to ask her."

"Let's just go. Hank is waiting for us at the Lion's Pub and you know Hank doesn't like to be kept waiting."

"Hank won't care if we bring him company for those that we have locked in the pub's basement."

That last comment caused the hair on my arms and neck to stand on end. My gut was telling me these men were dangerous, very dangerous. I squinted for a better look then involuntarily squealed aloud as I noticed the men were all wearing black masks. A flashlight momentarily blinded me.

"It is a woman! There behind that tree!"

"Come on out you pretty thing. We won't hurt you…much."

I took off in a blind run into the impenetrable darkness of the thick forest. Within minutes I must have bled from a half-dozen cuts and scrapes to my face and arms but I did not care and I did not stop.

Behind me I could hear the voices of the four men as they took up the chase while hooting and hollering. They were taunting me and telling me that I could not escape. They were saying that running will only make it worse for me and that I should just give up.

I knew immediately these were the men that Mr. Stone had witnessed and they must have been connected to the cult abductions and murders. I came looking for an interview concerning this case and wound up becoming a part of the story.

It was dark, so dark, and I had no idea where I was or which direction I was headed, but I just kept running. And so did the men, no doubt following the sounds I made of snapping twigs and crushing leaves underfoot. As fast as I was running, which under the circumstances I felt was quite fast, their voices were getting closer and closer, but I dared not look back.

Then an unfortunate thing occurred, which I supposed should have happened earlier but didn't; my foot caught on the thick root of a tree and down I went striking my head against a stone. Bright lights danced in front of my eyes and a sharp pain shot through my skull as I attempted to lift my head.

"Quickly girl, over here, and don't make a noise."

To my credit, I did not scream out as that voice whispered to me a few feet away to my right. I could not see the person but there was something about the tone of the voice that I felt I could trust. In any event, I possessed no other options as bobbing flashlights and the voices of the four men were nearly upon me.

Despite the searing pain in my head, I crawled dizzily

towards the whispered voice. A dark figure sat crouched in a natural ditch and I soon joined him.

"Lay still and don't say a word."

I was completely out of breath and it took every ounce of effort to try and control my breathing and stifle the noise. I heard my pursuers very close by. They had stopped, noticing that they could no longer hear me running.

"Where are you woman? Where did you go?

"Come out, come out, wherever you are."

"We have all night to look for you, we will find you."

I trembled uncontrollably in fear, while the shadow of the man kneeling next to me remained still and calm. For once, on this dreadful evening, I was afforded a bit of luck, as the men moved off in other directions, away from the ditch where we hid. They continued their taunting but their voices were becoming more distant.

I allowed myself to exhale and breathe a giant sigh of relief. I was certainly not out of danger yet but was given a moment's reprieve.

"What is your name?" the stranger in the dark asked of me.

"April."

"Alright, April, we need to move from here. Are you still able to walk? Are you hurt?"

"I hit my head, I can feel it bleeding, but my legs are fine I can walk."

"Good, come along then. Follow me and make as little noise as possible."

"Who are you?"

"My name is Henry, now let's go."

I had a dozen more questions to ask Henry, foremost

being, what was he doing out here by himself at night, but they would have to wait for now. As we rose from the ditch I was able to get a better look at the mysterious man. He didn't stand much taller than me and had a slim build. He wore brown pants and a thick brown coat. On his head was a fur hat with a raccoon's tail hanging from the back of it. He had a bushy brown beard and kind blue eyes. I thought he looked very much like a hunter and then that was confirmed as he picked up a long musket-style rifle.

"You have a gun. You can shoot those men then, if you have to."

"I hunt animals, April, and then only out of necessity. I do not hunt people."

"They are not people, they are monsters."

"Regardless, let's hope it doesn't come to that. Now let's move."

Henry crouched low to the ground as he moved away from the ditch and I followed suit. He would stop often to make sure that I was still close behind. We could no longer hear the men or see their flashlights and I hoped that was a good thing.

I was relieved when we emerged from some thick bushes to find a clear pathway. Enough of the moon was peeking through the clouds so that I could make out a trail that cut through the forest.

"We will follow this trail and it will lead you out of the forest. There is a ranger's station where you will be safe."

"Thank you, Henry."

"This is a strange place for a woman to be wandering around by herself at night. Did something happen to your metal wagon?"

"My what?"

"Your means of transportation."

"You mean my car? I got a nail in my tire, it's flat. What are you doing out here?"

"I live here."

"Here? Like in this forest?"

"Yes, here in the forest. It has been my home for a very long time."

We heard voices approaching and we stepped off the trail, crouching behind a bush. We could see two flashlights and they were coming straight for our position.

"We can hear you, missy. Just give yourself up."

"We know you are close."

"Quickly April, pick up that stone and throw it over them," Henry whispered.

"What?"

"Throw it so it lands behind them."

I did as Henry instructed and threw the stone with all my strength to land it a fair distance behind the two men. They whooped with excitement and spun around, running off in the opposite direction, thinking their quarry was close at hand.

Henry and I immediately sped down the trail away from the men, not stopping until the forest thinned and ahead of us was a clearing. In the distance, I could make out the lights of a small cabin, the ranger's station. I almost could not contain my elation. We had managed to elude those vile murderers, and best of all, I had their license plate and the name of the pub it seemed they used as their base of operations.

"Henry, I cannot thank you enough…Henry? Henry?"

I looked about for my rescuer but he was nowhere in sight. "Henry, where are you?"

I dared not linger for too long searching for Henry, lest those men come this way and find me. I dashed across the clearing and pounded with both fists upon the door to the cabin.

A man dressed in a ranger's uniform opened the door wearing a shocked expression. I am sure they were not used to visitors frantically knocking on their door at this hour of the night. I was brought inside and found there were two men on duty, and to my relief, several rifles hung on the wall.

I told the rangers of the men who pursued me and that I suspected they were involved with the recent cult murders. They immediately radioed the police and officers were on their way.

"I would never have found that trail and escaped those men if it were not for Henry. I want to be sure that he is hailed as a hero and gets a reward for saving my life."

"Where is this Henry now?"

"When we reached the clearing, I turned and he was gone. I don't know where he went."

Then I noticed a most curious sight. On the wall hung a painting, depicting a man who looked very much like Henry, standing next to a log cabin with his rifle in hand.

"That's him, that's Henry."

The rangers looked to each other, seemingly unconvinced. "That's the man who led you out of the forest? That's your Henry?"

"Yes, he was dressed exactly like that and even carried that rifle."

"That is Henry McAbbott. The trail you used to exit the forest is the famous McAbbott trail."

"He told me he lived in the forest, that's him!"

"Henry McAbbott was one of the first pioneers in this region. Miss Showers, Henry has been dead for one hundred and thirty years."

JUNGLE JOHNNY

Some of you may choose to think my words false, that I have imagined this tale or embellished it to the point of ridiculousness. I can assure you that is not the case. Sadly, I possess no photographic evidence but I was present for Johnathan White's last adventure on that dreadful island. My name can be found in the ship's ledger and the magazine that I work for can vouch for having sent me to travel with Jungle Johnny.

Why have I waited so long to tell this tale, you ask? Simply put, I have just arrived back to civilization after months lost at sea. I am no seaman, nor am I versed in the ways of nautical navigation. Aside from the odd fishing trip as a young lad, I had not spent any time on a boat. I hardly consider the daily ferry commute from Glorchester to Avindale as boating experience. Indeed, I am fortunate to have found my way back to land before my food stores were completely depleted.

Now that I am returned, I am obligated to apprise the details of Jungle Johnny's fate, along with the members of his crew. That I am even here to impart this information onto you is no small matter. I could have easily met my end on that selfsame island, though for whatever the reason, and maybe that reason is to tell this tale, I was spared a ghoulish fate.

Many of you are familiar with the Jungle Johnny of film and radio fame. I mean, who hasn't seen one of the many fine Jungle Johnny movies, where he was portrayed by the strapping young actor, Claudio Hart? And how many of you may have huddled around a radio, listening to the Jungle Johnny program, voiced by the remarkable, Stewart Rayne?

At the risk of damaging his reputation, Johnathan White, the real Jungle Johnny and the inspiration for those films and programs, was not the most pleasant of men. He was not the handsome and amiable fellow of fame, and certainly was not the brave and fearless leader most of us had thought.

I found the man to be brutish and his demeanor most unendearing. This revelation may come as a shock to most but I am sure those of you who have actually met the man, would wholeheartedly agree with that sentiment.

But I must apologize, my goal here is not to bash the character of perhaps the world's greatest explorer, I am simply here to relate the events that I am unfortunately the sole witness to.

I was first introduced to Jungle Johnny in Port Rock. His small ship was docked there while restocking their supplies. My initial feeling was one of slight disappointment. I realize Claudio Hart was just an actor but the two looked nothing alike. Jungle Johnny was a large man, though not muscle-bound like his counterpart in the pictures. He had a protruding stomach and a scruffy beard. Granted, the man was now in his late fifties, but he certainly did not care much about keeping up appearances.

Nor did he care much about making new friends. I found him quite rude and dismissive. A cantankerous fellow who was not overly pleased at having me join them for their next excursion. While I had mixed feelings myself about joining them and sailing into potential danger, the thought of discovering some new species of primate was admittedly exhilarating.

Some fisherman had stumbled upon an uncharted and unexplored island only recently. They reported witnessing a strange type of white ape, roaming about the beach. They claimed it looked something similar to a gorilla, only slightly smaller and possessed hair of the purest white. They dared not land on the beach for fear of these apes and what they may be capable of. They did, however, snap a photo, albeit fuzzy, but their claims appeared trustworthy.

Now it was the duty of Jungle Johnny, the famous explorer, to visit this island and bring back one of these white apes for study. In the past, Johnny had been responsible for the capture of many wild and rare animals from all over the globe. From the biggest of cats to the most dangerous of reptiles, Johnny had hunted and captured them all. An expert hunter, if you will; seemingly fearless.

The Jungle Johnny of the films wrestled tigers and bears with his bare hands. He once knocked out a gorilla with a punch, to save the lead female in the film. I highly doubted that the man I met was capable of any of those feats, though he was successful at what he did.

The magazine I worked for was interested in getting an exclusive story of this adventure, and the seemingly inevitable capture of this new species of ape. Thus, I was dispatched to Port Rock to rendezvous with Jungle Johnny before he set sail. I caught up with him, and his crew of five, while they were loading the last of their supplies onto the ship, and we set sail the following morning.

Disappointingly, the ship was not large enough for me to have my own cabin and I was forced to bunk with the other members of the crew. They were not the friendliest lot, mimicking the poor behavior of their captain. I did make some headway, mind you, with Borga, a black-skinned man who was said to be an unparalleled tracker and an expert marksman. He had been in the employ of Jungle Johnny for nearly thirty years and provided me much insight into some of their previous adventures.

Nickolas and Tomas were clearly sailors and did most of the work on the ship. They poorly hid their distaste for me and would not speak with me unless it was to tell me to move out of their way.

Kenneth was also an expert marksman and spent the majority of his time on the ship cleaning a variety of rifles. Horacio was the youngest of the men, only in his twenties, and the butt of much amusement and jests. From what I gathered, he was the "pack mule", as the others referred to him. He would be overburdened with packs and supplies and do his best to follow the others and keep up.

Thankfully, I was left well enough alone and was not assigned any extra duties while aboard the ship. Most often

I was making notes while speaking with Borga, and other times I was doing my best to elicit information from Jungle Johnny, which was no easy task by any stretch of the imagination. He tended to grunt his replies quite frequently, avoiding the use of actual words whenever possible, at least in my company.

That made for an uncomfortable trip. Though after two and a half weeks of sailing, and three unsettling storms, Tomas shouted that he had spotted land. The crew had little solid information to go by in locating this mysterious island. The coordinates provided by the fishermen had not been accurate and we were forced to change course several times. Though luck was with us and it appeared that we had found our island.

I was a little nervous, though quite relieved to have land once again in my view. It was no secret that many sailors had gone missing in this area of the ocean. So I was happy to learn that we had not become hopelessly lost.

I leaned over the rail of the ship as we approached the island, searching for any signs of the white apes that were previously spotted roaming the beach. At this moment, the beach was devoid of activity, and I supposed I felt that was a good thing, since we were almost ready to disembark.

Nikolas dropped the anchor a good hundred yards from the beach, then he and Tomas stayed with the boat as the rest of us paddled to land on a bright yellow dingy. Borga and Kenneth were the first on the beach, rifles in hand and on high alert.

I remember feeling surprised, thinking that Jungle Johnny would have proudly strode first onto the beach, chest puffed out like the brave explorer of the big screen.

Instead, Johnny remained in the dingy with myself and Horacio, until given the signal by Borga that all was clear. He doubled checked that his shotgun was loaded, then exited the dingy and proceeded to the beach.

"Come along, writer," he called back to me. "We have an ape to catch."

Horacio motioned for me to go first and then he followed, dragging the dingy onto the beach. I noticed Borga kneeling on the ground, inspecting strange footprints in the sand.

"Ape tracks," he said. "The fishermen were right. Looks as though several passed by here only recently. It would seem they are slightly smaller than we are, if my guess is correct."

"Excellent. Smaller means a good shotgun slug should take them down," Johnny said, tapping his gun.

"Are we not to capture one alive?" I inquired.

"If it's possible we will take one alive. We have no idea how vicious these animals can be. We also get paid quite handsomely by scientists for a dead specimen to study."

I was mortified. Here we were, on the verge of making contact with a completely new species of ape, and their plan was to kill one for no other reason than to sell it to a scientist. Claudio Hart would be rolling over in his grave. The Jungle Johnny of the movies did not even carry a gun. He would have been repulsed by the actions of his real self.

The midday sun beat down on us and the humidity of the jungle was near suffocating. When I wasn't wiping sweat from my forehead, I was swatting flies and mosquitoes, which could fly about at times in thick swarms.

Borga led the way, hacking at vines with a machete. Kenneth followed, with Jungle Johnny a good distance behind him. I was next, and poor Horacio did his best to keep up, hauling several packs and satchels filled with our supplies. I felt bad for the fellow. The going was tough for me and I only carried a pad of paper and a few pencils. I had to admire his dedication though; he marched on without a single word of complaint.

Soon, the three men in front of me were stopped and huddled together in conversation. I overheard Borga mention that the tracks disappeared, meaning the apes had taken to the trees. I glanced nervously upwards, expecting one of the hairy white beasts to descend on me at any moment. At the boat I was offered a pistol but had turned it down; dreadful things they were. Now though, I wondered if that was not the wisest of decisions on my part. I did not wish to harm anything, but at the same time, I did wish to get home in one piece.

It wasn't long before Borga was hacking at vines and trudging forward yet again, ever mindful of the trees. I was overwhelmed by an uneasy feeling of being watched. Surely we were being watched by several things simultaneously, as colorful birds and small monkeys were visible in the branches above, but this was a different feeling, almost as if there was an intelligence behind it. I know it is difficult to describe but I felt it all the same.

We had been moving deeper into the dense jungle for nearly three hours, though to me it felt as though it had already been days. We came across a clearing with a small pond and Jungle Johnny decided we would stop here for a time.

My heart threatened to leap straight out of my chest as Borga picked up a large snake that was as thick as my thigh and tossed it out of the way. Thank the lord it just decided to slither away and pay us no further mind. The sight of it alone was still enough to upset me and I was ever wary of my surroundings as I took a seat on the stump of a fallen tree.

Four of us had all taken a seat to rest our weary limbs. It took Horacio crashing into the clearing and finally collapsing with exhaustion, before I realized he had yet to join us. The poor lad, the others just laughed.

Jungle Johnny announced that the sun would soon be setting and that we would camp here for the night and resume our hunt in the morning. I had no complaints about that. My stamina was spent and I had no desire to be stumbling around this unforgiving terrain in the dark.

A little later, Borga got a small fire going and we were cooking weenies on sticks. There had been no further appearances of any slithering serpents, though I was still not at ease, and continuously glanced over my shoulder in an attempt to thwart their plot of creeping up on me. The bugs, however, I could nothing about. They were everywhere and beyond bothersome.

In my time on the boat, I had come to see Borga as a reasonable man. While everyone was occupied with their meals, I decided to take up conversation with the hunter.

"Borga, my good chap, you do not seem like the type of person who would wish to hunt and kill a new species of animal."

"People pay."

"Yes, people pay for a lot of things, that doesn't make it right to sell them what they want."

"When people stop paying, then that is the day I stop hunting."

"We are talking about an ape here, not some wild turkey that you would hunt and eat. This is a primate."

"An animal is animal."

"You are incorrect. Apes are highly intelligent. Why, we are not even sure yet of just how intelligent they could be. It's quite possible they are just as smart as we are."

Jungle Johnny laughed, a great belly laugh, with genuine amusement. "Listen here, writer. All animals are stupid. If they are as smart as us, then why do they live here in the jungle like savages? Why are we, humans, the dominant species on this planet? Why, because we are the smartest by far. These apes have eluded us today, but we are more intelligent, and by tomorrow, we will have one of these stupid creatures in a cage."

"Now it will be in a cage? You are not going to shoot one?"

"Had we spotted one of them today, I would have mostly likely had it shot. But they have proven elusive thus far. So tomorrow we will set a trap. A trap that works without fail, because all animals are stupid."

I decided not to press the debate. These men were thick-headed and any further conversation would only raise my ire. I did look over to Horacio, who merely shrugged his shoulders, denoting an indifference to the topic.

I found no sleep that night, so horrified was I by the thought of creepy crawlies. And they had not just been haunting my imagination, for I had seen a large hairy spider which had me standing and pacing for much of the night. I began to hope that we would catch one of these apes in the morning so we could get back to the ship, and thus, off this island.

With the arrival of morning came the suffocating humidity. We trekked for another hour, deeper into the jungle, until we found another substantial clearing.

"This is perfect," Jungle Johnny declared. "We will set our trap here."

I found a suitable log to place my rear and watched the four men go to work. I watched them, while again, I was assailed by that strange sensation that we too were being watched. I tried my best to shake those thoughts and retrieved a snack from one of Horacio's many packs.

The trap was fairly simple in design and one I had seen used many times on the big screen. On the ground of the clearing they placed a sizable net, which was then concealed with large green leaves. Ropes were tied to nearby trees and several bunches of bananas were placed in the center of the net for bait.

"There you go, writer," Johnny said, addressing me after they finished. "No guns needed. The stupid apes will not be able to resist those bananas. As soon as one gets to the center of the net, bingo, it will close around the ape and it will be ours. Works every single time."

Johnny then indicated to a group of tall trees with long thick branches. He thought that would be the best location for the five of us to lie in wait and remain out of sight.

Borga was up the tree first, securing a knotted rope to the trunk, making it much easier for the rest of us to climb up and join him. Of course I inspected the area thoroughly for snakes and spiders and breathed a sigh of relief that there were none. There were plenty of ants, but ants, I could handle. I tried my best to get comfortable and settle into what could prove to be a long wait.

Roughly twenty minutes into our vigil, I found myself glancing around nervously, when something shiny caught my eye. It was a fairly short distance away, behind us in another much smaller clearing. Something was reflecting the sun, something…metallic?

Borga had noticed it as well and was soon grabbing a pair of binoculars off of Horacio. He shook his head in disbelief and handed the binoculars to Jungle Johnny.

Johnny smiled ear to ear. "Gold! Look at all that gold!"

"Gold?" I wondered.

After Kenneth and Horacio had both taken a look, the young lad gave me the binoculars. I peered through the lenses and Johnny had indeed been correct. In the smaller clearing behind us, was a pile of gold coins. A wooden chest sat nearby, tipped over.

"Probably left here by pirates, long ago," Kenneth commented, barely able to contain his excitement.

The four men suddenly cared very little for the trap we had set and could not climb down out of the tree fast enough. It was the first time on this trip that I witnessed Jungle Johnny take the lead. In fact, in a most childish move, he even tripped Kenneth, who seemed to be passing him and might have made it to the treasure pile first.

I sat on the tree branch, watching the men hoot and holler as they reached the treasure and began scooping up gold coins with their hands. Johnny, who generally wore a scowl, laughed and even danced about with glee.

Unfortunately, their joy was not to last. I remember

watching the event unfold in utter disbelief. From under their feet, a large net suddenly wrapped itself around the four men, and ropes tied to nearby trees hoisted the net a good thirty feet into the air. A trap, just like ours. The gold was used as bait in the same way that we had used bananas.

A rumbling sound shook the tree I sat in and my heart stopped beating altogether at a sight that stole my breath. A monstrous, white-haired ape, marched into the small clearing. The ape, whose hair bordered on silver, stood about thirty feet tall and glared into the net which hung at eye level. It licked its lips as it regarded the trapped morsels within.

Soon, a second gigantic ape walked into the clearing, carrying two others that were much smaller, just a little smaller than us. Babies, I soon figured. The small apes the fishermen had seen, and the small tracks we had found on the beach, were the babies.

I positioned myself out of view and trembled as the first ape untied the ropes from the trees, then slung the net over its back with its speechless prisoners trapped inside. The two apes then plodded off into the jungle, and I know how strange this must sound, but I could swear they were giggling.

It took half a day before I found the courage to climb down out of that tree and make my escape. Thankfully, I grabbed one of Horacio's packs, the one that contained water, before dashing off in a mad run. I followed the trail that Borga had hacked all the way to the beach.

To my dismay, I now noticed several giant footprints in the sand. They led to the water, then back into the jungle. I did not even bother with the dingy and swam my way back to the boat and climbed the rope ladder that still hung down the side. I found the boat empty and knew the apes had taken Nickolas and Tomas.

I raised the anchor and managed to figure out how to start the boat. As I mentioned before, I know nothing of nautical navigation and just picked a direction, any direction away from that nightmarish island.

As I sailed away, I kept hearing Jungle Johnny's voice in my head, talking about stupid animals and how that trap always worked without fail.

THE PANHANDLER'S WILL

"Good afternoon, everyone. As most of you may already know, my name is Markus Shaw. Many years ago, I sat in this very same auditorium where you all sit now, as a student, like yourselves. And now, I am a huge success."

And that was the honest truth. I had been invited to come speak to these students from my former school, to show them that with hard work and dedication, they too could be as successful as I. I had grown up in the same neighborhood as them and had attended the very same school.

I knew the teachers present didn't care much for hearing this fact but I never bothered attending college. Several years after graduating from the high school that I was currently addressing, I started my own small printing company. Clients came easily and soon I was having trouble keeping up with the demand. I was forced to expand and even hire staff to help me. Over the next fifteen years, I moved the company location five different times, requiring a bigger warehouse with each new move.

I got into the stock trade and made some extremely wise decisions. Now I lived in a penthouse suite, in one of the most favorable areas of the Big City, with my gorgeous wife, Veronika.

Ahhhh Veronika, what more could I say, but she was the kindest and most beautiful woman on the planet, with her long raven-black hair. Veronika and I had met through a mutual friend, back when my company was still young. I was not yet wealthy, the opposite in fact. I was quite penniless in those days, having invested everything I owned into my budding company. Veronika didn't care about that though.

She came from a simple family and didn't require much to keep her happy. Her smile was radiant and infectious, lighting up any room she entered. She was a social butterfly, having the ability to strike up conversations with anyone at any time. She was genuinely interested in other people's stories and helping those in need.

Oh, if I could have only been like her, but I just didn't have the time. My company demanded most of my attention, as it had right from the very beginning. But my uncompromising dedication is what has led to my success. And as they say, the more money you have, the more money you want. I continued to pour my heart and soul into my company and it continued to prosper as a result.

After finishing my hour-long presentation, I left my old high school and hoped that I had been an inspiration to those young students. It was important that they heard that nothing had been handed to me in life; I worked for every copper coin.

Speaking of copper coins, I fished my hand around inside my pocket, looking for any spare change, as I approached the front of my apartment building. As per usual, Old Stan sat on the ground, his back resting on the brick wall of the building. He was like a permanent fixture in the neighborhood. Day in and day out he sat there, always wearing a glowing smile, despite the poor hand that life had apparently dealt him.

I couldn't exactly guess at Old Stan's age, much of his face was concealed behind a scruffy, greying beard, but I would place him somewhere within the seventies range. A frail, skeletal body, lay buried underneath layers of sweaters and a thick parka, which he seemed to wear no matter the season, along with a grubby blue toque, invariably affixed to the top of his head.

Like my adorable wife, Old Stan would talk to everyone, but then, I guess you would have to when attempting to elicit spare change from each person that passed you by. He did love to talk and could continue on endlessly unless you found a way to disengage yourself from the conversation.

"Good afternoon, Mr. Shaw," he said, his face aglow at my approach. "A fine day isn't it? Perfect weather for a walk, I see."

"Hello Stan, yes it is a very nice day indeed," I answered, dropping a handful of coins into an empty tin cup that sat on the ground directly in front of him.

"Ah, bless ya, Mr. Shaw. You are always so kind to this old man."

I smiled and nodded, then proceeded past to the lobby door.

"Oh, I almost forgot, Happy Anniversary to you as well. Lucky fella you are to have a wife like that Mrs. Shaw. Lucky man indeed," he said.

I paused before the lobby door. Good lord, it was our anniversary and I had completely forgotten, being so focused on my speech at the school. Old Stan said something else but I did not hear it as I rushed into the building towards the elevator. What would I do? I had no gift and no time to run back out to the shops.

The elevator ride was painstakingly slow, as one of the annoying children from the second floor of the building thought it would be amusing to push all thirty buttons. I could have pinched him for that but it did give me more time to contemplate my predicament. Then the simple solution came me and my problem was solved. Who didn't like money?

"Happy Anniversary, my dear," I announced upon entering our suite.

"Ahh, you remembered. I didn't think you would," she replied delightedly.

"Of course, how could I forget the day that I married the world's most wonderful woman?" Then I presented her with several hundred dollars in cash, a most impressive stack of bills. "Here you go, I want you to get whatever you like with that, but it has to be for you. Don't go giving it to the poor and don't buy anything for the apartment, it's all for you."

"Oh, how thoughtful. I don't know what to say."

Money always did the trick. I kissed her and offered to ring for some food to be delivered.

Several months later, I exited the building lobby one morning in search of a cab to hail. I owned my own car, of course, but most times it was easier to just walk to your destination, or grab a cab, within this area of the Big City.

"Good morning, Mr. Shaw," Old Stan called over. "Off to work, are ya?"

"Yes, Stan," I replied, cursing inwardly as I had forgotten to bring some change down with me in my rush.

"Anything big planned for tonight, for Mrs. Shaw's birthday?" he asked.

Unbelievable! Her birthday had completely slipped my mind. I had spent the last several days stressing over three different meetings that I had scheduled for today. How could I be such a fool?

"You know what she would really like, I bet...is...."

"Sorry Stan, we'll have to talk later," I cut him off as a cab pulled up in front of me. I simply could not be late for my first meeting of the day.

The meetings went better than I had even expected and I managed to secure three new large clients for the company. The day was a great success. I had sent my assistant, Olivia, out that afternoon to go and purchase my wife an extravagant diamond ring for her birthday, the biggest the store carried.

That night I slipped it on her finger over dinner. "It was the biggest diamond in the store," I said. "Olivia picked it out and assured me that its style was the latest craze."

"Yes...well...it's lovely, thank you," she replied.

I knew how much all women loved diamonds. Only the best for my most amazing wife.

"I was thinking we could do a dinner cruise tomorrow night. They have just started a new one down by the Third Street harbor," she suggested.

"Tomorrow is no good, my dear. I have to meet Maxwell about signing the new contracts."

"Of course, I understand."

She always understood, she was the best.

Business was booming and once again I was considering the purchase of a larger property for the company to keep up with the rising demand. This evening, Veronika and I had planned to go to the picture show. A new one was just opening by Otto Friedhelm and was starring Maude Levine. It was a werewolf picture that was already receiving much buzz. Veronika expressed great interest in seeing it and making a night out of it. I spent most of the day pouring over papers and contracts in my office at work, and when I glanced down to my pocket watch, I realized I would be late in picking her up.

Dammit, I thought to myself. I still had much to do before I could leave. Then I was struck with an exquisite idea. Veronika always enjoyed riding in a limousine. I would ring for one to be sent to pick her up and take her to the show. That would cheer her up undoubtedly and she probably wouldn't even notice that I wasn't there.

Later that night, when I got home, she was already in bed asleep, so I did not wish to wake her. She slept quite long into the morning and had not yet awakened by the time I decided to head out and grab a coffee with a business associate. This day, I made sure to grab some loose change before stepping out.

"Good morning, Stan," I said to the old man, dropping some coins into his cup.

"Ah, good morning to you too, Mr. Shaw," he replied. "I hope Mrs. Shaw enjoyed the show last night?"

"She told you about that, did she?" I asked.

"Oh yes, she was quite excited about the night out you both had planned. She was out here waiting for you to come by, so we got to chatting."

"Yes, I got held up at work. I imagine she was quite excited to ride in that fancy limousine, eh?"

"Well, I am not so sure I would have used the word excited."

"Overjoyed, perhaps?"

"Well…"

"Markus! Over here, Markus!" someone shouted.

The friend I was meeting for coffee, Franklin, was attempting to flag me down from the opposite side of the street.

"Sorry, Stan, we'll talk another time."

When I returned home later that afternoon, Veronika had just woken up. She complained of some headaches and said she just wasn't feeling too well. For the next several days she slept much and I worried for her health.

"You know what you need?" I said one morning over breakfast. "A good vacation. You can do nothing but sit on the beach all day and read a good book. How does that sound?"

Her face brightened, a sight I had not seen in some time. "Really? That does sound nice."

"Yes, really. I will buy you a plane ticket this very afternoon and book you the finest hotel available."

"Oh, you won't be coming then?"

"Dear, you know I cannot leave work in Harold's hands for more than a few days, no telling what mess I would return to. But you go and have a wonderful time. I will spare no expense to see you happy."

She smiled, women loved to travel.

I remember it clearly; it was a cold winter's day, when I was sitting in my den with a warm fire burning in the hearth. I received a peculiar telephone call, asking me stop by a lawyer's office later in the afternoon to speak with a Mr. Halstead. Curious to see what this was all about, I attended at the appointed time.

"You must be Markus Shaw. Please, have a seat," the well-dressed, middle-aged lawyer, with the bushy moustache said to me.

"What is this about, Mr. Halstead?" I asked. "Is someone suing my company over something?"

He chuckled. "Be at ease, Mr. Shaw, nobody is suing you. This has to do with Stanley Wright."

"Stanley Wright? Who on earth is Stanley Wright?" I had to wonder.

"Well you must have known him, your name is the only one listed in his will."

"His will?"

"Yes."

"Stanley Wright is dead then?"

"Oh yes, most regrettably. You wouldn't have been called here if he wasn't."

"What did he die of?"

"The doctors weren't too sure. One suggested he died of a broken heart. Personally, I believe it was the elements that finally got him, living on the streets as he did."

"Stanley Wright lived on the streets?"

"Oh yes, for many, many, years."

"Ohhhhhh…you must mean Old Stan?"

"I believe some called him Old Stan, yes."

"Hmmm, I did find it strange that I had not seen him in front of my building for several days. Stan had a will? I didn't think he owned anything."

Mr. Halstead produced a small wooden box and sat it on the desk in front of him. "It's not much," he said, opening the box. "There was just this silk handkerchief, and a sealed envelope, a letter, I believe."

He handed the items to me and I held the handkerchief awkwardly between the tips of two fingers. I couldn't imagine the germs that could be found on a panhandler's hanky. Oddly, it looked fairly white and unused, with several blue butterflies stitched on both sides as a pattern.

I thanked Mr. Halstead and promptly left his office. As I approached my building, a feeling of sadness overcame me while I looked to the now empty spot, where Stan had sat for years. It would feel strange not seeing his face every morning when I left and every evening when I returned. Though, I supposed, I would save more money now, not that I needed it.

I sat in my den, which doubled as a library, with the hanky and Stan's envelope resting on top of an opened book. I was curious about what Stan would have had to say in a letter to me. Probably thanking me for all the money I had given him over the years. Lord knows he could have probably afforded to stay in a hotel instead of living on the street.

The smell of scented candles filled the room and I was enjoying some music on the record player when Veronika entered. Dark rings were visible under her eyes; she had not been sleeping well lately.

"What are you doing?" she asked.

"Oh, nothing, was just looking through some old books," I said, closing the book to conceal the hanky and the envelope. I knew how much Veronika was fond of Old Stan and didn't want to upset her tonight with the news of his demise.

I returned the book to its proper place on the shelf and took Veronika by the hand, leading her to the kitchen where I could pour her a glass of wine.

Her next birthday came and went, and I disappointingly did not remember it until two days later. I joked to myself that I needed Old Stan around to remind me of these important events. I made it up to her though with an astonishing, custom-made diamond necklace. What a piece it was. It was certain to make all women jealous.

Now, that dreadful week in July had been one of the busiest for me at work. A few nights I was even forced to sleep in my office so I was admittedly inattentive at home. In hopes of cheering up Veronika, I booked her a trip to a world famous resort and spa at some exotic southern island for the week; a most expensive trip. Sadly, she had not felt up to going.

The Friday of that week was the worst day of my entire life. The scene in front of my building will forever be etched into my mind, playing itself out continuously in my dreams, both while sleeping and during the kind you had throughout the waking day.

A crowd of people was gathered around the lobby door as police attempted to clear a path for the medical crew. They were pushing some unfortunate person on a stretcher towards the waiting ambulance. The significance of this scene before me was not yet evident, until one person in the crowd pointed at me with a most distressed expression and said to a police officer, "That's Mr. Shaw."

The officer approached me, his face pale, visibly uncomfortable at having to be the bearer of bad news. "Mr. Shaw, let's take a walk."

I was told that it was a deadly mix of alcohol and drugs which had finally led to Veronika's untimely departing of this life. Alcohol and drugs?? That was not the Veronika I knew. She enjoyed her wine but certainly not to excess. And drugs? How on earth did she even acquire such horrible substances?

The officer said a great deal more after that but I heard not a word of it. My mind was already on a downward spiral to the very pits of despair. I did remember the man grabbing me by an arm to help keep me on my feet, as my legs had given out and I nearly crumbled to the street.

The next few weeks, even months, were a blur. It was difficult to tell what was real and what was a dream, as I spent most of the waking hours heavily intoxicated and never leaving the apartment. Even after a year had passed, my grief was still too much to bear. I longed for some memento, something personal that had belonged to Veronika, so that I might hold it, and in so doing, perhaps feel as though she was near. But alas, I had none, save for the treasures made of gold and diamonds that I had purchased, but she had not worn too often.

I was neglecting my company and in my absence, the imbecilic Harold, was running it into the ground with poor judgment and empty-headed decisions. My stocks also suffered at the hands of my disregardance. By the end of the second year, all that I had spent my lifetime building, was in ruin. There were repeated knocks at my door, which I had ignored, and many letters were then shoved underneath.

It took police officers breaking down my door, before I learned that I was being evicted from the apartment, my funds having completely run out. I was given two days to pack up what I could and not an hour more.

On the second day, in one of my rare, semi-sober moments, I stood in my den with a fire burning, packing away some books into a box. That's when I found it. One particular book slipped from my grasp to tumble and lay open on the table beside the box. Looking down, I spotted that odd handkerchief with the blue butterflies and the sealed envelope that was left to me in Old Stan's will.

The fire was burning low, so I tossed the hanky into the hearth, having no foreseeable need for an old panhandler's hanky, and then opened the envelope to find a handwritten letter inside.

Dear Mister Shaw,

I hope this letter finds you well. Weller than I, since if you are reading this, then I have finally left this miserable existence and hopefully have gone to join with Harriet. I wanted to thank you for all the years of kindness and the coins you had always so thoughtfully given to me. I was once very wealthy, like yourself, but the grief of losing my wife, Harriet, was too much for me, and I subsequently lost everything. So unfortunately, I have nothing left to leave to anyone in a will, save for some advice, and this I leave to you. I can say I was very blessed to have met your lovely wife, Veronika. What a kind and gentle soul, so full of compassion for everyone. It was many a day, that Veronika stood and spoke to me about life, when everyone else would rush past, pretending not to see an old beggar on the street. I know I always put on a smile for everyone who walked by but I was not a happy man. One day, Veronika had caught me in one of my weak moments. She offered me the handkerchief, which I have left for you, in order to dry my tears. So lovely an item it was, I could not use it, but I kept it and treasured it, as it was a gift of great kindness. You see, it was her favorite, made by her mother and given to her as a child. Veronika has a passion for butterflies and loves them very much. Are you aware of that, Mister Shaw?

I was not.

I see the fancy jewelry you have purchased for your wife but these expensive trinkets are not what she truly enjoys. You need to take the time to learn these things, things like butterflies. Veronika wears a distant stare now; she is losing her love of life. Yes, you are a busy man, but do not let your work get in the way of your personal life. Do not allow yourself to lose Veronika, as I had lost Harriet. It is not too late, Mister Shaw. So my advice to you is, get to know Veronika, the real Veronika, before she forever slips from your grasp and you spend the rest of your life regretting it. Do not become like me.

*   *   *   *

A chill December wind blew down from the north and I shivered slightly as I leaned against the wall of a building. A well-dressed man in a long brown overcoat walked down the street swinging a briefcase. He was approaching my direction.

I put on my best smile. "Excuse me, sir, can you spare any change?"

ONE LESS HUNTER

The fog rolled in from the water of the harbor in thick waves, substantially limiting my visibility. Dark clouds had already hidden the moon and stars behind a heavy blanket and now the fog was blotting out the light from the street lamps.

This evening had proven to be quite uncooperative and was seriously impeding my search for Erwin Baardwik. I had spent the better part of a year tracking the man to this town which was comprised mostly of fishermen.

This was now my second night in town and I had yet to set my eyes on Baardwik, but my extensive information gathering had led me to firmly believe that he was indeed here. He was most likely using an alias, as I had learned that the man rarely, if ever, went by his real name. And therein was my biggest challenge. I had never seen Baardwik in person and had to rely on second-hand descriptions of the man.

Thankfully, he possessed a scar which ran down the right side of his face from his temple to his jaw. That provided me with considerable aid when inquiring about the man and if anyone had seen someone matching that description.

In Belborn he went by the name Christian Kranz. In Red Valley he was Demetrius Kloeten. In Cantos he was Albert Peeters. But each of those men was tall, dark-haired, and bore a scar that ran down the right side of their face.

In each of those places, someone went missing and was never found. The monster that was named Erwin Baardwik left a trail of death everywhere that he went. Now he was here in Vandenbourg and I needed to find him before he chose his next victim. I just hoped that I was not already too late.

A bell tower that was obscured by the fog gonged to announce the tenth hour. The evening was still fairly young and I was positive that Baardwik must have been about. The monster moved around and hunted only at night, which suited me just fine. I understood the dangers that the night brought on but did not fear them as others did, or should.

Vandenbourg was not a big town and only had a few places that catered to a night life. I chose to visit the largest of the pubs this night, as I felt that would have been Baardwik's choice as well. I had to get into the monster's mind and think like him. The largest pub simply meant more people to choose from for his next potential target.

Despite the low visibility of the night, I successfully

navigated my way from my room at the inn to the pub known as *Robin's Rest*. I paused at the door for a moment only and then entered.

My senses were immediately assaulted by a cloud of pipe smoke which left the pub in a haze that was no different from the fog outside. I possessed a sensitive nose and my eyes were soon watering from the sheer amount of smoke.

The spacious taproom was extremely busy. Most of the patrons looked like the gruff sailors that made up most of the population. Given the port here in town, strangers were not uncommon in Vandenbourg, arriving in various ships. So fortunately for me, nobody paid me much attention as I entered. A few gazes shifted my way but they did not linger and soon returned to their own business.

I wondered where I might sit as all the tables and chairs were taken, when a large man seated at the bar vacated a stool and stumbled for a side door. He appeared to be in a hurry and looked as though he was about to lose his dinner and everything he had been drinking thus far.

I quickly moved in and took his seat at the bar. The man to my left guzzled a large mug of ale, spilling more onto his long disheveled grey beard than actually went into his mouth. To my right was a hard-looking man with a flat nose, doing his best to impress the equally as hard-looking woman beside him.

Life in these types of towns was tough and produced a tough breed of folk. It didn't seem like the type of place for Baardwik to hunt for another victim, but then so far, his victims did follow a certain pattern. Some were old and some were young. Some had been male and some had been female. His lack of a preference only made my job here more difficult.

I rested an elbow on the bar and casually scanned the faces in the room. Not all were locals. It was a simple thing to pick out the visitors by their attire, just as my long black overcoat announced my status as a stranger to town. I sighed as nobody fitting Baardwik's description stood out.

The busy barkeep eventually made his way over to me and I ordered a mug of ale for the simple reason of blending in. I did not drink but did not want to appear out of place while waiting to see if the monster showed his face.

Twenty minutes passed when a tap on my shoulder startled me. I was so focused on one end of the room, and with the volume of voices around me, I had not even heard the approach of the large man whose seat I had taken.

He appeared less intoxicated from the time he had stumbled out. I supposed most of the alcohol in his body now coated the ground of the alley beside the pub. He was large with a substantial gut. His forearms looked as thick as tree trunks and he frowned from beneath a bushy black beard.

"I believe you are sitting in my seat," he growled.

"I did not see a name on it when I sat down."

"A smart guy, eh? A smart-mouthed city guy, by the looks of you."

"I just came in for a drink, I am not looking for any trouble."

"Well trouble is gonna find you if you don't get up

off that stool."

"There is a seat over in the corner," I pointed to a recently vacated chair. "How about you just go over there."

"Because that is not my seat. This one is."

I could have easily got up and went over to the other chair but I had an immense distaste for bullies. I found it too difficult to ignore their behavior.

"No, I think I am comfortable right where I am," I said.

"I was hoping you were going to say that," he smiled wickedly.

He grabbed the left shoulder of my coat with his meaty right hand and he possessed an iron grip. Undaunted, I stood and brought my own right arm around in a circular motion, my wrist slamming into his. My fingers wrapped around his thick wrist as best they could and I slid my body to the side of him, while twisting his arm at the same time.

I used his size and strength against him, bringing his arm around painfully behind his back. He howled as he was forced to take a knee. Before he could spit out a curse, I snapped his arm, breaking it at the elbow. He fell to the floor with a roar that now had every face in the pub focused on us.

"Sorry for the trouble," I said to the barkeep.

I tossed a few extra coins onto the bar and casually walked out, leaving the obnoxious man rolling about in agony. It was not my intention to cause such a scene but I decided it best to continue my search for Baardwik elsewhere.

He could have been in any of the other pubs, or in none at all. He could very well be out prowling the fog-shrouded streets. The next closest pub was only a block away, so I first paid a visit there, and when Baardwik did not appear to be present, I decided to tour some of the dark alleyways.

I found the usual drunks and homeless populating many of the alleys. I stumbled across a few shady dealings and drew perturbed stares but I would run into no further trouble this night.

However, in the last alley I had decided to walk through, I did find something out of the ordinary. I spotted a small pool of blood, with drops leading to the far end of the alley. While following the trail I noticed one woman's shoe. I began to wonder if maybe I had been too late. Perhaps Baardwik had already chosen his next victim.

I followed the trail to the street and that's where it ended. Obviously, I couldn't be certain that this was Baardwik's doing, as street fights and bar brawls were common in this town. The shoe made me wonder, though it could have been lost by a drunk.

As dawn approached, I knew Baardwik would be retiring to wherever he was hiding out, so I decided to do the same. I would continue the search tonight, when the monster would be hunting again. I suddenly realized how hungry I had felt but the hour was too late now and I did my best to ignore the pain.

I awoke on the third evening and immediately set out from the inn. It wasn't as foggy this night which would make things a little easier. Anger filled me with determination as I thought of the woman that Baardwik had murdered in Red Valley. While I had not known her personally, she was by all accounts a decent woman. Beautiful and intelligent. She owned a chain of well-to-do clothing shops and was highly respected.

I spat on the ground when I considered that terrible loss of life. There were many inns in this town, given the amount of ships that came and went, so I decided to hit a few more and make some inquiries.

I had no luck with the first three but then I entered the fourth, *The Red Herring Inn*. It was a four-story building that looked out over the harbor. I found a tiny, mouse-like man, seated behind the reception desk reading an old book.

"Hello stranger, need a room?" he asked, putting his book down.

"No, sorry. Just some information if you have a moment to spare."

The innkeeper frowned so I produced a large silver coin to brighten his mood, and it worked.

"I am looking for a man who may have checked in within the last several days. His name is Erwin Baardwik, though I doubt he would have used that name."

The man leafed through a ledger that sat on the desk then shook his head. "No, nobody by that name has checked in here. At least not within the last month."

"He is a tall man, a little taller than me. He has dark hair and a scar that runs down the side of his face."

The description elicited a curious reaction from the innkeeper, though he shook his head, *no*.

"Please, good sir, it is of the utmost importance that I find this man. He is a danger to your town."

He visibly paled, which told me that he also must have believed this to be true, but out of fear, shook his head again. This man knew something and I wasn't about to leave without finding out what that was.

I changed my tone and stared menacingly into his eyes, leaving him no doubt that I was quite serious. "You will tell me what you know. This man needs to be stopped and I am the only one in this town capable of it."

Sweat formed on the innkeeper's brow and his lips twitched as he fought some internal struggle. Despite his apparent fear of Baardwik, I won over.

He glanced about nervously and lowered his voice. "Three days ago, a tall man with a scar checked in. He is in room 410. He unnerves me something terrible. He demands not to be disturbed at all during the day and he is out all night."

"I would like to get a room beside his."

"W-well, 409 is already occupied and 411 is booked for an early morning arrival tomorrow."

I placed a small pouch of coins onto the desk and made sure to jingle it before putting it down. The innkeeper's eyes lit up as he undid the pouch and peered inside.

"I-I-I will make other arrangements for that guest. You may have 411," he stammered as he handed me the room key. "P-please, sir, I don't want any trouble in here."

"Then pray that I am on time."

I silently ascended the steps to the fourth floor and with extreme caution, approached the door to room 410. I placed an ear against the door and listened intently for any noise from inside. There was nothing. As quiet as a church on Monday.

Once I was positive that Baardwik must have been out, I carefully tried the doorknob which of course was locked. I pulled out two small pieces of wire from a pocket within my coat and quickly set to work on the lock. The building was old and the lock unsophisticated. In mere moments I was inside the room, quietly closing the door behind me.

A quick scan of the room confirmed I was alone. The only other door in this room led to a privy, and that door was open, revealing that it too was empty. Some clothes were strewn about on the floor and a black hat hung on a wall hook. The hat did match those that Baardwik tended to favor and a pair of pants on the floor would indeed have been his exact size.

A black leather bag lay open on a writing table near the window, so I walked over for a peek inside. I spat again in disgust as the bag was filled with the various tools of Baardwik's revolting trade of dealing death. I had indeed found my man.

At a glance, it did not appear that any fresh blood coated his implements of murder. The fact that he was still here in town told me that he must not have taken a victim as of yet. He would be out there, at this very moment, prowling about.

He could be anywhere, I figured, and decided to head over to my room next door and wait. I should be able to hear his arrival with these old thin walls and I knew he would be back to his room sometime before dawn.

If there was one thing I possessed an overabundance of, it was patience. I sat on the edge of the bed in my room, unmoving for hours, until I was finally rewarded with the sound of voices next door. It was a man and a woman speaking in hushed tones. Baardwik had returned and brought company with him.

With the stealth and agility of a cat, I was into the hallway in a flash, standing before the monster's door. There was a conversation going on within the room but I could not make out the details. I pressed my ear against the door hoping to gauge the monster's intentions.

I jumped back as the woman inside the room suddenly let out a blood-curdling scream. I cursed myself, I was too late. I was positive that I was too late. I tried the door but Baardwik had locked it behind him.

With all my strength, I kicked the door down, taking the hinges right off the aged frame. Barely able to contain my rage, I stalked inside.

The woman lay sprawled on the floor near the window and a tall, dark-haired man, with a scar that ran down the right side of his face, spun around to glare at me in surprise.

"Who the hell are you?" he demanded.

"My name matters little, but I have come a long way to find you, Erwin Baardwik."

He did well to hide his shock at the mention of his real name but I noticed the subtle change in his expression. He narrowed his eyes as his mind raced through all the possibilities of who I might be.

Baardwik backed up, moving closer to the writing

table, closer to his bag of deadly weapons. As he moved further from the body of the woman, I noticed the wooden stake protruding from her heart.

"You monster!" I roared.

In my fury, two of my teeth elongated into razor-sharp fangs and I dove at Baardwik with inhuman speed. He managed to reach the writing table but it was too late. I sunk my fangs into his neck and tore a hole in his throat.

Baardwik choked and sputtered for air as I dropped him to the floor and laughed at him.

"You have hunted your last vampire, Baardwik. No longer will you murder my kind."

With one hand, I lifted the dying human into the air and then finished the job I had set out to do.

VANDEGALD'S GLOBES

The chimes above the shop's door played their soft
melody to announce the arrival of another potential
customer. The middle-aged man behind the counter
looked up from a dusty tome and straightened his black
robe.

The customer was female and fairly attractive, with
her auburn hair tied up into a bun. It was a simple enough
task to deduce that she was well off. Perhaps not the status
of a Lady, and yet still upper-class. Her clothes were
obviously expensive and she walked with an air of nobility;
of someone who was used to getting what she wanted.

The woman browsed through a few of the shop's
knick-knacks before the man behind the counter spoke.

"Excuse me, my dear, is there anything that I may
help you with?"

The woman looked up with a start, not having
noticed that there had been someone watching her. The

shop was so cluttered with various items that the man behind the counter had just blended in with the scenery. He had a neatly-trimmed salt-and-pepper beard to match his hair of the same color. After seeing nearly fifty-three years, his hair was now more salt than pepper.

He wore a simple, nondescript black robe and several silver rings were visible on both of his hands. His smile was a friendly one and his eyes bespoke of a calm, gentle, demeanor.

"I am sorry, I did not notice you standing there."

"I apologize for giving you a start. I am Vandegald, the owner of this den of antiquities. Is there anything you were looking for in particular?"

"Nothing specific, no. My nephew's birthday is approaching and I just wanted to get him something more unique."

"How old is your nephew, if I may inquire?"

"He is turning ten."

"And his interests? Knights, perhaps? Gladiators?"

"Monsters," the woman blushed.

"Ah, not so strange for a lad of ten," Vandegald smiled. "I can recall my own interests in the creatures that prowled through the shadows of my room and hid out of sight beneath my bed."

"Yes, you boys."

"We are guilty of silly interests. And I am afraid we carry those on into our twilight years, as well."

"So, do you have anything monster related at all? Perhaps a carving, or even a painting? Nothing too gruesome, mind you, I don't want to be the one responsible for giving him nightmares."

"Indeed, I do have a few such things laying about.

Though, depending on your budget of course, I have something that he may find of particular interest."

"Oh?"

"Yes, please step this way, I keep them on the shelf here behind the counter. They are quite fragile so I prefer to keep them out of reach."

The woman approached the counter and watched the man pull down three objects from the shelf, very carefully, and one at a time. He sat them on the counter in front of her for inspection.

"How lovely. What are they exactly?"

"I call them Vandegald's Globes."

The items were indeed glass globes, resting on ornately-carved wooden bases. They almost appeared similar to a wizard's crystal ball, only the globes were not empty. Each globe consisted of a different scene. The first one held the ruins of a tiny castle, the second had a mountain with a dark cave at the base, and the third housed a tiny cabin, surrounded by a swamp.

"Good heavens, what is that?" the woman said, jumping back.

She had spotted movement from the second globe, with the cave. From within the cave, emerged a tiny bat-like creature. It hovered in front of the cave entrance with black wings and looked up at the woman with sickly-yellow eyes."

"That is a bolgrock, or I should say, the illusion of a bolgrock."

"A bolgrock?"

"Yes. A bolgrock is a type of minor demon that roams the Abyss. As you can see it would have a certain appeal to a child of ten."

"I find it hideous, but yes, I see what you mean. It isn't real, you say?"

"No, no, of course not. A bolgrock is nothing you want to toy with, I assure you. You see, I studied magic in the City of Seven Towers for a time. I studied illusion, to be exact. I have cast a spell of illusion on the globes. Each globe consists of a different creature and that creature will move about from time to time and behave as if it is very much alive. Sometimes the bolgrock will hide within the mountain cave, and other times, like now, it will fly about the globe."

"Why, that is brilliant. What is in the other two globes?"

"The globe with the castle contains the illusion of a ghost. When there is little to no light in the room, the ghost will appear from within the castle and roam about. And the third, well there you go, the third contains a troll as you can see now."

The woman's eyes widened as she watched a miniature troll shuffle through the scenery of a swamp.

"I must know how much these cost."

"I am afraid they are not very budget-friendly, but I assure you they are unique. You will find nothing quite like them anywhere in Zalhandria or Tauros. Or the rest of the world, I might add."

"So, how much?"

"Well, I sell them for one hundred gold pieces each. The bases are all hand-carved by me, as well. Much work goes into the construction of just one globe. But seeing as how I can always use some word-of-mouth advertising, and seeing as how it is your nephew's birthday, I would be willing to sell you one for fifty."

"Fifty gold is a lot more than I was expecting to spend on my nephew but that is a good deal you have offered me. I am sure this could guarantee that I become his favorite aunt."

"Of that I have no doubt."

"Does your offer apply to two of them? My brother is always reading tales of ghosts and I am sure he would enjoy your ghost globe."

"Absolutely. Two globes for one hundred gold pieces, today only. I would appreciate if you not tell any others of the deal I have given you. The price goes back to one hundred each once you exit my shop."

"Understood, and I thank you."

"So, the ghost for your brother, and have you decided which one your nephew may like the most?"

"Hmm, I do know he is fascinated by trolls but that, bolgrock, you said? Yes, the bolgrock is positively frightening. I think I will take that one."

"A fine choice, my dear. Your nephew will be delighted, I can guarantee it. Allow me to package them up carefully for a safe journey home."

"Much appreciated."

Vandegald wrapped each globe individually with paper and placed each within its own box. He made sure it was a snug fit to prevent them from being jostled about. The woman counted out one hundred gold pieces, a large amount for one person to be carrying around at any one time, and thanked the man for his generous deal.

Once she had exited the shop, Vandegald took the gold into a back room and stored it away inside of a safe he had hidden under a floorboard. The man smiled. That made six globes sold just this week. He did not mind selling the last two at a discounted price. It meant that one of them was going to be showcased at a birthday party. He was confident that when others got a peek at one of his globes, there would be more people wishing to purchase one for themselves. His troll globe was the last one left in stock, which meant he had better get started on crafting several more. He would need to start tonight.

The afternoon passed slowly, with only a few minor sales the rest of the day. Night descended on the city of Moorstead and Vandegald closed his shop. He found that very few decent folk roamed the streets at night. The night belonged to vagrants and undesirable types. Three different locks were used to secure his front door from curious thieves.

Vandegald lived within his shop. He had a small apartment located directly above the shop and a basement below, where he did his work. After filling his belly with some leftover stew, he retired to the basement for the rest of the evening.

The narrow winding stairs to his basement workshop creaked noisily as Vandegald descended. He had always mused that no burglar could catch him unaware down there. Not even a master thief could navigate those stairs silently, he figured.

The workshop was devoid of any windows and was cast in complete darkness. Vandegald utilized a small lantern in order to move about and light some candles. The candles managed to chase away much of the shadows and provided enough light to read by.

Fortunately, he had several carved bases already finished, along with a few globes that contained their scenery. Now all they required were their occupants. The bolgrock was one of his more popular globes so he decided to craft one of those ones first.

Vandegald Skaldanos was a sorcerer of no small measure. While it was true that he spent most of his life studying magic in the City of Seven Towers, it was not actually the art of illusion that he studied. Vandegald's main interest was in odd creatures, and more specifically, creatures from other worlds and planes of existence. He was most fascinated by those creatures that made the

Abyss their home; all varieties of demons and devils. The bolgrock, of course, was one of those creatures. Bolgrocks were considered a demon of lesser-note but Vandegald found them fascinating all the same.

The City of Seven Towers, located in the southern nation of Zalhandria, was a haven for wizards and sorcerers of all levels of expertise. The city itself was ruled by seven wizards who occupied the seven towers. Vandegald had studied under Torglad the Mad, a great summoner who was rumored to have gone mad from his many dealings with denizens of the Abyss.

With sorcerers being a silver coin a dozen in that city, Vandegald had decided to leave when he felt he had learned all that he could from Torglad. He sought out a city where he and his magical skills would be seen as more unique. The sorcerer settled in the city of Moorstead, which sat in the northern reaches of Zalhandria, just beyond the Zal-Baron Desert and bordering with the lands of Tauros.

Vandegald was also a collector of strange items from all corners of the world and had opened a shop to deal in such things. It was only within the last year, that he begun crafting his globes and making them available for sale. So far they had been selling well with the residents of Moorstead and with travelers and merchants who were only passing through.

Vandegald opened an old tome that rested on his workshop table and turned the yellowed-pages to the appropriate spot. He paced around the room, inspecting the circle he had painted on the floor, to be absolutely sure that it was perfect. He also ensured that every candle and every painted rune outside the circle was in their proper place. It was crucial that everything be exact. One small mistake could prove disastrous.

Once everything seemed to be in order, Vandegald retraced his steps and checked everything over a second time. Many were the tales of wizards, who in haste, and lacking patience, had rushed into a spell that brought doom upon them. Vandegald never wanted to star in his own tale of a foolish wizard. He had always been meticulous in his work.

Nodding in satisfaction, he picked up the tome and began reading a spell aloud. Torglad the Mad had this particular spell committed to memory. It was a fairly complex spell, written in an unused language, so Vandegald always felt more comfortable reading from the book.

Beads of sweat formed on his forehead as his voice rose, nearing the end of the spell. He closed his eyes and then spoke the final word, slamming the book shut. A blast of hot air buffeted his face, messing his hair, slightly.

When his eyes opened, he was greeted with a familiar sight. Inside his summoning circle hovered a bolgrock. The black-skinned creature of the Abyss was held aloft by its bat-like wings. The three-foot tall demon cast him a hateful stare with its sickly-yellow eyes. It glanced about, immediately recognizing that it was trapped within the wizard's magical circle.

The bolgrock let out a skin-shivering screech, and then moments later, was sucked into the nearest globe. Vandegald walked over to regard his newest creation. The bolgrock flew about in a frenzy, looking for any way out of its tiny prison, but of course, there was none.

Each globe was painstakingly warded with protective spells prior to the summoning. The globe was able to suck in its occupant but nothing could leave. Inside the globe, time seemed to stand still, or at very least, slow down, quite considerably. The globe's occupant could survive without food and water for an indefinite amount of time. Torglad had perfected this spell in order to imprison demons and devils for study. He wished to keep them alive for great lengths of time, without having to feed or hydrate them. Vandegald was unsure of just how long the globe's occupant could survive but he had yet to witness one perish.

The sorcerer smiled; he was pleased with his work. Casting the spell was taxing, so Vandegald gave himself a break before summoning a second bolgrock and making another globe. He retired to his bed for the night, after also summoning a troll from the Whisper Marsh. Three globes in one evening was a fine accomplishment.

The next few weeks flew by and business was good. Vandegald was averaging one globe sold per day and some days he sold two. Each evening was spent carving new bases, enchanting globes, and then summoning the appropriate creature. Bolgrocks and trolls continued to be a customer favorite and some folk were beginning to make requests.

"Can you make one with an ogre?"

"How about a wraith?"

"I would like one with a dragon," they said.

Summoning different types of creatures was no simple task. One had to know of a location to summon them from. Vandegald had studied a variety of books on the Abyss which made summoning the bolgrocks much easier. He had made several excursions into the Whisper Marsh where many trolls made their home. He gathered ghosts from the Pallantyr Valley, the site of an ancient battleground where tens of thousands of warriors lost their lives.

The sorcerer knew of only one location, where dwelt a dragon, but he dared not attempt that summoning. He was not even sure if it was possible, and even if it were, he would not risk it.

One quiet afternoon, a potential customer made a most curious request. His young son was fascinated by gladiators and offered to buy a globe that featured one. Vandegald informed the man that he did not have such a globe and that the illusion required to create a gladiator was not a simple one. The man was quite wealthy and offered three times the normal amount if Vandegald could craft one for his son. The sorcerer lay awake all night, pondering that request.

The following day, Vandegald paid a visit to the city of Gladenfar. Gladenfar was a port city along the southern coast of Zalhandria and was famous for its gladiatorial arena. Travel to that city by normal means could have taken a month but Vandegald had a spell that made it instantaneous. He opened a magical gate in his basement and when he stepped through, he was instantly transported outside the walls of Gladenfar.

He was granted entry into a holding area which housed many gladiators. Gladenfar's gladiators were all slaves and Vandegald posed as a potential buyer. When the timing was just right, and no prying eyes were about, the sorcerer cast the necessary spell that sucked one of the poor warriors into the globe that he had brought with him. Vandegald was back in Moorstead before the man was ever missed.

The globe featured an arena scene, and much like any of the imprisoned creatures, the gladiator explored his new prison, seeking a way out of his living nightmare. Vandegald made sure the man was unarmed so he would be unable to take his own life if madness took him.

It was the first time that he had crafted a globe using a human and he had mixed emotions about it. There was a moral line that he had never crossed before; only using savage creatures for his creations. Though, the three hundred gold pieces helped quiet his conscience. The customer was pleased and his son was ecstatic. So, Vandegald continued on with little regard for the trapped gladiator.

A month later, another request was brought to his attention. This customer, much like Vandegald himself, was well-versed in the creatures of the Abyss. He was a wealthy lord who studied demonology.

"A ghastly hobby, some people say, but I collect all things Abyssal," Lord Ryerdon stated. "Tomes, statues, weaponry. Any relic, really, that relates to the Abyss."

"I can quite understand your interest, really I do," Vandegald replied. "I have read a book or two and developed more than just a mild fascination."

"Ah, a brother-in-demon-arms."

"Quite. So what can I do for you?"

"Well, I have seen your globes. Fantastic creations, if I may say."

"Thank you."

"I would love to purchase one to display with the rest

of my collection."

Vandegald lifted one of the globes from the shelf behind the counter and placed it in front of Lord Ryerdon. "This bolgrock might interest you, then."

"Hmm, well, as interesting a creature as the bolgrock is, I know of several other people who own a globe just like it. I was hoping for a globe a little more unique. Perhaps a globe better suited to my tastes."

"I am afraid as far as denizens of the Abyss go, the bolgrock is the only globe I have available."

"Is crafting the illusion of another creature really that difficult? Pardon my ignorance, I know nothing of magic and its workings."

"Without going into the boring details, it certainly can be, yes. I have perfected the illusion of the bolgrock. Creating a different creature for the globe is a longer and more difficult process."

"I will gladly pay."

"It is not just a matter of…"

"How about one thousand gold pieces?"

"One thousand?"

"Yes, one thousand. But I want it unique. I want a four-armed zairgoth, or a xano-fiend, or even a devil."

Vandegald paused to consider whether he could even pull it off and Lord Ryerdon took his silence as a reluctance to accept the gold he offered.

"Two thousand, then. I want a one-of-a-kind demonic globe that nobody else possesses. It will become an honored piece in my collection."

The sorcerer rubbed his chin and nodded. "I will certainly give it my best effort."

Lord Ryerdon placed a piece of paper onto the counter. "Splendid. This is my address. Have a message sent to me when it is complete. But please do not make me wait too long, I beg."

Vandegald nodded again and Lord Ryerdon took his leave. The sorcerer sat down in his chair behind the counter to ponder his situation. Two thousand gold pieces was far too large an amount to pass up, but could he do it? He knew it was possible. He had witnessed Torglad summon several greater demons and even the odd devil. But to summon those, he required the creature's name.

In the world of sorcerers, names brought power. Vandegald knew he had recorded the names of a few demons and devils in one of his own notebooks, before he left the City of Seven Towers. He also possessed tomes which named a few others. Summoning those types of creatures, devils especially, who ruled over the Abyss, was something that could not be taken lightly. Vandegald did believe he was capable, though. He would need to strengthen the wards surrounding his summoning circle and prepare a few other defenses, in the event that something unforeseen arose, but he felt he could do it.

Vandegald's shop was open for business but he spent much of the next day behind the counter, pouring over numerous books. Customers came and went and he paid them little heed. His mind was consumed with the task ahead. He searched his library, desperately, seeking a name to use for the summoning. He decided against using any of the names he had recorded in his own notes. Those names were taken from Torglad and Vandegald had no idea whether any of those creatures were still in existence. Also, if he had made any mistake in recording the name correctly, the consequences could prove horrendous.

Late into the night, before retiring to bed, Vandegald smiled; he had found what he was looking for. The old tome was titled, Valysha's Guide to the Abyss. Valysha was apparently a sorceress of immense power who had traveled to the Abyss on many occasions, recording her experiences, and most importantly, the names of those she had encountered. Satisfied with his find, Vandegald planned to read further in the morning and turned in for the night.

As the following morning became afternoon, Vandegald had a name. Xalboda Vaxalian, a devil of considerable power and influence, and a prince among devils. Not only did the book provide Xalboda's full name, but detailed his castle and its location within the Abyss. Vandegald felt he had everything he required to summon and trap this particular devil. He believed he would be ready to attempt the summoning in two days' time.

"Ah, excuse me, I hate to interrupt," a voice suddenly said.

Vandegald looked up from his seat behind the counter to find three gentlemen standing in his shop. How long they had been there, only they knew.

"Sorry, I was little preoccupied with my reading," the sorcerer said, standing up.

The tall man in the middle was very well-dressed, a lord no doubt. The two men flanking him wore chain mail vests with swords hanging by their sides; bodyguards most likely.

"How may I help you gentlemen?" Vandegald inquired.

"You must be Vandegald?"

"I am."

"It is a pleasure to meet you. I am Lord Stainford. It would seem your globes are the talk of the town. I am quite impressed with your work."

"Thank you, you flatter me."

"My daughter is even more impressed, than I. In fact, your globes are all she can talk about, as of late. I am here to place an order as a gift for her."

"I have several on the shelf here behind me."

"I have seen most of your work so far. However, my daughter has very little interest in monsters. By chance, do you have any other types of globes? Something less frightening for a young girl?"

"I am afraid I do not. Not currently. I would have to craft a new globe, just for her. It would be slightly more expensive."

"I am sure we can come to an arrangement. This would mean a lot to me and to her, if you could do that."

"I could do it for two hundred gold pieces."

"That sounds reasonable to me."

"Excellent. Give me two days, Lord Stainford, and I will have a globe here for your daughter."

"Thank you, Vandegald. We shall return in two days."

When Vandegald was alone again, he figured crafting a globe for the man's daughter would be simple enough. If she wasn't interested in monsters, he would find her a bunny, or perhaps a fox. He thought he may even be able to acquire a fairy.

The sorcerer cast aside all thoughts of the young girl's globe and dove back into Valysha's book, concentrating fully on the more difficult task in front of him. He closed his shop early that day and went straight to the basement to make the necessary preparations. On the following day, when he was absolutely positive that everything was ready, he decided it was time for the summoning.

Vandegald's hands trembled slightly as he held the spellbook in front of him. He took a few deep breaths and then began the casting. This spell was more involved and took longer than usual. The casting ended as Vandegald shouted the name, Xalboda Vaxalian. For a few brief moments, the candles in the room were extinguished, leaving the sorcerer standing in pitch-darkness. When they flared back to life, Vandegald gasped, his jaw hanging open in surprise.

Standing in the center of his summoning circle was not the devil-prince he was expecting, but a stunningly-attractive human woman. The raven-haired beauty immediately looked about at her surroundings, wearing a look of surprise that was equal to Vandegald's. Her eyes went wide when she noticed the sorcerer.

"Am I free? Have you really rescued me from the vile clutches of Xalboda? I cannot thank..."

The woman's sentence was cut short and replaced with an ear-splitting scream as her body was sucked into the globe that Vandegald had prepared. Vandegald was speechless and watched in horror as the innocent woman now stood next to a castle of red brick within her tiny glass prison. She fell to her knees and wept, not understanding what had just happened to her.

A million thoughts ran through Vandegald's mind. How had his spell gone awry? Apparently he had summoned a prisoner from within Xalboda's castle and not Xalboda himself. And it was a woman, a human woman of exceptional beauty. Vandegald could not leave this woman inside the globe and immediately set to work on dispelling the protective wards around it.

With the wards eliminated, the sorcerer did the only thing that he could; he teleported inside the globe. He planned to grab the woman and teleport them both back outside. Once inside his own globe, Vandegald took a moment to look around and finally get the view of the world that all the other occupants of his globes shared. Everything outside of the globe appeared giant-sized, and slightly distorted, due to the shape of the glass.

"Who are you?" the woman said, standing and wiping tears from her beautiful green eyes.

"I am Vandegald and I have apparently made a huge mistake. Take my hand and I will get us out of here."

The woman accepted Vandegald's extended hand and the sorcerer was surprised by how warm her skin felt against his. It sent a soothing feeling up his arm and spread throughout his body. She leaned in to kiss her would-be rescuer and Vandegald was helpless to resist. His lips tingled and went numb when she placed hers against his. She kissed Vandegald deeply and his knees went weak. The sorcerer slowly slumped to the ground, feeling completely paralyzed. He was unable to move or even to speak.

The woman smiled wickedly as her pale skin turned a shade of red. Two small horns sprouted from her forehead and black, leathery wings, unfolded from behind her back. She spoke a few words in a demonic language and vanished. Only Vandegald's eyes could move and he shifted his gaze upwards, noticing that the strange woman was now outside the globe, looking in.

Possessing an extensive knowledge of magic, the woman picked up one of Vandegald's spellbooks and renewed the protective wards onto the globe. The effects of her paralyzing kiss soon wore off and Vandegald got to his feet, staring up at her. He attempted his spell of teleportation, but of course, it had failed. The demonic-woman laughed.

She picked up Valysha's Guide to the Abyss and held it toward the globe. "I see you have read my book," she laughed again. "There is no Castle Bloodborn and there is no devil-prince that dwells there. I am Xalboda Vaxalian, a succubus. I wrote that book and saw to it that it reached the land of mortals. I wanted fools like you to summon me and fall prey to my charms. Thank you for freeing me from the Abyss, Vandegald. And know that your name is well-known among us. Did you think that your summonings would go unnoticed by the powers of the Abyss? It was only a matter of time before one of us got you. I am pleased that it was me. Now, how will you like living in your tiny little prison, I wonder?"

Xalboda picked up the globe and made her way into Vandegald's shop. A knock at the door surprised her and she placed the globe on the counter. By the time she unlocked the door, she resembled a human female once more.

A young man wore a shocked expression at the sight of the woman in Vandegald's shop. "H-hello, g-good afternoon, my lady. Is Vandegald about?"

"Oh he is about, but is unable to receive company. I, on the other hand, am free," she purred.

"Excuse m-me?"

"I am new here and would like a tour of your city. Would you be so kind as to show me around?"

The young man found the woman's request irresistible and nodded, foolishly, like a young school-boy. The succubus smiled widely and took the man's arm in hers, strolling from the shop.

*　　*　　*　　*

"Hello? Hello? Vandegald? Are you here?" Lord Stainford called.

The wealthy lord had returned to the shop with one of his men-at-arms. They found the door unlocked, though Vandegald was nowhere in sight. The pair had waited, impatiently, until they decided to take a look around.

Lord Stainford stuck his head into the back room. "Vandegald? Vandegald, are you there? I have returned for my daughter's globe."

"My lord, this must be it here on the counter," the other man said.

Lord Stainford joined him at the counter.

"See here, there is a packing box with your name on it. Something must have distracted Vandegald and he never got around to it. This globe must be yours."

"Hmm, you must be correct. I wonder what he has created for me."

Lord Stainford peered into the globe, admiring the craftsmanship of the tiny red castle. He tapped on the glass of the globe and then lifted and shook it when no illusion had first appeared.

"My goodness, how exquisite."

The wealthy lord marveled at the sight of a miniature Vandegald, exiting the little castle. The illusion of the wizard jumped up and down, waving his arms in the air, almost as if it was actually aware of the two men looking down upon it.

"Magnificent. Look at the detail. It's a spitting image of the man himself. Oh, Vandegald, you old rascal, you have truly outdone yourself this time. My daughter will love it. Vernon, leave the payment behind the counter some place where Vandegald will find it when he returns. I can't wait to get home and give Nella her gift."

THE POSSESSED

It was always hot here but today was unusually hot. The sky was a deep red and I knew I had my work cut out for me this time. We approached the ancient keep and there was a hesitance to my step. Not because I was afraid, no, but because I had a reputation to uphold. The information I was given by the temple told me this case would be a difficult one.

I paused at the front gate and turned to my coworker. "Perhaps, you should wait out here. This may get a little rough."

"Are you positive? I can help."

"No, trust me, you will be safer out here. I must do this one alone."

He reluctantly nodded and I proceeded through the gate, which had been left open in anticipation of my arrival. I knew my longtime friend wished to help but I truly felt that this time he may only get in the way. I did not wish to worry for his safety as well. I knew the risks and I was better prepared for all outcomes. He was still young and inexperienced. This one I would have to do alone.

I ascended the stone steps to a set of iron-bound double doors. I reached for the door knocker but the entrance way opened. A servant nodded and indicated for me to follow. There was no need for introductions. He knew who I was and time was of the essence.

The servant held a candle to light our way through the dark corridor. We passed several lavishly-furnished rooms but I had no time to admire the décor. My mind was set on the task ahead of me.

My escort unlatched a thick door and led me down a narrow winding staircase. I assumed we would have been heading upwards toward the living quarters in the keep's tower. The fact that we were now heading down into the dungeons told me this was serious indeed.

It was an unpleasant thought that the daughter of a powerful lord had to be humiliated and locked in a dark dungeon. I felt for the family. This was a difficult time for them. The lord of the keep held much influence in this region and if word got out about his daughter's condition, it could prove damaging. Discretion was paramount. My lips were sealed about such cases and I felt it was nobody else's business anyhow. Once I was called in to deal with a situation, I knew the family had exhausted all other resources and were now at their wits' end. I would do everything within my power to remedy this as quickly and as quietly as possible.

A few twists and turns brought us into a dank chamber that was illuminated by four torches; one per wall. The room was devoid of furnishings, save for one table that sat in the center. The poor unfortunate lord's daughter lay on the table, chained down by her wrists and ankles. Her parents stood close by; weeks' worth of worry was etched upon their faces. This had taken a toll on them. They appeared to have aged over this ordeal.

The lord's face did brighten, somewhat, as he turned to regard my arrival. He came toward me and meant to speak, but I held a finger to my lips and indicated he remain silent. There would be time for pleasantries later, I had hoped. Now was not the time.

The servant bowed and exited the room. I made a gesture with my hand, suggesting that the others follow him but they shook their heads. They were determined to see this through. While I thought it best that they leave, I could not argue with a parent's desire to remain by their daughter's side in such a time as this. I would have probably done the same, despite the perils that were present.

I placed my bag onto the smooth stone floor and decided to inspect the lord's daughter before beginning anything further. So far, I only had second-hand information that was given to me about her condition. I needed to determine how grave this was for myself.

Her eyes were closed but her limbs were in constant motion, fighting against the iron restraints that kept her immobile on the table. The lord was wise to restrain her as such, to prevent her from harming herself, and most definitely others. A necessary precaution with these extreme cases.

Her skin color appeared off. It was paler than it should have been and it seemed as though she had lost much weight. Her once pretty face now looked gaunt, with protruding cheek bones.

I placed a hand on her forehead and it felt chilled. Not a good sign at all. The lord may have waited too long in sending for my help but I truly hoped that was not the case.

I attempted to lift an eyelid with my thumb, when both her eyes shot open and she snarled, causing me to jump back with a start. Her pupils had vanished behind a silvery glow. I silently whispered a prayer to a specific god. This was worse than I had originally thought. The monster inside her had already taken a firm hold.

I composed myself quickly, not wishing to overly alarm the lord and his wife. It was time I began.

"Amelaxia," I said, using her name. "I am here to free you of this monster. I know you are still in there, somewhere. I need you to be strong and hang in there. Only together, with our strength combined, will we prevail here."

She snarled again and spat at me, threatening to break free of her restraints. For a moment, I worried, but they seemed to be strongly-built and held her in place. She was small but the beast inside her provided supernatural strength. Were she to get free, it would create a world of problems for us all.

I pulled out a carved symbol from my bag and held it over her. I began chanting in an ancient language that was seldom used. Very few even knew of its existence, as it was from a time long forgotten. Each syllable caused Amelaxia to thrash about. She growled; her eyes glowing brightly with a silver radiance.

"The spirit that resides inside the body of Amelaxia is

not welcome!" I shouted. "You must leave her! You must leave this world entirely and never return! Do you hear me?"

"She is mine now," she spoke, but the voice was not her own. It was a soft melodic voice that caused my skin to crawl. "Her soul is mine and you cannot have it back."

I chanted louder and began circling the table. The lord and his wife clung to each other tightly; their faces were masks of horror. Amelaxia howled in distress.

I took a black-bladed dagger from my bag and sliced into my thumb. As it began to bleed, I pressed my thumb onto her forehead and drew a symbol. Her body immediately convulsed with pain.

"You unholy priest!" she screamed. "You cannot have her back!"

The lord shouted a warning as her right hand broke free. The iron shackle around her wrist shattered and she reached for me. Fortunately, I proved the quicker and pulled back in time. She ripped a strip off my black robe but that was all. I nodded a silent thanks to the lord.

I crouched down and searched my bag for a particular vial. It contained water that I had cursed just before leaving my home. I pulled out the cork and downed a mouthful of the liquid before handing it toward the lord and his wife.

"Take a sip, each of you. When that monster leaves her body it will seek another to inhabit. This will prevent it from entering ours."

With trembling hands, the lord's wife drank first. After the lord had also taken a sip, he handed the vial back to me. I quickly grabbed Amelaxia by the jaw and forced the rest of the liquid down her throat, being mindful of her right hand which was looking to claw at my skin.

The girl vomited a black acidic substance that burned small holes into my robe. The table smoked where drops of the vomit had landed. It was time for the final stage.

"Please, my Lord, some assistance."

"What do you need?" he asked, with a quiver in his voice.

"Grab her arm and hold it down, while I draw the last symbol. Careful, now, do not let her grab you."

The lord was imbued with great strength and did as instructed. He grabbed his daughter's wrist and held her arm down, though, it took all of his immense strength to do so. His arms shook and he gritted his teeth, growling.

I tore Amelaxia's nightshirt and used my thumb to draw the final symbol with my own blood, directly above her heart. She screamed and trashed and spat but I finished the symbol and chanted the last words, loudly.

As the last syllable left my lips, a great wind roared through the chamber and extinguished the torches. The room would have been cast into total darkness if it were not for Amelaxia's glowing silver eyes. Her back arched and she squealed with an otherworldly shriek.

Amelaxia vomited again, only this time, a golden mist shot forth from her mouth. It sparkled with a radiance so bright that it stung our eyes to behold it. The mist took on a humanoid shape with two large wings. It floated around the room, seeking a new host, but found no vessel with which to inhabit. The cursed water had done its duty.

A mouth formed on its misty face and it opened in a silent sigh of disappointment. Then it was gone.

"Quickly, the torches," I said in the pitch darkness that followed the monster's departure.

I heard the lord fumbling around until the first torch flared back to life and allowed us to assess the situation. Amelaxia laid on the table, panting quickly with exhaustion. Her eyes were closed and she had ceased her attempts to break free of the remaining shackles. Her right arm rested limply by her side.

The three of us rushed to the table and Amelaxia suddenly sensed our presence.

"Mother? Father?" she said weakly, in her own voice.

Her eyes fluttered open and her previous silver orbs were now blood red. I let out a giant sigh of relief. She was saved.

The mighty demon lord turned to me and placed a strong hand on my shoulder. "I do not know how to thank you, Xoraxelstein. I was told you were the best exorcist in all the Abyss and you did not disappoint."

"I am glad I could help. Fear not, that angel has no more hold on your daughter."

LAKE OF EVIL

"Really, Harry? You are just going to sit there and watch us?"

"You don't know what horrors lurk below the surface, watching you from below and waiting for the right moment to drag you under."

Rachel rolled her eyes and tossed her paddleboard into the lake. The raven-haired beauty was expecting that type of response. Harry had been paranoid of water ever since watching *The Monster of Avery Lake* at the picture show. It was frightening, understandably, but it was just a film, after all.

"Fine, sit there and fry in the sun, then, see if we care," Jack remarked.

"A far better fate than becoming the next meal for some diabolical aquatic beast."

Janice smirked. "You really are something else, Harry. Enjoy the summer while it lasts. Before you know it, it will be too cold to swim or paddleboard and then you will regret it."

"I will live to see another summer and that is good enough for me," Harry responded.

The others shook their heads in disbelief and splashed their way into the lake with a chorus of laughter. Janice and Erin found the water too cold and attempted to ease their way in, ankle deep at first, and then to their knees. Jack thought them silly and jumped in, splashing them both and eliciting high-pitched squeals.

Harry sat in a lawn chair on the beach, keeping a healthy distance from the water. He felt that he was just far enough away to make good on his escape, if a lake monster emerged, seeking an easy meal. His friends, however, were doomed. They were just blissfully unaware.

All over the world, scientists had discovered pre-historic creatures that should have been dead billions of years ago, but somehow they had survived in the ocean's depths. These lakes were no different. This particular lake was even deeper than most. It was impossible for anyone to have explored the bottom. So, who knew what could be living down there since the beginning of time?

It was not unheard of for people to go missing in these parts. Harry knew there was something up with this lake. It was a lake of evil. The others teased him but he did not care. There were public pools when the urge to swim overcame him. It was not necessary to risk his life in the dark waters of the lake.

"Harry, why do you even come to the lake with us if you have no intentions of going in?" Agatha asked, after returning from the water and wrapping herself in a towel.

Why, indeed? Harry had to wonder. But what else

could he do on a hot summer's day? The best radio programs did not come on until the early evening. He did not possess enough money to sit at the malt shop every day. And besides, the few friends that he had were here at the lake. Maybe he felt it was his duty to keep an eye on them; to watch for strange ripples in the water or bubbles rushing to the surface, revealing a possible threat from below. Perhaps, he could shout a warning in time for his friends to get back to shore safely.

Harry shrugged a reply to the young girl, not willing to explain his reasons. They all thought him silly and a coward. Donald even accused him of being embarrassed about not being able to swim. He could swim, of course, just not in dangerous lakes.

This day was a particularly hot one and Harry walked over to the vendor who was selling snow cones out of a truck parked next to the beach.

"Be careful with that, son," the man in the truck said. "I hear lake monsters love snow cones."

Most of the regulars at the beach were aware of Harry's story by now. The man chuckled while Harry walked away, ignoring the jest. Harry didn't mind. Everyone was just ignorant to the dangers. That would be their undoing.

As Harry walked slowly back to his chair on the beach, something odd grabbed his attention from the corner of his eye. He spotted his friend Rachel on her paddleboard and she appeared to be in some type of distress. Harry ran closer to the water, though not too close, and squinted for a better look.

Rachel clearly appeared panicked and was frantically attempting to paddle away from something. Then Harry saw it too and his jaw dropped. His mind reeled. What was it? He swore it was a tentacle and it was moving toward his friend on the surface of the water. He could only imagine what nightmare that tentacle was attached to.

Rachel screamed out and Harry flew into action. He ran up and down the beach shouting that his friend was in trouble and someone needed to help her.

"Someone call the police!" he screamed. "The monster is going to get her!"

Folk who had been lounging lazily on the beach, all jumped up with fright. Panic overtook the beach and people scrambled about. Two gentlemen ran straight for the water and jumped in, swimming bravely toward the girl in grave danger.

Harry pointed to the snow cone vendor who had left his truck to see what all the commotion was about. "Don't just stand there, go get help! Call the police!"

When the concerned boy turned back to the dire situation in the water, he was surprised to notice everyone laughing. Even Rachel was laughing, albeit with a touch of embarrassment written upon her face. Jack was now holding the monster's tentacle aloft and that tentacle was nothing more than a long stick.

"I thought it was a snake," Rachel admitted.

The friends continued to laugh in the water for quite some time. The others on the beach were not too impressed and glared at Harry with angry eyes. Some of them had been blissfully asleep on their towels, until rudely awakened and put into panic mode. One woman even dropped the snow cone she had just purchased. Luckily for her, the man replaced it at no cost.

"A monster, eh?" the vendor shouted in Harry's

direction. "Call the police, eh? They need to arrest that stick before it causes anymore harm today."

Even Harry felt embarrassed, and when he returned to his lawn chair, he found that he had lost interest in consuming his snow cone. Soon enough, his friends ventured back to the beach to dry off and lay in the sun.

"Good thing Harry stands watch," Jack joked. "He will keep us all safe."

The others laughed.

"I appreciate it at least, Harry," Rachel said. "I could have sworn it was a snake."

"What did you think it was, Harry?" Agatha asked. "A giant squid? Some demon octopus?"

The others laughed some more.

"It's better to be safe than sorry," he finally replied. "Today it was a stick, tomorrow, who knows?"

The rest of that day passed uneventfully, along with the following week. One day, when it was mildly cool and Erin didn't feel much like getting into the chilly water, she hung back and sat with Harry in his usual spot on the beach. She had always found Harry to be a tad odd but harmless. They had all grown up in the same neighborhood and gone to school together. Erin felt sorry for Harry at times; he never seemed to have any fun.

"Harry, surely you have to know there are no monsters in the lake. How long have we all been coming here? Years, Harry, years. I have been swimming in there since my parents used to put floaties on my arms. Fish, Harry, there are just fish in there."

"You don't know that."

"Yes, I do. None of us have ever seen anything other than fish and none of us have ever been eaten."

"How many people have gone missing over the years? Quite a few."

"And?"

"What happened to all those people?"

"I don't know. Nobody knows. Runaways? God forbid, even a serial killer? But I am positive it was not a monster in the lake."

"I have kept newspaper clippings of everyone that has disappeared. All of their last known whereabouts were in this area, near the lake."

"So that means a monster took them?"

"Makes sense to me. There is never any trace of them, afterward. No clues at all. I bet whatever is left of them is at the bottom of that lake."

"Harry, police have searched the lake."

"The lake is too big and too deep. The police divers have never been able to search the deepest parts."

"Alright, but they went pretty deep and nothing ever ate those divers."

"Because the monster had just eaten. They were lucky."

"Ugh, you are impossible. Every summer you waste it away sitting here in your lawn chair, worrying."

"You will thank me when I spot something in time to save everyone."

"Like the stick that nearly ate Rachel?"

Harry blushed.

"Come on, go for a swim today."

"No."

"I will hold your hand, nothing will get you, I promise."

"No."

"I give up. A day will come when you look back at all the summers you wasted and regret it. I guarantee that."

The next weekend, the friends all went to a Saturday matinee at the picture show. A new film had just opened from the director, Otto Friedhelm, titled *Fangs*. It was the story of an overly large shark that was terrorizing the beaches along the southern coast. Not the best film, the others soon realized, to have brought Harry to see.

When the friends exited the theater, they were all forced to listen to Harry ramble on and on about the dangers of the lake and how that film had just reinforced all his deepest, darkest, fears. He was becoming increasingly difficult to be around. His paranoia was reaching epic levels and the others soon worried whether their strange friend might be suffering from a disease of the mind.

After watching *Fangs*, Harry now sat even farther away from the lake, with his chair nearly in the forest beside the beach. A pair of binoculars hung around his neck so that he could still watch his friends and keep an eye out for danger.

One warm afternoon, Jack joined Harry in order to retrieve a cold soda from their cooler. Jack never minded much that Harry would only ever sit and watch, because then he could also keep an eye on their coolers and clothes. The fact that Harry had been moving farther from the water and now sat with binoculars, though, was beginning to get people talking.

"You know, people are starting to talk about you."

"What do you mean?"

"Well, you sit here with binoculars. At a beach."

"So?"

"So, people think that is creepy. They think you are spying on girls with those."

"That's ridiculous, I am watching the water for trouble."

"Yeah, I get that. Your friends get that. The other people around here don't. All they see is a guy who comes to the beach all the time and never goes in the water. They see someone sitting way back here with binoculars and they think that is creepy."

"Yeah, but I am only…wait…what's that??"

Harry leaped up from his chair, gazing through the binoculars. Not far from Janice, something was just below the surface, and moving quickly toward her. Something dark and something about the same size as her.

"Oh, good heavens! Janice is in trouble! Look!"

He handed the binoculars to Jack who accepted them and took a look for himself. Jack shook his head and tossed the binoculars back to Harry.

"Maybe you should go sit in the shade, I think the heat has fried your brain."

Harry, feeling a touch perturbed that Jack was not as worried about their friend as he was, caught the binoculars and looked again. His shoulders slumped as he noticed another boy, near Janice, who had been snorkeling and swimming around under the water. He had just come up and removed his mask and snorkel. Jack left Harry alone and grumbled to himself all the way back to the water.

Harry, again, felt embarrassed. Even he was beginning to doubt himself now. What if he was just being too paranoid? What if it was just his over-active imagination? All these years he was positive a monster lived in that lake but was it possible that maybe he had been wrong?

Harry took Jack's advice and decided to get out of the sun and headed for the shade of the forest. He needed to walk and sort through his thoughts. There was immediate relief from the sun once he entered the forest. The leaves of the trees were full and effectively blocked much of the light.

Harry was no more than twenty feet in, when he heard a loud rustling sound behind him. Something was moving toward him and quite rapidly at that. He spun just in time to witness a blur of black fur and fangs reaching for him. The beast stood on two legs, much like a human, but was covered head to claw in black fur. It had pointed ears and fangs as long as his fingers.

Harry didn't even have time to scream, before the beast took him and he was never seen again. For much of his life, Harry worried about what lived beneath the surface of the lake and never once considered what lurked in the dark forest behind him.

GUT FEELING

It had been a long day of mostly paperwork and I was quite relieved to leave the office and breathe in the fresh summer air. I had almost forgotten what the world outside our musty records room smelled like. The sun was still out and it was a rare day indeed when I was able to leave work at a decent time.

I generally worked long grueling hours, which were not conducive to maintaining a relationship, thus, I was single. I needed to consider where I would stop for a bite to eat to quiet my angry stomach, given that there was nobody waiting for me at home.

"Excuse me, sir, but are you Detective Edward Kane?"

I turned to regard a lovely young woman with long dark hair. I would guess that she was somewhere in her twenties, and I was positive that I had seen her face somewhere before, but at the moment, I could not place it.

319

"Yes, ma'am, it is me. Have we met somewhere before? You seem familiar for some reason."

"No, Detective, we have not."

"How do you know me?"

"I have seen you in the papers a few times. You have been involved in some very bizarre cases over the years."

Wasn't that the truth. "I sure have. Was there something you needed?"

Her eyes darted back and forth, as if to ensure that there was nobody about to listen in on our conversation. She was visibly nervous.

"I was wondering if I could enlist your help in finding someone?"

"Well, usually you would file your case with the police and they will assign a detective to investigate. Have you spoken with the police?"

"They wouldn't listen to me."

"That doesn't sound right, are you…"

"They didn't want to listen to me, I swear it. But I really need some help."

"What about a private eye?"

"Please, Detective, I have read so much about you. If anyone can find this person, it would be you."

The woman appeared panicked; I could see it in her eyes. It was obvious to me that it meant a lot to her to locate whoever it was that was missing. I always had a good read on people, it was essential to my job. I could tell she was a kind and caring woman. She seemed educated and probably came from money, judging by her dress.

"Why don't you start by telling me who is missing?"

"He is just a friend."

"What is your friend's name?"

"Bernard."

"Bernard, what?"

"Just Bernard. I don't know his last name."

"He is your friend but you don't know his last name?"

"No, I don't. He never told me. We met a little over a year ago at the Big City Bus Terminal. He told me he was in some kind of trouble and until he knew me better, he could not reveal his last name."

"Where does he live?"

"I don't know."

"How would you keep in touch? Do you have a phone number?"

"No, I am sorry. We would just happen to bump into each other from time to time."

"So, you don't have a last name and you don't know where he lives? How do you know he is missing?"

"I just know it. I have not seen him around for over a month now. It is not like him. Like I said, he mentioned he was in some kind of trouble. People were after him. Bad people, I suppose. I fear they may have found him."

"What is your name, ma'am?"

"Amanda Finch."

The pause before she answered told me it was a fake name but I played along.

"Well, Amanda, you do not have much information to help anyone locate this man. He may not even be missing. You don't have a phone number or an address, so perhaps he has just moved on."

"No, something has happened to him, I just know it. I have this gut feeling that something is terribly wrong. Please, Detective, I beg you to help me."

"I need a coffee. How about we walk over to a diner and you can tell me more there?"

"I would rather not. Can we just talk somewhere more private?"

"Alright, how about Edgewood Park? It's just down the street there. We could find a bench."

"That would be fine."

"How about you go find a suitable bench and I will go grab a couple of coffees and meet you there shortly?"

"I could do that."

"What do you take in your coffee? It's on me."

"Oh, no thank you, Detective, none for me thanks."

"Are you sure?"

"Yes, but thanks for asking."

Amanda, or whatever her name was, left in the direction of the park and I walked to the nearest diner. I grabbed a coffee and a donut to go, and grumbled to myself over the thirteen cents I had to pay. Everything was just getting so damn expensive in the Big City, it was ridiculous.

I took my time in walking to the park, processing my interaction with the woman. I was definitely not getting the whole story but she was indeed desperate to find this man, that I was certain of. Now, I just had to figure out why. Jilted lover was my first instinct. I assumed Bernard never told her his last name or where he lived since he was most likely already married. He probably got whatever he wanted out of this "Amanda" and then disappeared back to his normal life. I was willing to bet that Bernard made her great promises, but of course, followed through with none of them.

And why the fake name? It occurred to me that

perhaps she was also married and wished to keep this as discreet as possible. Or perhaps she was a person of note within the Big City, which is why I had this strange feeling that I had seen her somewhere before.

Edgewood Park was quite large and I found Amanda sitting on a bench in a fairly secluded area of the park, overlooking a duck pond. I sat down beside her and sipped my coffee.

"As I have said, you have not given me much information, Amanda. Do you have any idea at all where Bernard could be?"

"He had a cabin just outside the city where he liked to spend most of his time."

"Now we are getting somewhere. Where is this cabin?"

"I don't know."

I sighed. "That doesn't help me much."

"He brought me there once, but I am terrible with directions. I could not tell you where it was at all. It was very dark when we went but if I had to guess, I would say it took us about forty minutes to get there."

"Forty minutes from where?"

"The bus terminal."

"He drove?"

"Yes."

"What kind of car does he have? Do you remember a plate number?"

"No, I am sorry. It was a dark-colored car and had four doors. That is all I remember."

This was a hopeless case. "Well, Amanda, how about you leave me with a description of Bernard. I can check to see if we have any reports of any missing Bernards, or anyone of interest fitting his description. Fair enough?"

She appeared devastated. "I suppose."

"It's all I can offer you right now. How can I get in touch with you?"

"I will just come find you in a couple of days to see if you have heard anything."

"It would be easier if I just called you or paid you a visit, if I find out anything worth reporting."

"That's ok, Detective, I will find you."

Amanda got up and walked away. Her head was down and she walked slowly, as if her shoes were filled with lead. I know she wanted a more positive reply from me but I just could not give one with so little to go on. She was withholding information, I was certain. For some reason she was afraid, or perhaps too embarrassed to tell me the full story.

I waited for her to disappear around a hill before following her. I thought if I found out where she lived, it might better help me to understand her situation. I kept a good distance between us and followed her out of the park and down Applefield Way. She walked at a snail's pace and I was getting frustrated. This was not exactly how I planned to spend my evening. It figures that the one day I left work at a decent hour, I would get caught up with something else.

It was dark by the time she entered the bus terminal and that's where I lost her. I was fairly confident in my ability to follow people without being noticed, but I had to wonder if she had spotted me and hid. I even asked an employee to check the women's restroom, but no luck. Amanda had vanished in the bus terminal and I was out of options.

I made the long walk back to the office where I had parked my car and returned home for the rest of the evening. The following day, I did investigate into any interesting reports involving anyone named Bernard, but found nothing. I also ran a check on Amanda Finch but found nobody by that name matching her apparent age. My strange encounter with Amanda soon left my mind as I became wrapped up once again with my ongoing cases.

Three days later, as I exited our office building, I ran into Amanda once more. I noticed she was wearing the same blue dress. Distress was plainly visible on her face.

"Did you find out anything at all?" she asked.

"No, I am afraid not. I have found nothing of interest concerning anyone named Bernard, or anyone fitting his description. You haven't given me much to go on, Amanda."

She began to weep. I attempted to place a hand on her shoulder for comfort but she turned and walked away. I shouldn't have felt so concerned but I did. There was definitely things she was not telling me but she was genuine in her desperation to find this man she believed missing.

"Amanda, wait. About this cabin, is there anything you can tell me about it at all? What did it look like?"

She turned and wiped away some tears. "Can we talk in the park?"

"Absolutely."

We returned to the same bench in the park and she did her best to recall any details about the cabin.

"I don't remember much about the outside of the cabin. It was very dark when we got there and still dark when we left. Inside, it had a kitchen and two separate bedrooms. It was fairly small."

"Alright, how about sounds? Was it near any water?"

"No, I don't remember hearing any water but I heard a train from time to time. It was faint, but definitely a train."

I rubbed my chin. "Well, you said it was about a forty-minute drive from the city. If you remember hearing a train then you could have been near Oakbridge. The Tanner Line runs east and west through there. Or perhaps Fernwood. The Blue Grass Express runs north and south through there. What about the drive? Do you remember anything about it? Smooth roads? Gravel roads?"

"I do remember the road sounding different at one point but it only lasted a minute or so. It sounded like we passed over a bridge."

"How long into your drive?"

"Maybe twenty minutes."

"Hmm, if you traveled twenty or so minutes west towards Oakbridge, you would cross the O' Connor bridge. Amanda, would you care to go for a drive? Perhaps it would help jog your memory."

"Yes, sure."

We walked back to my car and then headed west. It was late, so thankfully there was no traffic when leaving the city. As we approached the O' Connor bridge, I asked Amanda to close her eyes and listen while we passed over it.

"Yes," she said, excitedly. "That was what I heard."

"So, you reached this cabin roughly twenty minutes later?"

"I think so."

We drove for another ten minutes until there was a

fork in the road. I noticed several farms on the left-hand side, with many cattle roaming about the fields.

"Amanda, do you remember hearing any cows? Or perhaps smelling a farm?"

She shook her head. "No, I don't."

So I turned north, away from the farms. Shortly after, we arrived at a four-way intersection and I stopped. Bond Lake was to the east but Amanda did not recall being near to any water. The Tanner train line ran east and west just to the north of us. Amanda said the sound of the train was faint so I turned west instead of north. Several dirt roads branched off from the road we traveled on, and in the distance, a heavily wooded area sat on our right side.

"I do remember the road getting a little rough and bumpy before we stopped at the cabin."

I chose a dirt road and turned onto it. The road appeared to be seldom used and ran straight into the woods. It was a cloudy night to begin with, and when combined with the thick trees of the forest, the road would have been pitch-dark without the headlights from my car.

There were no cabins or cottages in this area of Oakbridge, as far as I was aware, but then again, I rarely had any reason to be out this way. I have had several picnics over at Bond Lake in the past, though, I was largely unfamiliar with this area.

We drove for a few minutes longer until the road ended. I grabbed a flashlight from my glove compartment and exited the vehicle.

"Did you have to walk very far from the car to the cabin? Do you remember?"

"Vaguely. It was perhaps five minutes."

Well, I had already come this far so there was no

sense in leaving now. The forest was as black as could be and all we could hear was a chorus of crickets. I chose a direction at random and plunged into the dense woods. I walked about for nearly ten minutes before I realized I was alone. Amanda must have gone back to the car, I imagined. The forest was too much for her to handle and she was not properly dressed for a hike in the woods.

I doubled back a ways and then chose a different direction, searching around some more. It wasn't my idea of a fun evening but I was committed. After another ten minutes, I was just about to head back to the car when I saw it. Faint lights in the distance where there shouldn't have been any lights.

I decided to investigate and crept as silently as I could toward the light. I exercised caution, in the event that whoever was out here, did not wish to be found. It was indeed a cabin, I soon realized. It was fairly small, about the size that Amanda had described. The windows were boarded shut but a definite light source emanated from inside.

For some reason, goosebumps ran their way up and down my arms. I touched the handle of my revolver within the shoulder holster inside my jacket, taking comfort that it was still there.

I left the cover of the forest and crept through a clearing, toward the front door. A twig snapped a few yards behind me and I whirled around to face a large, disheveled man, that fit the description of Bernard.

"Who are you?" the man demanded. "What are you doing here?"

I took note of the hatchet that he carried in his right hand.

"My car broke down a little ways away. I am lost and was looking for help," I decided to lie.

"You shouldn't be here."

"I would like to phone for a tow truck but if you don't have a phone in the cabin, I will be on my way."

"There is no phone here. Who else is with you?" he asked, looking around suspiciously.

"I am alone. It's just me. But I am leaving now, don't worry."

"You have already seen too much."

"Pardon me? I haven't seen anything. I will leave you to your privacy. Sorry for disturbing you."

"I can't let you leave."

The man suddenly ran towards me and raised the hatchet above his head. I quickly drew my revolver and shot him three times in the chest. He didn't immediately fall and actually continued to stumble forward. I backed up and fired two more shots. This time he went down and did not move again.

I kicked the hatchet away and nudged him with my foot. When he didn't move, I risked bending over and checked his pulse. He was dead. I stood and reloaded my gun as fast as possible. I had no idea who was inside that cabin.

I banged on the door and then stood back and pointed my gun. "This is Detective Kane. If there is anyone inside that cabin, exit slowly with your hands in the air."

There was only silence.

"We have the cabin surrounded. Come out with your hands up," I shouted once more.

After a few more moments of silence, I kicked the

door wide open and entered. An awful smell assaulted my nostrils immediately and I gagged. It was the unmistakable stench of death.

The kitchen and living area of the cabin was a disgusting mess. I covered my nose with a handkerchief and kicked open the doors to both bedrooms. The sight that awaited me will forever be burned into my mind. I discovered the bodies of five women. All were deceased. My jaw hung open in shock as I closely inspected the woman in a blue dress. She appeared to have only been dead a week and was the spitting image of Amanda. Even the dress was exactly the same. A twin? I wondered.

I hastily removed myself from that cabin of horrors. I had to get back to my car and radio for help. I had to check on Amanda. A million questions swirled around inside my mind. When I reached my car, I found that Amanda was nowhere in sight. Now, I am no tracker, but I could find no footprints, or any evidence of which way she may have gone. In fact, I found that only my footprints existed in a muddy area, where I remember distinctly that Amanda was with me.

I shook my head with confusion and waited for backup to arrive. An hour later, the cabin, along with the forest, was swarming with police and detectives. I soon found out why Amanda's face looked so familiar. Amanda was not Amanda Finch, as I had suspected. She was Amanda Jones and a photograph of her face hung in our office along with the four other women who had been missing for months. Amanda had been the last one to go missing and the last one to have been murdered.

Bernard's car was located not far away on a different road leading into the forest. A woman was found locked in the trunk of his car, still alive. She would have been victim number six, if I had not happened by.

I attempted to piece together this riddle in my mind but it made no sense at all. There was no trace, whatsoever, of the Amanda that helped me locate the cabin. It was as if she was a phantom. There were no footprints. There were no fingerprints. Nobody else had seen her except for me. My skin prickled at the notion that the ghost of Amanda had helped me track down her murderer.

My captain approached me. "Congratulations, Kane. This was one hell of a find. How did you know where to look?"

"Let's just call it a gut feeling."

EIGHTY-EIGHT
BARNWOOD WAY

It was without a doubt, the creepiest house anyone had ever laid eyes upon. I can only imagine that the sole reason it was not condemned and torn down, was that the town officials were just as frightened by the witch that dwelled there as the children in the area were.

The two-story ramshackle house was located at the very end of Barnwood Way; a dead end street where the road was swallowed by the surrounding forest. During the summer months, while the leaves were thick on the trees, the house was not visible by any of the neighbors, and they were glad for that.

The exterior was in such a state of disrepair that none understood how the house had not yet collapsed upon itself, and yet, there it still stood. The paint was peeling. Shutters hung at odd angles. The eaves trough on the south side of the house had completely come loose and lay on the ground. And speaking of the ground, nothing grew within a twenty-foot radius of the house. Grass did not grow and the plants and trees nearest the home were dead and decayed.

That unsettling phenomenon was of course attributed to the curse of the witch. Black magic and foul rituals had ruined the land, everyone was certain of it. There was no other logical explanation. It was said that even animals shunned the area around the house, except for the large black crows which loved to perch on the roof. They were commonly believed to be the eyes of the witch, spying on those nearby.

Old Miss Hawthorn was as old as the hills for as far as anyone could tell. Nobody could remember a time when she did not live in town, and in that house, specifically. Her birthdate or even her place of birth was not on record. She had just always been a permanent fixture in Floral Green, a sleepy little rural town just west of the Big City. No husband. No children. Just her in that creepy old house on Barnwood Way.

I remember the first time I had ever seen Miss Hawthorn like it was just yesterday. I was in the fifth grade and at the grocery store with my mother one afternoon. I grew bored while my mother gossiped with another woman in the vegetable section, so I wandered off in search of sweets to drool over.

It did not take me long to find the jar of licorice sticks and I thought to go and beg my mother for a penny. It was then that a can of soup fell out of someone's basket and rolled toward me. I did the gentlemanly thing, of course, and picked it up in order to return it to its owner.

"Excuse me, ma'am, you dropped…"

My sentence was cut short as the elderly woman turned to regard me. My jaw dropped and the can of soup nearly fell from my grasp as I stared into the face of Old Miss Hawthorn. She had wrinkles upon wrinkles and her nose was long and crooked, sporting a wart on the end. Her snow-white hair appeared coarse and straw-like and stuck out from beneath her tattered black hat in odd angles. She smiled down at me and her teeth, the ones that were still left, were yellowed like old parchment.

I recall being frozen in place; paralyzed if you will, with fear. The stories about the witch claimed she ate children. Every story I had ever heard of Old Miss Hawthorn flashed through my mind while I stood only an arm's length away from this monster in human guise.

"Thank you, deary, I am so clumsy," she said with a hoarse voice, reaching for the can of soup that I still held.

The sound of her voice raised goosebumps all over my body, similar to listening to someone scrape their nails down a chalkboard. I smiled, stupidly, a vain attempt to mask my fear, and handed her the soup.

"And just what is your name?" she asked.

I opened my mouth but nothing came out. The thought also struck me that telling her my name was a bad idea. Perhaps my name would be used in some terrible spell or curse she could put upon me.

"Timmy, there you are."

NO, I silently screamed. My mother had just inadvertently given the witch my name. I was doomed, I knew it.

My mother also tensed up at the sight of the old hag. "Ah, come along now, Timmy, it's time to go."

Old Miss Hawthorn sighed and wore a disappointed expression on her aged face. She managed to flash me a weak smile as my mother pulled me away and dragged me to the closest cash register.

Later that evening, while I was reading funny books in bed with a flashlight, I replayed the encounter with the infamous witch in my mind. I figured if I survived the night without being turned into a frog or sprouting boils all over my skin, I should be alright.

And indeed I was alright the next morning and each morning that followed that. Life continued on as normal. In fact, when enough time had passed, my memory of Old Miss Hawthorn had faded completely, until years later when our paths crossed once more. I was riding my bike with three of my friends, when we found ourselves on Barnwood Way.

"I bet Rory is locked up in that witch's house," Bob commented, referring to Rory Baker, a boy our age who had gone missing a week prior.

"Nah, it's been a week already. Old Miss Hawthorn would have eaten him by now," Nick reasoned.

"We should go look around for clues," Fred suggested. "I don't think the police ever went there. Even they are afraid of the witch."

"I think that is a bad idea," I replied.

"Me too," Nick agreed. "You want us to be added to her menu?"

"Ah, come on. It's the middle of the afternoon. Witches are not active during the day, their powers are weak. They are only really dangerous at night," said Fred.

Nick, like the rest of us, was unconvinced. "Where did you hear that?"

"I read it in books. Witches draw their power from the moon. While the sun is out, she is just a frail old woman. Think of every picture you have ever seen drawn of a witch. It is always dark. They are always flying their broom through the night sky, passing over the moon."

Fred made a good point. Thinking back, I had never seen a drawing of a witch that was out during the light of day. It was always a night scene.

"We could just go look around the property. Maybe we could find something of Rory's as a clue," he added.

I shook my head in disagreement, as I was still against the idea. Fred's logic won over my other friends, though, and I was out-voted. Not wishing to be labeled a coward, I followed the others to the creepy old house at the end of Barnwood Way. Even during the light of day, the sight of that house unnerved me; unnerved us all.

The house was surrounded by a thick forest but nothing grew near to the house at all. It looked every bit like a house taken from the horror films that we occasionally watched at the picture show. The four of us cautiously laid our bikes on the ground, facing them in the opposition direction of the house, in case a speedy getaway was required, then slowly creeped about.

"What are we even looking for?" I whispered, wanting nothing more than to be away from there.

"Anything out of the ordinary," Fred replied.

"Everything here is out of the ordinary," Bob correctly countered.

Fred shook his head. "We know Old Miss Hawthorn never had any kids. So let's see if we can find anything around here that might belong to any of the missing kids she kidnapped and ate."

I swallowed hard. That was a most displeasing image that Fred had just forced into my delicate mind. I imagined a giant woodstove in a dark basement, filled with cobwebs. And there was Old Miss Hawthorn, cackling away over a cauldron, while waiting for her latest victim to cook inside the stove. Needless to say, I tried very hard to expel that image and hung back closer to our bikes. If the witch came out of her house, I wanted a better head start than the others.

"Hey, look at all these frogs," shouted Bob, from the

right side of the house. "There must be about twenty of them."

I positioned myself in a spot where I could see where Bob stood but I was still closer than everyone else to our bikes. Bob stooped over a muddy pond and the others joined him. I kept one eye on Bob and my other on the decrepit front door to the house.

"I bet these are some of those kidnapped kids," Fred blurted, a little louder than I thought he should have.

"That's ridiculous," Nick countered. "They are just frogs."

"Witches turn people into frogs and then use their parts in awful recipes or as components for spells. Makes eating them easier too."

Bob jumped back from the pond; his face was as pale as a ghost. "Maybe we should go now. I think I have seen enough of this place."

I breathed a giant sigh of relief when Nick agreed. They began making their way back, quite quickly I might add, to where I awaited by the bikes. Then, to my ultimate horror, I watched in slow motion as Fred picked up a rock and launched it at a second-story window. Time slowed down as I watched that rock sail through the air and then crash through the window.

We scrambled to get on our bikes, bumping into each other and knocking each other over, like a slapstick skit from a film featuring the Four Imbeciles. I even punched Fred in the arm, so angry was I that he had put us all in jeopardy. I thought it could not get any worse, when my shoe lace became caught on my bike's pedal. My friends were off and racing away while I struggled to get myself free.

"My hat!" Fred yelled, with panic clearly evident in his voice. "Timmy, grab my hat!"

At some point during all the commotion, Fred had lost his favorite red hat. He never went anywhere without that hat, and in fact, he looked fairly odd to the rest of us anytime he was made to remove it. There it sat in the dirt, a few feet away from me.

I cursed myself for my kindness. As I finally freed my lace, I dove and grabbed the hat before turning back to my bike. That's when I heard that voice again. That same voice that was like fingernails on a chalkboard and it took me right back to that encounter in the grocery store. I froze in place like a statue.

"You there. What is this about?"

For some reason, in my child's mind, I thought if I just remained still and did not answer, she would not notice me and go away. I was wrong.

"Well? Answer me."

I slowly turned. My friends were gone and out of sight, and the feeling of dread threatened to stop my heart and kill me right then and there. Old Miss Hawthorn stood in her front door with her hands placed angrily on her hips.

"I-I-I…well…w-w-we…," I stammered.

"I remember you. Your name is Timmy, isn't it?"

Oh good heavens! She remembered my name!

"Y-yes, ma'am."

"What were you boys doing here?"

"Ah...well...w-we were j-just riding our b-bikes in the area and somehow ended up h-here." Then I hastily added, "I didn't throw the r-rock."

"I know, it was that other boy, the trouble maker."

"Y-yes, it was Fred who did it," I blurted, and did not care one bit about being a snitch. Fred would have done the same if the situation was reversed.

I shivered at the thought that she had been watching us this whole time. I could have sworn I scanned every window for faces. Then I spotted a crow perched on the roof and remembered that folk said the crows acted as her eyes.

"You punched the other boy, too. Why?"

"W-well I was mad that he threw the r-rock. I didn't know he w-would d-do something like that. I am v-very sorry."

She waved me away. "Run along, Timmy. And tell your friend, Fred, he is not welcome around here."

"Y-yes, ma'am."

I could not get out of there fast enough. My friends were nowhere in sight and I found out later that they just assumed I was captured so did not stick around. You certainly learn what your friends are really like when faced with a witch crisis.

Fred, of course, was deeply upset that I told her his name. I explained I could not be held accountable for anything said, since everyone left me behind. I had even saved his hat, for which he was most grateful.

That very next summer, though, Fred went missing. He had left Nick's house one evening, sometime before midnight, but had never made it home. Posters went up everywhere and police combed the neighborhoods. Nick stopped by my house later that second night, holding two flashlights.

"Come on, let's go join in the search for Fred."

"Where would we even look that the police have not already tried?" I wondered.

"Old Miss Hawthorn's place."

"Pardon me? Surely you are kidding."

"It has to be her. She wanted Fred for breaking her windows."

"That's nonsense. That was a year ago."

"Well, he had apparently done it a few more times since. He always told me that if he ever went missing, to make sure I went to Hawthorn's place to look for him."

"But, it's so dark out."

He handed me the flashlight. "Yeah, so I am not going alone. Take that and let's go. Look, it hasn't even been twenty-four hours yet. If he is there, we could be in time to save him."

Nick had a point. I was not sure how long it took before a witch devoured her captive but it somehow made sense that it was not done immediately. Age had made me braver, or dumber, perhaps. While butterflies still flew around my stomach at the thought of visiting the witch's house at night, I still followed Nick down the driveway.

We got on our bikes and approached the dead end of Barnwood Way, not more than twenty minutes later. We decided to ditch the bikes farther from the house and then creep in on foot. If we had thought her property was frightening during the day, words could not describe how terrifying it was at night. And eerily silent, we both noted. Even the chirping of crickets was absent.

As we exited the forest and made our way across the muddy expanse toward the house, I quickly scanned for any crows perched on the roof. Birds were generally not seen at night and tonight was no exception. I don't know why that made me feel so much better but I figured there was less of a chance for the witch to be alerted to our presence.

The front of the house was dark and appeared devoid of life. Nick tugged on my sleeve and I followed him around the back of the house. It was there that we spotted a light source from a first floor window. The window was covered with an old worn curtain but there was enough of a gap to allow someone to peek inside. Nick pointed to the window and I nodded, indicating for him to lead the way and I would follow. My heart thumped in my chest and I was sure that even my friend could hear it.

I followed him toward the window, albeit a little slowly. He looked back and motioned that he was going to peek in. Again, I nodded. As he did his best to move as silently as possible, I took note of the strange patch of straw that covered the ground in front of the window. I crept in for a closer examination.

Nick paid the straw patch no heed and placed his face against the glass of the window to peer inside.

"No, Nick, wait," I said desperately, trying to keep my voice to a whisper.

It was too late. Nick's full weight caused the straw patch to give way and he vanished into the ground. I reached for him but he was gone before I could grab onto anything. Unfortunately, I was now off balance and also tumbled into the pit that had been previously hidden.

Somehow, I managed to latch onto the lip of the hole and there I dangled; my fingers dug deeply into the earth, holding on for my dear life. Below, I heard Nick groan.

I hazarded a look below me and the hole led straight into what appeared to be a cellar beneath the house. A light source came from a burning fire; a fire that sat below a large black cauldron. Beside that cauldron, stood Old Miss Hawthorn, dressed head to toe in black. She held a large jar in her withered hands and the contents of the jar nearly stopped my heart. Inside was a frog, but not just any frog. It was a frog that wore a little red hat. A tiny version of Fred's favorite hat.

"My leg," Nick moaned below me on the cellar floor. "I think I broke my leg."

Old Miss Hawthorn cackled and that cackle nearly stole the strength from my arms and forced me to let go. Some inner-strength I did not even know I possessed, allowed me to hang on.

She flashed a wicked smile my way. "Your friend on the floor there is now mine, Timmy. Now, be gone from here and never let me see you again. And if you tell anyone about what you have seen, I can promise you that you will be next."

That was all I needed to hear. I was suddenly imbued with the strength of Hercules as I climbed out of that hole. Her horrible cackle chased me through the forest and even down the street. I ran right past my bike, not wishing to waste any time in picking it up. I ran and ran and ran. Just when I did not think I was able to run anymore...I ran some more.

IN DESPERATE NEED OF
PRAISE

Butterflies flitted about in my stomach. I was about to give
the most important performance of my life, so naturally, I
was nervous to the point of vomiting. I waited backstage
and paced back and forth, wearing a path into the wooden
floor. I dared to take one final peek around the curtain and
excitedly observed that it was a full house. Mind you, the
venue was quite small but there was not an empty seat to
be found.

Admittedly, the Big City housed many grand theaters
that could have served my purpose but there had always
been a certain charm about The Emerald Theater. True, it
had been abandoned for years, but I had spent months,
painstakingly fixing it up for my big show. And to my
credit, I had done it all on my own. I had no help,
whatsoever. This was going to be a solo performance. A
daunting task that I had never before attempted.

From the time I was a young lad, I had wanted nothing more in life than to be a stage performer. I started out with school plays as a teen and then slowly progressed to more elaborate productions. There were many theaters throughout the Big City but every performer, without doubt, dreamed of working on the big stages in the theater district, or at one of the large casinos. That is when you knew you had made it. The whole city watching you. Journalists. Critics. Everyone.

For years, I was part of the Flying Flamingo troupe. We performed a wide variety of different plays, ranging from serious dramas, all the way to outrageous comedies. I was having the time of my life and we had met with some mild successes. Two years ago, our group was invited to perform at the very prestigious Grand Royal Theater. It was our shot at the big time. It was the goal we had been working our whole lives to achieve and we flopped.

The media blasted us. We had performed a touching tale of two lovers but the Big City Times titled their review, A Horror Show. Other papers and magazines similarly ripped us to shreds, calling us amateurs and a waste of good money. I truly felt I gave the performance of my life and it was my colleagues who had caused us to flounder on stage. Several critics, though, had singled me out in reviews, naming me as the weakest link. My name was dragged through the muck of the city's gutters. I was devastated.

Shortly thereafter, I had a falling out with the rest of the group and was expelled for reasons I would rather not get into. They can say whatever they want about me. They can tell as many lies as they like but I was going to quit anyway. They were a bunch of immature whiners who only brought me down. My performances and my good name were tarnished by their lack of acting skills and professionalism. I should have left them long ago. I am on a level far above them all and did not need them in the slightest.

I have now spent the last year writing my own original play. A tragic tale of a misunderstood man. Someone with so much potential but never accepted by those around him. The story consists of several different characters, of which I have elected to play all, myself. I will be damned if I allow the incompetence's of others to ruin this night for me. Tonight is my night to shine, alone. Tonight, I elevate myself to stand above all other performers. Tonight, nobody will be able to deny my thespian talents.

It was almost time to begin and my level of nervousness was through the roof. It was not going to be easy running a one-man show, but I envied those performers who could pull it off. People like the ventriloquist, Sullivan, of Sullivan and Micky. Magicians like, The Great Fazoo. Their shows lived or died by their performance, alone. They had nobody else to rely on if the going got rough. But I knew that I could do this. I had trained my entire life for this. That crowd out there was in for a real treat.

ACT 1, SCENE 1

(Stage lights off except for the spotlight on center stage. Rufus walks into the light with head down and opens with a soliloquy.)

RUFUS: I don't know why people don't understand me. I don't feel as though I am all that different from everyone else. Is it because I am a recluse? Because I don't often socialize with others? Has anyone ever stopped to consider why I don't care to socialize? Maybe it is society that has molded me into the person that I am. The ridicule. The whispers behind my back. The sneers. People treat others like outsiders and then wonder why they behave the way that they do. Thinking back, though, perhaps my mother may have played some small part.

I attached fishing line to several of the light switches and subtly tugged on one to turn off the spotlight, casting the theater into total darkness. I had memorized the walk from center stage to back behind the curtain, so even without the use of my eyes, I made it unhindered.

I quickly changed into my next costume and was quite proud of myself for the ingenuity of it. The left side of my body was dressed as Rufus' mother and the right side of my body was dressed as a young Rufus. Now, I could stand on stage and carry on a conversation between two people, by simply switching my stance. I flipped on two stage lights and went back out. Rufus' mother was facing the audience.

ACT 1, SCENE 2

(Dorothy enters. Stamps foot on floor while making the motion of knocking on a door.)

DOROTHY: Rufus? Rufus? You open the door this instant. Rufus? I know you are awake, I can see the light from your lamp under the door.

(Rufus turns to audience. Unlocks the door.)

DOROTHY: I knew it! You were reading those awful magazines again. You are filling your fool head with nonsense. Monsters, Rufus? Really? Those monster magazines are pure rubbish.

(Dorothy makes the motion of ripping the magazines.)

DOROTHY: There! That takes care of that! There will be no more reading in this room. Do you hear me? Bedrooms are for sleeping in. If your father was still around you'd get the belt, mark my words. But disobey me again and see what happens. Don't push me.

RUFUS: But, Mom, there is nothing wrong with those magazines.

DOROTHY: NO MORE READING! (Dorothy shouts and raises her hand in a threat.)

Then I did something that no stage actor should do. I hazarded a glance at the audience to gauge their reactions, thus far. An actor should focus on the task at hand. A really good actor gets lost in the role and is not even aware that there is an audience present. The audience can be a distraction if one tends to overly worry about how they perceive the performance. A negative reaction could have a profound effect on an actor and jeopardize the show. I truly felt I could take the risk, though. I needed to see their faces, as they had been fairly quiet to this point.

The first face I recognized, sitting in the front row, was William Freeman. He worked for the Daily Globe and had trashed my last performance. He said that his child in kindergarten could have done a better job than I did. His face was difficult to read. I moved on to the next.

In the row directly behind William, I noticed Nancy Blain. She wrote a column for the Venus Tribune. She had said she would have walked out of that performance, if she was not getting paid to be there in order to write a review. Her eyes were wide. Wide with wonder? Wide in awe of the show so far?

To her left was Neil Bradshaw. He wrote reviews for Global Entertainment and said that I had single-handedly brought down that last show. Now he was witnessing how I could single-handedly carry an entire show. He was stone-faced for the moment but I was sure that would all change by the second act.

I found Donald Donaldson among the crowd. He was a reporter for BCTV news on the television. I had never owned a picture tube but I had heard that he referred to my acting as pure rubbish. He sat there wearing a poker face. Perhaps it was too early to gauge their opinions.

Before finishing the current scene, I spotted Barry Addams. He was probably the biggest deal of them all. He reviewed movies and plays for the Big City Times. Of course, he sat dead-center in the middle of the theater, having the best view. He would be the toughest nut to crack. He loathed my performance in that last show and had said the most hurtful things. He did not appear too impressed at the moment. I would need to step up my game.

ACT 2, SCENE 2

(Children walking about in the schoolyard.)

KID 1: Hey, look. It's weirdo Rufus.

KID 2: Weirdo Rufus. Weirdo Rufus.

KID 1: Is he talking to one of his imaginary friends again?

KID 2: He must be, cuz nobody else wants to be friends with such a weirdo.

Much of Act Two focused on the steady decline in Rufus' social life. At home, his mother pretty well had him confined to his bedroom, where even the simple act of reading was strictly prohibited. So, he did indeed invent imaginary friends to talk and play with, in order to pass the time away. At school, he kept to himself and tried to avoid the other kids whenever possible. The only thing he enjoyed about school was drama class. In drama class, he could pretend to be other people and could leave the life of Rufus behind, even if it was for only a short while. He grasped at any opportunity he could to escape.

Act Three jumped ahead several years and now

portrayed Rufus as a lonely young man. After the untimely death of this mother, he truly had nobody left. He found it difficult to hold down jobs for any length of time. People thought him strange and socially awkward. His life had no purpose until he joined an acting troupe. Now, he could escape being Rufus once more. Now, he could be anyone but Rufus.

Acting yielded a paycheck but it was not much. It afforded him a tiny apartment in the slums of the Big City; a neighborhood that was referred to as the Junkie Jungle. Despite his surroundings, Rufus never partook in any illicit activities and even refused to imbibe any alcoholic beverages. He still did not socialize outside of his acting group, and even within it, conversations were kept to the work at hand. He had no desire to discuss his life outside the theater.

As the third act came to a close, I pulled the string that would darken the stage and once again allowed myself a moment to study the audience. Wide-eyed and stone-faced, still. All of them. I suppose I could understand. The content thus far had been fairly deep and somewhat depressing. The plight of Rufus would tug at the heartstrings of any feeling individual. The fourth act would see a change in tempo. The fourth act allowed for a bit of comedy and wit on the part of Rufus. Now, I would showcase my comedic abilities after dazzling them with my dramatic skills.

During the second scene of the fourth act, I launched several clever quips but could not elicit any change in expression from the audience. Not a single laugh. Not even a mild chuckle. I can admit it was quite disheartening. Scene three provided me with the best joke yet and still the room remained silent. I was convinced these critics possessed no sense of humor, whatsoever. That was quite evident. The fourth act closed with Rufus earning chastisement by critics for perhaps his greatest performance on stage. Their verbal and written barbs caused tremendous damage and attributed to the actor departing from the group. Without acting in his life, Rufus walked a dark path, while harboring even darker thoughts.

Act Five was the final act, consisting of a single scene. It also included the most elaborate costume yet. If nothing else had impressed the critics to this point, then my Grim Reaper costume was sure to inspire a sense of awe. I wore a long and flowing robe of black, with a frightening mask that transformed my face into a grinning skull with glowing red eyes. In my right hand I carried a long scythe.

ACT 5, FINAL SCENE

(Theater goes dark. One single light on stage. Grim Reaper appears through a cloud of smoke to deliver final speech.)

GRIM REAPER: And now, my friends, we come to the end. The end of the line for poor Rufus. Rufus will suffer no more at the hands of idiotic critics. Those bitter men and women who could obviously not act, themselves, so choose to write about it instead. Choosing to lambaste those hard-working individuals who poured their entire souls into their craft. To belittle those that they look down upon. No more, my friends.

No more.

With my left hand, I produced a book of matches. The lack of empathy from the audience for the fate of Rufus disgusted me. I had not noticed one single smile from any faces, for the entire show. Not even a nod of approval. They should have been astounded by this night's performance. I could not fathom any one of them ever seeing anything as marvelous before. What other actor could pull off an entire play by themselves? None, that's who. Well, to Hell with these critics. To Hell with them all, quite literally.

Before I could strike a match, a loud thump came from a side door, just to the right of the stage. It startled me and I momentarily lost my train of thought.

"Who would dare interrupt the final scene?"

*   *   *   *

Several officers burst into the decrepit old theater, once the battering ram made short work of the barred side door. Upon spotting the lone actor on stage, they raised their revolvers and took aim. One of the new arrivals, wearing a long brown trench coat, took in the scene around him and shook his head in bewilderment. He too, pointed his gun at the actor.

"Drop the broomstick and put your hands in the air," the man shouted. "My name is Detective Edward Kane and you are going to want to do exactly what I tell you."

A uniformed officer sniffed the air, curiously. "Ah, Detective? I smell gasoline."

Detective Kane made the same horrendous discovery

and then his eyes went wide as he noticed the book of matches in the strange man's hands. This entire theater was ready to go up in flames.

"Drop the matches, NOW!"

The man on the stage had his face painted with white makeup. Sweat was causing the makeup to run down his face. It dripped onto the black garbage bag he wore, with holes punched through for his arms. He threw down the broomstick he held in one hand but kept ahold of the matches.

"I am not playing any games here. Drop the matches," Kane demanded.

The strange man frowned. These officers had ruined his finale. The Grim Reaper was to transform the entire theater into the final set, Hell. Rufus was going to Hell and he was going to take those ungrateful critics with him.

No matter, he thought to himself, the police would just have to join him.

BLAM! BLAM!

The man attempted to strike a match and Detective Kane shot him twice in the chest. He stumbled about, as if enacting a dramatic death scene, and then dropped the matches and fell to the stage.

The officers held their breath, expecting the sparks from Kane's revolver to ignite the theater, but luck was with them and nothing had happened.

Kane exhaled and again took in the scene around him. "Jones, see if he is dead. The rest of you untie everyone and see if anyone is injured."

The detective approached the nearest audience member and removed the woman's gag. "What in the hell was going on here?" he asked, while untying her wrists from the arms of the chair.

"That raving lunatic kidnapped us all and held us hostage. He forced us to watch his horrible last performance. I have never seen anything this bad in my entire life. Words can't even describe the insanity we just sat through."

Officer Jones approached the bleeding man on stage and noticed his shallow breathing. He leaned over the fallen actor who was attempting to speak.

"Did they like the show? What are they saying down there? Was it the best they have ever seen?"

The man closed his eyes and breathed his last breath.

FAIRBROOKE:
HOME FOR SENIORS

"Welcome to Fairbrooke, Doctor O'Hara. I believe this place is much smaller than what you are used to but I trust you will enjoy it here."

I smiled and nodded. "Thank you, Miss, ah, Miss…"

"Mrs. Shay."

"Thank you, Mrs. Shay. Yes, this is certainly a drastic change from the Big City General Hospital but a welcomed one. I look forward to a more relaxed environment."

"Well, we may not have many residents here yet, but the ones we do have can be demanding at times. Nothing serious, really, but they do so love to complain."

"Complainers I can handle."

Mrs. Shay smiled. "You say that now." Then she lowered her voice. "Speak of the devil. Here comes one of our resident hypochondriacs now. Henry Briar has something different wrong with him each week."

Henry Briar shuffled toward us, obviously displaying a pain in his legs. He was tall and lean, and I soon learned was eighty-eight years old.

"Good afternoon, Mister Briar, how are you feeling today?" Mrs. Shay asked.

"Oh, it's my legs. A terrible pain in both my legs. I fear I shall lose my ability to walk, I just know it."

"Well, Mister Briar, I am Doctor O'Hara and I will be working here from now on. How about I stop by your room this afternoon and we will have a look at those legs?"

"You can come by but there won't be anything you can do. You'll probably need to saw them off. Probably infected that's what's wrong, I just know it."

Henry shuffled off down the hall, grumbling to himself as he went.

"Last week it was his left shoulder. The week before that his right eye," Mrs. Shay told me.

"I will examine him later and see what I can find out."

The two of us walked through a lounge area and I was introduced to another resident.

"Good morning, Mrs. Henson. This is our new doctor, Doctor O'Hara."

"Pleasure to meet you, Doctor. Maybe you can do something about my chest pain before I die. The last doctor was useless and couldn't do anything for me."

"I would be happy to give you an examination this afternoon, once I am settled."

"Mrs. Henson is always dying. She has been here just over a year and a half and has been dying, according to her, every day since her arrival," Mrs. Shay explained, as she escorted me to my new office. "Here you go, this is your office. I would suggest you keep your door closed or you will have everyone in here at all times, complaining about their problems."

I thanked her and set about organizing my new office and making it feel more like mine. I hung a few certificates and awards on the wall, and displayed a photo of my wife and two kids on the desk. Several other staff members dropped by to introduce themselves and welcome me to Fairbrooke.

I found myself enjoying a moment of silence, which was not something I had while working at the Big City General. The pace there was fast and exhausting. It was an environment better suited to the younger doctors. I put in my time there, twenty-three years to be exact, now I deserved a little break and looked forward to a more relaxed environment.

Later that day, I looked over Mister Briars legs, and as was suggested by Mrs. Shay, I could find nothing wrong.

"But I can barely walk," he told me. "The pain is terrible."

I was informed that last week he was saying the same thing about his left shoulder. "How does your shoulder feel, Mister Briar? I was told that you were having problems with it last week."

"Ah, well, it seems fine now. But it will flare up again, you can bet on that."

"How about I get you a walker to help you move around? And I will keep a close watch on those legs in the meantime."

"The last few doctors couldn't do a damn thing for

me either. A bunch of useless quacks, I say," he grumbled.

"I just don't see anything wrong with your legs. Let's give it a few more days to see if they get better on their own."

"It will be too late in a few days. I will lose both my legs."

I left Mister Briar's room and asked one of the nurses' to have a walker brought by to help him in the meantime. As with most hypochondriacs, they could convince themselves that something was wrong. His legs may be perfectly fine, but he has created this pain in his mind, so for him it is very real.

I made the short trek over to the room of Mrs. Henson and gave her a thorough examination with the same results. She complained of a pressure on her chest which was making it difficult for her to breathe. She was certain that the reaper of death was knocking at her door. I could find nothing to suggest there was a problem with her chest or her breathing.

"I think you will be staying with us a lot longer than you think, Mrs. Henson."

"I don't see how. I can barely breathe. Tonight is probably going to be my last night here. Will you phone my children and inform them?"

"Hmm, maybe we should not alarm them so soon, huh? I have been doing this doctoring thing for quite some time now and in my expert opinion you are going to live."

Soon after, I met with Mister Seagal, who said the pain in his right hand was so great that he could not even move his fingers. Then Mrs. Ruttle dropped by my office, complaining of an intense headache that would not go away, no matter what pills she took.

I, of course, could find nothing to suggest that any of these people suffered from any afflictions. In my experience, I found that many of the lonely seniors in these homes were just looking for attention. Perhaps, they had no family to fuss over them so they sought the attention elsewhere.

One evening, when most of the residents were asleep, I stayed late in my office and poured through the records left behind by the previous doctors. Mister Briar had complained of something different nearly each week, and as expected, nothing was ever truly wrong. Once a doctor determined that he was fine, he just moved on to a different body part and began the whole complaining process anew.

Mrs. Henson was always dying, in her mind, from one excuse to the next. Mrs. Ruttle, who came to me with a terrible headache, only recently complained about a terrible pain in her back, which was determined to be nothing as well.

I could see from the notes made by the other doctors that they were frustrated and growing rather irritable from the constant phantom complaints. Over the next few days, I made some inquiries and discovered that the last four resident doctors before me had all quit. Apparently the folk here had driven them out.

One afternoon, I sat in a lounge area and questioned

Mrs. Shay. "How did the residents get along with the previous doctors?"

"They weren't too fond of them, I would say."

"I have found that seniors can be rather stubborn at times. I wonder if perhaps they did not like any of the other doctors, so decided to force them out?"

"What do you mean?"

"Well, I have been reading over a lot of notes and could feel the growing frustration that these doctors were feeling. They all quit, did they not?"

"Yes, that is correct."

"So, my theory is that the residents decided to drive these doctors crazy with phantom afflictions, until they were forced to leave. Perhaps, these doctors were not giving them the proper attention that they felt they deserved."

"Hello, Doctor. Hello, Mrs. Shay. Care for some apple pie? Baked fresh today," a small woman with short white hair said.

The woman held a tray with a warm, freshly-baked apple pie, that smelled wonderful.

"Thank you, Mrs. Walters, we would love some pie," Mrs. Shay replied.

The elderly woman smiled and placed the pie on a table and walked away. I had not met this woman yet and surprisingly, she did not come to me with any complaints.

"Mrs. Walters, you said?"

"Yes, such a sweet woman and always baking things. Her pies are fantastic."

"She doesn't complain of any pains or say that she is going to die?"

"No, actually she says very little at all. Spends most of

her time in her room baking."

"You see, this supports my theory. Mrs. Walters bakes and everyone enjoys what she makes. She gets attention from that and is satisfied. She does not have to make something up in order for people to fuss over her."

"You may have a point. No other doctor has ever found anything wrong with anyone here, aside from the normal effects of aging."

I returned to my office and pondered an idea I had rolling around inside my mind. If the residents wanted to play games then I could play one of my own. If all they wanted was attention then I would give it to them. I feel that the other doctors failed because they dismissed all the phantom ailments as being just that. They were telling these people that they were wrong. That was not the reaction the residents were looking for. I decided I would play along with their personal diagnoses and attempt to treat them.

I made a phone call to a pharmacist friend of mine and placed an order for some harmless vitamins that would act as a placebo. Maybe if I could convince folk that these pills were treating their pain, they would believe it and it would have the desired effect.

My shipment arrived a few days later and I paid a visit to Mister Briar's room. I planned to begin with him and quickly started examining his legs.

"They are still hurting you, are they?"

"Tremendously. You are going to have to cut them off, won't you? There must be some kind of infection that you cannot detect."

"Actually, I notice some swelling here. Yes, yes indeed. I believe this is your problem."

Mister Briar appeared shocked.

"Really? You mean you can see something wrong?"

"Yes, most definitely. It is only a slight swelling, which is why I must have missed it before. But there is definite swelling and would contribute to the pain and trouble you are experiencing while walking."

"Can anything be done about it?"

"Of course, this is very treatable. I just happen to have a pill that will reduce the inflammation and remove the pain within an hour." I searched around inside a small black bag I carried with me. "Ah, yes, here it is. Now, Mister Briar, take one of these with some water after your next meal. This should make you feel much better."

"Umm, ok, well if you say so."

"Yes, I will check on you first thing in the morning."

I was most excited to see how this miracle pill was going to work and went in search of Mister Briar, as my shift began the next morning. I found him up and about in the hallways, without the use of his walker.

"Good morning, Mister Briar. How are you today?"

"My legs feel fine. No more pain. You did it. I can't believe you really did it. You must be the world's best doctor."

I smiled. "Thank you, but I am nowhere near the best. But I am so happy you are feeling better."

"None of the other doctors ever believed me. They said the pain was all in my head. My head, can you believe that?"

"I suppose they did not examine you as thoroughly as they should have."

"Quacks. All of them."

I proceeded to track down Mister Seagal and repeated

the same process, finding some swelling on this right hand which did not actually exist, and prescribing the same placebo. I checked back with him much later that afternoon and was pleased to find the pain in his hand had completely disappeared. As with Mister Briar, Mister Seagal went on and on about the incompetence of the other doctors and praised me for believing him and fixing his problem.

I was now satisfied that I could treat the rest of the residents here with the same pill. I was truly convinced that pretending to believe in them was the key to this plan's success. Elderly folk did not want to be constantly told that they were crazy and imagining things. Once I got on their good side, I believed things would change around here. I would try to give them the attention they deserved, to prevent any more mystery ailments.

The next morning, as I was about to leave my office in search of Mrs. Ruttle with the awful headaches, Mister Briar entered. He was holding his throat and looked quite distressed.

"What's wrong, Mister Briar?"

"My throat," he croaked. "Hurts to swallow and I can barely talk."

I sighed. The pain in his legs was gone so now he had a pain in his throat. Mrs. Shay had warned me of this. I examined his throat, and of course, there was no redness or inflammation. There was no indication at all that his throat should be in pain.

"It's bad, isn't it?" he asked, after I finished my exam. "This will be the end of me, won't it?"

"Your throat is very red," I lied. "But I have another pill that should clear this right up."

"That looks just like the other one for my legs."

"True, they look alike, but I assure you this one is made specially to deal with throat pain. Trust me, it should do the trick."

"Well, alright, if you say so," he whispered.

Mister Briar accepted the pill and left my office. Shortly, thereafter, Mister Seagal marched in.

"I can't move the fingers in my left hand now!"

"Hmm, but your right hand is fine, is it?"

"Yes, no pain at all. But now I have the exact same pain in my left hand. What's wrong with me, Doc?"

"It is very common for the pain to switch hands. I was expecting this. You will just need another pill and this time it will eliminate your pain completely."

"I am left-handed. I am useless without my left hand!"

"Just take this pill and I promise you will regain the use of your hand."

With the departure of Mister Seagal, I tracked down Mrs. Henson, who was listening to the Jungle Johnny program on the radio. I gave her the same pill and told her it would help her chest pain and she would soon be able to breathe normally. Later, I found Mrs. Ruttle sitting outside and prescribed her the pill for her terrible headaches.

To my total dismay, they were all complaining of the same symptoms the following day. I did not know what went wrong. My plan seemed to be working.

"I still can't breathe, I am going to die today," Mrs. Henson said.

"My head feels like it will explode," Mrs. Ruttle added.

"I can't swallow," Mister Briar complained.

And of course, Mister Seagal could not move the fingers on his left hand. I really had no other option but to prescribe them all another pill and send them on their way.

I sat alone in my office and ran through everything in my mind. I thought I had them all figured out. Could I have been wrong? I thought that believing in them and prescribing them the placebo would have worked. Mister Briar, it would appear, was just determined to have something new wrong with him all the time. It was clearly a mental disorder. And Mrs. Henson seemed to want to live with her doom and gloom thoughts that she was dying every day. I would need a new plan. But what?

Mrs. Shay burst into my office and startled me from my thoughts.

"Doctor O'Hara, we are worried about Mrs. Walters."

"Why, what has happened? There is never anything wrong with Mrs. Walters."

"Nobody has seen her since yesterday. Mrs. Walters never misses a meal and she will not answer her door."

"It's locked?"

"Yes."

"Well, have security get the key and meet me at her room. We will have to go in and check on her."

"Yes, Doctor."

Mrs. Shay ran down the hall and I packed a few things into my little black bag. I made my way quickly to the door of Mrs. Walter's room, and was soon joined by Mrs. Shay and the security officer with the key. I decided to try knocking again first, before we entered.

"Hello? Mrs. Walters? Are you there? This is Doctor O'Hara. Hello?"

When we received no response, I nodded to the other

man to open the door. I entered directly behind the officer and my heart sunk as my worst fear was realized. Mrs. Walters was lying face down on the floor. I rushed to her side and checked her pulse, but unfortunately she was dead. A heart attack was my initial guess.

"Umm, what the hell is all this?" the security officer asked.

When Mrs. Shay gasped, I stood and took a look around. I was shocked to find the room full of small dolls. But these were not just ordinary dolls. These dolls resembled many of the folk that lived in Fairbrooke. So much so, that they were readily identifiable. Their likenesses were uncanny.

I picked up a doll that was the spitting image of Mister Briar, only to find that an elastic band was tied tightly around his throat. Then I spotted the doll of Mister Seagal. His left hand had been flattened by a hammer that rested nearby. A rock was placed on the chest of Mrs. Henson's doll. My mind reeled at this discovery. I looked around further and found the doll of Mrs. Ruttle, sitting in the sink, with water dripping onto the doll's head.

Voodoo dolls? The quiet and sweet Mrs. Walters was making voodoo dolls? How could I ever enter this into my records? An uncompleted doll sat on an end table next to her rocking chair. It's face resembled mine.

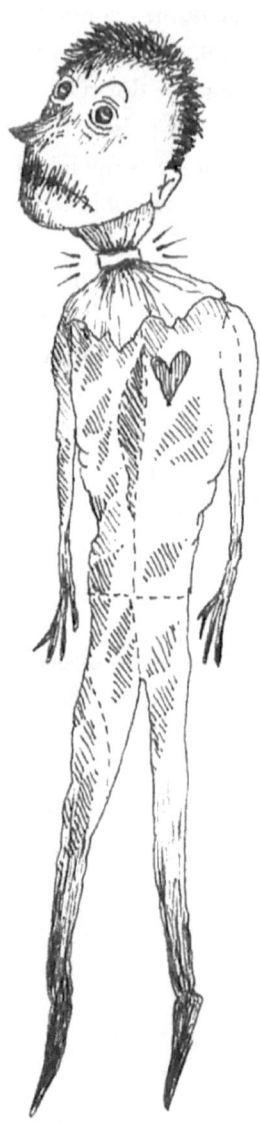

THE WOMAN ON THE BEACH

My first day of the boring conference was finally over. Listening to endless lectures, and watching horrendous slideshows with graphs and flowcharts, certainly takes its toll on one's mind. My brain checked out somewhere after our lunch break and I am not sure if I could recall a single word said after that point.

Fortunately, for me, I was staying in the same hotel as the conference, so I did not have far to travel to get back to my room. I could not complain one bit about the accommodations. From my window, I had a perfect unobstructed view of the beach and the boardwalk. My only problem was that it got dark fairly early this time of year, and by the time the conference was over, I did not have much daylight left to enjoy the quaint scenery.

I changed into something more comfortable and decided to get out for some fresh air. I thought a nice walk

369

would do me some good and help clear my mind before the sun vanished.

The boardwalk here seemed to stretch on for miles. I passed many small restaurants and vendors selling food, and while each one smelled amazingly delicious, I was regrettably not very hungry. I had snacked on too many pastries all day at the conference and it ruined my appetite for dinner. But it was good to know that many options existed if I were to grow peckish later that evening.

I loved watching the waves roll onto the sand. There was something about the sound of it that could just wash away the troubles of the day. I could just stand there with my eyes closed and listen to that for hours.

I had walked nearly an hour in one direction and the sun was beginning to rapidly set. I reckoned it was best to head back to the hotel before it got too dark. I was unsure of just how I would pass the rest of the evening. Were I at home, I would be listening to radio programs, but my hotel room lacked a radio. It seemed as though I would miss my favorite program tonight, Jungle Johnny, unless the lounge area at the hotel had a radio. I picked up the pace as I considered that a strong possibility.

Last week's episode ended with Jungle Johnny surrounded by a group of angry apes. The rest of his crew had already left to return to their ship, so I had no idea how Johnny was going to escape this harrowing situation. The thought of missing this week's episode was enormously distressing.

As the lights of the hotel came into view, an odd sound from the beach caught my attention. Amid the crash of the waves, I thought I heard someone sobbing. I paused for a moment, attempting to shut out everything else and focus on that strange sound. I heard it again, and it was definitely someone upset, and a woman, I was certain of it.

I left the boardwalk for the sand of the beach and followed the sobbing through the darkness.

"Hello? Hello? Is everything alright?" I called out.

I received no response, but then suddenly leaped aside to avoid stumbling into a woman, who was sitting in the sand nearly ten feet from the water's edge.

"Oh, pardon me, I didn't see you sitting there," I apologized. "Miss, are you okay? I heard you sobbing from over on the boardwalk."

"I doubt that I will ever be okay again," the woman answered in a soft voice.

"Why would you say such a thing? Are you hurt?"

"My heart is hurt and I fear it shall never mend. Not until Donald returns."

"Donald? Who is Donald, if I may ask?"

"Donald is my husband."

"Donald is away? Traveling, perhaps?"

"He left on a fishing boat. He fishes for a living. I am waiting here for his return."

"Ah, I see. How long is he usually gone for?"

"A few days. A week at the most."

"Well, has it been a week yet? I am sure he will be back soon."

"He has been gone for three years now."

I wasn't quite sure if I had heard her properly. I thought she may have said three years.

"I am sorry, did you say three years?"

"Yes, three years," her sobbing renewed.

Now I understood her distress.

"Oh…ahh…I am sorry to hear that," I wasn't sure

what I could possibly say in response to that. "You believe he is coming back?"

"He will come back. He would never leave me. He loved me dearly."

"Then I am sure that he will too. I bid you a goodnight, miss, I must be returning to the hotel now. I mustn't miss Jungle Johnny if it can be avoided."

"Goodnight to you, sir."

With that, I took my leave and hurried back to the hotel with great haste. I navigated my way to the hotel lounge but was horrendously disappointed to learn that their radio had not been working. There would be no Jungle Johnny this evening. Wearing a long face, I returned to my room and decided to order some room service.

I changed into something more suitable for lying about in bed, and once I had devoured my cheesesteak sandwich, my mind drifted back to that poor woman on the beach. She was obviously not in her right mind. A man gone for three years was not going to be showing up on shore anytime soon. I could not be sure of their marital situation, but he had either decided not to return, or something unfortunate had befallen him. I chose to believe the latter. It was not uncommon for ships to go missing at sea. Victims of some terrible storm or something unforeseen had caused the ship to sink.

I could relate, somewhat, as to how that woman felt. I had lost my wife to the disease, six years past. It had been one terribly awful ordeal but at least I had had some closure. For better or worse, I was aware of my wife's fate. I could not imagine what it would be like to not know. To always wonder what happened to them. Were they alive? Were they dead? It broke my heart to think of that woman sitting on the beach, hoping that her husband would sail back at any moment.

Once my eyes had adjusted to the gloom on the beach, I had noticed that the woman was roughly the same age as I. Mid-to-late forties, I would guess. She was quite attractive with long dark hair. Her eyes were brown, I believed, with a lovely shape to them. She intrigued me and occupied most of my thoughts, before I drifted off to sleep that first night.

The second day of the conference was long and seemed to have dragged on endlessly. I was famished by the time we were let out and this time I did accompany some of the others to a nearby restaurant for dinner. I had a delicious lobster bisque, socialized for a spell, and then decided to call it a night.

After washing up and changing back at my room, I felt like a little fresh air before getting into bed. I stepped outside the hotel and closed my eyes, listening to the waves as I had done the previous night.

My eyes shot open as I heard a familiar sobbing sound. Good heavens, that woman must have been sitting on the beach again. I followed the sound and found the same woman sitting in the same general area.

"Pardon the intrusion, miss, but I couldn't help but hear you again as I stepped out for a bit of air. You may recall me from last night."

"I do, and I am sorry to have disturbed you."

"No, no, you did not disturb me at all. May I sit?"

"You may, although I don't make for great company."

Not caring about getting sand in my trousers, I took a seat on the beach next to the woman. We were facing the ocean, though, at this time of night there was nothing to see. Of course the sound of the waves was indeed soothing.

"I am Albert," I said. "May I have the pleasure of your name?"

"My name is Anna."

"A lovely name. Tell me, Anna, are you out here often? Waiting, like this?"

"Every day."

"Every day? For three years?"

"Yes. Every day."

The poor, poor girl. I truly felt for her.

"Have you ever considered why Donald may have been gone this long? An accident, perhaps?"

"There was a terrible storm the night he and the others had left. Some of the locals say the storm took them but I don't believe that."

"Well, if I may ask, what do you think happened, then? I don't want to appear pessimistic, but three years is a long time, and the timing of that storm is a tragic coincidence."

"Maybe their ship did get damaged and it made getting home more difficult. There are a lot of islands out there, they could have been stranded on one. Someone could find them any day now."

I could understand her not wishing to think of the worst scenario but three years was a long time to try to fool one's self. I decided to change the subject.

"You must live in town, do you?"

"Yes, we have a small house just five minutes from the beach here. Are you a tourist?"

"Well, I am here for a conference. It's rather boring,

to be honest, but sometimes it is nice to get away. I am from the Big City and don't often get to enjoy the sights and sounds of the ocean."

"Ah, a Big City boy. What do you do there?"

"Please don't hate me if I tell you, but I sell insurance."

"Nothing wrong with that."

"I am here for a dull sales conference and it takes considerable effort to remain awake in there all day. I really don't know how I manage it. And what about yourself? What is it that you do, well, when you aren't here at the beach?"

"I spend most of my time here. I want to make sure I am the first one that Donald sees when he gets back."

"You know, Anna, I know how you feel. I, too, have lost someone. The grief is terrible and it does take a long time to get over. I understand that people all deal with it in different ways."

"Was it your wife?"

I then proceeded to tell Anna about my wife and what happened all those years ago. She listened intently and we shared more than a few tears. We talked for hours until I really had to get some sleep. She remained at the beach, staring out into the blackness of the sea, waiting.

The following day dragged on dreadfully. All I could think about was Anna and how I wanted to join her at the beach and talk some more. Watching the clock only seemed to make the time pass more slowly. Regrettably, the sun had already set by the time I was released from my daytime prison, and I thought I would forego any plans for dinner and head straight to the beach. In short order, I found Anna, sobbing as usual.

This night, I changed up the topics and steered clear of dead loved ones and missing husbands. I got Anna to smile and even laugh. She had a stunning smile and it felt marvelous to be able to cheer her up. She clearly did not have anyone else in her life to provide that for her.

"I really appreciate these talks, Albert. It has been a pleasant distraction. When do you leave?"

"Friday is the last day of my conference," I said with a sigh. "And I have really enjoyed these talks as well. I believe the sun will be coming up soon and I should try to sleep for an hour or two at least. Shall I join you again, when the conference is done for the day?"

"Yes, of course, I would like that."

I was unable to sleep for even a minute when I got back to my room. My every thought was of Anna and of that smile of hers. As per usual, I attended the next day of the conference in body only, as my mind was elsewhere. We even broke into groups for a project and I was utterly useless. I stared blankly out the window, wondering what Anna was doing at that very moment.

When the conference finally concluded for the day, I dashed toward my room to get changed. I was intercepted by one of the employees who worked for the hotel.

"Ah, pardon me, sir, I have some good news."

"Oh?"

"Yes, we have fixed the problem with our radio and they are doing a rebroadcast of the Jungle Johnny episode you had missed from the other night. It will be at seven this evening."

"Oh, ah, yes, that is fantastic. Thank you for the news."

As I was changing, I considered this news but found

that I had no interest in Jungle Johnny this night. I had not even given Johnny a second thought since I had gotten to know Anna. I still didn't know whether Johnny escaped the angry apes, and for the moment, that was not a priority to me. I wanted nothing more than to spend every free moment with the woman on the beach.

I had room service deliver two ham and cheese sandwiches and promptly headed to the beach. It was quite dark again and I cursed the conference and its long hours. I located Anna, who was again sobbing, although her face did brighten this time at my arrival. Ah, that smile.

I offered her my second sandwich but she said she had already eaten. I hadn't realized how famished I was, until I finished both sandwiches in record time. We then spent many, many hours, talking as we had done the previous nights. We talked about family and friends and just life in general. I learned that she loved to garden and that she felt awful for neglecting hers these last few years. We even laughed some more and she seemed in better spirits.

"Anna, tomorrow is the last day of the conference. Would it be alright if I asked you to dinner? Some of the other folk have been raving about this seafood place just down the boardwalk. You are probably familiar with it but I would love for you to join me."

Her smile faded. "I would enjoy that, Albert, but Donald could be back any time now and I should be here."

"Anna, it has been three years. We could just be an hour and then come right back here."

"I am sorry, I had better not. Just in case."

I sighed. "Ok, well, how about I get some take out

and we will just have our dinner here at the beach? How does that work?"

"That works, I would like that," she nodded.

We spoke for a while longer, before I really did need to try and sleep. I had been attempting to function on little to no sleep this week and it was beginning to catch up to me. I fell asleep with Anna on my mind and she was the first thing that entered into my thoughts when I awoke.

An idea struck me that morning and I ran to use the telephone in the hotel lobby. I made arrangements to extend my trip until the end of the weekend and paid out of my own pocket to keep my room for another two days. I was hoping Anna would be as excited as I was. I felt we had made a genuine connection. I thought maybe if I spent the weekend at the beach with her, I could even manage to get her away for a short time. To show her that there was still a life to be lived away from the beach. After three years, she needed to understand that Donald was not coming back.

To my absolute joy, the conference ended early that Friday. It was only noon when they bid us farewell. I had not yet had the pleasure of really enjoying the view of the beach during the daylight hours, and of course the best part was that I now had more time to spend with Anna.

So excited was I, that I did not even bother to change. I made my way down to the beach in my jacket and tie, in search of this woman that I had come to…love? Yes, love, I could admit it. She had an extraordinary personality and every moment we spent talking was a delight.

With the sun high in the sky, I was finally afforded a perfect view of the beach. There were several people lying in the sand this day but Anna was not among them. I searched up and down the area where she always sat, without an ounce of luck. I even called out her name. I supposed she might not have come yet, after all, the woman needed her sleep as well.

I was about to approach a couple and ask if they might have seen Anna, when something strange caught my eye. I walked over to a spot on the beach to inspect what appeared to be some kind of memorial. A wooden cross was stuck into the sand and various types of flowers had been laid all around it. When I knelt down, I could see something written on the cross. It read, "Anna Hallworth. Forever Waiting."

I stood, utterly confused. Looking to the boardwalk, I spotted the hotel employee who had relayed to me the good news about the repaired radio.

"Hello? You there, hello?"

He stopped and I joined him on the boardwalk.

"Hello again, sir, what may I do for you?"

"That cross over there on the beach, what can you tell me about it?"

"That is a sad tale, to be sure."

"It says Anna Hallworth on it. Forever Waiting. What does that mean?"

"They say that Anna Hallworth died from a broken heart. She used to sit there, every day, waiting for her husband to return. He had gone out on a fishing vessel and a wicked storm capsized the ship and killed all on board. They say Anna could never accept that news and sat there every day, believing he would still come home to her."

"She died? When did she die?" my heart skipped a

beat.

"Oh, about fifteen years ago. Some people say at night, if you listen very carefully, you can still hear her sobbing."

MISTY MCDONNELL AND THE EXPERIMENTAL TREATMENT

The doctor was wearing his serious face today and Misty knew that was not good. She guessed that in his mind, he was wearing his poker face, which would be impossible to read. But when the usually jovial doctor was not smiling, that gave it all away.

"I am afraid I don't have good news, Misty. I am sorry."

Misty sighed. It was not like it wasn't expected anyway. "How long do I have?"

The doctor fidgeted with a pen and found it difficult to look the older woman in the eyes. He hated this part of his job the most. "A month. Maybe two, if I had to guess."

"Well, it's not really a surprise, is it?"

"Misty, I am sorry, we have tried everything. I just

wish we…"

"It's alright," she cut him off. "I understand. I know you have done all that you could. That's just life. And I am old."

Misty McDonnell was eighty-six years old. She felt fortunate that her sight and hearing had stuck with her for all these years but the disease had finally claimed her. She had spent the last six months of her life bed-ridden and requiring aid for even the smallest of tasks. The Fairbrooke senior's home in the upper-east side of the Big City is where she now called home. There were certainly worse places that one could live but she disliked it here all the same. She viewed it as just a place where people came to die. Almost everyone around her complained of phantom aches and pains. They were all positive the end was near, though, the doctors never found anything wrong with them. Misty only wished she had phantom problems; hers were all too real.

Later that evening, after receiving her most terrible news, the other reason she hated living in this home walked into her room.

"I hear you won't be with us for very much longer. It's about time," said the male nurse.

Misty frowned. "I thought you didn't work on Saturdays, Kevin."

"I don't, it's Friday. Your old brain has stopped working again. Want me to give it a shake?"

"Friday?" Misty looked up to the clock on the wall. "Oh, I almost forgot. Quick, turn on the radio. It's almost time for Detective Darke."

Since the disease had stolen the strength from her body and she could no longer walk, the only enjoyment

Misty got was from her radio programs. Detective Darke was her absolute favorite. He was such a clever detective and each week he had to solve the most bizarre crimes. It saddened her to think that soon she would not be able follow the exploits of Detective Darke and the wild adventures of Jungle Johnny.

"I am afraid the radio doesn't work."

"Don't be absurd. It was working just fine yesterday."

"That was yesterday. Today it's not working."

"You never even tried it."

"There was a note from another staff member. Said it wasn't working."

Misty was not a hateful person but she hated Kevin. He was a miserable wretch who took great joy in tormenting her, and the other seniors, she imagined. She was fearful of mentioning it to anyone else in case it just made the situation worse. Kevin had even said as much on several occasions. Many of the other nurses were quite rude as well but Kevin was the worst of them all.

"What's for dinner? I am hungry," Misty asked, after giving up on pressing the issue of the radio.

"Here, have some crackers."

Kevin threw a small package of crackers at the older woman before leaving the room. Fortunately, the crackers did land on top of her, within reach. She fumed inside, knowing that Detective Darke was about to start and that horrible man refused to turn the radio on for her. For a moment, she even considered crawling to the radio and turning it on herself, but quickly dismissed that notion. The program would probably be over by the time she made it that far. And it was no use ringing the bell for assistance since Kevin would be the only one to respond.

Misty sighed and ate her crackers, then attempted to get some sleep.

Days later, when Kevin was off work, one of the other nurses turned on the radio. Of course, there was nothing wrong with it and it worked just fine. That just made Misty all the more angrier. But at least she was able to listen to the Jungle Johnny program that evening. It was a thrilling episode with its usual cliff-hanger ending that left the listeners craving to know what would happen next. Johnny was alone in the jungle and surrounded by savage apes. How could he possibly escape this time, she wondered.

Sadness overcame Misty once again. She did not have any family left alive and her friends were few, but she counted Jungle Johnny and Detective Darke as part of her family. Life inside Fairbrooke was not great, but she so thoroughly enjoyed her radio programs that she found she was most distressed about leaving this world and never hearing them again. The joy those shows brought her, outweighed her loneliness.

The next few weeks that passed with Kevin on duty were miserable. Misty learned a valuable trick, though, she had the morning nurse leave the radio on all day and then Kevin could not claim it was broken when he came in. That did not prevent him from tormenting her in other ways but at least she did not miss her programs.

One somber afternoon, Doctor Whethers paid Misty a visit. He had not seen her since delivering her the bad news.

"How are we holding up?" he asked.

"This waiting to die is horrible," she replied.

"I can only imagine. Aside from that, how are you

feeling?"

"Weak. Just very weak."

"No pain?"

"Not yet, no."

"That's good, then."

"Doctor, I am not ready to die. My life has become miserable but the thought of being without Detective Darke and Jungle Johnny pains me the most. I so enjoy listening to those programs. I don't have any family left but I feel as though they are my family."

"I apologize if this question sounds a tad inappropriate, but do you have much money in savings?"

"Well, I do have a tidy sum left but I have not yet written a will. I know I can't take the money with me but I haven't yet decided what to do with it. Why do you ask?"

"I was just curious. I was reading something the other day that perhaps you might find interesting."

"Oh?"

The doctor closed the door to her room and pulled a chair up next to her bed. Misty had been fortunate to get her own room and have the privacy it afforded. She could not imagine what the doctor had to say, while exercising such caution. He even lowered his voice as he explained.

"A colleague of mine had suggested I read something quite recently. This is not widely known, as it is being kept only within certain circles."

"Yes?" Misty sat up, fully intrigued.

"Well, in Eastern Europe, apparently, a small group of doctors have been working on an experimental treatment for the disease. For many terminal ailments, actually."

"Experimental treatment? To what end?"

"From what I have read, they can prolong life and improve upon the quality of life. They claim to have achieved success so far with a few patients."

"Are you saying they have found a cure for the disease?"

"Something like that. They are not calling it a cure, just yet, but essentially it would be the same thing."

"Are they bringing this treatment here? Will it be available in the Big City?"

"I am afraid not. They are closely guarding their techniques. They are quite secretive about the details but boast success with it. They also charge a large sum to those seeking this treatment."

"So, it is of little use to me here, then."

"Well, not quite so. That is why I inquired about your financial situation. As you said, you cannot take the money with you after…well, after everything. And if you have no family you wish to leave the money with, then it may be possible to take a gamble."

"A gamble?"

"Yes. If you have nothing to left to lose, and you possess the necessary funds, you could utilize that money for the flight over there and the treatment. I say gamble because I have not seen the results of this treatment, firsthand, so I cannot say whether it really works or not. I can only go by what I have read, though, the source is reliable."

"How much would this be?"

"It's a lot. How about I write the sum down for you, along with a phone number and other contact information, and just leave it here on your nightstand. Look it over and give it some thought. I wish I could have been more help to you, Misty, I am sorry."

The doctor scribbled down the information he promised and left the piece of paper on the nightstand, within reach. He smiled at Misty and left her alone. She spent the next few hours mulling over the doctor's words before picking up the piece of paper. It was a considerable amount they were asking but could you really put a price on life? Misty would not have been so keen to extend her bed-ridden life but they were claiming to improve the quality of life and not just prolong it. Perhaps it would be possible to live on her own again and leave Fairbrooke. As hefty a fee as it was, Misty did have enough money saved to cover the cost of the treatment and a flight, with some left over. There would not be much left but she was sure she could manage something if the treatment was successful. If it was not successful, then it would not really matter to her anyway.

The following day, it was as though Misty was not present at all. Nurses came and went and she paid them little heed, so lost in thought was she. It was not until much later, that she noticed she had been oblivious to the radio and missed the Ollie Organ show. Ollie was a brilliant accordion player and always brought on fantastic musical guests. As Misty awoke from her deep thoughts, she caught Ollie Organ just as he was signing off for the evening.

She looked to the clock and could not believe she had spent the entire day inside her mind, working out all the pros and cons of this possible treatment. She was not even sure what the treatment entailed. Would it be painful? Was it a lengthy procedure? Had there been many failures thus far? So many questions swirled about her head.

Misty had made up her mind during Kevin's next shift. He had brought her soup for her dinner and purposely spilled it all over her and left her like that for the rest of the evening. She figured she was dying anyway, so why not take the trip, regardless. If the treatment failed, then at least she would have escaped Kevin and could die someplace else with some relative peace. Surely, that alone was worth every cent of the costly endeavor.

In the morning, Misty asked one of the more pleasant nurses to bring her to one of the sitting rooms so she could look out the window. She strategically requested her wheelchair to be placed within reach of the phone in that room. Once the nurse had left, and once she was sure that the few other folk in the room were preoccupied with conversation, she picked up the phone and dialed the number the doctor had left her.

A kind man answered her call and was pleased to hear from her. He had a thick Eastern European accent but spoke English very well. Misty explained her situation and how she had obtained the number. The man, who identified himself as Victor, was quite helpful and related to her all the steps that would be required, were she to proceed seriously with this treatment. She attempted to get details of the treatment, itself, without much luck. Victor was vague when it came to the procedure but assured her that it had been perfected and would be successful. He guaranteed her an immense improvement on the quality of her life and the disease would hinder her no more.

The man suggested she take some time to give it further thought but Misty's mind was made. She informed him that more time was unnecessary and she was ready to proceed with whatever needed to be done. A second phone call was required the next day, as Misty had to get her banking information in order. The considerable fee for the treatment included the flight and chauffeur service from Fairbrooke.

Victor requested that the full amount of the cost be wired to him before any plans could be made. Misty was hesitant at first, wondering if this was some scheme to swindle seniors out of money, but went ahead with it anyway. She reminded herself that she was dying so nothing really mattered. The disease would claim her whether she had money left in the bank or not.

Two long days went by, as Misty waited impatiently to hear any news from Victor. At least she found a pleasant distraction with Detective Darke on the radio, well, that is until Kevin arrived and unplugged it.

"What do you think you are doing? I was listening to that."

"Sorry, too many complaints about the noise."

"The noise? It wasn't loud at all. And besides, Mrs. Heinrichs and Mrs. Florence can't even hear."

"Yeah, well, too many complaints. Nothing I can do about it."

"You plug that in right…"

"Ah, hello? Ms. McDonnell?"

Their conversation was interrupted by the arrival of two men dressed in dark suits.

"Visiting hours are over," Kevin stated.

"Yes, I am Ms. McDonnell," Misty replied, ignoring Kevin. "Who are you both?"

"We work for Victor. It is time, Ms. McDonnell."

"Time? As in right now?"

"Yes. We can gather up any belongings you would

like to take. Your flight leaves in two hours and we will be transporting you to the airport."

"Leaving? What is this nonsense?" Kevin demanded to know. "You know you are not allowed to go anywhere at this time. You have not gotten any approvals from the office staff."

"Kevin, go to hell," Misty smiled ear to ear; that felt wonderful.

"We will see about this," he said, storming out of the room.

"Pay him no mind. I don't own much. Just a handful of clothes from the closet over there and a few knick-knacks from my drawer. I wasn't expecting things to move so quickly."

"Your money transfer went through so Victor did not want to waste any time. We were told to retrieve you. Is this an inconvenient time?"

"No, no, not at all. Time is something I don't have a lot of, so the quicker the better."

Butterflies danced about in Misty's stomach as she watched the two men pack up her meager belongings into two small suitcases she had stored away. It was happening so fast but it was for the better, she kept reminding herself.

They avoided Kevin and the other staff as Misty was wheeled out to a waiting limousine. She had never been in such a fancy car in her entire life. The two men were very gentle and patient as they helped her get inside. It was not until Fairbrooke was far behind them, that Misty thought she should have left a note for Doctor Whethers. A thank-you letter or at least a good-bye. She could very well die at her appointed destination and nobody would ever know where she had gone. Oh well, she thought, she had bigger concerns now.

Then it dawned on her that she did not even know where she was going. "Pardon me, gentlemen, but where is it exactly that I will be going to?"

"Far from here," one of them answered.

"Yes, but where exactly? Victor was never clear about that."

"Eastern Europe."

"I figured that. Whereabouts?"

"We honestly don't know, ma'am. We just take you to the airport."

Misty remained quiet the rest of the way, just enjoying the drive and getting what could very well be her last look at the Big City. She was quite surprised that the limo brought her straight to a runway with a small private plane.

"Wow, my own private plane?"

"All part of the fee you paid."

The two men helped get her settled onto the plane and introduced her to the captain and a woman who would see to her needs during the flight. They wished her a safe trip and the plane was in the air in no time at all. Misty tried to elicit more information out of the female crewmember but she was as much in the dark about everything as the other two men. She knew nothing else about what was going on except to make Misty comfortable during the fifteen-hour flight.

Misty hoped she could just sleep most of the way but sleep would not come to her. Her mind was working on overdrive as the reality of this bizarre situation was kicking in. She did not know where she was going. She did not know the people she would be meeting. She would be undergoing some secret experimental treatment to rid herself of her disease. She had every right to be terrified and the closer they got to their destination, that immense feeling of nervousness grew tenfold.

The flight passed without incident and she was soon sitting in the back of a small car. The driver was an extremely pale young man who appeared emaciated. She wondered if he had the disease as well but withheld her questions as he was not the friendliest of fellows. He spoke not a word and focused solely on the winding road ahead of him.

He would not even tell her what country it was that she had landed in. The landscape was beautiful, though, wherever she was. Forests of tall green trees. Distant mountains in every direction she turned. She did her best to focus on the scenery and think less about her creepy escort. It was best for her not to second-guess her decision as it was far too late for that now. Her body was getting weaker by the day and the sand in her hourglass would soon run out.

With the combination of the long flight, her weakening body, and the jostling of the car, sleep finally claimed Misty. When her eyes had finally reopened, it was dark outside and the car pulled into a long, gated-driveway, which ended in front of a magnificent-looking mansion. It was all made of stone and had the feel of a castle, only on a smaller scale. Green ivy creeped its way all over the house, threatening to engulf it entirely.

Misty's initial thought was that this looked nothing like a hospital, or a senior's home, for that matter.

"Driver, are you sure you have the right place? I am here in search of a medical procedure."

The driver said nothing and exited the car, retrieving

Misty's suitcases from the trunk. Another man, as equally pale and as equally unnerving, came and helped Misty out of the car and into her wheelchair. Without a word, that man brought her to the beautifully-carved, wooden front door. Two stone gargoyles clung to the wall on each side of the door, leering down at her.

She was about to ask the strange man if they would need to knock, when the door opened. Out stepped a tall and gaunt middle-aged man. His salt and pepper hair was combed perfectly back and his pale complexion matched that of the other two men. He was very well-dressed and obviously wealthy.

"Misty McDonnell, it is a pleasure to finally make your acquaintance," he said in a familiar voice. "I am Victor. I trust that your journey was uneventful?"

"Yes, yes, it was fine, if not a touch too long."

"Yes, it is quite a distance from the Big City to here."

"Where is here?"

"Why don't we bring you inside, away from this chill night air. I am sure you have many questions and we can begin your treatment straightaway."

"Do you really think you can cure me of the disease?"

"My dear, I guarantee it."

*　　*　　*　　*

The sound of a radio from down the hall grabbed Kevin's attention. Further investigation revealed that it was coming from Misty McDonnell's old room. Curious, Kevin entered the room and gasped.

"What are you doing here? I thought you left? How did you get back in here?"

Misty lay in her bed, buddled up with a thick blanket, while listening to Detective Darke on the radio. It was a particularly interesting episode and she grew upset that Kevin had interrupted. She mouthed a reply but no words came out. She appeared paler than he had previously remembered.

"What are you saying? I can't hear you. Explain yourself, you old witch."

Again, she attempted to answer but it only came out as a faint whisper. Frustrated, Kevin stood beside her bed and leaned over.

"What are you trying to say?"

Misty smiled and spoke in a perfectly calm voice. "I said, shut up. You are interrupting Detective Darke."

"What did you just say?" Kevin roared. "You miserable old....GACK!"

Misty rose from her bed and grabbed Kevin by the throat, cutting off his sentence. His eyes bulged from his head in shock. Misty stood and held Kevin off the floor with one hand, then threw him against the wall with such force, that he nearly crashed straight through.

Before he could even think to cry out for help, Misty hoisted him from the floor as if he weighed nothing at all. She smiled at him, revealing razor-sharp fangs, and then sunk those fangs deep into Kevin's throat. Misty drank his body clean of blood and then cast it aside.

She sat on the edge of her bed until Detective Darke had solved this week's murder. With the program over, Misty exited through the room's window and never returned to Fairbrooke again.

SNAKE OIL

It was an oppressively hot afternoon and Sheriff Ward sat outside his office, fanning himself in a poor attempt to cool off. He had made a tactical retreat from the office, as he had found it hotter inside than it was out. The main thoroughfare was nearly devoid of townsfolk this day and the Sheriff chalked it up to the heat. It was normally hot this time of year but today was extremely so. At least the heat kept most people indoors, out of the sun, and not out and about causing trouble. It would be a lazy day, or so he thought.

"Sheriff! Sheriff!" a familiar voice shouted from down the road.

Sheriff Ward turned to regard Doctor Tuttle shuffling his way through the dusty street. He leaped to his feet, as the old doctor rarely moved that fast unless there was an emergency.

"What is it, Doc? Someone hurt?" he asked, after

meeting the other man in the middle of the thoroughfare.

The doctor motioned for him to wait a moment while he caught his breath.

"Well, spit it out, Doc. What happened?"

"A stranger in town…"

"Yes, and?"

"He is out past Miller's Grocery Store…"

"Alright, yes, and what has he done? Come on, Doc."

"Well…he…he is out there peddling snake oil."

The Sheriff relaxed and shook his head. "Snake oil? You come running down the street like the devil is behind you because some stranger is selling snake oil? Gosh darnit, Doc! I thought someone got shot or robbed."

"Well, they are being robbed. A mob of folk are over there right now buying up all that rubbish."

"If someone is not holding a gun to their fool heads to make them buy it, then no, Doc, they ain't being robbed, they are just plum stupid."

"It is illegal all the same! He is claiming his tonics can heal all sorts of ailments."

"Yeah, it's still fraud."

"What are you going to do about it? Huh?"

"Now, you just simmer down. I'll head over there and take a look-see for myself."

"I am sorry I have to take you away from your nap over there in front of your office."

"I wasn't napping. And you better get yourself out of the sun before you keel over dead and we need to find ourselves a new doctor."

The usually grumpy doctor mumbled something under his breath and shuffled into the closest saloon to get some shade and possibly a drink, since he was there.

Sheriff Ward elected to walk and made the fifteen minute trek out to Miller's Grocery Store. Sure enough, he spotted a large crowd gathered around a wagon in a pasture, just out behind the store. So, it wasn't the heat after all that made the town appear to be dead. Most folk were here, listening to the sales pitch of the tall, white-haired stranger.

The man stood on a stool at the back of his large, enclosed, weather-beaten wagon. On the side of the wagon, written in red paint, was "ALL ELIXIRS – ONE DOLLAR." The back doors were wide open, with many cases of a bottled liquid visible within. The magical elixir. The stranger held a bottle in each hand and addressed the crowd like a carnival barker.

"That's right, folks, it's only one dollar to cure any ailment. I have an elixir for everything. Have a bad back? Sore neck? Trouble walking? You tell me what's wrong and I will fetch the bottle that will fix it."

The Sheriff watched old Andy Anderson hobble his way to the front. Andy owned a farm on the outskirts of town and was thrown from a horse many years ago. He had broken his leg in the fall and it had never healed properly.

"My leg is in constant pain," he told the stranger. "I don't get around as well as I used to."

"Leg pain, you say? Have trouble walking? I have just the thing for you."

The stranger rummaged through the back of the wagon until he produced the bottle that he was looking for. The Sheriff thought the bottle looked exactly like all the rest.

"Here you go, my friend. This elixir is specifically for leg pain. Drink three mouthfuls a day until the bottle is empty and your leg pain will be gone. Why, you will be running around in no time. That'll be one dollar."

Sheriff Ward smirked. He guessed that three mouthfuls a day would take about a week before the bottle was empty. Snake oil salesmen never promised instant results. They needed to get as far away from town as possible before the unfortunate individual realized they had been taken for a fool. In a week's time, this stranger would be clear across the territory, peddling his wares to another group of ignorant folk.

"Alright, who's next? Who needs a cure? Ok, you sir, what exactly is bothering…oh, hello, Sheriff, a pleasure to make your acquaintance."

"Okay, everyone, go on about your business. Show's over. Go on now, get!"

"But, Sheriff, you know how bad my back gets around this time of year, you know that. I was gonna purchase one of these here bottles."

"Not today, you won't. Go on home, Teddy. I know you still owe Mr. Oswald three dollars so it seems to me that you could make better use of the dollar you were about to give this charlatan."

The stranger pressed a hand against his heart. "Charlatan? Now, Sheriff, you wound me. I am here only to help these good folk."

"And you are gonna help them by closing up that wagon of yours. What's your name, stranger?"

"Gabriel."

"Gabriel, what?"

"Why, I never thought to give myself a last name. I just go by Gabriel."

"Where are you from?"

"Far from here."

"Look, I wouldn't keep cracking wise if I were you, I ain't in a good mood today."

"I wasn't causing any trouble. I told you, all I was doing was trying to help these people."

"The folk around here don't have a lot of money. They are decent hard-working folk that can't afford to just go throwing away a whole dollar."

"It's not throwing it away when they are cured of their aches and pains."

"You and I both know your snake oil ain't gonna heal anyone of any aches or pains."

"Snake oil? You insult me again. Why, I will have you know I have been curing folk all over this glorious country."

"How long were you planning on staying here in town?"

"Well, not long. I have to be on my way tomorrow morning. Lotsa sick people need seeing to."

"I am gonna invite you to stay with us for a week."

"A week? Sheriff, I am afraid I really need to be on my way tomorrow."

"I insist."

"Am I under arrest or something?"

"Not yet, you ain't."

"A whole week?"

"Yup. You are gonna hang around here until all those people you sold your elixirs to are finished drinking those bottles. Should be pretty satisfying for you to see all those happy faces from all those cured people. Right?"

"Well, of course it would be but I have to be elsewhere. A week is a long time, Sheriff."

"You can stay at the hotel just over yonder. Their rates are quite reasonable and I imagine that won't be a problem with all the sales you made today already."

"I don't sell my elixirs for profit, I will have you know. The money just covers my expenses and keeps my old mule here fed. I sell these for the pure joy of helping those in need."

"And that's another thing. You won't be selling another bottle for the rest of your stay. Got it?"

"But, Sheriff!"

"Don't you but Sheriff me. No more peddling your snake oil. You hear me? Or you can spend your week in a jail cell instead of the hotel."

The man grumbled while he began packing up his wagon.

"And don't think about skipping town. I am gonna have eyes on you. One week and then you can go."

"Fine."

Sheriff Ward waited around until Gabriel finished packing up and then watched him make his way over to the hotel, tethering his mule just outside. Satisfied that the stranger wasn't going anywhere, anytime soon, the Sheriff returned to his office and went through a pile of wanted posters. He was curious to see if Gabriel's face had decorated any of them. One came close, a wanted murderer from the northern territories, but the nose and eye color were not quite a match. Not enough to warrant suspicion, anyhow. Either way, the Sheriff would dispatch a few men to keep eyes on the stranger and prevent him from leaving town until a week's time had gone by.

The next few days passed lazily until Doc Tuttle burst into the Sheriff's office, startling him.

"I thought you were going to get rid of that snake oil salesman!" he said, in quite a perturbed tone. "Why is he still here in town? You should have either run him out or locked him up."

"Now, Doc, I just can't lock people up for no reason."

"You have a reason. He is a fraud and stealing money from the folk around here."

"Well, it just so happens that I have asked him to stick around for a week. I reckon that's just enough time for people to realize his elixirs don't work. Then I can call him a fraud with proof. But don't you worry, I have told him not to sell any more of those bottles."

"And a fine job of sheriffing you seem to be doing. That weasel is over at Fanny's Saloon peddling his wares again. Got a line going straight out the door, he has."

"What?"

"Go and see for yourself, if your naptime is over. I saw Wilbur Harrison this morning and asked him why he hadn't come to see me about his headache pills. He told me he wouldn't need headache pills anymore. And would you like me to tell you why Wilbur Harrison doesn't think he needs his headache pills anymore?"

"You are gonna tell me anyway."

"Because Wilbur Harrison told me he got an elixir from over at Fanny's and it's gonna cure his headaches for good. That fraud is gonna have people giving up real medicine for his snake oil."

"Alright, alright, I am going over there right now."

"You see to it."

As much as Sheriff Ward wanted to rush over to Fanny's, he took his time, only to anger Doc Tuttle. His own anger level rose, however, when he spotted people lined up out the door of the saloon and onto the street, just as the Doc had described.

"Get out of here, all y'all," he shouted to everyone outside the saloon. "Don't go throwing your hard-earned money away on snake oil. Come on, now, I ain't kidding. Get."

Just then, a young woman came rushing out of the saloon holding a bottle of elixir.

"Madison?" the Sheriff looked at her, bewildered. "You are young and healthy, what are you doing with that bottle?"

"Well, Sheriff, you know my Ma can't see all too well. That nice man in there gave me an elixir that will bring her sight back."

He shook his head. "Is there no end to what you folk will believe?"

Sheriff Ward stormed into the saloon and began pushing people out of the way, shouting at them to go back home or to go back to work. He seethed with anger as he approached the stranger and grabbed the wrist shackles from his belt.

"You are under arrest, Gabriel," he declared.

"Arrest? Whatever for?"

"I told you days ago that you were not to peddle any more of that snake oil while you were in town. You were not to take any more money from these people."

"But, Sheriff, I wasn't selling any of my elixirs."

"Huh? I just caught you red-handed."

"No, I was not selling them. I was giving them away, for free."

"For free?"

"I told you, I am just here to help people and there are so many here in need."

The Sheriff called over Fanny, the saloon's owner. "Is he telling the truth? Did he take money from anyone?"

"No, he didn't, Sheriff. In fact, a few folk were insisting on paying him and he refused to even accept a cent."

"See? I haven't committed any crimes here. I didn't sell any, just like you told me."

"You get back to the hotel and take all this snake oil with you. I don't want you selling it and I don't want you giving any of it away. You are filling folk's heads with your fool ideas of being cured."

"But, Sheriff."

"No buts. This is your last warning."

For the next several days, Doc Tuttle was relentless and was a constant thorn in the Sheriff's side. He wanted Gabriel out of town, something fierce. Sheriff Ward was finally beginning to understand why. The folk in town were turning to the stranger to fix their various problems and were ignoring the Doc, altogether. Business had dropped for almost a week now. The doctor made money from visits and prescribing medicine. The Sheriff figured that Doc Tuttle dealt in a little bit of snake oil himself and now he had some competition.

The week was nearly up when the peace and quiet of one afternoon was interrupted by frantic shouting.

"Murder! Murder! Oh dear Lord, Murder!"

Sheriff Ward found Virginia Blake, sobbing in the street with folk beginning to gather around.

"Sheriff, there has been a murder!" she proclaimed, between sobs.

"Who was murdered, Virginia?"

"Clarence. Oh dear Lord, he murdered Clarence."

Clarence was Virginia's husband and had been bed-ridden and knocking on death's door for months. The Sheriff was surprised that Clarence had even lasted this long.

"Who murdered him, Virginia? How did it happen?"

"That stranger," she continued to weep. "I sought him out for his help and he poisoned my husband, Sheriff. He murdered poor Clarence."

"I saw the stranger in the hotel lobby just moments ago, Sheriff," a man said.

"Do you need any help?" another asked. "Need us to help you string him up?"

"Nobody is stringing anyone up, just yet. You men help Virginia here over to my office. I will see to the stranger."

As suggested, Gabriel was found sitting on a sofa in the hotel lobby, sipping some tea. Concern was written on his face as he looked up to regard the arrival of Sheriff Ward.

"Afternoon, Sheriff. Is there a problem?"

"Virginia Blake is accusing you of murder. She says you poisoned her husband."

"That is simply not true. That woman asked me if I had an elixir to help her husband."

"You were told not give anyone else that snake oil of yours," the Sheriff growled.

"She was so desperate for help, so I went with her. Have you seen her husband lately?"

"I have."

"Then you know how badly off he was. There was

nothing I could do to help. I did not have an elixir that could fix him but I did have one that could ease his suffering."

"So you admit you poisoned him?"

"No! I didn't say that. I gave him an elixir for the pain, that's all. He died all on his own."

"So, he drank some of your snake oil and then died, shortly thereafter."

"He would have died anyway. I merely took his pain away, as per his own request."

"You are under arrest. Come with me."

"I didn't murder that man! I helped him!"

"Let's go. You have some new accommodations."

A mob had now gathered around the Sheriff's office as he approached with his prisoner. Doc Tuttle was there and apparently had been prodding the group into a frenzy.

"Murderer!" they shouted. "Hang him!"

After Gabriel was securely locked away in a cell and Virginia was given a cup of tea and a place to sit and rest, Doc Tuttle pulled Sheriff Ward out the back door.

"I warned you about him. Now you have a murder on your hands."

"Doc, you and I both know that Clarence could have gone any day now."

"Nonsense. I had kept him alive this long with real medicine. He could have gotten better."

"I highly doubt that."

"It doesn't matter what you doubt, you have to look at the facts. That man gave Clarence a drink of his elixir and Clarence died right after. That was poisoning. That was murder."

Sheriff Ward could not deny those facts but it did not

make his job any easier. Gabriel continued to plead his innocence and that he was only here to help people. The Sheriff delayed any type of trial until the week had passed, hoping to gather further evidence. A day after the week's deadline he had given the stranger had come and gone, a mob, once again, gathered outside the office, shouting. Doc Tuttle, of course, was among them, but a few of the others surprised the Sheriff.

"Andy? You seem to be walking just fine. Mrs. Rosewood? You can see?"

"The pain in my leg is gone," Andy replied.

"I can see again," Madison's mother added.

"So, the elixirs worked? Why are you here, then?"

"Witchcraft!" shouted Doc Tuttle. "How long before these so-called healed folk just drop dead like poor Clarence did? Witchcraft, I tell ya!"

"I have been poisoned, Sheriff," said Rory Tate. "I don't have any ache or pain left in my body. It's gone completely numb from that poison, I just know it. I wanna see that man hang before I meet my end."

"Hang him!" someone else yelled.

"Hang him, now!" a few others joined in.

"You all just simmer down. There is gonna be no hangings until there is a proper trial."

"How many more folk are going to be poisoned before that time, Sheriff?" Doc Tuttle shouted. "Witchcraft! He could cast some terrible spells from his cell. Perhaps he should be burned like a witch!"

"Burn him! Burn him!" people chanted, as they began to swarm toward the front door.

Sheriff Ward had lost control and retreated into the office, locking the door behind him. Fists pounded on the door, while the frenzied townsfolk demanded instant justice. And instant justice for what, the Sheriff had to wonder. Somehow, and quite miraculously, people had been cured of their ailments after drinking Gabriel's elixirs. He needed answers and quickly.

"Your elixirs actually worked," the Sheriff stated, standing in front of Gabriel's cell.

"Just as I said they would."

"But...how? How is that possible?"

"Why should it matter, how? They work and that is the important thing."

"It matters because there is a mob of folk out there accusing you of witchcraft."

Gabriel shook his head in disbelief. "So, I have helped people. I have cured them of their maladies and now they are angry with me? They are healed, permanently."

"Folk become easily spooked by things they can't explain. You have done things that nobody else could achieve. They are scared and are looking for answers."

"Sheriff!" a voice was heard shouting from outside. "If you don't bring that stranger out here right now, we are gonna break this door down."

"What is it that they want?" Gabriel asked.

"They want to see you hang."

"But...I told you, I helped them. All I wanted to do was help them."

"And I told you, they are scared of things that cannot be explained. Would you care to explain to me how you can create elixirs that heal?"

Gabriel hung his head in defeat and sorrow. He let out a loud sigh before speaking again.

"I can see that this world is not yet ready for explanations, or help, for that matter."

"Huh? This world?"

"Humans are so mistrusting and so quick to anger. If you do not understand something, your first instinct is violence. I have done nothing more than to show kindness and heal those people in need, and now those same people wish to see me dead? As I said, this world is not ready. Perhaps myself, or others like me, will return here one day. Or, perhaps not. Maybe humans will never be ready. Farewell, Sheriff, I will leave you to your mob."

Sheriff Ward took a step back and shielded his eyes as a blinding, golden light, emanated from the stranger. Once the Sheriff was able to safely open his eyes again, he gasped. Gabriel still resembled Gabriel, but was outlined with a glowing, silvery radiance, and appeared almost translucent. Magnificent white wings sprouted from his back. The stranger nodded to the Sheriff before passing straight though the cell wall, like a ghost, and disappearing into the sky above.

Sheriff Ward stood frozen in place like a statue. He blinked his eyes several times and attempted to process what he had just witnessed. As the front door to his office threatened to burst open, from the repeated kicks of the angry mob, the man had to wonder how he would explain the missing prisoner.

SIR STEELHEART

I rode atop my muscled steed, along a lonely dark road. I was flanked on both sides by a murky swamp and the long weeping limbs of trees had blotted out most of the sunlight. I had grown somewhat accustomed to the stench by this point but the biting swamp flies threatened to push me over the edge of madness.

Fortunately, my horse, Ned, paid the flies no heed. Ned was as fine a horse as any; strong and fast and black as coal. I knew that Ned was his name and I knew that he was my horse, only I could not recall naming him or how he even came into my possession.

In fact, I was having trouble remembering anything of late. I was not sure why I was even on this road that cut through this accursed swamp. And where had I been before this? I could not recall. My memory was just a swirl of grey fog. Try and try as I might, I could remember nothing.

I shook my head in frustration and spurred Ned on to move a little more quickly. The sooner we exited this swamp the better. I knew of the ever-present dangers around me and kept my hand close to the hilt of my sword. Remaining in this swamp after the sun had disappeared was not a good idea at all. Trolls and things much worse than trolls prowled the swamps at night in these lands.

An hour or so later, Ned and I were granted a reprieve as the swamp gave way to an empty field of brownish grass. Mountains loomed like dark shadows in the distance and the lights from some kind of settlement could be seen near the base of the closest mountain. The sun had nearly disappeared, but I guessed that I could reach the settlement before it got too late, and kept Ned running at a steady pace.

It was clearly a town up ahead. It was protected by a high wall and I observed smoke rising from several chimneys within. With luck, I could find an inn to rest my weary bones and possibly get some answers as to my whereabouts.

I misjudged the distance of the town and darkness fell before reaching its gates. Two sentries armed with loaded crossbows looked down upon me from their stations along the wall.

"Who goes there?" one of them shouted.

"I am Sir Steelheart and I am in search of an inn."

"From where have you come?"

"I-I…don't know," I admitted.

"Drunk, already?"

"No. I am just having trouble with my memory, I apologize."

"Do you work for him?"

"I am sorry, work for who?"

"Darvaan, that sorcerous dog."

"No, I have never even heard that name before."

"Alright, we will open the gates but we are going to be keeping an eye on you. Do not attempt anything foolish."

"I wouldn't think of it. I need some cold ale and a place to rest my bones."

The front gates creaked open and another guard holding a spear motioned me in.

"You can leave your horse at the stables on your left, and that large building you see over there, that's the Flameguard Inn. You can get a drink and a meal and a small room there."

"My thanks."

I left Ned at the stables as instructed and made my way over to the inn. I could hear music from outside and was greeted to a busy taproom, bustling with activity, when I entered through the front door. A fair-sized crowd had assembled this night, and was being treated to entertainment provided by a bard, who was singing and playing the lute. Coins were scattered all over the floor around him, due to the intoxicated patrons who were unable to toss the coins into the man's hat that sat in front of him. Each time a new coin was tossed, the bard gave a slight nod without breaking a note from his song.

Several stools were vacant near the bar so I decided to choose one and sit myself down. I was dying to get out of my armor but quenching my thirst was my highest priority.

"A flagon of ale, please," I requested, once the

bearded man behind the bar had noticed me.

He was a large man with a grubby apron. He gave me a nod and fulfilled a few other orders before coming back my way and sliding over my drink.

"There you go, stranger. Five silver."

I took out six silver coins and deposited them onto the bar. I wore a pouch on my belt filled with gold and silver coins, though, for the life of me, I could not recall where I had earned them.

"Pardon me, my good man," I said to the barkeep, after downing my first mouthful of that much-needed drink. "What town is this?"

"Brockton. Not from around here, huh?"

"Ah, no, I am not."

"Well, welcome to Brockton, then. I am Bryan and I manage this establishment. What's your name, stranger?"

"Sir Steelheart."

"A Sir? You are one of the King's knights?"

"Ah, I am not sure."

"Eh? You have a title."

"This is true, but my memory is failing me of late."

In truth, I had no memory of where I had received that title, I just knew that it was indeed my name.

"Oh. I was hoping that you had been sent to save us."

"Save you from what?"

"That evil sorcerer that has been a plague upon these lands."

"Darvaan?"

"Ah, so you have heard of him?"

"Well, not really. One of the guards at the front gate had mentioned the name. What is the trouble?"

"That foul wizard has destroyed our crops and cursed our livestock in demand of gold. Each time he is paid, he grows greedier and demands even more the next time. The town cannot keep up with his demands, so he punishes us ever more."

"I see many capable-looking men in this room, as well as guards along the wall, why has nobody attempted to rid the world of this sorcerer?"

"Some have tried."

"And?"

"They were never seen again. The wizard is powerful."

I felt an anger boiling inside me. I did not know the folk in this town and yet I felt for them. Nobody should have to live under such tyranny. I was willing to bet these were all decent folk just struggling during the best of times.

"Where can this Darvaan be found?" I asked.

"He lives in a tower within the swamp, just south of here."

"Yes, I know that swamp all too well and was looking forward to never returning there."

"What are you saying? You will seek out this devil?"

"I cannot sit idly by while this is going on. Someone needs to put a stop to him. I feel as though that is why I am here."

"You are mad to go alone, Sir Steelheart. Nobody would fault you for leaving here and never coming back."

"I will seek out this tyrant and a put an end to your town's suffering, if I am able."

"Rest the night, at least. Your room and a warm meal will be on the house. It's the least I can do."

I accepted the barkeep's offer and after a delicious

meal, and another flagon of ale, I retired to a quiet room on the second floor of the inn. It was situated at the far end of the building. Far enough that I could no longer hear the songs of the bard or the voices of the other patrons. I lay in bed pondering my situation.

Again, I felt this overwhelming feeling that it was my duty to help these people whom I did not know. I felt that something had guided me to this town for this very reason. But what? And how? The barkeep mentioned a king, but I could not recall any king. I knew for certain that my name was indeed, Sir Steelheart, and that name did seem to belong to someone who would have been a knight in the employ of a king. I wish I knew what was going on. I wish I knew why I could not remember anything.

I tossed and turned and found little sleep that night. Strangely, though, I found that I was not worried about the prospect of facing some evil sorcerer who dwelled in that dreadful swamp. I felt confident that I could deal with this man when I found him. I was either extremely brave or extremely foolish, and I could not, at this point, say which.

That morning, I donned my armor, strapped on my sword, and exited the inn to a chorus of cheers from a gathered crowd. It appeared the barkeep had spread the word about my impending mission.

"May the gods bless you."

"Please save us."

"A thousand thank yous, Sir Steelheart."

"All hail, Sir Steelheart!"

The streets were thick with people, all witnessing my departure. I will admit it emboldened me even further. A young boy had already gotten a well-fed Ned ready for me, and had him waiting at the front gates. I mounted my faithful steed and gave one last wave to the townsfolk, before setting off through the gates.

As I traveled back the way I had come, back toward the swamp, I first considered the size of the swamp, and wondered where I would even begin my search. I had never noticed any tower from the main road and thought I could spend hours, or even days, in search of the sorcerer's home. But an odd feeling struck me. I felt as though I knew where to begin my search. It was as if that strange invisible force that had brought me to that town, was now guiding me in the right direction.

Long before reaching the swamp, I veered off the main road and took an alternate route. Within an hour's time, I reached that most unpleasant bog and noticed a pathway leading into its depths. It appeared seldom-trodden, but was definitely a path, all the same. I am not sure how I knew just where to locate this spot but perhaps the gods were guiding me on this noble quest.

The ground was uneven and fairly muddy, so I made the decision to leave Ned in the field and continue on foot. I did not bother to tether him to any tree, as I knew that Ned would wait for me to return.

Concern crept back into my mind, while I trudged through that horrendous landscape; concern over my failing memory. Why could I remember nothing from before the moment I found myself riding through this swamp the previous day? I have lived a life that eludes my recalling, no matter how hard I try. I know that I have lived for thirty-five years and yet I am not even sure as to how I know that. Where have I been for all that time? Why am I here now?

The harder I thought about it, the more frustrated it made me feel. I shook my head and decided to concentrate solely on the job before me. If Darvaan was indeed some terrible sorcerer, then I would need all my wits about me.

I hacked at rotten vines that almost appeared to reach for me, while doing my best not to inhale too much of the foul stench that permeated the air in this place. Swamps were not the loveliest of places to begin with but this particular one had to be among the worst. The smell of death and decay was almost unnatural and I was willing to wager it had something to do with this sorcerer. An awful necromancer would be my guess.

I worried at times, when I sunk nearly knee-deep into thick mud, but still I continued on, undaunted. After an hour into my torturous trek, the trees and reaching vines gave way to a small clearing. I was rewarded with the sight of a tall stone tower that rose straight out of the muck. The brick was as black as night. One single window was visible high up the tower.

I wondered if the sorcerer was aware of my approach, as their kind was apt to such knowledge. I frowned as the double doors to the tower suddenly flew open and a maniacal laugh confirmed my thought.

A black-robed man appeared in the doorway, where one did not exist a moment before. He held a long black staff in one skeletal hand. The hood of his robe concealed his face in darkness but two glowing red eyes were visible from within. A chill ran down my spine. I had found the sorcerer. He cackled and spoke with a raspy voice.

"So, Sir Steelheart, you come here thinking that..."

"How do you know my name?" I cut him off.

My question appeared to have given the sorcerer

pause. He stood in silence for a moment before speaking again.

"I will admit that I do not know how I know your name, but only that I do. You are Sir Steelheart, a meddlesome do-gooder who thinks he can just walk in here and save those pathetic townsfolk."

"You will leave those people alone from this day forward and you will leave these lands and never return. This deal I give you in exchange for your life."

Darvaan began that maniacal laugh once more and threw back the hood of his robe to reveal the head of a skull. "I abandoned my life long ago, foolish knight."

"I can destroy you all the same," I pronounced, as I drew my gleaming sword.

"You can try."

The sorcerer held his staff aloft and chanted in some unknown language. Before I could charge toward him, the muddied ground around me erupted, and several decayed corpses began to climb their way out.

"By all the gods," I whispered.

The blade of my sword was now glowing with a bluish hue and I did not hesitate in attacking the undead abominations. My weapon sliced through rotted flesh and bone as if it was mere butter. As I hacked three of the creatures to pieces, another three rose up from the ground. They scratched and clawed and bit at me, but could not penetrate my armor.

I sent ten of them back to their boggy graves before turning my attention, once again, to the sorcerer.

"Impressive indeed, Sir Foolheart," he taunted me. "But now you will die and become another of the undead guardians of my home."

He pointed a bony finger toward me and a bolt of black energy flew forth. I held up my sword, confidently, and stood my ground. The bolt of deadly magical energy struck the blade of my sword and was immediately absorbed into the weapon.

"My magical blade can absorb your spells, foul wizard. Now, I will run you through."

I charged the evil thing before me and he shouted, "NO!"

I raised my sword and brought it down with a chopping motion. Darvaan held his staff out in a feeble attempt to block my strike. My blade cut through his staff with a shower of blue sparks and bit into a bony shoulder. The sorcerer cursed and fell to the ground, just inside the doorway to the tower.

I lifted my sword for a final strike and Darvaan vanished. His laugh now echoed from everywhere around me. It did not come from one place in particular but from everywhere all at once.

"You have defeated me this time, Sir Foolheart, but this is not over. One day, I will return and I will make you pay for this."

His laughter faded into the distance and I knew the sorcerer was gone. For now. I was certain that he would indeed return and we would battle again. Somehow, I knew that he and I were destined to be enemies forever, and would have many more spectacular battles throughout the coming years.

I made the journey back to the field where I had left Ned and there he stood, patiently waiting for me, as I had known he would. I returned to the town of Brockton and was hailed as a hero during two days of celebration. I allowed myself some enjoyment, but in the back of my mind, I knew I needed to remain vigilant. I knew that round two between Darvaan and I was not far off, and I needed to be ready.

*   *   *   *

"Michael? What are you doing in here, I have been calling you for five minutes? What is this you are working on? The Adventures of Sir Steelheart: Part One - The Sorcerer in the Swamp. Well, you certainly do have quite the imagination. I am happy to see that you are making good use of those pencil crayons we bought from that really strange woman at the garage sale. Anyhow, dinner is ready and is getting cold. Now, come down and eat and you can work on your comic book after."

THE FORTUNE TELLER

It was a wonderful summer's day without a cloud in the sky. I navigated my way through the crowded midway, while attempting to finish my ice cream before it melted and dripped all over my hand. I generally did not crave the frosty dessert but had observed some children indulging in the sinful sweets. I found that it was beyond my control to resist in purchasing my own. Mint chocolate chip was my favorite.

The carnival barkers were relentless as I passed the varied tents and game booths.

"Come on, sir, take your chance in the shooting gallery. Three shots for a nickel. Hit two or more ducks and win a prize."

"Right this way, mister. Ten cents to view the hideous lizard man. Half man, half lizard, all terrifying."

"This could be your lucky day. Just get the ball in the basket and you win a prize."

Perhaps a younger version of me might have been interested in playing games or taking a peek at the many oddities hidden away within the tents, but I was focused on finding only one attraction this day. I had already dallied enough by allowing the ice cream vendor to distract me. While I was enjoying the tasty treat, it was an unplanned detour from my course.

I am a writer for The Big City Times newspaper. I write the popular, Skeptical Skeptic column. As the title suggests, I am a profound skeptic and took immense delight in exposing various myths and fraudsters. "Stop the Bunk" was my famous catch phrase. Fortune Tellers were my preferred targets. They tended to irk me the most. Whether they claimed to be speaking with dead spirits returned or simply reading palms, I detested them all the same. Bottom dwellers, I considered them. Preying on the weak minded and foolish.

The Big City Summer Fair lasted the entire summer and lured out all types of charlatans. One in particular had gained my attention. Ms. Nayomi was a fortune teller who set up her own tent, a month past, at the opening of the fair. She had quite the reputation for accurate palm and card readings and I even had a few coworkers who swore she gave them accurate information. They claimed she must have possessed wonderful powers. My colleagues were not unintelligent folk and it continued to baffle me how even normal people were susceptible to the glib tongue of a trickster.

As I finished my ice cream, I spotted Ms. Nayomi's large red tent. Fortune Telling, Five Cents, the sign read. It amazed me that it was such a nominal fee to pay, for a look into your future. Who wouldn't be tempted? But of course, it's a large amount to pay when it's all false.

I had done some extensive investigative work prior to my arrival at the fair. Ms. Nayomi was really Natalie Schwartz, a former scientist with a large company based here in The Big City. The circumstances around her departure from the company were unclear but it appeared as though she may have quit. From scientist to fortune teller, that was an odd transition. Desperate times called for desperate measures, I suppose.

As I approached the tent, two giggling teens emerged from within. Looks of wonder were clearly evident upon their faces.

"I can't believe she knew all that," one girl said to the other.

"Ah, pardon me, girls, but you just had a reading with Ms. Nayomi?"

"Yes we did, both of us."

"And she was accurate, was she?"

"Oh my god, yes!" the brunette exclaimed. "She knew my name and even that tomorrow was my birthday!"

"Have you ever been here before? Seen Ms. Nayomi?"

"Never," the second girl answered. "We don't even live in The Big City. We took the train in from Floral Green, just to come to this fair for the first time."

"I see. Well, thank you both."

The girls walked away discussing their fortunes with excitement. The tent appeared empty of any other victims so I entered. The smell of burning incense immediately assaulted my nostrils. The smell wasn't unpleasant, but I did find it a little overwhelming. The inside of the tent was dimly-lit. There were no windows and only three candles set on the cluttered table in the middle of the reading area.

The table where Ms. Nayomi was seated was covered in a long red tablecloth, where sat decks of cards, a crystal ball, and other various knick-knacks and tools of the trade. The area where I stood was only half the size of the entire tent. The other half of the tent, behind where Ms. Nayomi sat, was curtained-off. A sign was hung stating that entry beyond the curtain was strictly prohibited.

Ms. Nayomi flashed me a welcoming smile. "Please, sir, have a seat."

She looked very much like I imagined she would. She wore a long black gown with large gaudy earrings hanging from both ears. Several chains also hung around her neck and each of her fingers was ornamented with jeweled rings. Fake jewels, of course. Her lipstick was black and matched her black hair, which she wore back in a ponytail. She appeared somewhere in her forties and was mildly attractive. Of course, the whole fortune telling thing lessened a person's look in my eyes, but I suppose if I had spotted her dressed normally, at a dinner party, or perhaps the picture show, she might have caught my fancy.

I did as instructed and took a seat opposite her at the table. I grinned like a foolish child who was here to eat up whatever slop she was about to dish out. I placed my nickel on the table beside her silly crystal ball.

"So, Bradley, are you interested in your future, or are you looking for guidance with your love life? What can I interest you in today?"

I stopped short from blurting out my first reply, as to why a fortune teller was asking me what I was interested in, since she should have already known, but something else caught me off guard.

"You know my name, so obviously you have recognized me."

"I am sorry, no, I have never seen you before."

"Sure you haven't. You must read The Big City Times and recognized my face from my column."

"As strange as it might sound, no, I do not actually read the Times. I get all the information I need, elsewhere."

"Right. So of all the names in the world, you correctly guessed mine? Amazing."

"Well, you have the feel of a Bradley."

That made me laugh. I felt like a Bradley.

"Alright, continue. Tell me my future."

"I sense you came here for other reasons, really, and not to hear about your future. You are somewhat skeptical, aren't you?"

"Somewhat?" I chuckled. "That's putting it mildly. You are clearly familiar with the column I write."

"I have never read it before, I told you. Believe it or not, I have never even read the magazine you wrote for before you joined the Times."

"Ah, I see now. One of my coworkers has given you some background on me in a vain attempt to impress me," I stood up then. "This is pointless. Someone is playing a joke on me. I will find out who."

"Don't you want to get even a small glimpse into your future before leaving?" she asked, as I had turned to exit.

"Not really, but go ahead anyway."

She closed her eyes in some ridiculous gesture of meditating and then opened them a moment later. "Bring a spare shirt to work tomorrow."

"What is that supposed to mean?"

"Enjoy the rest of your day, Bradley. Maybe even get a second mint chocolate chip ice cream since that is your favorite flavor."

I stormed out of the tent and headed straight home. I was fuming. Some office prankster was trying to sabotage my piece on Ms. Nayomi. My first instinct told me it was Frieda. She seemed offended when I laughed at her for believing in the fortune teller. I must have offended her so she went back and gave the clever woman information about me to try and convince me of her powers. That was it.

Of course as Monday morning arrived, Frieda denied all accusations and even feigned being more offended than she had been previously. In fact, the entire office denied any accountability over the information Ms. Nayomi had acquired.

I sat at my desk stewing. Perhaps it wasn't anyone here. It was obvious she knew my name from the paper and had recognized me from a photo. It was not secret information that I had worked for a magazine before coming to the Times. Anyone could dig that up with a little effort. And as for the ice cream, well, she must have seen me eating it before I entered her tent. It would be a simple assumption that I would have purchased my favorite flavor. Either she had seen me eating it, or more likely, she had an accomplice that watched people outside the tent. Someone that probably stayed hidden behind that curtained-off area.

The phone on my desk rang and pulled me from my contemplations. As I grabbed the receiver, I accidentally knocked over my cup of coffee and spilled the entire contents onto the front of my white shirt. Fortunately, the coffee had long since gone cold, but my shirt was soaked and stained. I cursed to myself and then suddenly remembered Ms. Nayomi's words.

"Bring a spare shirt to work tomorrow."

But how? I could see if someone was in on the joke and they had spilled the coffee on my shirt but I had done this myself. Or did someone strategically place my coffee mug closer to the edge of the desk, during a brief moment of absence. That was it.

"Ha ha, very funny everyone," I announced.

"Wow, look at your shirt," Francis said. "You are very clumsy."

"Yes, look at my shirt. Was it you, Francis? Was it?"

"Was it me, what?"

"She put you up to this, didn't she? You moved the mug on my desk, huh?"

"I beg your pardon? I have been at my desk all morning."

I heard Neil laughing. "It was you, then, Neil? You think this is funny?"

"I didn't do anything but yeah I think it is pretty funny. This woman has really gotten into your head. I guess she does have a gift."

"No!" I shouted. "She does not have a gift. One of you did this, I know it."

The following day I left the office in the morning and spent three hours watching Ms. Nayomi's tent from a distance. I remained out of sight, standing between the tent of the bearded lady and a stall selling caramel apples. I watched for anyone suspicious coming or going from the tent, someone that could have been in league with Ms.

Nayomi. I saw nobody. Ms. Nayomi never emerged from the tent at any time either.

Frustrated, I waited for the latest victim to leave the tent before entering again.

"So, who is in on this? Francis? Neil? Herbert? Which one?"

"In on what, exactly?" she feigned ignorance.

"Don't play dumb with me."

"Are you going to stand there accusing me of nonsense, or are you going to sit down for a reading? We both already know you are going to sit down."

I took a seat. "Fine. Tell me something else that is going to happen."

"That will cost you five cents, Mr. Fluke."

"Oh right, you have never read my column before. I guess I also feel like a Fluke, huh?" I tossed a nickel on the table. "There. Amaze me."

I snorted as she cupped her crystal ball with both hands and gazed into nothingness.

"Can you get tonight's boxing match on that thing? My radio at home has been acting up."

She ignored my comment and continued with her absurd spectacle.

"I see you are on the east side of the city tomorrow. A meeting, perhaps?" My eyes narrowed. "Wait, I see you standing beside your car. You are not happy. One of your tires is flat."

I had a meeting on the east side of the city tomorrow, concerning an article I was planning to write but I had not told anyone in the office about that yet. How could she have known? Who would have told her?

"What color is my car?"

"Blue."

I marched out of the tent without another word. Someone was playing games with me and I was not impressed with this. Someone must have been spying on me or going through my appointment book, which was locked in my desk drawer at the office.

The next morning, before leaving for my meeting, a thought struck me and I inspected every inch of every tire on my car. I was certain someone would have stuck a nail in one, or possibly slashed it; done something to cause a flat. I could detect nothing with the naked eye but that didn't mean there wasn't a small hole somewhere, causing a slow leak. So, I stopped at the closest gas bar and filled each tire with air, to be on the safe side.

I was about ten minutes from my appointed destination, when an oblivious kid, stupidly rode his bicycle off the sidewalk and into my path. I swerved just in time to avoid the boy and ran into the curb with a loud thump. I honked and cursed, simultaneously, then jumped out to inspect the damage. My front passenger tire was ruined. Flat.

The boy rode his bike over to where I stood.

"Gee, mister, I am sorry. I swear I didn't see you coming."

I grabbed him roughly by the arm. "Did she tell you to do that? She told you to ride in front of me, knowing I would have to swerve?"

"W-what? She, who?"

"Tell me!" I shouted.

"Mister, you are hurting my arm."

I let the boy go and told him to beat it. He couldn't ride away fast enough. Needless to say, I missed my meeting. It was nearly an hour before I got the spare tire on my car, and by that time, the individual I was to meet had given up and departed.

The next day, I was once again seated across from Ms. Nayomi. I slapped a nickel on the table, as she was reluctant to answer any questions until I had done so.

"I could have killed that boy. You told him to ride in front of me?"

"I have done no such thing, Mr. Fluke. I saw the flat tire in your future, nothing more."

"You couldn't have known that would happen unless you planned it!"

"Please, lower your voice. I am a fortune teller, this is what I do."

"You were a scientist, not a fortune teller. What did you do for IvoryTech before leaving, Ms. Schwartz? Yes, I know all about you too. I must be a fortune teller myself, eh? You graduated with honors from right here at the Big City University. A brilliant mind, by all accounts. A budding scientist. Now you sit here in a tent, next to the cotton candy stand, and you peddle in deceit at a fair."

"I realized that wasn't the life for me. I had a gift, so I decided to pursue that."

"Your only gift was your understanding of technology and your intelligence. You cannot read minds or see into my future. It is all a scam, Ms. Schwartz. I have been debunking this rubbish for years."

"Because you don't believe in it, it immediately becomes rubbish, does it?"

"It's rubbish because that is indeed what it is. Rubbish."

"Very well, you are entitled your opinion."

"Look into your little magic ball there and tell me something else," I tossed a second nickel onto the table.

The woman sighed and again proceeded with her laughable performance with the ball. When her eyes opened, she spoke.

"I am afraid I see your father, he is in distress."

"Oh, he is, is he? He is quite healthy for his age, with no signs of leaving this existence any time soon."

"I just see him in a hospital bed, that is all."

That weekend, when my mother called to say that my father had been feeling very ill and was taken to the hospital, I rushed right over. The doctors suspected food poisoning. From the hospital, I drove straight to the fair.

"You poisoned my father in order to convince me?" I accused.

"Excuse me?"

"My father is in the hospital, as you said, sick with possible food poisoning."

"Yes, I saw that scene. I told you."

"I know you told me. So you had him poisoned, didn't you? I will have you arrested and locked away for this."

"Calm down, Mr. Fluke. I haven't gone anywhere near your father."

"You had someone do it?"

"I work alone."

"Sure you do," I threw a nickel on the table. "Tell me what you are planning next. What do you see this time?"

"There is no need to behave in this manner."

"Tell me."

She proceeded with her carnival act once more and I laughed at the incredulity of it all. This time she wore a mask of confusion, as if something troubled her. She shook her head and looked again. The same expression remained.

"Your magic ball is not working? Want me to fix the antenna on the roof? Might be a reception issue."

"I don't see any future. It's all just white. I don't understand."

"What does that mean? It's all just white?"

"It means simply that. Inside the ball is white, everywhere I look, it's just white. That is all I can see, nothing more."

"I should demand my nickel back but I think you are in more need of it than I am."

Disgusted, I turned to leave as a woman was entering at the same time.

"I am sorry, miss," Ms. Schwartz said. "Do you mind coming back in about fifteen minutes?"

"She has to fix her magic ball," I commented on my way out.

I was about halfway to my car, when I turned back around. I found another place to sit out of sight and watched the tent. This time I was going to wait until Ms. Schwartz left. I was curious to see where she would go or who she would speak with. Hours passed and she never left once. Pitiful victims came and went, each emerging with expressions of awe.

Night was falling and the fair was beginning to close. I had waited hours and Ms. Schwartz did not appear. The tent went dark and she still had not made an exit.

With my patience worn out completely, I marched into the tent. It took a moment for my eyes to adjust to the darkness but there was some light coming from behind the curtain that cut the tent in half. Perhaps, Ms. Schwartz slept overnight on the other side. It was time for a peek. What was she hiding over there?

I approached the curtain, when a sudden flash of light, and a loud crackling sound, actually sent me to the floor on my buttocks, out of fright. The flash momentarily blinded me and once my vision returned, I stood and pulled the curtain aside. I was stunned by the scene in front of me.

There was no other exit from the tent and yet there was no Ms. Schwartz. It was as if she had simply vanished. A small table was the only furnishing on this side of the tent. On that table sat the weirdest contraption I had ever laid eyes upon. It had buttons and dials and two objects that appeared to be handles. As I moved in for a closer inspection, I could see a small screen right above a series of numbered buttons. Displayed on the screen was a date. I had to think for a moment but the date was tomorrow's date. Just what in the hell was this thing?

*   *   *   *

"Hey, Frieda, have you seen Bradley today? I have looked all over the office."

"You mean you didn't hear?"

"Hear what? I was in a meeting all morning. He is home sick?"

"He was picked up by the police last night."

"The police? For what?"

"Well, as I heard it, at first they thought him wandering around drunk. He was babbling incoherently."

"I didn't think Bradley even drank."

"He doesn't. Apparently they found nothing in his

system but he continued to babble and make not a word of sense all night long. I heard he was admitted to the Big City Asylum and is sitting in one of those white padded rooms."

"Goodness, me. He hasn't said anything at all that has made sense? Nothing to explain what happened?"

"Nothing, as I heard it. They found him not far from the fair, and he keeps going on and on, babbling about time travel."

THE GRAVE OF OLD MAN FINKEL

Journal Entry #167 – June 4

I had no luck again today. I spent thirteen hours standing in that barren river, panning for gold, that would appear does not exist. I suppose it is the varied tales of men striking it rich in these parts that keeps me going, but I have yet to find even the smallest amount of gold. Do I regret leaving my farm? Every day. The work was hard and the hours long but it put food in my mouth. What little money I have brought with me is nearly spent. All the tools I have bought have so far proven useless. I had even purchased a large wagon, dreaming that I would require it to carry all my gold back into town. A fool's dream, perhaps. I have traveled too far to give up just yet. Tomorrow is another day. I will venture further up river in the morning and see if my luck changes.

Journal Entry #168 – June 6

I stood in that gods-forsaken river until well after dark tonight with nothing to show for it but a grumbling stomach. I encountered two other prospectors that had also met with the same luck as I. I can't be doing this wrong as there is no other way to be doing it. Using that stupid pan to sift through the mud at the bottom of the river. I traveled further north the last two days, for all the good that did me. It was at Johnson's Bend where I crossed paths with Alfred and Benjamin. At first the meeting was tense and my hand drifted to the handle of my six-shooter. Gold prospectors were generally territorial, but seeing as how they had also found nothing, I was not viewed as any sort of threat. We exchanged depressing tales and agreed to share a fire and some drinks tonight. I am off to join them at their campsite.

Journal Entry #169 – June 7

Another fruitless day, I regret to report. Thank god for the willow tree that offered me some relief from that awful midday sun. At least I am not alone with my misfortune. I learned last night that Alfred and Benjamin are also in dire straits. Both left decent-paying jobs and gambled everything on traveling to this region to make a fortune in gold. Like me, their dreams have been dashed with weeks of nothing to show for their work. Alfred even left a wife and children behind, with the thought of returning to them a rich man. My food stores are running drastically low. I can't afford to waste time making the two-day trek back into town. Additionally, I have almost no money left to replenish my supplies. I don't know how much longer I can last out here.

Journal Entry #170 – June 11

I have not written for several days now. Recent events have unnerved me and I have gotten very little rest. I have been sleeping with one eye open and with my six-shooter resting on my chest. Two days ago, I came across a grisly discovery. I found Benjamin hanging from the branch of a willow tree, overlooking the river. A handwritten note was left nearby, stating that he had gambled everything and lost. He no longer possessed the will to continue and felt shamed to return home empty-handed. Poor Benjamin. I attempted to locate Alfred but his partner was nowhere to be found. I waited near their camp until nightfall but the other man never returned. I felt conflicted, but with the death of Benjamin and the disappearance of Alfred, I helped myself to what little food and drink they had left at their campsite. The following day, while continuing my futile search for gold, Alfred appeared from behind a tree and nearly put a bullet in my head. The man looked disheveled, and fortunately, his shaky hand spoiled his aim, causing that bullet to whiz past my ear without harm. I ran for the woods as he fired two more times, while shouting that I was a dirty thief. We have been playing a game of hide and seek ever since. I know he is still out here, searching for me. I can hear him still, from time to time. I do not wish to kill the man who is clearly distraught by the death of his friend, but I will be damned if I am going to let him shoot me. The food I took from their camp is nearly gone. I think I am going to be forced to journey back into town. Maybe tomorrow I will attempt to catch some fish.

Journal Entry #171 – June 12

Well, that lunatic Alfred forced me to kill him today. While I was trying to catch some fish, which proved a waste a time, Alfred found me. Thankfully, I was fast on the draw and was able to shoot him dead. I didn't want to kill him. I was hoping we could have talked but he was beyond reason. I found some money in his pockets but there was regrettably no food in his possession. I spent two hours burying the man. I think I will leave for town in the morning. I cannot go much longer without any food. Clearly, I am no fisherman. What a nightmare my life has become. I considered bringing the bodies of both men into town but I do not wish to have any suspicion placed on me. Benjamin obviously killed himself and I killed Alfred in self-defence, but that could be difficult to prove with no witnesses. It is best that I leave them out here and claim no knowledge of their whereabouts, if ever brought to question.

Journal Entry #172 – June 13

It would appear that I have been the victim of thieves. All the money I owned, down to the last coin, was missing as I awoke this morning. Footprints led away from my camp and disappeared in the woods. I know this region is thick with would-be prospectors and thievery is not uncommon. I will have to postpone my trip to town. With no money to purchase food, it would be a useless journey. I will have to find food somehow and keep up the search for gold. That is the only chance I have.

Journal Entry #173 – June 15

No gold. I am convinced now that this river hides no fortune below its watery surface. I am starving and cannot last much longer. I may have to consider selling what little equipment I have in town, in order to buy food. My wagon is worth a few meals at least. A small part of me still clings to the irrational thought that if I stay just a little longer, I am bound to find gold. That is the gold fever talking. It is a sickness, I realize now, but a sickness that is hard to shake. I am feeling weaker. No more can I write this evening. I need rest.

Journal Entry #174 – June 16

I have done something despicable today. I hate myself for it but it has bought me a few more days to remain at the river in search of gold. I packed up my gear this morning and headed onto the road leading back to town. An hour into my journey, I came across a stagecoach. There was three well-to-do travelers plus the driver. Without even thinking it through, I drew my gun and robbed them. They stopped to offer me a ride into town but I robbed them of a few days' worth of food and some cash. I have since returned to my campsite and spent the rest of the afternoon panning for gold. I found nothing today but I have to find something soon. I just have to.

Journal Entry #175 – June 19

I find myself once again questioning my sanity. The food I robbed from the stage is gone and I have found no gold in this rotten river. This river will be the death of me, I am certain of it. I am beginning to believe that either all the gold that was here is gone, or I was provided false information and there was none in this region to begin with. I have found several abandoned campsites, which lead me to believe that others have already been here ahead of me and taken whatever there was here to find. Or, they had more sense than me and knew when to give up and leave. Each time I decide I have had enough, a nagging feeling tells me to wait just a little longer. I am trying to show patience but my patience is wearing dreadfully thin.

Journal Entry #176 – June 20

This morning I found a most curious item floating down the river. It was a clear bottle and I almost paid it no mind. As it floated past, I noticed there was a piece of paper inside. Naturally, I scooped it up and pulled out the paper to find out what it was. It was a letter. The handwriting was almost illegible but I believe I was able to decipher it. It was written by a prospector, like myself. The man claims that he struck it rich, finding a major deposit of gold up river. He goes on to say that he received major injuries in a bear attack. He forced the bear to flee but he believes he will succumb to his injuries. A poorly drawn map was included at the bottom of the letter. The man says that he has hidden his gold in an old graveyard near the river. He placed it in the grave of Old Man Finkel. He ends the letter by saying that he will attempt to crawl to the road for help but does not truly believe that he will make it. He hopes that somebody will find this letter and the gold will not go to waste. Dirty fingerprints were found all over the paper and also contributed to a difficult read. The letter is not dated, so I have no idea how long ago this was written. But the fact that I found the letter still within the bottle, makes me believe that I am the first to read this.

According to the map, this graveyard is about a half-day travel from my current location. I will attempt to get a good sleep this night and set out at first light.

Journal Entry #177 – June 21

It is late in the afternoon and I have located the graveyard. There is approximately sixty headstones spread out in an area fairly close to the river. Using the poorly drawn map, I was able to locate the grave of Old Man Finkel easily enough. The grave is open and a plain wooden coffin rests inside the hole. I observed many footprints throughout the graveyard but nothing to indicate that anyone had recently visited the grave of Old Man Finkel. I firmly believe the gold must still be intact within the casket. I passed several other prospectors down river, not far from here. I do not wish anyone to see me opening a coffin in the graveyard. I have decided to return to the grave later tonight and conduct my business in the dark, away from prying eyes.

Journal Entry #178 – June 22

It is well past midnight and I firmly believe that there is nobody else in the vicinity. I have heard nothing save for the sound of the river and the chirping of crickets. There is no glow from any campfires. I believe my luck has finally changed. I am starving and this is my last-ditch effort to salvage anything from this expedition. The author of the letter mentioned he had found a fortune in gold. Now, all I have to do is retrieve it from that grave. I am leaving now. I will write again when I return with good news.

* * * *

The undead creature finished eating the last remaining bit of the unfortunate prospector and tossed his clothing behind a thick bush. Filthy and rotted fingers placed the letter back into the bottle and it shambled over to the river, tossing the bottle in. Through black pits for eyes, it watched as the bottle floated down the river and out of sight. Satisfied, the horrible thing returned to the grave of Old Man Finkel. It climbed back inside the coffin to await the arrival of its next meal

HAROLD THE CONQUEROR

I sheathed my sword and entered the keep when I was told the fighting was over. Greymane Keep was the seat of power for Baron Stromwall but Baron Stromwall was no more. Three hours after storming the immense keep, the Baron and his forces had been defeated. My brothers and I had won.

Our victory was never in doubt. Stromwall was weak and foolishly thought to rule these lands with kindness and compassion. Two qualities that should never be attributed to a ruler. People were more inclined to work harder and talk less when motivated by fear. I wonder if Stromwall came to realize his folly just before my brother Curtis removed his head.

A soldier approached me and it was obvious that he was fresh from battle. Blood still dripped from his silver armor but he himself showed no wounds. He bowed his head and took a knee in front of me.

"My Lord, the entire keep is secure and Lords Curtis and Stephan await you in the throne room."

I nodded and waved the man away. I took my time, strolling through the hallways, admiring the carnage around me. My brothers could wait. A lord never hurried.

"Oh, look who has finally arrived now that the battle is won," my brother Curtis said, once the three of us were alone in the throne room.

"Not a drop of blood on his armor," Stephan added, with a sneer.

Their verbal barbs did no harm. "Someone had to ensure that nobody escaped this keep. My men and I had the place surrounded. Can you imagine the chaos that would ensue if Stromwall had somehow gotten away?"

Curtis laughed. "A convenient excuse, dear brother. There was no hope of escape for that weakling."

"Underground tunnels, perhaps? We don't know the full layout of this place."

Stephan rolled his eyes. "You are always late to battle. It is always one thing or another. You never want to dirty your hands. I have half a mind to call you a cow…"

I placed a hand on the pommel of my sword and cut him off right there. "Careful, brother. Choose your words wisely."

"Or what? You plan on running me through?"

Curtis stepped between us. "Enough with the bickering. We have won and that is all that matters. Now we have to focus on the King and his reaction to our coup."

"As long as we can convince the King that we have no ambitions beyond Stromwall's lands, there should be no need to fear any retaliation," I figured. "Our forces are too large for the King to easily defeat us, so the intelligent route is to accept us as the new barons and life continues on much as it did before. The higher taxes we will impose, will only mean more coins in his coffers."

"He has a point, I hate to say," Stephan reluctantly agreed. "Stromwall was too lax in his rule and the King was ultimately losing wealth as a result. That greedy pig of a man shouldn't care who rules this region as long as he sees more coins flowing over to him."

Curtis nodded. "Alright, maybe we send a nice tribute over immediately, as a friendly gesture? It won't take long for him to hear of what happened to Stromwall, so it's in our best interest to make first contact and start things off on good terms."

"Once we locate the vault in this place, I will assemble some trusted men to make the delivery."

"Excellent, Stephan," Curtis smiled. "Tonight we feast and celebrate like barons."

I was not one for celebrations and ducked out early that evening, just as the alcohol consumption was reaching an epic level. I decided to lay claim to one of the better bedrooms in the keep before Stephan could. Stromwall's room now belonged to Curtis. Curtis was the biggest and strongest of us three, and by far, the fiercest warrior. We all agreed to rule as equals, but some things still went to the strongest. That was just the way of the world and the chief reason Stromwall was now without his head. He was weak, so the strong swept him aside. There was no place here for people like him. The strong is entitled to take what they want and that is exactly what we did. After two years of planning, the keep and these lands were ours.

As I explained to my brothers, the King should not

become a worry of ours. Stromwall was a fool. In an act of insane kindness, he lowered the taxes of the people living in this region. He lowered the taxes on merchants operating in this region. He wanted to make life easier on the people and alleviate their suffering. He gave away lands owned by the crown. He reduced punishments for many of the petty crimes that ran rampant in this region. What manner of man would do such a thing? A man unfit to rule, that was who.

My brothers were more brawn than brain. They could take the keep and hold onto it but I would suggest the best ways to govern. There is going to be a considerable tax increase on everyone, for starters. Merchants are going to be taxed heavily and will also need to purchase a permit to sell anything within this region. And the death penalty will be imposed on all crimes, no matter how petty. The folk in these parts are going to learn very quickly that we are not to be trifled with.

I found the second largest bedroom on the top level of the keep to my liking. The previous owner would have no more use for it. We had Stromwall's brother executed before the celebrations began. The skinny fop had surrendered during the battle but I suggested that no person from this keep be left alive. The room was large enough for my needs but the décor would need to change. The bed, however, was indeed quite comfortable.

I lounged around for some time before sleep eventually overtook me. I spent that time considering the future. We had taken over Stromwall's keep with such ease, that it made me think that we could turn our attention to other barons. Targeting the King at this point was far too great an ambition to undergo, but it was not entirely out of the question in the future. I thought if we removed several other barons first, then we could amass the men and the wealth necessary to dethrone the King.

Men flocked to my brothers and me. We may have been born into a poor family but we were also born to rule. It was just a part of our very souls. Soldiers listened to us and rallied to our cause. To this point, we had gathered men with great promises. Now that we had captured the keep, we had the coins to make good on those promises, and this was just the beginning.

My brothers would be satisfied with just ruling Stromwall's region but I had much grander goals in mind. Curtis would be the easier of my two brothers to convince. The man loved fighting more than anything else in life. He was a brute that stood several inches taller than I and built like a stone house. If he believed that victory would be ours, then his bloodlust would secure his compliance. Stephan, on the other hand, would be more difficult.

Stephan and I butted heads often. Most of the time he argued with me just for the sake of arguing. If I made a suggestion, he would take the opposite stance, just for the sole reason that it was my idea. He was a year older than me, and had the mind that since he was the oldest, he should ultimately be in charge. He hated that I was the smarter of the two of us. I was positive that Stephan would be happy with what we had gained so far and not wish to press our luck further. He would be a problem.

The next few weeks went well during the transition of power. The people in these lands came to know that we now ruled and we meant business. I ordered the dungeons emptied and we held a mass hanging in front of the keep, to rid ourselves of prisoners. Why should we waste perfectly good food to feed criminals? Word spread that we would no longer arrest criminals; they would be executed on the spot. That order had been carried out a half-dozen times already to prove that this was no jest.

After a month of tense waiting, a messenger arrived with the news we had been hoping for. The King did express his disapproval of our methods of deposing Baron Stromwall, but there would be no action taken against us. The King accepted our tribute and would be expecting more where that came from. He would get his coins, for the time being.

As expected, Stephan made agreeing on any plans extremely difficult. He fought me every step of the way, simply because I had thought of them. And it came as no surprise to me that he was opposed to eliminating the barons closest to us.

One cool night, I found my troublesome brother pacing the battlements of the keep.

"Do you hear that, brother?" I asked.

"Hear what? I don't hear anything."

"Precisely. There is nothing but silence out there."

"And your point?"

"The people in these lands have fallen in line. They are too busy working hard for us all day long, to drink and revel at night. They are sleeping, so that they may wake early and begin their work day anew."

"And if we expand, as you suggest, it will be harder to keep everyone in line. Be happy with what we have."

"Why should we settle with what we now have, when we could have more?"

"Because Stromwall was a fool and never saw us coming. The other barons are already fearful of our potential ambitions and are no doubt preparing for us, in the event of us wishing to expand. Do not think that everyone will be so easily defeated."

"Bah! We have the men and the coins to buy more men. None of these barons could resist us."

"And what of the King? You think that he will just sit idly by and watch us slowly take over all his lands?"

"Soon enough, the King won't be able to stop us either."

"No. I will never agree to your plans. This region is large enough for us to rule and live as kings, anyhow. That is good enough for me."

"We could have more," I implored. "So much more."

"Not interested in your ideas of conquest."

"Fine. But you see that solider down there in the courtyard?"

Stephan leaned over, squinting his eyes. "Which one?"

"That one. The one right below you."

As my brother leaned over a little further, I grabbed him by his shirt and threw him off the battlement. His scream was cut short as his body broke against the ground of the courtyard. I spotted the closest solider to me, patrolling the battlements, and an idea quickly came to mind.

"Guards! Guards!" I shouted. "There has been an assassination! Guards!"

The closest guard arrived first, wearing a mask of confusion. I drew my sword and cut a line of blood across his left arm. He jumped back with a yelp. Three more guards rushed to our position and I pointed my blade at the wounded soldier.

"This man has killed my brother! Take him!"

"My Lord?" the bleeding man went pale. "I did no such thing. I ran over here as soon as you shouted."

I ignored him and continued to address the others. "He pushed Lord Stephan over the side! Drag him to the dungeon. He is a Stromwall sympathizer!"

The soldier was disarmed and roughly taken away. He shouted his innocence the entire way. Approximately an hour later, Curtis found me in the corridor outside my bedroom. Blood was splattered on the white shirt he wore.

"Would you like to know what that soldier said while we tortured him?" he asked me.

"What?"

"Nothing."

"Nothing?"

"He maintained his innocence, right until the moment he died."

"Who knew that Stromwall had such fanatical supporters?"

"Yes, brother, who knew?"

"We will need to be more mindful of traitors in our midst."

"Indeed. I suppose it had nothing to do with the fact that Stephan opposed your ideas of expansion?"

"How dare you accuse me of murdering our brother. Despite our differences, he was still family."

"I sincerely hope you would do no such thing, since I oppose your plan as well."

"What? Baron Eriksson is the perfect target for our next move. He will crumble before us and his region will be ours."

"And then the King will sweep through here and

crush us. Stephan was right. We have all the land and wealth we need right here. Enjoy it, brother. We only have to divide things two ways now."

Curtis took his leave and I stood there for some time, immensely disappointed by his words. I was certain that he would see things my way and be eager to get out there and fight. This was going to be a serious problem. I took a brief moment to consider that nameless soldier. Did I feel bad that an innocent man was tortured to death for my crime? No. It was necessary. He was just a small pawn in the grand scheme of things. I slept just fine that night.

Curtis proved to be the new thorn in my side over the course of the following few weeks. His attitude toward me had changed. He constantly threw out comments that implicated me in Stephan's murder. He was certain that I was behind it.

I never shed a tear when I was informed that Curtis was murdered. Another of Stromwall's supporters had poisoned him, or so the story went. He was adamant in his opposing stance of attacking the other barons so he had to go. I would have preferred to have both my brothers beside me in the coming wars but it was not meant to be. They did not share my visions of conquest. It was truly unfortunate.

A year later, I was touring the new lands under my control, following the defeat of Baron Eriksson. I dismounted my horse and approached a haggard-looking woman who refused to bow before me and just glared with pure hatred.

"This is your farm?" I asked her.

"Yes it is," she spat. "All mine since my husband died. Worked to death."

"You will take a knee when faced with your Lord."

"I see no Lord here. Just an evil tyrant."

My patience was wearing thin. "You should rejoice. Your previous baron was weak. Now, you have a strong leader who is capable of protecting your land."

"It won't be my land for much longer. I can't keep up with your taxes."

"A pity."

I snapped my fingers and two soldiers shoved the woman into the mud, forcing her to kneel before me.

"Next time, I will not be as forgiving," I warned her.

I turned back toward my horse and that witch produced a blade from under her dress and dove at me. My guards were too slow to react and she drove that blade hilt-deep into my back. I shrieked in agony and fell to my knees. My men threw her back down in the mud and began to beat her near senseless. With unimaginable pain, I pulled the dagger from my back and rose to my feet, seething with anger. I approached her, grimacing with every painful step.

"Any last words before I cut your throat?"

"Yes! A curse upon you, you horrible tyrant! I curse you to suffer in this life and every life you live after this one!"

*   *   *   *

"Alright, Harold, I am going to count to three and snap my fingers, and then you will open your eyes. One. Two. Three."

SNAP.

"Hey, Doc. Did it work? Did you find out anything

useful? This pain in my back is something terrible."

"Ummm…"

"No? Geez, no medical doctors can ever explain my pain. I was really hoping your hypnosis thing could help me remember if I ever injured it somehow and just plum forgot."

"Well, Harold, I really specialize in past life regression. Under hypnosis, I generally bring people a lot farther back in time than what you were hoping. Do you have any brothers, by chance?"

"Yes, two. My older brother has a gift for arguing and actually became a lawyer. My younger brother is a brute of a man and is a professional boxer. We never really got along and I don't talk to them much. Why?"

"Oh, just wondering is all. Sometimes chronic pain can run in the family. I was just curious if your brothers suffered from the same pain."

"No, not that I am aware of. This pain is really affecting my work, Doc. Makes it so difficult to bend over when I clean the toilets at the schools."

"Maybe you need a longer handle on your brush?"

DINNER AT THE WAINWRIGHT'S

Robert Wainwright paced back and forth in his living room, occasionally glancing outside the front window. It was a quiet Sunday and the afternoon was quickly turning into evening. He was about to take a seat and pick up a magazine, when a sound drew his attention back to the window. He spotted a vehicle pulling into his driveway and he called out.

"Dear, the King's have arrived."

Prescilla Wainwright emerged from the kitchen and inspected her dress and hair in front of a mirror. Once satisfied, she joined her husband at the front door just as the doorbell chimed.

"Well, go on, open the door," Prescilla urged, after her husband had hesitated.

Robert inhaled deeply, nodded to his wife, and then opened the door, while wearing his biggest smile.

"Good evening, George, Clara, you found the place, alright?"

"Of course, ole sport," George King replied.

Clara rolled her eyes. "Now, George…"

"Alright, well, we may have made a few wrong turns but a chap at the gas bar down the road pointed us in the right direction. We just don't get out into the country very often. You know, life in the Big City."

"Understandable, yes. Well, do come in, won't you?"

The King's were invited in and prompted to take a seat in the living room.

"Dinner will be ready shortly," Priscilla announced, before disappearing back into the kitchen.

"It's good to see you both again. What has it been? Two years? Three?"

George had to think for a moment. "Closer to three, I would have to say."

"The last time we saw you and Prescilla was at that art show," Clara added. "So, yes, three years."

"Time just flies, doesn't it?"

"You've got that right, Rob," George agreed. "How are you adjusting to life in the country?"

"Quite well, actually. It's quiet out here. As you have noticed there is no traffic out this way. The pace is very slow and leisurely. We like it."

"The scenery on the way here was lovely, I must say," Clara commented.

"Indeed, so. After we eat we can give you a tour around. The lake in the back offers a breath-taking view. There is nothing like sitting by the lake with a coffee in the morning."

"Dinner is ready," Prescilla called. "Bring our guests

to the dining room, Rob."

Robert guided his guests into the dining room where Prescilla had set a marvelous table. Fresh buns right out of the oven. Salad with a savory dressing. Shrimp galore. And a mouth-watering main dish of roasted chicken with mashed potatoes and mixed vegetables as a side.

"This looks fantastic, Prescilla."

"Thank you, Clara. Sit wherever you like."

"It's your house, Rob should get the head seat."

"It matters not."

"No, no, it's guest etiquette," George insisted.

George and Clara took the two side seats at the rectangular table, leaving the end seats for the hosts.

Prescilla motioned for everyone to start. "Dig in while everything is nice and hot."

The two couples filled their plates and began to eat.

"My goodness," Clara said. "I don't think I have ever tasted a salad this fresh before."

"We grow all the vegetables ourselves," Prescilla replied.

Silence reigned for a short time while all four were enjoying their meals. Robert spoke next.

"So, how is everyone at the old company?"

George paused for a moment. "Good. They are good."

"Splendid. Nice to know that all is well."

"Tell us, how do you pass the day away now, with no more hustle and bustle of the Big City?"

"Lazily, truth be told. We have our coffee by the lake in the morning. Then I do some gardening until the afternoon gets too hot. I take a nap or read a magazine. We have dinner and then listen to our radio programs in the evening. Nothing too complicated."

"We love our programs too. Clara enjoys the orphan, Beatrice, or Jungle Johnny. I am more partial to Invaders from Space. That Commander Foxx is something else, isn't he?"

"We don't much care for the ones with aliens," Prescilla replied. "Detective Darke is our favorite."

"What? Who doesn't love a good story with aliens and monsters from other worlds?"

"Now, George, stop that. Not everyone enjoys your enthusiasm about aliens from outer space," scolded Clara.

"I did as a young lad," Robert said. "Just, not so much anymore."

"I guess I have never grown out of it," George admitted.

"I just don't seem to have the same interest that I once did."

Robert stared off into space, deep in thought and far from the dinner table. George's voice brought him back again.

"What was all that hubbub about something falling from the sky out this way? It was in all the Big City papers."

"I am not sure what you are referring to."

"How could you not have heard about it?"

"We don't read any of the papers. I have wanted to leave the Big City behind."

"Well, something unexplained apparently fell from the sky and landed out here in the country somewhere. They even had the military out looking but turned up nothing. Enough people had seen it to make the story sound fairly credible. Isn't that right, Clara?"

"It was all over the papers, yes. Just some falling star, if you ask me."

Prescilla shook her head. "We heard nothing about it. But then, as Rob said, we don't read any of the papers and even stay away from the news programs on the radio. Life just seems simpler this way."

"You didn't even notice all the military presence lately?"

"We rarely even leave our own property," Robert replied. "Maybe the odd trip to the grocery store but other than that we have everything that we require right here. Not much reason to leave."

"Well, I envy you guys, there. It would be nice to be able to escape the hectic city life. One day, perhaps, eh, Clara?"

"Yes, dear. That would be nice."

"Are we ready for fresh coffee and dessert?" Prescilla asked, once everyone's plates were empty.

"Sounds good to us," George clapped. "Your banana bread is legendary. Rob used to bring some by the office from time to time and nearly cause a riot from folk fighting for a piece."

Prescilla blushed. "I hope it's as good as you remember."

Prescilla returned from the kitchen, promptly, with a pot of fresh coffee and a tray of her scrumptious banana bread. George wasted no time in attacking the bread. It was as good as he remembered.

The Wainwright's and the King's enjoyed some more small talk during dessert. Afterwards, in the interest of being more comfortable, Prescilla suggested they finish their coffee in the living room.

"That was a fine meal, Prescilla, my compliments to the chef," George said, taking a seat on the sofa.

"Yes it was, indeed," Clara added.

"Thank you, I am glad you all enjoyed it."

"We did. And it was mighty big of you, Rob, to invite us out here like this, after all that mess at the office."

Clara paled. "Now, George, this is not the time for such talk. You'll have to excuse…"

"No, no, Clara. We can't all just sit here and ignore the elephant in the room. Rob and I have been friends from way back, good friends, and it just makes me happy that he was able to look past everything that happened. Warms my heart."

Robert shifted uncomfortably in his chair across from the sofa. "Yes, well, as we get older I think it's silly, and quite frankly unhealthy, to hold onto such grudges. I was pleased you both accepted our invitation."

George nodded. "How could we not when remembering all the good times we had? And look at you both, now. You guys are living this wonderful laid-back life out here. Why, it was probably even a blessing that you had gotten fired. You would have been miserable in the Big City."

Robert smiled, weakly. "You are right. I suppose I should even thank you for the part you played in that. We do enjoy our lives out here."

George stood and walked over to where Robert sat, extending his hand out in a friendly gesture. "Put her there, ole boy. Let bygones be bygones."

Robert accepted and shook his hand. "To old friends. Um, how about we show you around before the sun disappears completely?"

"A splendid idea," Prescilla said. "You both will love the view of the lake. The sunset is beautiful."

"Sounds fantastic," Clara said, just happy to be off that uncomfortable topic of Robert's dismissal at the hands of her husband.

The Wainwright's guided the King's back through the kitchen and out a side door. They walked around to the backyard where the Wainwright's had erected a magnificent garden, but as it was suggested, it was the view of the lake that truly grabbed their attention. The sun was just setting beyond a distant wooded-hill and the water was as calm as could be, like a sheet of glass.

"Good heavens, it's beautiful. Isn't it George?"

He had to agree with his wife. "Indeed, so. I can see why you sit out here every day with a coffee. I must say I am jealous."

The two couples strolled down toward the water's edge, where Robert had built a small dock that extended about fifteen feet out.

"May we?" George asked, motioning to the dock.

"Absolutely. Go see how crystal clear the water is. There is a fairly steep drop off near the end of the dock where the lake gets quite deep."

George and Clara made their way, hand in hand, to the end of wooden dock. It was no lie, they were both quite jealous. They both thought, at the same time, how serene it would be to sit here each day, soaking in this view. George was marveling at how still the water appeared, when he suddenly noticed ripples just below them. Large bubbles were coming up to the surface from some unknown source, deep within the lake.

Clara was the first to notice and gasped out loud. A

hideous tentacle soon broke the surface and writhed about in the air. It was followed by several others and Clara finally screamed with horror, as something large came forth from the water. George was rendered speechless and was paralyzed in place.

The creature was enormous with slimy-green skin and great wings. It possessed a bulbous head with many tentacles where a mouth should be. They wiggled and writhed as if sniffing the air. Giant, milky-white eyes, gazed down at the terrified couple and Clara fainted. With hands, much like a human, it grabbed the King's, who were helpless to resist.

With mouths agape, the Wainwright's watched the spectacle. Nothing could be done to stop this monstrosity that was already old when the Earth was considered young. It spoke, then, in some sickly-gurgling language that was never meant for the ears of humans. The Wainwright's heard this speech in their minds. Despite the indecipherable sound of the language, somehow, Robert and Prescilla knew exactly what it was saying.

"MORE FOOD."

The elder one sunk back beneath surface of the lake, taking the King's with it.

After standing speechless for some time, the Wainwright's turned back toward their house. It was Prescilla that finally broke the silence.

"What happens when we run out of people we don't like?"

Robert looked at his wife but had no answer for that.

"Let's get the table reset. The Wallace's will be here in about an hour."

A DISEASED MIND

Aaron was a troubled soul from the time he was very young. While other young boys took care of their action figures, Aaron pulled his part. He took pleasure in destroying things and imagining their distress, had they been real. His parents hadn't notice anything too out of the ordinary, until they took note of his malice toward animals. Young children generally adored animals and yet Aaron was not among that group. He made an odd request one day, asking if they could get a puppy. His parents, making a wise decision, denied that request, questioning his motives.

So, Aaron just continued to destroy toys in gruesome fashion. Hacking off limbs. Lighting them on fire. Dragging them behind his bicycle while tied to fishing line. The older he got, the more creative his methods became.

In school, he was the quiet kid that kept mostly to himself. The other children found him strange. Nobody could pinpoint one particular thing about him that creeped them out, it was just the general sense of unease they felt in his presence. He appeared to lack emotion. The teachers would gossip with one another about the odd boy. He possessed a cold stare and never smiled, that is until the day they dissected a frog in science class.

Aaron was in his glory, and for the first time, people saw him smile. None would say that it was a warm smile, in fact, the smile only further creeped the others out. While most of the kids found this particular lesson revolting, Aaron obviously enjoyed it, and a little too much.

"Will we be dissecting a human in a future class?" Aaron asked his science teacher.

"Good heavens, no!" his teacher replied, and immediately noticed how truly sad the young boy appeared from the answer.

As a teenager, Aaron was still a recluse. He felt awkward in the presence of others and found it difficult to maintain eye contact. He passed away his free time with monster magazines and watching scary movies at the picture show. Most of the movies he was too young to see, so he found ways to sneak in. Slasher films were his favorite, like, The Red House on the Corner, or The Shadows Have Eyes. He could watch the same films over and over and barely blink an eye. He didn't even purchase popcorn as that was a distraction that took his attention away from the screen. He would sit, motionless, completely transfixed on the film, from start to finish.

His bedroom was adorned with the posters from his favorite films or grisly pictures he cut out of the monster magazines. It brought the boy great joy to be surrounded by such imagery. His mother disapproved but it was not uncommon for kids to be drawn to such movies. The films and magazines were successful for a reason, she figured. There was obviously a market.

As Aaron grew into a young man, he found it increasingly difficult to live at home and get along with his opinionated parents. He managed to secure himself a job in a local butcher's shop, after the butcher found that he had a natural talent for the kind of work required of him. Aaron earned just enough so that he could afford a small one-room apartment above a beer store.

He no longer attended school and when he wasn't working, he was always home. Alone. Aaron still had no friends and family did not visit him. He spent many hours looking out his window, watching drunks come and go from the beer store below. Some of them appeared homeless, purchasing a bottle, or sometimes a case of beer, after they had begged for enough money to do so. Aaron often wondered if anyone would miss them, if they were to suddenly disappear.

His thoughts were becoming darker. His obsession for slasher films became greater. He found himself, more frequently now, imagining those scenes from the movies, playing out before his very eyes. He imagined himself wielding a variety of different weapons with deadly proficiency. He envisioned expressions of fear. Screams of horror. How different would they be, he wondered, when it was real, and not just performed by an actor or actress?

Aaron decided he needed to experience it for himself. Films and magazines were failing to satisfy his hunger. He borrowed a meat cleaver from work one evening and followed a man who exited the beer store, carrying a case under one arm. The man's clothes were ragged and his shoes torn. He looked as though he might live on the streets and therefore would not have anyone waiting for him to return home.

The evening was warm but Aaron wore a long dark jacket, regardless. He kept his head down and followed the man for several blocks, keeping a fair distance between them, so as not to raise suspicion. His heart raced with a mixture of excitement and nervousness. His right hand, which gripped the handle of the cleaver hidden within his pocket, trembled.

Aaron began to quicken his pace, shortening the distance between him and his prey. He smiled at the analogy, that he was now a predator and the man he followed the prey. He was no longer the shy, strange guy, that felt awkward in social situations. Now, he was a hunter. He had a purpose.

His prey turned into an alleyway between two stores which had closed for the night. This was it, Aaron thought, time to make his move. He sped around the corner after the man and then stopped short. His prey had sat down next to two other men who were drinking bottles from brown paper bags. Aaron immediately spun around and headed back the way he had come. He had to abort.

He was overwhelmed with the feeling of disappointment and eyed other people that passed him by, considering a new target. Aaron shook that notion away and returned home. He could not just choose a target out of haste. Hasty decisions could lead to mistakes and he could not afford to make any mistakes.

Aaron lay awake that night, deep in thought. The adrenaline from the hunt was still coursing through his veins. The more he thought about it, the more he realized he had come very close to making a major mistake. If the body of the homeless man had ever been discovered, the police would retrace his steps and look for suspects within that general area. Aaron lived above the beer store that these vagrants frequented, so perhaps this was too close to home. He would need to choose someone further away.

Several days later, Aaron received a letter from his landlord that the cost of his rent would be rising next month. For a brief moment, he considered making his landlord his next target but he quickly realized that was a poor decision. After raising the rent, anyone affected would be prime suspects in the man's disappearance.

Aaron picked up a newspaper that afternoon to browse through the classified section to see if he could find a cheaper place to rent. There were several possible options and he circled a few of interest. He learned that renting a room or a basement in someone else's house was less expensive. The place with the cheapest rent was the farthest away from where he worked, but it was not out of the question. The bus was easy to get to and it would be possible to ride a bicycle if the weather permitted.

That evening, he took a trip out to see the house that was on the far side of town. It was located on a quiet street, a fair distance away from neighbors. It was a small bungalow house that was offering a basement apartment for rent. From Aaron's vantage point, he could see clearly through the front window of the house and observed a couple having dinner. They appeared to be somewhere in their thirties and Aaron found the woman with the long blonde hair to be quite attractive.

Dark thoughts creeped their way into his mind and a

new plan began to formulate. Here was a house far from where he lived, where a couple was allowing random strangers into their home to view the basement. If he was careful about it, there would be no link between Aaron and this couple. The strong desire to become the predator returned and he knew now that he had his new target.

Aaron had the next few days off work, so he went back to the house early the next morning, finding a good spot to watch and remain out of sight. He thought it best to study any routines this couple might have. He observed the man leave the house at 8am with a briefcase and get into a car, no doubt to head off to work. The woman remained home for the entire day and the man returned at 5pm. The next day was the same routine as the first. On the third day, the woman left for two hours and returned with grocery bags, but that was the only deviation.

Now, Aaron was thinking to move on the woman when she was alone during the day. He could pose as a potential renter to gain access to the house. As long as he was careful that nobody noticed him come and go, or leave any clues behind, he could be in the clear. There would be no link to make him a suspect. In fact, in most cases involving a missing or murdered wife, the husband was always the prime suspect.

Due to his work schedule, Aaron returned to the house the following week and was satisfied to observe the same routine. He picked up a newspaper to confirm that the basement was still listed for rent and it was. He decided that Wednesday would be the day.

He would sleep not a wink that Tuesday night. His level of excitement was off the charts. He worked through a variety of scenarios while he replayed many of his favorite movie scenes in his mind. This would be the first adventure of many, he thought. He wondered if others before him had thought of the idea of posing as a potential renter. It was the perfect way in.

That Wednesday morning, Aaron packed a bag with the things that he thought would be essential. Meat cleaver. Gloves. Duct tape. Garbage bags. Change of clothes. Scissors. A container of bleach. He pulled on an old pair of boots and wore his long black jacket. He got off the bus several blocks from his destination and walked the remainder of the way. It was fairly early in the morning and Aaron saw very few people up and about.

He found his way to the desired street without incident and took up watch from his usual hiding place behind a tree. No neighbors had seen his approach, as far as he was aware. It didn't take long before he was watching the man of the house pull out of the driveway in his car and head off to work. Aaron smiled a wicked smile. It was time.

He steeled his nerve and approached the house, ever mindful of any neighbors. There was none. He took a deep breath and knocked on the front door. His heart beat so rapidly that it threatened to leap out of his chest. When there was no immediate response, he knocked again.

Aaron was finally rewarded when the woman of the house opened the door. She appeared surprised that someone would be here this early in the morning.

"Yes? Can I help you?"

"Um, good m-morning to you. I am here about the ad you placed for your basement apartment."

Aaron always found interacting with others to be an awkward thing and he shifted from foot to foot and could not look the woman in the eyes. He could sense that she felt uneasy.

"Our ad said evening appointments only. My husband will…"

Aaron cut her off. "I am sorry I did see that, but I work evenings all this week and that would be impossible."

"Perhaps, you could come back next week?"

"I really need to find a place this week. I have to leave my current place by this weekend, so I am really in a jam here."

"My husband usually handles these things."

"That's alright, I just need to take a quick look at the basement and then I could call him later to discuss the details. I just need five minutes of your time, that's all. Just a quick peek."

"Well, I suppose that would be alright."

"Thank you so much, I really appreciate this. I need a place as soon as possible and your house is the perfect location for me with regards to work."

She nodded. "Come in."

The woman closed the door behind them and Aaron found it difficult to breathe. His hands, which he kept buried in his coat pockets, trembled with nervousness. He dared not remove them from his pockets, as he didn't wish to touch anything accidently, until he could put his gloves on.

His legs trembled and he did his best to appear that nothing was out of sorts, as she motioned for him to follow her over to the basement door.

"There is a separate entrance at the side of the house," she said. "But we will just use this one."

The inside of the house smelled sweet. Something

delicious was baking in the oven. The living room they passed through was spotless and elegantly decorated. Aaron tried not to get distracted by his surroundings and focused on the attractive woman he followed. She opened the door that led to the basement and flicked on a light.

She went first, down the narrow stairwell, with Aaron closely behind. The perfume she wore was intoxicating. They passed the side door and then descended further to the basement. The woman flicked another light switch and Aaron could now see two doors. He tightly gripped the handle of the meat cleaver which was concealed in his deep right pocket. The woman opened the door on the left and motioned for Aaron to take a peek.

"It is a small room, but tell me what you think. There is another switch just inside on your left."

Aaron still had not put his gloves on, so he carefully used one of his knuckles to flick the light switch to illuminate the room. What he saw in the room puzzled him.

"Ah, what is all this?"

Something struck the back of Aaron's head hard and the floor rushed upward to meet his face. When he opened his eyes, he could not tell how much time had passed. Every slight movement sent a sharp, searing pain, throughout his head. He came to realize that he was in a standing position and shackled to the wall of that small room. His vision was blurry but he could make out two people standing in front of him. As his eyes slowly came into focus, he recognized the man and woman who owned the house.

"He is awake?" she asked.

The man was holding Aaron's bag and was looking

through its contents. "And just what were you planning to do with all this stuff, young man?"

Aaron couldn't muster the where-with-all to respond.

The man smiled, evilly. "I have a feeling I know exactly what you were planning. So I am willing to bet that nobody knew you were coming here today. I am also willing to bet that you were careful that nobody saw you enter our house. That tells me that nobody will be looking for you here when someone realizes that you are missing."

The woman produced a kitchen knife and matched her husband's evil smile. "We have all the time in the world to have fun with this one."

CREEP'S MOTEL

The rain was coming down with a vengeance. The windshield wipers were barely able to keep up, making visibility nearly non-existent. Gordon could see very little of the road ahead and his wife Martha was now in a state of panic.

"You can't even see the road. I think we need to stop."

"Stop where, Martha? I can't just stop, this is a highway. You want some truck to come up from behind and run right over us?"

"Well, pull off the road at least. I didn't mean to stop right here in the middle."

Their weekend trip from the Big City to Shallow Lake had gone horribly awry. What should have only been a two-hour drive was now four, and they felt they were no closer to their destination than they were two hours earlier.

"I told you that road didn't look right back there. You

should have just kept going straight."

"Well, the directions said to make a left off of Highway Nine."

"Yes, but it said to make a left onto Kingsway. That road you took didn't say Kingsway and I think that turn came a lot sooner than it should have."

"I was told the first left was Kingsway. The sign must have come down in this storm, perhaps. That should have been the correct turn."

"Obviously it wasn't."

Thunder cracked overhead and it was so loud that Gordon nearly veered right off the road. Martha shrieked.

"Alright, we really need to stop somewhere," she implored. "Where do you think we are?"

"I haven't seen a sign in hours. I was thinking we should be near Bridgeway Township but none of this looks familiar to me."

"I haven't even seen a street light or a gas bar in over an hour. Please, we need to stop at the next one we see."

"At this point, I will gladly stop at the next gas bar. We are going to run out of a fuel if we don't find one soon."

Martha's face turned a whiter shade of pale, if that was even possible. "Oh, Gordon, why didn't you fill up before we left?"

"It should have only been a two-hour drive. We had enough for that. Look, there is another road up here on the left."

"Can you see a sign? What road is it?"

"I can't see a sign at all. I think we should take it, though."

"No, Gordon, no more side roads. Let's just stay on

this main highway."

"But maybe we could find some houses and ask someone where we are."

"It's almost midnight. You think we are just going to go knock on some stranger's door in this kind of weather? Who in their right mind would answer? Just stay on this road and we are bound to come across something soon."

"Fine."

Gordon gripped the steering wheel so tightly his knuckles were white. He had never driven in such a storm before. Lightning arced across the sky and momentarily lit up the road ahead, as if it were the middle of day. Both their hearts sunk at the sight before them.

"Did you see that, Martha? The bridge is completely flooded."

Martha sighed. "I suppose we will have to go back to that last turnoff then."

"Maybe if I get a good run at it, we can make it across the bridge."

Martha appeared mortified. "You will do no such thing! The last thing we need right now is for our car to sink in there! Gordon, turn around."

"Fine."

Gordon doubled back and turned down the nameless side road. They were in a heavily-wooded area which made everything appear that much darker. The road was not paved and his new worry was getting stuck in the mud, though, he did not voice that aloud. Martha was already in such a frenzy that one more thing could send her completely over the edge. He also thought it best not to mention that the needle on the fuel indicator was now in the red. That was a major concern.

Twenty minutes later, the woods thinned and the road came to a four-way intersection. Gordon and Martha both smiled and allowed themselves a moment to laugh at their sudden good fortune. On the far side of the intersection, they spotted a motel. The neon vacancy sign was on, though, two of the letters were burnt out. And to put the couple in an even better mood, there was a gas pump at the motel.

"Someone is looking out for us," Martha said, jubilantly.

Gordon exhaled, the timing could not have been better. He turned in to the empty parking lot and another flash of lightning lit up the night sky.

"Oh, good heavens," Martha said. "Did you see that sign?"

Gordon had. "Creep's Motel? Who would name a motel that?"

"That's absurd. I don't see any other cars here. Strange for a Friday night."

Gordon was just thinking the same thing. But then, they did not even know where here was. Another thing they both noticed was the state of the motel. To suggest it would need some fixing up would be an understatement. It was a long, single-level building, with what appeared to be ten rooms and a main office. The only visible light came from within the office.

Gordon parked the car in front of the first room, which was adjacent to the office. His headlights revealed a broken window and a door that did not sit properly on its hinges.

Worry crept back into Martha's mind. "Ah, I don't think I like the look of this place. It has the right title because it gives me the creeps."

"Don't be so silly. A lot of the old motels out in the middle of nowhere are like this. This storm is just making it appear creepier than I am sure it really is."

"I don't know. I think it would look just as creepy in the middle of the day. How about you just get some gas and find out where we are, then we can leave."

"Martha, I am exhausted and this storm is horrendous. We are going to need to wait somewhere for it to clear up."

"Not here."

"Nonsense. A place like this will probably cost next to nothing for a room. I can see someone in the office. Are you coming in with me?"

Martha reluctantly nodded. She had no real desire to get out of the car but they had been driving so long she figured she should at least use the restroom while they were here. The pair ran the short distance from their car to the office and still arrived inside, soaking wet. It was as if they had both just jumped fully-clothed into a pool.

Chimes jingled on the door and startled the middle-aged man, who moments before, had been asleep behind the front counter.

"Oh my, where did you folk come from?" he asked, rubbing his eyes.

"That's a long story, my friend. First we need to know where we are," Gordon replied.

"The middle of nowhere," the man joked.

Gordon was not in the mood. "We are from the Big City and we're trying to get to Shallow Lake. How far are we from the lake?"

"Shallow Lake? Hmm," he scratched his chin in

thought. "I don't reckon I have ever heard of Shallow Lake."

"Never heard of…oh never mind. What town are we in?"

"Oldhill."

"Oldhill? I have no idea where Oldhill is. How far away are we from the Big City?"

"Oh, I would say purdy far."

Gordon was finding it difficult to keep his eyes from the man's stained shirt. His grubby appearance was a distraction. The office was in disarray and layers of dust lined every surface. Perhaps Martha was right, Gordon thought.

"Look, maybe we could just get some gas and a map, and then we will be on our way?"

"Our pump is empty."

"What?"

"Hasn't been used in years."

Gordon noticed his wife tense up as she realized they were not going to be going anywhere, anytime soon.

"Joe? Who are ya talking to?" a woman said, as she entered the office from a back room. "Oh, howdy folks."

The woman's hair was disheveled and she had an equally as grubby appearance as the man behind the counter. She was picking at the remnants of a recent meal from her teeth with a toothpick.

"This is my wife, Maude. Maude, these folk just arrived from that wicked storm."

"Ah, be needin a room, will ya?"

"Well, we were just hoping to get some gas and directions and be on our way."

"Our pump is empty," the woman restated.

"Yeah, we just heard that grim news."

"So, ya best be bringin yer bags in. Ya got the pick of any room ya like. The storm should clear come mornin, don't ya be thinkin, Joe?"

"I reckon so, Maude."

"Got some leftovers in the back room here that's still warm. Once ya get settled I can bring some to yer room."

Martha paled. She could not imagine the state of the kitchen in this place. "That won't be necessary, we had a big dinner before we left and had some snacks in the car."

"Suit yerself."

"Since you are kinda in a jam, with the storm and all, I will even offer you our best room for regular price," Joe smiled.

"Ah, much appreciated. I suppose I will go grab our bags from the car."

Martha grabbed Gordon's arm tightly. "I am coming with you, I, ah, forgot something."

"Nonsense, Junior can fetch your bags. Maude, go wake Junior."

"Oh, no, no. No need to wake anyone. We are fine," Gordon insisted.

Before heading back out into the rain, Gordon turned, with a burning question on his mind.

"Just curious, what's with the name of your place? Creep's Motel? Really? Are you trying to keep people away?"

Both Joe and Maude bristled at the comment. "Well, that is our name. We are Joe and Maude Creep."

Martha pinched Gordon's arm to the point where it hurt and then dragged him out the front door. The rain had not let up one bit so they both ran as fast as they could back to the car. Once inside, Martha whirled on her husband.

"As if the Creep's weren't creepy enough, you had to go and insult them!"

"How could I know that was their name? Who has the name, Creep?"

"They do!"

"Suits them, too."

"We are not staying here tonight."

"What? We have no choice."

"I cannot sleep in this place. I have a very bad feeling. They give me the heebie jeebies."

"Well, we have no gas and have no idea where we are. Not to mention this storm."

"Didn't you say once that you drove a half hour with the gas needle on red?"

"Yes, but we have already been driving with it in the red. We won't get very far."

"I don't care, anywhere is better than here."

"You say that now. You will change your mind when we are sleeping in the car out on some dark road somewhere."

"No I won't."

"Dear, be reasonable. It's not safe for us out there. Now, we have to stay here tonight and then we can assess things in the morning. Hopefully the storm will stop by then. We found this place so I am sure there is somewhere else close by where we can get gas, but we can't just go driving blindly in the dark."

"My gut tells me something is off about this place."

"Don't be silly. It's dark, it's stormy, and the owners are a touch creepy. You are letting your imagination run wild."

Suddenly, Martha screamed at the top of her lungs, which caused Gordon to shriek as well, though, he was not quite sure why. His wife had been looking behind him, so he turned and shrieked a second time at the sight of a face pressed against the glass of the car window.

"I got the key to your room," Joe said, from within the hood of his raincoat. "It's right over here if you want to follow me with your bags."

It took several moments before the couple got their breathing back under control. Martha gave her husband a glare that told him she did not want to get back out of the car but they really were not presented much of a choice.

"Come on, it will only be a few more hours until morning, then we'll leave. I'll grab the bags from the trunk. Let's go."

Gordon grabbed three bags and they both ran for the cover of the motel's awning, and then followed Joe down to room 105. Gordon was pleased that at least this room's window was intact and the door sat properly on its hinges.

Joe unlocked the door and invited the couple to follow him inside. The room was quite dark, so the couple hesitated by the doorway until their escort had entered and turned on a small lamp next to the double bed. This was their best room? Gordon and Martha thought silently in unison.

"Is there anything else you need?" their host asked.

"I think we will be fine, thanks," Gordon answered.

"Once you get settled, you can drop by the office and get things squared away. We accept cash and charge cards."

Gordon nodded and closed the door quickly behind

the departing Joe Creep. He turned back and surveyed the room again. Dust covered every surface within the small nondescript room and the awful choice in wallpaper was peeling in several places. There was one double bed, a side table with the lamp, and a writing desk under the window, next to the front door. A tiny bathroom was located at the back of the room and there was a door that linked this room with the one on the left, which was typical in some places. A horrible painting of a family standing in front of a farm hung crookedly on one of the walls. It looked as though a child had painted it with their fingers.

Martha inspected the bed and wrinkled her nose in disgust. "The sheets are all stained. I can't stay here."

"We have no choice, I already told you. We can sleep on the floor, if you prefer. We can pretend we are camping."

Martha was in no mood for jokes.

"I am going to go pay, so you get comfortable."

Thunder cracked outside and caused Martha to jump in fright. "Don't leave me in this room alone."

"I will just be a minute. Lock the door behind me if you like. And stop worrying."

Gordon left and Martha did indeed lock the deadbolt. Her heart was racing a million miles a minute. She had not been exaggerating in the least when she said her gut told her something was off about this place. It was just a nagging feeling that would not let up or allow her to relax.

She walked about the room, conducting a thorough inspection. Even the carpet was stained, she noticed with disgust. Martha stopped in front of the ugly painting and something odd immediately drew her attention. Three people stood in front of a farm, and one of them had a hole for an eye. An actual hole through the painting. Curious, Martha pulled the painting off the wall and her stomach did more flip flops as she found there was a small round hole in the wall. The perfect peep hole, she figured, from the room next door.

She quickly retrieved a tissue from her purse and stuffed it in the dark hole. Goosebumps ran up and down her neck and arms. She glanced at the door that connected the two rooms and her heart skipped a beat at her discovery. There was no lock. She carefully tried the door knob and found that door was indeed locked, but from the other side.

A knock on the front door nearly had Martha jumping straight through the roof of the room. Once she recovered, she quickly unlocked the door and pulled it open.

"Gordon, I nearly…," Martha's sentence was interrupted by another scream.

It was not Gordon who was standing outside the door, but a very large person whose face was concealed behind the hood of a raincoat. Martha was frozen in place with fear.

"W-who are y-you?" she managed to ask.

No answer.

"My husband will be b-back any m-moment now."

No answer.

"P-please don't h-hurt me."

"Junior! You get away from there now. Stop scaring the nice lady!" Joe shouted from outside.

Martha breathed a giant sigh of relief when the silent individual walked away and Gordon came back into the room.

Joe stuck his head around the doorway. "I apologize, Miss. Junior was just curious to see the new guests, is all."

"He doesn't say much, does he?"

"Junior is a simple lad. Well, goodnight folks. Give a holler if you need anything."

Once the door was closed again, Gordon noticed the frantic look on Martha's face.

"I am not staying here tonight," she stated, with a quiver in her voice.

"What? I just paid."

"We are leaving."

"The man apologized for his son. He didn't mean to scare you, you heard him, he is just simple."

"It's not just that, Gordon, come here. I found a peep hole in the wall. It was disguised with the painting."

"You are jumping to conclusions."

"Am I? What about this door that connects to the next room? It's only locked from the other side. Anyone could come in here from the other room."

"Oh, stop it. Come in here for what purpose?"

"To murder us in our sleep!"

"Do you realize how ridiculous you sound? You watch too many of those late night movies."

"Something doesn't feel right. These Creeps are real creeps."

"It's just their name! You are letting this storm affect your judgment. This is all in your mind. Granted, the room could be a little better but…"

"A little better?"

"Fine, the room is a dump. The whole place is a dump. But we are stuck here, just for tonight."

"I refuse to stay here. We are leaving."

"But, dear! We won't get far before we run out of gas!"

"We will be away from here and that's all that matters."

"Oh for Pete's sake!"

*   *   *   *

Maude rushed into the main office and the sound of her shuffling slippers jolted her husband awake, who had just nodded off behind the counter again.

"I thought I heard something," she said. "Joe, that young couple just drove off."

"Eh?"

"That couple. They just left."

Joe joined his wife by the front window and caught a glimpse of tail lights just before they faded from view.

"Hmm, you're right."

"Dang it! I bet Junior plum scared them off. I told ya that ya should hit that one in the head with the shovel when he was in here payin."

"Now, Maude, you know I prefer to get them in their sleep."

"Maybe we ought to send Junior after them? They might not get far with little gas."

"We don't want Junior catching a cold, it's miserable out there."

"Well, there ain't much left from that last couple. Ya want us to starve?"

"Don't forget we still have that traveling salesman in the cold storage."

EYES THAT FOLLOW

From my vantage point, I had the entire library in view. Although the room was quite large, there was nothing that could escape my notice. At this moment, I was observing a secret meeting between Davral, the resident sorcerer, and Lucia, the Queen's sister.

Davral was a sly and meddlesome man. He was afforded much freedom here in the castle, as the King trusted him, foolishly. The man was an outsider and dabbled in dark magic. I believe nobody, save myself, knew just how dark. I was only aware of the sorcerer's less-than-desirable studies and secret meetings through spying. I was an adept spy and gathering secrets was my specialty.

I was born right here in this very castle and have lived all of my twenty-three years here. Make no mistake, though, I am not royalty or nobility. I am still only a commoner. Both of my parents worked here at the castle.

My mother was a chambermaid and did laundry and made beds. My father, before his untimely death from disease, swept the hallways and cleaned windows. From a very young age, I took after my father and wielded a broom as soon as I was able to lift one. Since that time, I have added window cleaning and a little gardening to my daily duties.

While life inside the castle was much better than life anywhere else in the realm, I was still only a commoner and I was paid and treated as such. I wasn't happy with my lot in life. I wanted more. Most castle workers dreamed of one day becoming a steward and being in charge of all the other workers. While that did pay more, and offer a tad more prestige, it still wouldn't satisfy my desires. I wanted to be rich like the lords and ladies that frequented the halls of this castle. I craved gold and all the things that it could buy.

Having lived in this castle for my entire life, I had become quite familiar with every corner. I was trusted and granted access to many rooms that were off-limits to most. I studied the complete layout of the immense building and learned of all the secret passages and corridors. The castle was riddled with them. Some were common knowledge and others, as I discovered with layers of thick dust, were only known by me. The castle was built hundreds of years before the current ruling King and Queen, so the architect, and those that commissioned these secret passages, were all but dust in the wind.

Years ago, while exploring these hidden ways quite often, I was able to unearth many secrets. Not secrets of the castle, itself, but secrets about its residents. Shady dealings. Torrid affairs. Nefarious plots. The kinds of things that people would pay to find out. And pay in gold.

Lots of gold.

I hid in corridors, out of sight. I spied with peep holes, or merely listened through walls. I gathered information that was never meant for ears outside the appointed meeting rooms. At first, I cleverly sold my secrets anonymously, through letters, requiring payments to be left in secluded locations. I was fearful of retribution. Later, as I amassed greater amounts of information, I dealt with a select few people in person. To some people, I was too valuable an asset to lose, to others, I was too dangerous a person to dare inflict harm upon. To cross me, was to find all your secrets laid bare, for all to see. Some people paid me for secrets. Others paid me to keep their secrets. Business was good.

I was becoming so good that I had caught the attention of the royal spymaster; the man who was charged with protecting the King from plots against his life. This was a deadly man, full of resources at his disposal, and unlimited coins to see his job was done well. And it was this very man who quite often would enlist my aid. He allowed me to keep my own secrets as to how I obtained the knowledge that I did. Although, I truly believed that he already knew, but crawling through dusty passages was beneath him. He let me do the dirty work but compensated me handsomely for my efforts.

The spymaster was becoming increasingly suspicious of Davral and had tasked me to keep an eye on the sorcerer. It was an impossible task when the man was inside his own private chamber. There was no way to get eyes and ears in there at all. Fortunately, for me, he spent much of his time in the castle's library. The library was seldom used by others and made a great place for the sorcerer's dark studies and secret meetings.

Davral was not the only one who used the library for reasons other than reading. There was the time I observed one of the castle's guards writing a letter to an acquaintance on the outside, which contained details of the castle's layout. That man was later hung for treason. I had also observed several rendezvous between Lord Brass and Lady Gwendolyn. The problem there was that each was married to someone different. Lord Brass was beheaded and Lady Gwendolyn was publically flogged for their indiscretions. There was also the former steward of the castle, who would use a corner of the library to sleep most of the day away, while he was paid to be working. He was stripped of his job and exiled from the realm.

Davral was up to something but I had yet to uncover what it was. He spent long hours poring over the pages of dark texts, researching such awful topics as demonology and necromancy. He appeared to be most interested in the summoning of demons to extract information on the casting of certain spells. It was said the sorcerer wielded terrible power. I had never witnessed any, firsthand, but the tales were many of the unfortunate fools who ended up on the wrong end of one of Davral's spells. He was a master of transmutation and had a particular love of transforming people into other things.

Spying on the sorcerer was not a job I took lightly. He was a guarded and paranoid individual on the best of days. Most people with secrets generally were. If it wasn't for my knowledge of hidden passageways, I would never have even gotten close to the man. Most often, I made a note of which books he read in the library and where he returned them to on the shelf. Afterwards, when he was gone and I deemed it safe to do so, I would creep in from my hiding place to locate the books.

Just recently, he had spent nearly two hours reading through an old tome of poisons, which contained many home-brewed recipes of deadly concoctions. That raised red flags in my mind. I felt that this was something that the spymaster would need to know. Was Davral plotting to poison someone? The King, perhaps? So engrossed in thought was I that day, that I had not even noticed that Davral had returned to the library and stood directly behind me.

Now, I looked down on Davral and Lucia, who were seated in a shadowed-corner of the library. They were speaking in hushed tones but my acute hearing picked up most of the details. The rest I pieced together from my years of reading lips. The spymaster's greatest fears were confirmed; Davral was plotting against the King, and with the Queen's own sister, no less. The sorcerer had somehow enlisted the aid of Lucia, who planned to administer a lethal dose of poison into the drinks of the King and Queen. Davral had manufactured the concoction in his private laboratory and now it was Lucia's job to get it into the hands of the royal couple. This was the greatest secret that I had ever uncovered, but nobody would ever learn of it.

Davral and Lucia concluded their private discussion and walked in my direction. Lucia kept eyeing my location, suspiciously, until she approached for a closer look. The sorcerer joined her with a smug smile upon his bearded-face.

"I have never noticed that painting before," she said.

"I believe it is a recent acquisition," Davral replied.

"I could swear those eyes moved. I felt like they have been following me around this room."

"Merely an illusion created by the talented artist, no doubt."

"That man's face looks vaguely familiar. Wait, it resembles that man that sweeps the halls. Don't you think?"

"I can definitely see the similarities but who would waste their time painting the portrait of a commoner and floor sweeper? Just a strange coincidence."

"I suppose. I haven't seen him around lately either.

Would be amusing to have him stand here and compare the two faces."

"Amusing, indeed. I heard the man has run away. I don't think we shall ever see him around again."

"Ah, well."

Lucia turned and exited the library leaving me alone with the vile sorcerer.

"You like to spy on people in the library," he stated. "Now you can hang there as a painting for an eternity and spy all you want."

His cruel laughter echoed throughout the room.

PENPALS

May 5

Dear Mr. Baxter,

I found the ad that you placed in our local paper seeking a pen pal. It wasn't an easy thing to spot, due to the fact that it was quite small and tucked underneath the giant ad for that sleazy auto dealer. But I am someone with a lot of time on my hands and I do read the entire paper, word for word, from cover to cover. I must admit, I lead a rather dull life and reading the morning paper is one of my favorite things to look forward to each day. Sad I know. So I can see by your mailing address that you are not very close to the Big City. About three hours by train, I believe. I am curious to know why you chose our paper here to post your ad? I suppose I should refrain from rambling on too much in my first correspondence, as I may not even be of much interest to you to elicit a reply. If you do,

however, care to respond, I will write more the next time, I promise.
Yours truly,
Margaret

*   *   *   *

May 19

Dear Margaret,
It was splendid to receive your letter in the post. Yours is the first reply I have ever gotten, and to be completely honest, I wasn't holding out much hope of hearing from anyone. I was unable to see where my ad was placed in your paper but someone found it at least, so it worked. Why you ask, did I choose your paper for my ad? Simply put, the Big City is far from my home. It is something different. I live in a very small town where everyone knows everyone. So the chances would be great that somebody responding to an ad near me, would most likely be someone I am already familiar with. There is not much thrill in corresponding with someone I already know. In addition to that, there are so many people in the Big City, that the odds were greater that someone would reply, and someone did. As stated in my ad, I am quite a lonely person and was seeking someone to converse with on a regular basis. Don't you enjoy the thrill of expecting something in the post? And then reveling in that joyous feeling you get when you notice that the postman has brought it for you? Admittedly, I was not expecting a reply, so my feeling of joy at noticing your letter in my box was that much greater. My hands were even shaking as I

opened the envelope. Silly I know. I live in a very small house in a thickly-wooded area. One might even consider it just a cabin. I look after my ailing mother, who is bed-ridden, and she is the only other person I really speak with. Unfortunately, she contracted the disease a year ago and her health has been on a steady decline. Most days now, she does not even have the energy to entertain a meaningful conversation. Speaking of which, I should cut this letter short and check on Mother. You were silly to say that I may not find you interesting enough to elicit a response. I look forward to hearing from you again and learning a little more about you.

Your friend,
Donald Baxter

*　　*　　*　　*

May 31

Dear Mr. Baxter,
It was lovely to hear back from you. I completely agree with you about the thrilling feeling of expecting something to arrive in the post. I know we have only just begun to converse but I found myself eagerly checking my box each morning to see if you had sent a reply. The feeling is foreign to me, as until now, all I expect to receive are my monthly bills. This is surely a welcomed change. I am terribly sorry to hear about your mother. It is good to know that she has someone there to care for her. Are you close to town? Close to your neighbors? How old are you, if I may ask? So a little bit about myself. I am in my mid-

forties and I live alone. I was an only child and both my parents passed several years ago. I was left with a large chunk of money as an inheritance so I currently do not work. I will be honest with you, I suffer from anxiety when around too many people, and sometimes find it difficult to leave my apartment. Once I had enough money to do so, I had to leave my suffocating place of work. I do not do much these days, and like yourself, find that I am very lonely. I read the paper in the morning. I water and talk to my plants. Some days I will take walks in a fairly-empty park near to my apartment. I read books. My evenings are generally spent listening to various radio programs, which I thoroughly enjoy. Then I sleep and repeat the whole process anew in the morning. Exciting isn't it? Well, today is looking like a very sunny day, so I suppose I may attempt to get out for a walk and some fresh air. Wish your mother well for me and write back whenever you have time.

Yours truly,
Margaret

*　　*　　*　　*

June 12

Dear Margaret,
Hello again, my new friend. Please, call me Donald. Mr. Baxter sounds far too formal. We are also not that distant in age, as I am closing in on forty-eight. I appreciate your concern and your warm wishes for Mother. Sadly, she has not been showing any signs of improvement and has

spoken very little of late. So believe me, your letters are a wonderful distraction. They come at a time when I need them the most. My neighbors are not very close at all. My house is somewhat secluded, located at the end of a bumpy dirt road. The forest is thick around me and a babbling brook provides a pleasant soundtrack. I don't own a motor vehicle but it is about a twenty-minute bike ride into town. It feels like it's been ages since I have been in town and socialized with anyone. Unfortunately, I do not own a radio either. This house is very old and there is no electricity, so you'll have to pardon me, but I am unfamiliar with your radio programs. What do you like so much about them? You seem to be a charming woman, have you never married before? Pardon me, if that is getting too personal. You may ignore that question if you wish. I can hear my soup boiling on the woodstove so I will end this letter now. I hope you enjoyed your walk in the park that day and each time since then. I eagerly anticipate your next reply.

Your friend,
Donald Baxter

*   *   *   *

June 23

Dear Donald,
How is your mother doing? How are you coping? I will just say that seeing your letter in my box this morning brought a huge smile to my face. Our correspondence has now become part of my routine and sometimes I check my

box several times a day. The postman is usually here by noon, but sometimes I imagine that he might arrive earlier, so I find myself repeatedly checking. So, no electricity? I admire you living the simple life, however, I do so enjoy my radio programs. Little Orphan Beatrice and Detective Darke are my favorites. I listen to them religiously each week, and while fictional, I feel their lives have become a part of my own. I cannot wait to hear what happens in each episode. They give me something to look forward to, much like your letters, now. And to answer your question, no I have never been married. I have never found someone compatible. Oh, I have to mention that the other day, I found myself looking into the price of train tickets to your town. The trip would be reasonably inexpensive. What do you think about meeting for lunch and a coffee one afternoon this summer? I think it would be wonderful to put a face to the letters. Let me know your thoughts, and I look forward to your reply.

Yours truly,
Margaret

*　　*　　*　　*

July 2

Dear Margaret,
I have been coping well, thank you for inquiring. Mother is the same, I regret to say. I, too, thoroughly enjoy receiving your letters and honestly it is the only thing I look forward to. I don't have much else going on in my life and as I

stated before, I don't have electricity in order to enjoy your radio programs. Though, they do sound quite interesting. Your idea does sound splendid but I feel it is just too far for you to travel. Three hours, one way, just for lunch? Then there is the issue of Mother. I shouldn't really leave her for very long. Perhaps, some other time in the future? In the meantime, I could describe myself, to give you an idea of who you have been conversing with. I am a few inches short of the six feet mark. I have salt and pepper hair, with a beard to match. Blue eyes. Let's see, what else? Oh, I am possibly a little heavier now than I should be, given my sedimentary lifestyle these last few years. Does that help? How has the weather been over there? Have you been enjoying your walks?

Your friend,
Donald

*　　*　　*　　*

July 15

Dear Donald,
I hope you are well. I have been enjoying my walks when the weather allows for it. It has been raining a lot this year, though. Well, I did something really spontaneous yesterday. I understand your concerns about your Mother and the travel time I would need to endure to visit you, but I went ahead and purchased a train ticket. I can read a book on the train so that does not bother me in the least. And I was thinking I could just visit your house. I would very much like to bring your Mother some flowers. I

wouldn't have to stay long at all. The idea is that could we meet face to face. I really hope you won't mind this, terribly. My ticket is for July 29. I timed it so that you should have already received this letter and will be aware of my impending arrival. I should reach the train station in your town by approximately noon. From there I can hire a motor car to take me to your place. I will bring the coffee. I have to say I am very excited. It's been so very long since I have ventured outside the Big City. I will keep this letter short, seeing as how we will converse in person quite soon. Looking forward to meeting you, Donald.

Yours truly,
Margaret

*   *   *   *

September 21

Dear Margaret,
First of all, allow me to apologize for everything. This has taken me longer to send than I had planned, but I wasn't sure how best to explain this. I feel terrible that you had to waste your time traveling here and I know you must have a million questions running through your mind. I truly hope that you did not hurt yourself when you fell, running from the cabin. It was wonderful for me to see you in person, it really was. You are even prettier than I had dared to imagine. I am sorry that you cannot say the same, as you were unable to see me. Oh, dear, where do I begin? I have been dead for a long time, Margaret, longer than I can even recall. Shortly after Mother had passed, loneliness and

despair got the better of me, and in a moment of
weakness, I took my own life. But that wasn't the end for
me, no, not at all. I am not sure if this was a punishment
handed down by God, or perhaps even the Devil himself,
but I was cursed to continue to live in this cabin, alone.
No, not live, sorry, I should rephrase that. I have been
cursed to exist, somehow, within this cabin. I cannot leave
and I cannot be seen by anyone. Margaret, I am so
dreadfully lonely. Were I able to end this existence in some
way, I would have, long before now. I did discover that for
some reason, I am able to manipulate small items, such as
a pencil and paper. The post office believes that someone
still lives here, and continues to drop off and pick up mail
from my front door. I watched you enter my cabin that
day, Margaret. I saw the confusion etched into your face as
you looked around. Nobody has dusted in here in so long,
I apologize for the state of the place. I wanted so badly to
communicate with you, to let you know that I was here. I
did the only thing that I could and began to write, "Hello
Margaret," on the piece of paper sitting on the dinner
table. I realize how startling that must have been to
witness. I didn't mean to frighten you so. I wished you had
not run away so quickly. I wished you could have stayed
longer so I could have written you an explanation. Please,
Margaret, can we not remain friends? I am so lonely.

THE MOLE PEOPLE

I awoke with such delighted excitement. The blazing sun
that sent forth its warm rays through my bedroom
window, confirmed that it was indeed morning. I thought
the morning would never come. The previous night, I
tossed and turned, with little hope of falling asleep and
speeding up the coming of the dawn.

I had waited for this day for so long that when I
climbed into bed, my mind would not allow sleep to come.
I spent the first hour just imagining what it will be like to
gaze upon real mole people for the first time. I had seen
drawings in school, of course, but nothing could compare
to seeing one of these elusive creatures in the flesh.

My cousin Stew claims to have seen one years ago,
over by the Bubbling Falls. Nobody believes him, least of
all me. Stew was a practical joker and apt to make up grand
tales. I had fallen prey to his tomfoolery enough that I was
almost certain he had never seen one of the mole people.

He could tell a convincing tale, I will give him that, but his past deceits were proof enough for my dismissal of his claim.

As Stew did not count, I did not know anyone personally who had seen a real mole person. They lived far underground, and the rare times that they did come to the surface, it was only at night. Their sensitive eyes could not handle the brightness of the sun, plus, the night allowed them the cover they required to sneak into towns in order to steal food and supplies. My town had been the victim of several raids by the mole people over the years, but it was not until recently, that one had ever been captured.

That mole person, a male it was said, was sold to the traveling carnival so that he could be put on display. While a proper habitat was being built, a second mole person was captured. Now, the carnival has two mole people and today is the first day that they will be on display to the public. There is a nominal fee involved with the pleasure of viewing them but I have been saving money for weeks now in jubilant anticipation of this day.

Even my brother, Ed, had trouble sleeping as his excitement nearly equaled my own. Generally, his snoring, or just heavy breathing, kept me awake at night but this last night he was silent. The few times I glanced in his direction, I saw his eyes wide open, much like mine.

We were typical brothers, in that we tended to annoy each other quite often and rarely could get along. But this day we had something in common. We were both dying to get our first peek at the mole people. Mother called us for breakfast and we made our way down to the kitchen.

"Are you both excited this morning?" Mother asked.

We both nodded in unison as we began to wolf down

our cereal. She taught us not to speak with our mouths full but we didn't need to, she could read the answer clearly on our faces.

"Your father has gone to fuel up and then will be back to pick you both up to take you to the carnival."

"Aren't you coming with us?" I asked.

"Oh, no, I don't think I need to see any mole people. Dreadful creatures they are."

"You mean you are not even curious to see a real one? Not at all?" my brother wondered.

"Not at all. You know, when I was a little girl, we had a farm over in the Barren Plains. The mole people would raid our farm at night, from time to time, and steal everything we had to eat."

"And you never saw one? Ever?"

"Heavens, no! The mole people are creatures of the night. I would never have left our house after the sun went down. I even had trouble sleeping at night. I was always afraid they would sneak into my room and snatch me away."

My brother's face paled. "They do that?"

"There have been rumors but nothing was ever proven. The mole people only seem to care about food and not taking humans, thank goodness for that. But as a child, I had an active imagination, and I was sure they were going to come and get me in the night."

"Why don't they make their own food?"

I shook my head. Sometimes my brother asked the dumbest things. "They can't grow any food underground, stupid."

"Mom, Willie called me stupid," he whined.

"Now, Willie, you know better than that. Apologize

to your brother."

I grumbled an apology but I still thought he was dumb.

"He is right, Ed, the mole people cannot grow anything underground. It's even very difficult for us on the surface, since the wars, but fortunately we have valuable livestock."

"If they got hungry enough, I am sure they would eat humans," I added, just to bother my brother.

"Stop that, Willie. The mole people might not eat us but they are still dangerous, none the less. I am just glad they finally caught two of them. Maybe that will send a message to the others and keep them away from us."

A horn blasted from outside and my face lit up.

"There's your father. Now, run along and enjoy yourselves today. And for heaven's sake, don't get too close to that cage, or whatever they are holding those creatures in. You just look from a safe distance."

We had no time to answer Mother as Ed and I went out the side door in a flash and raced down to the car, climbing into the back seat.

Father smiled at us from the rearview mirror. "I would say you boys are a little excited, eh?"

We nodded our heads in unison.

"Well, get comfortable, the drive is going to be about an hour. The carnival is set up just outside the ruins of the Big City."

That news was almost as exciting as going to see the mole people. I had only ever seen the ruins of the Big City once in my life. It was an area that most folk generally avoided. It was inhabited now by undesirable types, and it was said that the mole people traveled more frequently through there, using old sewer and subway tunnels. The carnival would draw a lot of visitors so I would think that it would be safe for everyone to be there.

In school, I had seen photos of what the Big City looked like before the wars. It was marvelous. It was hard to imagine that buildings stood so tall at one time and so many people lived together in one place. The once grand city was now a cesspool for degenerates and outcasts.

My brother Ed was always the worrier.

"Is it safe to go near the Big City?" he asked.

"Don't worry, boys, there will be a lot of security at the carnival. This is probably the biggest attraction they've ever had."

"Dad, do you think the mole people look as weird as they do in our school books?" I wondered.

"They sure should. Enough folk have seen them before. You know, your Grandfather shot one of them once."

"Really? Gramps saw a mole person?"

"Yes, really. This was a long time ago, mind you, while I was still young. Gramps heard some sort of commotion outside one night, from the cows. His first thought was that perhaps a coyote was out there. He grabbed his shotgun and headed out toward the barn. That's when he came face to face with one of the mole people. The wretched creature carried a pitchfork but Gramps had his gun and shot the thing in the leg. It managed to escape but they never did come back to our barn again."

"Wow, Gramps never told us that story."

"It's a true story. I remember that shotgun blast woke the rest of us up that night. We all ran outside but all that was left was a blood trail through the field."

"What color was their blood?" Ed inquired.

"It was just red, same as ours."

We spent the rest of the drive in relative silence. My mind was swirling with excited thoughts of seeing the mole people. No doubt my stupid brother was having the same thoughts.

My excitement rose to an entirely new level when the carnival came into view. Giant flags and brightly-colored tents were spread across an open field, with the ruins of the Big City as an awe-inspiring backdrop. So focused was I on the carnival, that I barely even took note of the ruined skyscrapers in the distance.

It seemed as though a million vehicles were already here at the carnival and we were forced to park a fair distance from the entrance. The sun was particularly hot this day but even that could not bother me. My skin felt as though it was on fire by the time we bought our tickets and walked through the gates into the carnival.

I am sure my smile nearly swallowed my face. I glanced over to notice that Ed had the same goofy grin. We were instantly intoxicated by the heavenly smells around us. Vendors were selling everything from roasted corn to candied apples. The midway boasted a variety of different games and barkers shouted to all the kids, attempting to lure them in with dazzling prizes that could be easily won.

My Father didn't even have to ask us if we wished to play any games first. He knew our main concern was getting to the tent that housed the mole people and that tent was not difficult to locate. We just had to look for the largest gathering of people.

Ed, however, did get distracted by an ice cream stand and begged our father for an ice cream cone. He bought us each one and it didn't take my clumsy brother very long before some of his ice cream dripped onto my favorite green shirt.

"Dad, Ed spilled ice cream on my favorite shirt."

"Now, Ed, you be more careful."

"It's so hot out. The sun is melting my ice cream faster than I can lick it."

"Well, we will have some shade when we get inside that tent. Come along, boys, let's see what we came to see."

This was finally the moment. All the exuberant buildup had led to this. I knew we were in for something special by studying the faces of those who were leaving the tent. Expressions of joy and wonder were clearly etched on all the faces, young and old.

Our timing seemed to be impeccable. Even before we could maneuver our way through the thick crowd toward a large cage, a carnival barker announced that they were about to introduce the second mole person into the same enclosure. We could be in for a real treat now, I thought. Perhaps the mole people would fight each other. It was said the creatures could be quite vicious when provoked.

Everyone inside the tent was attempting to get the best spot to view the attraction. Fortunately, my father was able to clear a path through the crowd so that my brother and I had an unobstructed view. Both our jaws hung open in amazement. The two mole people looked as equally bizarre as the photos from my school books. They wore human clothes to appear like us but looked nothing like us.

The two strange creatures just stood motionless

within their cage, staring out at the gathered crowd. It didn't appear that they held any animosity toward each other and a fight between the two did not seem to be imminent. I wasn't too disappointed, however, just to see these rare things in the flesh was a still joy for me.

I wanted to get closer to the cage for a better look but feared getting any of my ice cream on the people around me.

"Dad, can you hold my ice cream?"

"Mine, too," Ed echoed.

"Oh, come on now boys, I only have four hands."

*　　*　　*　　*

The second man was shoved forcibly into the cage. He quickly noticed that he was not alone but did not recognize his fellow prisoner. His gaze shifted to the ghastly gathering of surface dwellers that were all staring back at him with clear amusement.

The first man turned to regard the other and saw clearly the look of horror upon his face. "This was your first trip to the surface, was it?"

"Yes," the second man answered.

"I have been up here many times but I never get used to seeing them. Who knew the surface radiation from the wars could produce such abominations all these years later?"

"Good heavens, look at the small one with the green shirt, holding the ice cream cones. It has two heads!"

THE CEMETERY KEEPER

Thunder cracked overhead and my eyes flew open. I hadn't yet fallen asleep but I felt I was close. It wasn't the storm that was keeping me up this night, it was the unbearable heat in my apartment. I had two fans running, with little success of cooling me off. All they seemed to do was circulate around the hot air.

Wiping sweat from my forehead, I rose from my bed to fetch a glass of water. My throat felt parched. I had little trouble navigating my way through my dark apartment with the aid of the constant lightning flashes from this horrendous storm. I reached my kitchen and fumbled about for a clean glass.

As I downed a mouthful of the refreshingly-cool water, I nearly choked from a sight that caught my eye outside the window. My apartment overlooked the creepy cemetery across the street. A strange light bobbed up and down within the shadows of the graveyard, giving me quite a start. I froze in place, momentarily wondering if I was observing the glow of some spirit from one of the thousands of dead residents.

I exhaled a sigh of relief when the outline of a person came into view, carrying a lantern. I watched as the person patrolled the interior side of the cemetery's gate. I continued to observe until the person, and the lantern, eventually vanished from sight behind one of the many buildings within the property.

I felt embarrassed for my moment of silliness, thinking that the newly-hired cemetery keeper was some undead creature that had risen from a grave. An unfortunate rash of vandalism had prompted the cemetery to hire an overnight keeper to keep the young punks away. A group of rotten young brats had recently found fun in tipping over headstones and spray painting on others. Despicable acts, if you ask me. I couldn't understand anyone's desire to walk through a graveyard at night, and disturb the resting places of the dead, no less.

So now the cemetery had some poor fellow patrol the property each night to ensure those rotten kids caused no further trouble. I felt bad for the man. I didn't envy him on the best of nights, but tonight in particular, was an awful night to have to patrol a cemetery. This storm would only amplify the creepiness of that place, tenfold. Just gazing upon the graveyard from my apartment window this night, was enough to raise goosebumps along my arms.

My financial predicament allowed for my current living arrangement. The only job I was able to land since moving to the Big City was stocking shelves in a department store. A minimum-wage salary didn't make living alone an easy task. I absolutely refused to live in the Junkie Jungle, the poorest neighborhood in the city, so this apartment was the next best option. When I first noticed the ad in the paper, I thought there was a typo with regards to the cost of the rent. It wasn't until I came to view the place that I understood why. There was reluctance in most people to live so close to a cemetery. Perhaps, it was some childhood fear that the dead would one day rise up to feast on the flesh of the living, or perhaps it was the daily reminder of what awaited us all in the end. One day we would all take up permanent residence within those gates for our eternal sleep.

For me, I believe, it was a little of both. I grew up on monster magazines and horror films at the picture show. I admit that even as an adult, I felt uneasy around graveyards. In the back of my mind, there was always that lingering thought of a hand reaching up from the ground to grab my ankle. Silly, I know, but unavoidable due to all the films I had watched where just such a thing had happened.

And I did find it somewhat depressing to walk past that dreary place every day to go to and from work. It was a sad thought to think that I would slave away my life, working miserable jobs, only to end up buried in that cemetery with the rest of those unfortunate souls. That's what I had to look forward to.

But as I said, my finances dictated my decision to move into the apartment. I simply couldn't afford to live anywhere else. My apartment sat above a bakery in a two-story building, where all the apartments were situated above businesses. Far too many times, I was forced to purchase unneeded sweets, purely because of the aroma wafting through my windows. My waistline was also suffering as a result.

I would never be able to purchase a radio if those pastries kept dipping into my radio fund. With no radio, I passed away most evenings reading. And, at the sufferance of my imagination, all I had to read was my old monster magazines. Spooky stories and living next to a cemetery did not always make for a good combination. Horrible storms also did not help that equation. Thunder rumbled again and I made the decision to stop staring at the graveyard and get back into bed. I gave the cemetery keeper one last thought; pitying the man walking around out there in this storm, and then exhaustion set in and sleep claimed me.

Over the next week, the summer's heat attributed to more loss of sleep. I would toss and turn in my sweat-soaked sleepwear, until I was forced to the kitchen for a glass of water, or to place a wet towel onto my head. Each night, I took note of the poor cemetery keeper, making his rounds, ensuring the graveyard was free from vandalism. I had to wonder if this man was truly fearless, or was he simply that desperate for work? Often times, necessity drove people to do things that they would normally not. Personally, I could not imagine being desperate enough for money to patrol a graveyard at night. Not that I am belittling the work, or the good that that keeper is doing, but my mind would just not allow me to do it. So consumed would I be with childish thoughts of the undead, that I would most likely just flee in terror within the first half-hour. Clearly, this man did not harbor those same fears, or he found some way to successfully suppress them in order to collect a pay check.

Then I had to wonder, what one would be paid to perform that duty? I surely hoped that man was getting paid more than the minimum wage that I was making. Granted, the act of patrolling the property was not a difficult one, but the mental stress afforded by the frightening surroundings alone, should be worth a pretty penny. But, knowing today's employers, I was certain he was not making nearly enough as he should be.

One Friday, I was asked to stay late at work to help with an inventory count of the entire department store. I readily agreed, since the overtime money would be quite helpful in boosting my radio fund. Every day at work, I had to listen to my fellow coworkers discussing the previous night's radio programs, but of course, I knew nothing of what they spoke of.

The sheer amount of inventory at the store made for a very long shift indeed. I was not walking home until very close to the midnight hour. The darkness had not bothered me overly much; that is until the cemetery came into view. I promptly crossed the street to avoid being so close to the surrounding wrought-iron gate. Very rarely was I ever out after dark. Looking at the cemetery from the safety of my apartment was one thing, walking past it at night was something entirely different.

Goosebumps ran down my arms and I quickened my pace. I felt slightly embarrassed, harboring childish thoughts that the monsters were going to get me. I nearly stumbled with fright, when a bobbing light caught the corner of my eye. I was relieved when I realized it was just the cemetery keeper making his rounds. I was able to slow down to a normal walking pace, as I now possessed a buffer. Surely the monsters would get him first, before me, due to his closer proximity.

I continued along, while keeping a subtle eye on the keeper. As he neared the gate, closest to the sidewalk on the opposite side of the street, he appeared to notice me and pause in his patrol. For a brief moment, curiosity nearly got the best of me, as the thought crossed my mind to speak with this man. Perhaps, I could get answers to the myriad amount of questions that filled my head. Even putting a name to this person would be welcomed. But, my baseless fear of the cemetery drove away any notion of engaging that man in any form of conversation during the night-time hours. I walked straight home and went to bed.

The next morning, I sat in the malt shop a block away from my apartment and sipped a coffee while reading the paper. One of the front page stories had caught my attention. Three teens had gone missing the previous night and have appeared to vanish without a trace. Friends said the three were on their way to the cemetery to cause mischief sometime around midnight. None of them returned home. Detective Kane was urging anyone that may have witnessed anything, to come forward with information.

I scratched my head in thought. Reports would have put those kids in or near the cemetery approximately around the time I was walking past to get home. I did observe the cemetery keeper patrolling last night. I would think that if those kids were up to no good, they would have been spotted by the keeper. That is why he was hired, after all. And yet the article made no mention of any employees having seen these potential trouble-makers. Could they have possibly eluded the man while he was making his rounds? Or, dark thoughts came to my mind, or could the keeper have something to do with their disappearance? While the idea of kids vandalizing graves was disgusting to me, I did not feel as though they should have gone missing because of it. Punished, yes, kidnapped or killed, no.

The thought that the cemetery keeper had something to do with this case nagged at me for several hours. As I looked out my window toward the graveyard, I decided I should go speak with the daytime manager. My first instinct was to call this Detective Kane, to relay my suspicions, but I determined that doing a little of my own detective work first was best, before jumping to conclusions.

*　　*　　*　　*

I paced back and forth on the sidewalk in front of my building. It was getting close to midnight and I had yet to spot the cemetery keeper. After meeting with the cemetery manager earlier this afternoon, I had burning questions that required answers. My heart skipped a beat when suddenly the bobbing light from a lantern came into view.

I crossed the street immediately, making a straight line in the keeper's direction. I had uncovered some disturbing information and I felt that I was about to get to the bottom of this missing person's case. As the man neared the gate he appeared to notice my approach and I shouted.

"Hello? You there, hello? I need some answers from you."

The man remained silent and continued toward the gate with a slight stumble to his step. I bet he was drunk, I thought to myself.

"Just who are you?" I asked. "I spoke with the manager of the cemetery today and he told me they never hired anyone to patrol around here at night. He looked at me like I had three heads when I told him about watching you make your rounds each night."

The closer the man got, I nearly gagged from a god-awful stench. I managed to remain composed and continued with my questioning.

"I saw you here last night when those kids reportedly went missing. I am willing to bet that you saw them. I bet that you even know what happened to them."

The horrible smell intensified as the man reached the opposite side of the gate. He spoke not a word and reached for me through the iron bars with this free hand. I yelped and jumped back out of reach, to avoid being grabbed by a rotted hand. The light from the man's lantern illuminated his face and I quite nearly fainted from the mere sight of it. Like his hand, his face was rotted with his jaw bone clearly visible.

I am not above admitting that I screamed and ran for my life. The cemetery had never hired anyone to patrol at night. It would appear that the dead had unearthed their own keeper to take care of vandals.

THE WISHING WELL

Little Billy kicked a can through the field behind his house. Grasshoppers scattered in all directions at his approach. The afternoon sun had cooled off and made playing in the open field tolerable. Billy enjoyed spending time in the field and in the abandoned barn from the vacant lot nearby. He liked to pretend that the barn was a grand castle and that he was the king of said castle. Other times, he was a brave knight, dispatched from the castle to hunt down some marauding menace, like a fire-breathing dragon or a giant two-headed troll. He would find a suitable stick to substitute for his enchanted sword and slay the beasts to become the beloved hero of the realm.

Billy had very few friends, so he spent much of his time playing imaginary games alone. He and his mother lived in a ramshackle house on the far edges of town. The friends that he did have, lived too far away for him to visit. His mother did not own a car and they were too poor to afford a bicycle. When the school bus dropped Billy off at home in the afternoon, he would head out into the field and amuse himself. Today, however, he was not in the mood.

He continued to kick the can as if kicking it would solve his problems. Billy hated his math teacher. Mr. Dennis took great pleasure in terrorizing the kids and humiliating them whenever possible. He would laugh and call them stupid for answering questions incorrectly. In today's class, he pointed out the holes in Billy's shirt and told the rest of the students that Billy was an example of how not to dress. The only clean shirt Billy had available had holes in it. Mr. Dennis even inquired if Billy had been raised in a barn. The other kids laughed.

It was not the first time that Mr. Dennis had humiliated Billy in front of the others but the accumulation was beginning to take its toll. Billy dreaded going to math class and would feel sick to his stomach before entering the classroom. It was affecting his moods and he played less. Today, he just kicked the can about with his head down. He did not feel like slaying any dragons.

The can he had just kicked for the hundredth time, struck something solid, and the noise it made pulled Billy from his dark daydream. He looked around and realized that he was now on the far-western side of the abandoned barn. The side he never ventured to, as his own house and property was out of view. It always made Billy nervous if he couldn't see his property.

Curiosity defeated his nerves and he walked over to inspect an odd pile of tree branches. The can had struck something more solid than a branch and soon Billy was tossing them aside to reveal an old stone well, hidden beneath. He wondered why someone would have gone through the trouble of attempting to hide the well but then figured that perhaps it was for safety concerns. There were always stories of children falling into wells and Billy's own mother had warned him from time to time to be careful around them.

This particular well looked far older than any other well Billy had ever seen. There was something about the stones that it was built with. It stood nearly half as tall as the boy and the opening was roughly two feet across. Billy peered down the well but it was black as pitch and the bottom was out of sight. He found a small pebble and dropped it into the hole and was surprised that he never heard it land. No splash from water. No sound of stone on stone.

"Hello?" he shouted, and his voice echoed back at him five times.

Billy's stomach grumbled and he imagined that it would be close to dinner time. He stuck his hands in his pockets and turned back toward his house, kicking the can once again. His hand found the penny that he had hidden away in his left pocket. He generally kept his coins in his right pocket, a fact that was well known by Reggie, the school bully. Reggie had relinquished Billy of his nickel earlier that day, but Billy had stored a penny in the other pocket, allowing it to go unseen. He intended to buy a licorice stick with it, but after today's math class, he wasn't in the mood.

He paused for a moment to consider the words of his grandmother, who had said you could make a wish by tossing a coin into a well. She called them wishing wells. It was a difficult decision for Billy; make a silly wish or buy a licorice stick tomorrow. Under normal circumstances, Billy would never think to throw away a penny but these were desperate times. His mind was made when he considered that Reggie might just steal his penny tomorrow anyway. Better to throw it in the well than to hand it over freely to the bully.

Billy turned back to the well and leaned over. He spoke his wish aloud and tossed his only penny inside. It clinked once as it bounced off the side of the well but no sound of it landing was ever heard. He sighed and headed back home. He made it back just in time for dinner and to quiet his angry stomach.

The next day, Billy entered his math class accompanied by his usual feelings of anxiety. They awaited the arrival of Mr. Dennis, who was unusually late. As fifteen minutes went by, the class became restless. When twenty minutes had passed, Mr. Davidson, the principal, rushed into the classroom and informed them that Mr. Dennis was not in and proceeded to give the students some math problems to spend the rest of the class working on. Billy was obviously relieved to have a day without Mr. Dennis but it also made him curious about the timing of his absence. He pondered his wish, that Mr. Dennis would never bother him again, and then shook his head. It was just a silly wish. Wishes didn't really come true.

The following day, a substitute teacher was present in the math class when Billy arrived. He also noticed that police were inside the principal's office. The rumors around the school were that Mr. Dennis had just vanished. He was not at home and all attempts to find him had so far been unsuccessful. It was a complete mystery. Billy hated Mr. Dennis and did not feel sorry for him in the least, but his child's brain wondered, what would happen if anyone found out about his wish? Could he be held accountable for it? That was ridiculous, he thought, it was merely a coincidence.

A week passed by and still there was still no sign of Mr. Dennis. At lunch time on this particular day, Reggie was shaking down Billy for his lunch money, as per usual. This time, Billy had actually lost his nickel on the way to school. He had a newly found hole in his right pocket which must have attributed to the lost coin. Reggie, however, didn't believe the boy, and punched him hard in the stomach as a result. It took several moments before Billy could stand again and head for his next class.

After dinner that day, Billy begged his mother for a penny, which she reluctantly handed over, due to his skills of losing money. He then told her he wished to play outside before the sun disappeared and ran straight over to the old well. For quite some time, he just stood like a statue and stared at the well. Could it have really worked? he wondered. Or was it just a coincidence? Either way, he had decided to try it a second time.

Billy closed his eyes and spoke aloud. "I wish Reggie, the school bully, would disappear."

He tossed the coin into the well and again, heard nothing more. The sun was beginning to set behind a distant hill, so Billy ran home and spent most of the night awake, thinking about his wish.

When lunch time arrived the following day, Billy was shocked that Reggie was not waiting outside the back door of the school for him. He looked all over the schoolyard but the awful bully was nowhere in sight. Billy even decided to wait around, just to see if Reggie was running late, but the bully never showed up. The day passed with no Reggie and with no Mr. Dennis either.

Two days later, during dinner, Billy's mother noticed that her son was less talkative than usual.

"Something wrong, Billy?"

"No."

"Come on, you are even quieter than usual. Nothing you want to talk about?"

"Do wishes come true?"

"Wishes?"

"Yeah, like when you blow out the candles on your birthday cake and you are told to make a wish. Do those wishes ever come true?"

Billy's mother sat silent for a moment and considered the question. She figured her son was getting old enough now, that perhaps she shouldn't be telling him any more lies, and filling his head with fantasies. Life was not made up of fantasies and she supposed he should start getting used to that.

"Well no, Billy, those wishes don't come true. Believe me, if they did we wouldn't be living in this dump eating macaroni and cheese for dinner every night while your father lives in that mansion down the street, flaunting his wealth. That doesn't mean that the things you wish would come true, never will. You just have to make them happen on your own. There is no magical solution to make them come true."

"Oh."

"Why are you asking about wishes?"

"Well…"

"Yes?"

"Well, because I made two wishes and they came true."

"What wishes? What are you talking about?"

"I was playing over by the barn one day and I found this old well that someone had tried to hide."

"Now, Billy, you know you aren't supposed to wander away that far and you shouldn't be playing near any wells, they can be dangerous."

"I know but I was real careful. Anyway, I remember what Grandma said about wishing wells so I threw a penny in and made a wish."

"Is that why you asked me for a penny the other day? So you could throw it away into a well? You know we don't have a lot of money, Billy, you can't just go doing fool things like that."

"I know but Mr. Dennis was always so mean to me. Mean to everyone."

"Mr. Dennis? The missing teacher?"

"Yes. I wished that Mr. Dennis wouldn't bother me anymore and the next day he didn't show up to school. Nobody has seen him since I made that wish."

"Don't be so silly, that's just a coincidence."

"That's what I thought at first. So, I went back to the well and made another wish. This time I wished that Reggie the bully would disappear."

"Who is Reggie?"

"He is a bully. He takes my money every day at lunch time or punches me if he doesn't get it. I wished he would disappear and the next day he was gone. He also hasn't been seen since I made my wish."

Billy's mother tried to digest everything that she had just heard. It had to be a coincidence, wishes were not real.

She did her best to convince her son that those disappearances had nothing to do with his wishes and sent him along to his room to work on his homework.

Much later in the evening, when Billy had gone to bed, his mother threw on a sweater and went out the back door. The air was chill and the night was dark. The half-moon afforded little light, but once her eyes adjusted to the gloom, she set off in the direction of the barn.

Generations of her family had owned the land they lived on. After listening to Billy's story, she recalled a similar incident involving her parents. Her father had been a terrible drunk and physically abusive. Her mother used to say that she wished he would disappear one day, and then one day…he did. Billy's mother had always assumed that he just up and left. But, as Billy had reminded her, her mother used to tell them that if you threw a penny into a well and made a wish, that it would come true. She shook the nonsensical thoughts from her mind and marched toward the barn.

It took some effort to locate the well in the darkness but she eventually did. She stared at it for some time and wondered why there was a nervous feeling in her stomach. She thought to settle this silly notion of wishing wells and took a penny out of her wallet. She placed her wallet on the edge of the well and held the penny tightly, thinking of a stupid wish she could make. Her ex-husband was the first thought that came into her mind. Like her father had been, he was a drinker and a deadbeat. After abandoning her and Billy, he had come into some money and bought a large house just down the street. He never gave her a cent for Billy. She was positive that he only bought that house to torture her, as she had to pass it every single day on the way to work. Just the thought of him angered her so much. She was holding the penny so tightly, that it left an imprint on her palm. Her mind was made.

She closed her eyes and spoke her wish. "I wish my deadbeat ex down the road, Donny, would disappear."

She threw the penny into the well and waited to hear some kind of splash. There was nothing. She waited for…something…she wasn't sure what. She thought maybe there would be some kind of feeling that the wish worked. Perhaps, some kind of tingling sensation. When she felt nothing at all, she turned and walked back toward her house. She scolded herself for even coming out here and wasting a perfectly good penny. Earlier, she had been telling her son not to be foolish and believe in wishes, and then she had come out to the well and did the very same thing.

About half-way back, Billy's mother realized she had forgotten her wallet at the well. She cursed to herself and turned back. As she approached the well, movement caught her attention and froze her place. She was unsure if the darkness was playing tricks with her eyes but she stood motionless, nonetheless. Something crawled its way out of the well. Something dark and something vaguely humanoid. A horrendous stench suddenly assaulted her nostrils and she fought back the urge to vomit. It was the unmistakable stench of decay. Whatever that thing was, it smelled as if it had been dead for a very long time.

Its movements were jerky and sent shivers all over her body. She stifled a scream as it sniffed at the air, as though it detected her presence. She exhaled as it stood unsteadily, on two legs, and then shambled off away from her; off in the direction of Donny's house.

MONSTERS IN THE CLOSET

Mrs. Brookfield entered the office wearing a mask of concern. Behind her, she pulled her ten-year-old.

"Dr. Phinn, it has started again. Little Norbert thinks the monster is back in his closet. He hasn't slept in two days."

"I don't think it is there, I know it is there," her son responded.

Mrs. Brookfield shook her head in frustration. "You see? Whatever are we to do? I thought he was over this? He was doing so well."

"Alright, give Norbert and me some time to talk."

Mrs. Brookfield left the office muttering under her breath. "You think you have done everything right. Raised all our children the same way. You would think they would understand that there is no such thing as monsters. I mean really, monsters? Just ridiculous."

"Have a seat, Norbert," Dr. Phinn suggested, once his mother had closed the door behind her. "How have you been?"

"Okay."

"Just, okay?"

"Yeah."

"It doesn't sound like everything is okay. What's this about the monster coming back to your closet? I thought it left months ago?"

"It did."

"And you are certain it is back again? You are sure that maybe you just didn't imagine it this time, or maybe it was just a nightmare you had?"

"No. I heard it in my closet and then it even opened the door to peek at me."

Dr. Phinn opened a file folder on his desk and pulled out a sketch of Norbert's monster. "So, did it look exactly the same? A shadow creature with horns and wings and dull, red-colored eyes?"

Norbert fidgeted nervously with the buttons on this shirt. "Yes."

"So, now you are losing sleep again? You are worried it is going to get you?"

"Yes."

"I imagine you had your parents check the closet again? They didn't find anything, did they?"

"No. It leaves before they come."

Dr. Phinn nodded and wrote a few things down in a notebook. "These monsters are clever, aren't they?"

Norbert shook his head in agreement.

"So, when you left your lamp on at night, that seemed to work? Correct?"

"Uh huh."

"Yes, you see these shadow creatures fear the light. Even something as faint as a bedside lamp is enough to hurt their sensitive eyes. I am going to suggest leaving the lamp on again each night. I believe the creature will become frustrated eventually and leave for good."

"You still believe me?"

"Of course I do. You are not my only patient with monsters in their closet. It is actually a more common thing than folk want to believe."

"Why don't my parents ever believe me?"

"Well, there are some people who have never seen one of these monsters before, so for them it is hard to imagine that they exist. Then there are others who have seen them before but do not wish to acknowledge their existence anymore. It brings back frightening memories of when they were a child and they just want to forget about them and pretend it never happened."

"Have you seen them before, Dr. Phinn?"

"I will tell you something in confidence, Norbert, because we are friends. Yes, I have seen these shadow monsters before."

"Really? In your closet?"

"Yes, when I was about your age, one of them chose to visit my closet quite regularly. I can remember feeling very scared that it would get me and I lost a lot of sleep as well."

"What did you do?"

"As you can see, I am still here. It never got me. I left two lamps on at night for almost three months and the monster, I assume, grew too restless waiting for me to turn the lights off again and decided to leave me alone. It never returned to my closet ever again."

"My parents don't like it when I keep my lamp on. It disturbs my father's sleep and they say it is more expensive."

"You let me speak to your mother about that. Now, how about you go out there and tell her to come back in for a moment. And just remember, Norbert, the lamp will keep the monster away. I am positive that it will not be able to get you."

Norbert nodded and went into the waiting room to inform his mother that Dr. Phinn wished to speak with her. She returned to the office and closed the door behind her. Despite being offered a seat, the woman elected to pace about the room.

"Well? What are we to do? He is positive there is a monster in his closet and he simply cannot sleep because of it."

"I have advised him to just leave his lamp on for a while longer. That seemed to help before."

"That is easy for you to suggest, you don't pay our electricity bill. And my husband has trouble sleeping with that light coming from right across the hall."

"Mrs. Brookfield, I have told Norbert that the light from his lamp will keep the monster away. Allow him to leave it on for a while longer and soon he will forget about the monster."

"I admit I am no expert on such things but shouldn't you be trying to explain to him that there is no such thing as monsters? You tell him that the lamp will keep the monster away, so you are confirming that there is a monster."

"Can you not recall being that young? A child's mind works differently from ours. They still cannot differentiate between fantasy and reality. Norbert truly believes that there is a monster in his closet and you cannot convince him otherwise. The best thing to do is to play along and suggest things that will chase away the monster. He will be reluctant to share his concerns with you if you are always telling him that he is lying or imagining things. Norbert isn't the only child I deal with that believe monsters live in their closet. It is a common belief for children. They are either in the closet or hiding under the bed, just waiting for those lights to go off. Trust me, Mrs. Brookfield, I have much experience with this stuff."

"Oh I know, I have done my research. You are considered one of the best child psychologists in the Big City. Your fees can attest to that."

Dr. Phinn chuckled. "Believe it or not, I am trying to prevent you from having to come back here. Norbert is an otherwise very normal child. Just allow him to keep the lamp on and his problems will go away. As he gets older, he will forget about monsters and these worries will disappear. I see it all the time."

"We will see, I suppose. Well, thank you for your time again, Dr. Phinn."

"It is my pleasure."

The following week, another concerned parent brought their nine-year-old child to Dr. Phinn's office. Sammy had apparently gotten very little sleep for over a month, due to a monster in his closet. It was beginning to affect him at school as he would frequently doze off in class.

Dr. Phinn sat in his chair with a fresh new notebook, while Sammy sat on the sofa nearby.

"So, Sammy, your mother tells me you believe there is a monster in your closet?"

"Yes, sir."

"Do you just hear it, or have you also seen it, by chance?"

"Both, kinda. Sometimes I can hear it scratching around in there. Like it scrapes its claws on the back of the door. Sometimes, if I forget to close the door all the way, I can see it peeking out at me."

Dr. Phinn made notes while Sammy spoke. "And when it peeks at you, what do you do?"

"Um, well like sometimes I will run into my parent's room and like well other times I just hide under the blankets."

"And when you hide under the blankets, it goes away?"

"Usually, cuz then it can't see me."

"Yes, I have heard these monsters possess limited intelligence. They can be easily fooled by blankets."

"You know about these monsters? My parents say I am making it up. They say it is all because my older brother took me to the picture show to see a scary film."

"Oh, I see. What film was it?"

"The Creeping Thing."

"I wasn't aware they allowed children your age to see films like that."

"Well, um, my brother kinda snuck me in a back door."

"Ah. Did the film scare you?"

"Yes."

"And how long after that, would you say, that you started hearing the monster in your closet?"

"Um, a few days later."

"I see."

"I am not making it up. I saw it."

"Oh, I am sure you are not making it up. I can just understand why your parents might think it is related to the film you saw. But to answer your earlier question, yes, I do know a bit about these monsters. I believe you are telling the truth."

Sammy paled, slightly. "So, it is real?"

"I am afraid, so, yes. But these monsters are just curious creatures, and as you have already experienced, easily fooled. Have you ever wondered why it has never come out of your closet and, well, got you?"

"Cuz I am good at hiding."

"Well, that is part of it, yes. These monsters just like to observe humans and try to learn from us. They are content with only watching from the closet where they think that nobody can see them. Once you hide under the blankets, it believes you have disappeared, and then it will grow bored and simply leave."

"But even after I do that, it comes back again."

"Every night?"

"No. Every couple days."

"So, you have seen it a few times? Can you describe it to me?"

Dr. Phinn began sketching in his notebook as Sammy described the monster. "Um, it's like all black, like a shadow. Um, it has horns and wings."

"Wings like a bird?"

"Um, no. Wings like a bat."

"And its eyes? Can you remember?"

"Its eyes are red."

"Bright red?"

"Um, no. More dull."

Dr. Phinn completed a sketch that looked very similar to Norbert's monster. It resembled the monster of several other of his patients as well.

"Yes, these shadow monsters are quite common. And quite harmless, I can assure you."

"How come my parents can never see it? Even my big brother makes fun of me. He can't see it either."

"These monsters are afraid of anything larger than they are. They avoid adults and older children."

"How can I get rid of it?"

"Just keep doing what you are doing. Stay under the blankets where it cannot see you and eventually, as I said, it will grow bored and leave. It will find someone else's closet to visit."

"It won't get me?"

"No, it won't get you. It will not even know you are there if you remain out of sight under the covers."

Sammy's parents had to return two other times, as their son, while still hiding under the blankets, claimed he could still hear the monster scratching the closet door. The monster apparently left after Dr. Phinn thought to give Sammy a "magical" necklace that was created to ward off monsters. In truth, it cost a penny and came out of a vending machine.

Norbert's parents also brought him back several months later, quite frustrated. Dr. Phinn suggested using the necklace, and so far, to his parent's delight, Norbert's monster had disappeared.

One evening, Dr. Phinn stayed late at his office in order to organize some files. His office was located on the second floor of a building which housed various other offices. Dr. Phinn noticed the time and was running late for an appointment. He stepped out of his office and into the hallway, but before he could lock the door, a voice gave him a start.

"You are Dr. Phinn?"

The man appeared to be in his forties and glanced about nervously, with bloodshot eyes. If Dr. Phinn had to guess, he would say that the man had not slept for days.

"Yes, I am. What can I do for you, sir? I am running late for an appointment, elsewhere."

"My name is Franklyn Wade and I was told that you might be able to help me with a problem I am having. I have not been able to sleep as of late."

"Well, Mr. Wade, I am child psychologist. I do not have any adult clients."

"I figured that but I was told you are familiar with my problem."

"And what problem might that be?"

"I know how crazy this might sound but I believe I have a monster in my closet."

"I see."

"An employee of mine said that she brought her son here to speak with you about a monster. She told me that you were able to solve her problem and to make the monster go away."

"Well, as I said, I don't have any adult clients but if you wish to call in the morning and book an appointment, we could possibly have a chat."

"I can't wait until the morning. I haven't been able to sleep at all. Can we not just talk now?"

"It is after hours, Mr. Wade, and I have an appointment to get to."

"Please, I beg you! I am quite wealthy, I will pay double whatever you would normally charge for a session."

"Being after hours, my fee would already be double what it would be in the morning."

"I don't care. I will pay you double that, then. Please, can we just go inside and talk?"

"Very well, come inside."

Dr. Phinn turned all the lights back on and directed the man to have a seat on the sofa in his office. The money was definitely a contributing factor to his decision to entertain this individual, but truth be told, the doctor was a little intrigued to hear his tale. He picked up a fresh notebook and indicated to Mr. Wade that he may begin.

"You probably think I am nuts."

"No, Mr. Wade, I do not."

"I know what you must be thinking, though. You are thinking, what is an adult doing here complaining about a monster in his closet? That is the stuff of a child's imagination."

"I wasn't thinking that at all."

"Have you ever heard an adult say there is a monster in their closet?"

"Well, no, but there is always a first for everything. And as I said, I deal strictly with children. Tell me, Mr. Wade, have you been to the picture show lately? Have you watched any scary films?"

"Oh, I know where this is going. You think I am suffering from some kind of nightmare due to watching a horror film. I assure you, doctor, I do not frighten so easily. And no, I have not been to the picture show to see anything in quite some time."

"It was merely a simple question. I wasn't implying anything. Let's get right to the monster then, shall we? How do you know there is one in your closet? Have you seen it?"

"I have. I wouldn't be sitting here talking to you if I thought I was imagining the whole thing."

"Tell me about it."

"It started a few weeks ago. At first there was scratching sounds from inside the closet. My first thought was mice. So I would ignore it at first and then just look in the morning, but I could find no traces of mice."

"Did anyone else in the household hear these noises?"

"No, I live alone."

"So, when did you first see it?"

"I would say it was the fourth night of hearing noises when I finally got out of bed and opened the closet door," Mr. Wade visibly shuddered as he recalled that night. "It was standing right there in my closet. Right there staring me in the face."

"What was? Describe what you saw."

Mr. Wade stood up from the sofa and began pacing about. "You won't believe this."

"Try me."

"It was more of a shape in the darkness. Like a shadow. It felt as though if I reached out for it my hand would pass straight through."

"What did the shape look like?"

"It stood about as tall as me and was jet black. I could make out small horns and large wings."

"What about its eyes? Could you see any eyes?"

"Yes, they were yellowish. A kind of sickly yellow."

Dr. Phinn paused during his sketch of the monster and looked up. "Yellow eyes, you say?"

"Yes, yellow eyes. I can admit I yelled in fright and slammed the closet door shut. I ran downstairs and spent the rest of the night sitting on my sofa. I know what I saw. It was real, doctor. I know I am a grown man but there was no way I imagined what I saw. I was not dreaming. I was wide awake."

"No, no, I believe you, Mr. Wade."

"What can I do about this? Nobody else will believe me?"

Dr. Phinn scratched his head. "Well, there is a magical necklace, but it is not cheap."

The doctor explained the necklace and its success rate with warding off the monsters. Desperate, the man paid for the necklace and the session before leaving.

Dr. Phinn locked the door behind the man and then returned to his desk.

"Yellow eyes," he kept repeating to himself, as he flipped through the pages of his personal phone book. "Yellow eyes."

He found the number he sought and picked up his phone and dialed. It was late, he knew, but the detail of the yellow eyes bothered him. He needed answers.

"Hello? Dr. Ryanne?"

Pause.

"This is Dr. Phinn. I apologize for the lateness of this call but something has come up tonight."

Pause.

"Yes, well, I just had a client leave my office moments ago. He claims to have seen a monster in his closet with yellow eyes. Yellow eyes, Dr. Ryanne. And the client was an adult male. An adult. I thought we agreed to leave adults alone? We are only to frighten the children."

Pause.

"I don't care if you needed the extra money. The man came here to see me anyway, not you. We have built ourselves a remarkable business here by only scaring the children. Adults will only cause us headaches, believe me, Dr. Ryanne."

Pause.

"Well, I sold this man one of those ridiculous necklaces so just stay away from his house at ninety-one Wellsprings."

Pause.

"That's fine but let's just be smart about this in the future. I don't want to jeopardize what we have going here. We have the child come in for a few sessions, then cure them and stop visiting their closets. We need those word-of-mouth referrals that our therapy sessions actually work."

Pause.

"Alright, good. Now, I must be off. I am running extremely late. I was supposed to be in someone's closet hours ago. I hope they have not yet fallen asleep."

Pause.

"Yes, good night to you, Dr. Ryanne." Dr. Phinn hung up the phone, shaking his head. He removed his jacket and tie and placed them carefully on his chair, so as not to wrinkle them. His body began to shake and shudder until he transformed back into his natural form. A form that was more shadow than substance. The creature with the dull red eyes flew out of the office window, carried by bat-like wings, toward his appointed closet.

THE VOICELESS IN BENSHALA

Two horses pulled the large wagon along the bumpy road, making it difficult for the bounty hunters to get any rest. Each time Evonne seemed to drift off to sleep, a violent jolt from the wagon startled her awake. She sat up, thinking it best to remain alert, seeing as how they were traveling through unfamiliar territory.

Evonne and Vrawg were possibly the most famous bounty hunters in the western nation of Tauros, but they were no longer in Tauros. Recent encounters with assassins from the criminal organization, the Sundered Sons, had prompted their decision to do some traveling. The two bounty hunters were far from cowards but needed a break from watching over their shoulders. They knew that the world was full of wanted criminals so finding work anywhere should be a simple enough task.

The three merchants they encountered on the road had informed them of some trouble in the great city of

Stonewood, so that is where they were headed. With the King of Stonewood placing large bounties on the heads of thieves, Evonne figured the city was an easy place to make a small fortune.

During her time as a pirate, Evonne had sailed much of the Western Sea, but had never before traveled outside the borders of Tauros on land. The merchants had allowed her to peek at one of their maps and she hoped that she and Vrawg were going in the right direction. Vrawg, the giant half-ogre, was from the Grey Ash Mountains, just north of Tauros. He had traveled through parts of the Northern Wastes but was also unfamiliar with this wild and untamed territory between Tauros and the Stonewood lands.

Evonne glanced up at the black clouds and cursed. A storm was threatening to make their journey to the next town a miserable one. By her estimation, they were still about two days away from Green Harrow.

"I don't like the look of them clouds," she commented to her usually silent partner. "I doubt we will find any shelter from the rain when it comes."

Vrawg shrugged his shoulders. Storms did not bother him.

"Well, we all weren't raised in a cold and dreary cave like someone I know. If my cloak and clothes get wet I am not going to be the most cheery of traveling companions."

Vrawg smiled. His petite friend was never the most cheery of traveling companions, even on the best of days. The little human liked to talk tough but Vrawg knew she enjoyed his company almost as much as he enjoyed hers.

As predicted, the rain came down hard in the early evening and Evonne's mood had turned quite sour. She huddled under a tarp in the back of the wagon, doing her best to remain as dry as possible, while Vrawg held the reigns to the horses.

"Lights," he blurted, with his deep voice.

"What about lights?" Evonne responded, annoyingly. "See, this is what I mean when I say you need to learn to speak in complete sentences. When you just say lights, I have no clue about the context of what you are talking about."

"I. See. Lights," he said, very slowly.

Evonne crawled over to join the half-ogre at the front of the wagon, while attempting to remain under the cover of the tarp. Her partner was correct. Off the road and to the north, the glow of lights was evident from behind a large hill.

"City lights," Vrawg guessed.

Evonne shook her head. "There is no city around here. A town, perhaps, something small that was left off of that merchant's map."

The small bounty hunter spotted a fork in the road ahead. As they approached, Evonne noticed that the road continued east, but at some point in time, had also branched off to the north. The road north was now overgrown and appeared to have seen no recent traffic. A sign post still stood at the intersection but the sign that pointed north was torn down and missing.

"That road is fairly overgrown but I think our wagon can manage it. We could sure use a place to ride out this storm. What do you think?"

Vrawg shrugged his shoulders. He would do whatever Evonne thought was best.

"You know, you are allowed to have an opinion from

time to time. Well, let's see what's behind that hill. If it's nothing, then we only wasted an hour of traveling time."

The bounty hunters urged their horses to take the overgrown road to the north but slowed down their pace. The going was far rougher and Evonne had to hold on to keep from tumbling out of the wagon. They followed what was visible of the original road, which wound its way around a large hill and then descended into a deep valley.

Evonne's estimation had been correct; a small town sat in the center of this valley, with a most curious-looking tower at the far end. Lights could be seen from various windows within the town, while the tower was quite dark. It loomed like a terrible shadow, overlooking the smaller buildings. There were visible lights, though, so the place was inhabited and that was all Evonne cared about. There should be an inn, which meant a nice warm fire and bed awaited her below.

As they neared their destination, they spotted another sign post. This one had been pulled from the ground and tossed aside, face down in the grass. At Evonne's insistence, Vrawg climbed off the wagon and picked up the sign, holding it toward his friend.

"Welcome to Benshala. I don't remember a Benshala from that map and they don't appear to be very welcoming. If I had to guess, I would say we were the first people to use this road in years. Well, that looks like a stable over there. Come on, let's go."

The first building they reached was indeed a stable. Nobody was about, and the doors were unlocked, so the pair of bounty hunters let themselves in, then tethered their horses and unhitched their wagon. Before leaving the stable, Evonne grabbed her signature crossbow and slung it over her back, just in case. Likewise, Vrawg carried his massive war hammer.

Evonne realized how intimidating they would appear to the townsfolk but precautions had to be taken. The bounty hunters resembled a pair of gladiators, wearing mismatched pieces of a variety of armor types. Vrawg wore spiked pauldrons on both arms, running from his shoulders to his elbows. Black steel greaves protected both shins and black leather armor covered his chest. He wore a thick black girdle with a grinning skull etched into the front. The seven-foot tall, bald-headed and grey-skinned half-ogre, could make the most seasoned warrior tremble in their boots.

The much smaller Evonne wore a chain mail vest and tasset. Her right shoulder was covered with a steel pauldron, while her left was bare. She wore bracers on both wrists and greaves on both shins. A curved sabre, her favored blade from her time as a pirate, hung from her belt. Across her chest were five throwing knives. Despite her warriors-appearance, Evonne was quite attractive and wore her long blonde hair tied back into a ponytail.

"I haven't seen anyone around. I suppose this nasty storm has them all in hiding. Can't say I blame them. Let's see if we can find an inn."

They passed several homes and shops. The shops were all closed, and Evonne noticed dark forms peek from several windows, but disappeared the moment she turned to face their direction. A chill ran down Evonne's spine but she cursed herself for being silly.

Up ahead, the bounty hunters spotted a tavern which seemed to be open for business, though, eerily silent given the early hour of the evening. Evonne entered first, followed by Vrawg, who had to bend over and turn sideways to squeeze through the doorway.

They immediately noticed several cloaked individuals crowded around a fire, no doubt to warm up and dry off their rain-soaked clothes. Evonne was going to want a turn by that fire but first she needed a drink. She took a seat at the bar but there was nobody to take her order. A curious sight grabbed her attention. A thin layer of dust coated every bottle of liquor that sat on the shelves behind the bar. It was as if the bar was never used.

"Hey, does anyone actually work here?" Evonne called out. "Thirsty travelers here with gold to spend."

Evonne jingled a pouch full of gold coins and tossed it onto the bar. She grew annoyed when nobody in the room paid her any attention.

"Do I have to serve myself?"

A cloaked man finally extracted himself from the fire and walked behind the bar, though, his face was hidden within the darkness of his hood.

"A mug of ale for me and my friend here."

The man grabbed a dusty bottle of Hulbard Whiskey, along with two glasses, and placed them in front of the bounty hunters. He returned to the fire with the others.

"I said ale," Evonne called after him. She turned to Vrawg. "Can you believe this service? No tips for him. How can a tavern have no ale?"

Regardless, she poured a glass for her and Vrawg and downed hers in one gulp. Evonne got up from the bar and approached the six men around the fire.

"So, what's the deal with this place? Signs torn down. The road is overgrown. You don't like visitors?"

She was met with only silence.

"Is there an inn where we can get a room and wait out this storm?"

Silence.

"Hey, I am talking to you people."

Frustrated, Evonne grabbed the barkeep by the shoulder and spun him around. The hood of his cloak fell back and the bounty hunter gasped. She drew her sword and took several steps back. The other men turned to regard the stranger and Evonne noticed the same horrific sight within their hoods. These men had no mouth. Their faces were otherwise normal, they were just missing a mouth, as if it had merely vanished, leaving their faces featureless below the nose.

Vrawg gripped his hammer in both hands and growled, not realizing at first what had spooked his tiny friend. Then he noticed the same thing she had and wrinkled his face disgust.

"Ahh, umm," Evonne stammered. "Keep the change there on the bar and...ahh...we will be leaving now."

She quickly exited the tavern and Vrawg was right behind her. The rain had not let up but Evonne cared little about it.

"By Zalara's black heart, did you see their faces?"

Vrawg nodded. Evonne still held her sword and glanced about, nervously. She sheathed her weapon and replaced it with her loaded crossbow. As unnerved as she felt, Evonne was not about to give up on shelter from the storm so quickly.

She pointed to the closest home where lights could be seen behind drawn curtains. "Let's get some answers."

The pair approached and knocked on the door, keeping an eye on the tavern behind them. When no answer came, they knocked again. Evonne tested the door and found it unlocked. She decided to enter and ask a few questions.

Her arrival startled a woman that stood next to a warm wood stove. Evonne's skin paled again when she noticed the woman had no mouth. Two children that sat on the floor playing with a doll, looked up to regard the bounty hunter. They, too, were missing their mouth.

Evonne backed out the door and slammed it shut, bumping into Vrawg in the process. "No mouths, all of them," she said. "Let's get out of here, huh? A little rain never hurt anyone."

The proud bounty hunter refused to run but walked at a very brisk pace back to the stable. Vrawg kept up, watching intently behind them. Evonne shut the stable doors behind the half-ogre and for a moment, considered spending the night in the stable. She quickly dismissed that thought. She had seen enough of Benshala.

As they were untying their horses, an odd sound caught both of their attention. They thought it came from below them, and strangely, it resembled a muffled voice. The bounty hunters paused and stood silent. They heard it again. Vrawg scooped up a pile of hay and tossed it aside to reveal a trap door in the floor.

Evonne grabbed her crossbow and pointed it at the door. "You, in the trap door, come out slowly."

The trap door opened and a disheveled-looking fellow with white straggly hair and beard, slowly emerged. The first thing Evonne took note of was that he had a mouth.

The man's eyes went wide when he took in the sight of Vrawg. "What in the heavens is that?" he whispered.

"With all the bizarre things I have seen in this town, he is the least of your worries," Evonne answered.

"You have seen them, then? The voiceless?" he continued to whisper.

"If you are referring to the freaks with no mouth, then yeah, we've seen them. Why are you whispering?"

"So *he* doesn't hear me."

"Who is, *he*?"

"Who are you two?" the man ignored her question. "How long have you been in Benshala?"

"We are just travelers and wanted shelter from the storm. We only just got here but we have seen enough and are leaving."

The man looked them both over. "You don't look like the average traveler. Are you mercenaries?"

"We are bounty hunters, if you must know. What in the Abyss happened here and what are you doing hiding in the stable?"

"I am Winston and I have been hiding here for a long time."

"Hiding from what?"

"Hiding from Vandorn."

"Vandorn?"

"The sorcerer that lives in the tower. He is a wicked creature of immense power. He has cursed Benshala and he is the reason for the voiceless. I studied under Vandorn for many years and fled from his wrath just in time to hide here. I am the only person who still has a voice. He knows I still live and seeks me out so that he may steal my voice as well."

"What do you mean cursed the town?"

"He has cast an awful spell on every member of the

town, stealing their mouth and rendering them speechless."

"How do they survive? How do they eat?"

"The curse must preserve them in some way. Eliminating their need to eat or drink."

"Why would he do this?"

"A long time ago, Vandorn was a bard and sang in taverns, entertaining folk for gold. He already dabbled in magic at that time. Some unknown affliction robbed Vandorn of his beautiful voice and ended his career as a bard. He then dedicated his life to the study of magic in an attempt to save his voice. When he was unsuccessful, he turned to darker magic. Vandorn never was able to restore his voice, so in a jealous rage, he stole the voice of everyone in Benshala. Well, everyone but me. He could not bear the sound of others laughing and singing, so he punished them all."

"Why haven't you fled?"

"He is watching for me. Forever watching. And listening. So I have remained hidden and live every day in fear."

"You studied under him, you said? Studied magic?"

"Yes."

"And you have never thought to kill this sorcerer? Use magic against him?"

"You cannot kill that which is already dead."

"Pardon me?"

"Vandorn has used dark magic to preserve his life long after his body had died."

Evonne shook her head. "You have gone mad. Can you hear yourself?"

"It is true, I swear it. Vandorn is a terrible creature

and far too powerful for me, alone. During my time in solitude, I have devised a way to possibly defeat him but I am unable to accomplish this myself."

"Do tell."

"Vandorn's life-force occupies the body he is currently in. If that body is destroyed, his life-force will enter the next closest body. I have devised a spell that can trap his life-force." Winston retrieved a small box from his hiding place under the stable floor. "Ironically, I have chosen a child's music box. The spell is interwoven into the box and as the box plays its melody, it casts the spell. Once the spell is cast, Vandorn's life-force will become trapped inside the box. But, the melody must play to its completion for the spell to be successfully cast. I cannot keep Vandorn distracted long enough for that to happen. Perhaps the three of us…"

"Whoa, whoa, whoa, stop right there. The three of us?"

"There is nobody else we can turn to for help. People avoid Benshala."

"And for good reason, it would seem. Look, you can hide in our wagon and come with us."

"I cannot abandon my friends and family here."

"Suit yourself. We just wanted shelter from the storm. We didn't come here to battle some undead sorcerer. Come on, Vrawg, untie the horses."

Vrawg stood his ground, arms folded over his chest. Evonne knew that look on his face.

"Move it, you big oaf. Let's get out of here."

"Bad man," the half-ogre said.

"Yeah, but we don't go after bad men unless someone is paying us a lot of gold to do it."

"Please, Miss, I beg you. Benshala is not a rich town but I am sure we can give you something for your trouble. Please?"

"Bad man," Vrawg repeated.

Evonne looked to her stubborn partner and let out a giant sigh. "So, we just have to distract this sorcerer long enough for that box to play its melody?"

*　　*　　*　　*

Vrawg, with his massive war hammer held tightly in both hands, led the way into the tower. Evonne was closely behind, her crossbow held at the ready, and Winston with his magical music box, took up the rear. Fortunately, for the half-ogre, the tower boasted high ceilings and he was able to stand to his full height.

Evonne was pleased that torches lined the interior walls of the tower, as they had neglected to bring along any source of light. The main entrance had been left unlocked, which also worked in their favor. Winston, quietly, informed the bounty hunters that the sorcerer had little fear of intruders.

The first room they entered was devoid of any furnishings. The same black stones that made up the tower's exterior made for a very dreary and unwelcoming feeling inside as well. A single winding staircase led upward and Winston indicated that that is where they would find Vandorn. The sorcerer spent most of his time in the top-most room of the tower.

Despite Vrawg's protests, Evonne led the way up the stairs. They were dealing with a sorcerer, which meant ending the battle as quickly as possible was of the utmost importance. Evonne's crossbow was the best way to deal with dangerous adversaries from a safe distance. The former pirate was an expert marksman and deadly accurate with her preferred weapon.

The trio slowly ascended the stairs and wound their way up to the top of the tower. A large circular room, spanning the entire circumference of the tower, awaited them at the top of the stairs. The room was lit with several torches and resembled what one would expect a sorcerer's workshop to look like. There were overflowing bookcases aplenty and cluttered work tables with various jars and beakers.

The hair on Evonne's neck rose as she spotted an ornately carved chair against the far wall. A cloaked man sat in the chair with a hood concealing his face. What Evonne found to be most curious was that his wrists appeared to be shackled to the arms of the chair.

She took careful aim at the man. "Alright, Winston, open your little box."

Winston placed the box on the floor and opened the lid. Immediately, a haunting melody began to play. A maniacal laugh erupted from their new companion which gave the two bounty hunters quite a start.

Alarmed, Evonne spun to regard Winston. "What's wrong with you?"

He continued to laugh like a stark-raving lunatic and pointed to the cloaked individual that was chained to the chair. Evonne and Vrawg watched as the hood of the cloak was blown back by a mysterious wind. To their shock and surprise, the face of the man was the spitting-image of Winston, only he was missing a mouth. His eyes widened in some silent plea of warning.

Evonne whirled and aimed her crossbow at the laughing Winston, only, he no longer resembled Winston at all. In his place stood a skeletal individual wearing a black robe. His face was replaced with a skull and a red glow emanated from the black pits of his eye sockets. Goosebumps ran up and down the skin of both bounty hunters as they regarded this horror.

"So, bounty hunters," it cackled in a hoarse voice. "You have to survive until the melody plays out. Good luck."

Evonne pulled the trigger of her crossbow but was met with despair as the bolt passed harmlessly through the sorcerer's head to strike the wall behind. The sorcerer had vanished and now his mad laughter could be heard from all over the room. The bounty hunter quickly reloaded and she and Vrawg spun in circles, attempting to pinpoint the source of the laughter. It seemed to come from everywhere all at once.

Suddenly, and to the dismay of the two bounty hunters, they found themselves surrounded by ten images of the same sorcerer. Each laughed and appeared as real as the next.

Evonne picked one and fired again. The result, however, was the same; the image merely vanished. She dropped her crossbow and drew her sabre.

"Vrawg, just start swinging until we find the real Vandorn!"

The half-ogre roared and leaped into action, swinging his mighty war hammer at the various sorcerers. Each successful strike, passed clean through, but caused the illusion to vanish. Evonne followed suit, slashing through several fake sorcerers. A feeling of dread was building inside her as she considered the trap they had been led straight into.

She quickly dispatched three of the illusions with her sword and then drew a throwing knife with her free hand and dispatched another. Vrawg eliminated the last of the illusions and the bounty hunters looked to each other in confusion. The melody continued to play, and by Evonne's estimation, they still needed a couple of minutes.

She picked up her crossbow and reloaded, just as the sorcerer appeared again. This time, there was only one of him and he stood near the chair with the voiceless Winston.

"What do you think, Winston?" he said in his awful voice. "Have I played with them long enough?"

Evonne fired and watched her bolt bounce off some invisible barrier that must have surrounded the sorcerer. Vrawg charged forward with his hammer raised above his head. Vandorn laughed and said a few words in a language that neither of the bounty hunters understood. Suddenly, the floor beneath Vrawg's feet liquefied and the half-ogre sunk in, knee-deep. Another word from the sorcerer caused the floor to harden once more, effectively trapping the giant bounty hunter.

Evonne gaped with astonishment. An invisible force rendered her motionless and then pulled her towards the cackling sorcerer. She cringed as bony fingers probed her face.

"No voices allowed in Benshala," the sorcerer said.

He spoke the words to another spell and then to Evonne's complete horror, her mouth vanished. The spell holding in her place expired and she fell to the floor. She attempted to scream, but of course, could not.

Evonne watched as Vrawg roared with fury and raised his hammer in an attempt to throw it. She wanted to shout a warning to her partner that the sorcerer was protected by some magical barrier. The half-ogre threw his hammer with all the strength he could muster. Blue sparks exploded as it shattered the invisible shield and struck the sorcerer dead center in the chest. Vandorn flew back into a bookcase and his body broke apart. Bones lay scattered across the floor and his head rolled to a stop near the imprisoned Winston. The glowing red eyes dulled and then disappeared completely.

A most curious black mist rose from the broken body of the sorcerer and was then sucked straight into the music box as the melody concluded. The lid closed on its own, trapping the soul inside.

"I can't believe you really defeated him," a voice shouted.

Evonne noticed that the Winston chained to the chair possessed a mouth, once again. As did she, to her absolute joy. The destruction of the sorcerer had eliminated the curse he had placed on them. Vrawg, too, found that he was no longer stuck in the floor.

The half-ogre broke the shackles that imprisoned the white-haired man in the chair and he stood and danced about the room, singing and shouting at the top of his lungs.

"My voice! My voice is back! Bless you two strangers! You have saved Benshala from a terrible curse!"

Evonne rubbed her chin in thought. "I don't get it. Why would Vandorn approach us, as you, and attempt to bring us here in order to destroy him?"

"Because he never considered you both to have a

chance of defeating him. This was a game to him. You see, I constructed that music box in order to trap Vandorn. I attempted to do this myself but was unsuccessful. Vandorn imprisoned me here and each time strangers came to Benshala, he would lure them to this tower in the same way he did with you, in order to play with them and taunt me at the same time. I was chained here and forced to watch him kill or curse scores of people who were only trying to help by using the box I created. But you both have succeeded where all others have failed."

Vrawg retrieved his hammer and had a new found respect for it. It was forged long ago by dwarves using a strange metal that neither he nor Evonne was familiar with.

Evonne glanced over at her friend. "Bless those dwarves. Whatever that hammer is made of, it was able to shatter the sorcerer's magical barrier."

Curious sounds could be heard from outside the tower and the trio ran to the closest window for a look. Despite the rain that continued fall, hundreds of townsfolk filled the streets of Benshala, shouting and singing. Their voices had returned.

"What becomes of Vandorn, now?" Evonne inquired.

"The music box must be destroyed to prevent that evil creature from inhabiting another body. Come, let's join the others below and celebrate."

*   *   *   *

After an entire night of feasting and drinking, an elated Winston walked toward his home; a home he had not seen in so long. The morning sun had chased away the storm clouds and Winston smiled to himself. He was proud that his music box had actually worked; he just wished it had not taken so long.

Thinking of his music box, he searched his pockets but could not find it. He could not recall taking it from the tower but he was positive that the bounty hunters had. He had informed them that it needed to be destroyed.

Winston reached the front door to his small house and smiled again. He was finally home.

*   *   *   *

Evonne and Vrawg sat in their wagon as the horses turned back onto the road heading east. Evonne smirked as she noticed the look on Vrawg's smiling face. She knew that look. It was his, I told you so, look.

"Alright, out with it. Go ahead. I know you want to say it."

Vrawg looked at her curiously.

"I know you want to gloat and say you were right. Fine. He was a bad man and we saved the town, thanks to you. Feel better now?"

Vrawg smiled and nodded.

"By the way, what did you do with that music box?"

Vrawg shrugged his shoulders.

"What do you mean? Didn't you take it?"

"No."

"Well, I certainly didn't. I wasn't about to touch that thing. I suppose Winston did. He made it so I am sure he knows how to destroy it. Look, I am going to lay down back here. If you see anything strange, ignore it, huh? I have had enough excitement to last me a while. Let's just get to Stonewood."

*　　*　　*　　*

Ryval climbed in through the window and paused to survey the room before him. It took a moment only for his eyes to adjust to the darkness. It appeared to be some workshop. The thief had scaled the tower wall in the dead of night, hoping to bypass any sleeping residents or posted guards. Ryval was not even sure what town he was in, as it did not show up on any of the maps he had studied before.

He silently patrolled the cluttered room, looking for anything of value, when something on the floor caught is attention.

"What do we have here?" the thief whispered, as he picked up a small wooden box and opened the lid.

ZED'S TRAVELING PUPPET SHOW

There was a buzz throughout the town this fog-enshrouded morning. It had been some time since there was any cause for excitement. Generally, not much happened on the outskirts of this region, aside from the humdrum of daily life. And while the visiting entertainment was widely regarded as something aimed at only the younglings, adults enjoyed it all the same.

Zed's Traveling Puppet Show had come to this largely-forgotten town, situated in a mostly-unpopulated region of the world. Though, just because these folk were a fair distance from the next closest city, did not mean they were ignorant to the goings-on around them, and Zed's Traveling Puppet Show was known the world over.

Zed was a world traveler and explorer, and took his highly-entertaining puppet show everywhere, much to the delight of younglings across the entire planet. And much to the delight of most adults, as previously mentioned.

Zed's caravan had arrived in town two days prior and crowds of folk had flocked to the location to observe him and his assistant set up the stage and surrounding tent. Most everyone, whether they would admit it or not, were hoping to catch of glimpse of Zed's famous puppets, but alas, they were not to be seen. Tucked away securely, until it was show time.

The arrival of Zed's caravan had been a welcomed-surprise and the two-day wait was agonizing. But, the morning of the third day had finally come, and that meant the show was soon to begin.

Byff did not have to set his alarm this morning, as his two children performed their duties as the perfect substitute. He imagined that they found little sleep that night in anticipation of this morning's show. He had been fortunate enough to secure three front-row seats, dead center to the tiny stage.

Vendors had come out in droves and there was certainly no shortage of snacks and beverages, or even cheap souvenirs. Fortunately for Byff, his children showed little interest in the useless wares being hawked; they were determined to get to their seats to await the beginning of the show.

And they were not forced to wait too long. Just as the last individual from the sold-out crowd settled into their seat, Zed's lovely assistant appeared from behind a curtain to address the assembled audience. She thanked everyone for coming and assured them they would be thoroughly entertained for the next hour and a half, while Zed's puppets enacted the tragic tale of Marvin and Henrietta.

No sooner had she disappeared back behind the

curtain, the crowd cheered as two puppets climbed onto the little stage. Zed was known for his wild imagination and that became immediately evident at the sight of these two puppets. They were multi-limbed creatures with the most bizarre heads and eyes. One was supposed to be male, Marvin, and the other female, Henrietta, though which was which was not obvious until the puppets spoke. Henrietta's voice was of a higher pitch. Byff could not determine if Zed provided her voice while hidden behind the stage, or if it was that of his assistant.

The puppets moved about on stage in a very realistic manner. Well, realistic for creatures such as these. And that was the main allure of Zed's shows. His puppets appeared alive. Byff guessed that much of the audience might believe just that. But seeing as how he had the best seat here, combined with his impeccable vision, he was able to notice the nearly-invisible wires tied to each of the puppets limbs, allowing a hidden Zed to maneuver them as he wished. That did not ruin his experience though in the slightest. In fact, he was even more impressed with Zed's puppetry skills.

The first act started out slow and contained some light humor. It told the tale of how Marvin and Henrietta became acquainted. Marvin was a poor commoner, while Henrietta was royalty. It was love at first sight, though, their love was forbidden. Henrietta was being forced to marry a rich noble, for purely political reasons. Her parents cared nothing for their daughter's wishes or happiness.

The second and third act focused on the pairs blossoming but secret relationship. Byff could tell the adults in the audience were enthralled with the story, while the younglings were mesmerized by the puppets. The puppets did indeed make the show. One could easily forget they were puppets. The show would simply not be the same if Zed and his assistant acted out the story themselves.

There was a short intermission, while Zed closed a curtain to change the set on the stage. When the show resumed, they were treated to an elaborate set of the castle, where dwelt Henrietta.

The fourth act began with some action. Henrietta's parents had found out about Marvin and her father hired two assassins to eliminate him. Marvin was forced to defend himself with a blade and a fight ensued. The crowd gasped as Marvin slew his two would-be assassin's and an oddly-colored liquid poured forth from the slain puppet's bodies. It would have passed as blood for these strange creatures.

Another set change brought on the fifth act. The relationship between Henrietta and her parents was quickly deteriorating. She was being defiant and refusing to marry the noble, proclaiming her love for Marvin. Her parents were having none of that and she was now forbidden to leave the castle at all. But that did not stop the young couple from seeing one another. Marvin was an adept climber and was finding his way in.

Tension was building and the audience was on the edge of their seats for the sixth and final act. Most present were already aware that this was a tragic tale and there was to be no happy ending for Marvin and Henrietta.

Even Morg, who had seen this show before, from another location, was thoroughly enjoying it for a second time. Knowing how this tale concludes was not spoiling the experience. In fact, there were subtle differences, as

Zed was using two completely different puppets to play Marvin and Henrietta.

The audience sucked in air and held their breath when Marvin was captured within the castle. Henrietta's parents ordered the poor commoner to be hung. There was complete silence as Marvin gave his last speech, professing his love and that it was all worth it. He said he would do it all over again, with no regrets, even though it would mean his death.

Everyone gasped in unison as the platform dropped and Marvin swung from the rope, his eyes rolling back in his head. Henrietta shrieked from her balcony, having witnessed the entire horrific scene. She also gave one final speech, announcing that she was to join Marvin on the other side. The puppet fell from the balcony set to land on the stage with a sickening crunch. That same oddly-colored liquid began to pool under her head.

Byff found himself wiping a tear from his eye and then looking about embarrassingly to see if anyone had noticed. But there was nothing to feel ashamed about, there was not a dry eyestalk in the entire audience.

*　　*　　*　　*

As the last of the audience members had left, Zed's assistant began scrubbing the stage clean.

"I'd say that was a success," commented Zed, as he approached his assistant.

"Did you expect anything different?" she replied.

"We were very close to a catastrophe this time around."

"How so?"

"Our little Marvin had somehow cut three of the four wires attached to his limbs. He could have escaped. Imagine the panic that would have caused."

"Indeed. We should use a stronger material from now on."

"Perhaps we should use this story as well at next week's show? What do you think?" Zed wondered.

"Well, we are almost out of humans. I don't think we have any that would make a suitable Marvin or Henrietta."

Zed rubbed the side of his head in thought, with one of his many tentacles. "Alright, tomorrow we take a trip back to Earth to replenish our stock of humans."

Zed's assistant nodded and continued to scrub the disgusting red blood from the stage.

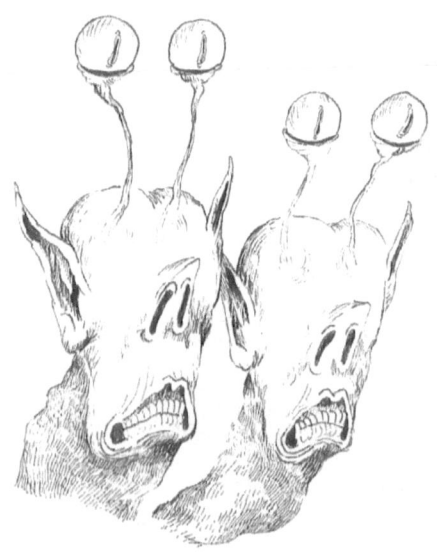

ALL THE SILVER IN
CLOVERTON

A fair-sized crowd had gathered inside the Foaming Mug
Tavern this night to wait out the horrendous storm, and to
down more than a few mugs of ale in the process. Shutters
rattled violently from the wicked wind and thunder shook
the very walls. But these residents did not care. Inside the
tavern a fire kept them warm and dry, and the drinks and
songs were flowing. All in all it was a joyous night, that is
until Joseph Benz arrived.

"Joe? What in the hell happened?" bellowed Norman
Bluth, who had been the closest to the front entrance and
the first to notice Joe enter.

Almost immediately, as other patrons turned to
regard the newcomer, the minstrels ceased their playing
and the townsfolk fell silent. All eyes were on Joseph, and
in particular, Joseph's rain-soaked, but also blood-stained
clothing.

"Joe, are you injured?" one man asked, as he rushed to the side of his friend, inspecting him for wounds.

"Not my blood," Joe finally answered. "It was from Markus Thornbury. Or, from what was left of him."

That drew gasps from the crowd and looks of astonishment and horror.

"What does that mean, Joe? What was left of him, you said," someone questioned.

Markus Thornbury was a farmer on the outskirts of Cloverton and a neighbor of Joseph's. He was a kind man and never wished ill-will on anyone. Those gathered in the tavern could not imagine anyone wishing to do the elderly farmer any harm.

"I-I heard a scream," Joe replied, eyes staring off into the distance. "Wasn't sure what I heard at first, what with this storm and all, but when I heard it a second time, I grabbed an axe and ran towards Markus's farm."

"And? What then, Joe? What did you find?" Adam pressed, when Joseph fell silent in thought.

The man swallowed hard and then continued. "Well, I am not rightly sure what I found, but I think it was whatever was left of poor old Markus."

"You think? What do you mean you think?"

"There was...pieces. I thought the carnage was from an animal at first, until I found articles of clothing amidst the gore. Markus's belt and strips from his favorite overcoat."

"What happened to him?"

"I think...I think something ate him."

Shouts of terror and shock reverberated around the tavern and one of the serving girls fainted.

"What could have done that?"

"Are you certain?"

"How do you know he was eaten?"

"A devil lurks in this storm!"

Panic overtook the townsfolk and the tavern erupted into chaos.

"Calm down everyone, calm down a moment," shouted Randal, an off-duty deputy. "Eric, go wake the Sheriff, the rest of us can grab our coats and go take a look-see for ourselves. Joe, can you show us where?"

Joseph reluctantly nodded, not wishing to visit the grisly scene a second time, but understood that others would need to investigate this mysterious murder. Eight men gathered their coats and followed Joseph out into the storm.

The following morning a mob of concerned citizens, presided over by Cloverton's mayor, met inside the town hall. Markus Thornbury was a very well-liked farmer, so naturally folk were upset and frightened.

"We want answers, Mayor!"

"Who did this?"

"Do we have a suspect?"

"There is a sadistic killer on the loose!"

"What are we doing to catch this person?"

"Nobody is safe!"

"Sheriff Blake and his men are doing all they can as we speak," Mayor Fenton reassured the gathering, once they had quieted down enough for him to be heard. "There is no reason for mass hysteria here. Whoever or whatever was responsible for this will be caught and brought to justice."

"Whatever? Are you suggesting an animal did this?"

"Because of the storm last night, no tracks anywhere

around Markus's property could be found. But the Sheriff's theory is possibly a bear, or even a pack of wolves."

"It was a werewolf," a deep voice stated from the rear of the crowd.

All heads turned to regard the imposing form of Bart Smithryn, a hunter and trapper who lived outside Cloverton and only made infrequent trips into town for supplies. He was reclusive and very few could call him friend.

"A werewolf?" someone responded. "Oh, good heavens, we are all doomed."

"Don't buy into this nonsense," the mayor said, rather annoyingly. "There is no such thing as werewolves. And Bart, stop feeding people with fool ideas."

"No man could have done that," Bart replied. "And there are no bears or wolves this close to Cloverton. I would know if there was."

"So that automatically makes this the crime of some mythical beast?"

"I have travelled much and seen many strange things. Some myths are not just myths. Two similar murders were reported in Westbridge months ago. My guess is that the beast has now moved our way," Bart reasoned.

"You have no proof of this. We have a wandering bear. You can't possibly know every animal that comes and goes around Cloverton. Now, everyone go back to your homes and stop worrying. Sheriff Blake and his men are on this."

As several tense weeks passed, the murder of Markus Thornbury remained unsolved, but the folk of Cloverton were settling back into their regular routines. Thoughts of some maniacal cannibal or a wild man-eating animal were pushed to the back of their minds. People were now walking the streets again at night. But the peace was not to last long. A relative found the remains of Bradley and Agatha Gates just outside their home. And much like the Markus murder, there was not much of them that remained.

Panic once again swept through Cloverton and an emergency meeting was called that very night in the town hall. Mayor Fenton found himself in front of an angry and frightened crowd for a second time. A grim-faced Sheriff Blake stood to his right.

"Settle down now. I am just as angry and disgusted as the rest of you. I want justice and gosh darnit we are going to get it," the mayor said.

"Anyone could be next!"

"Bradley and Agatha were good people!"

"We need to organize a posse and search the forests!"

"Never locked my doors at night ever. Now we all have to!"

"That cursed werewolf has struck again!"

"Who said that?" the mayor asked, furiously. "Who said it was a werewolf?"

Farmer Addams raised a hand but shied away.

"There is no such thing as werewolves! That is just a ridiculous myth. Children's stories!"

The hunter, Bart, shouldered his way to the front of the crowd. "I have spotted some peculiar tracks around the Gates's home. Prints the size of a man and sporting claws. The werewolf came in from the east and fled to the west. I lost the tracks in the rocky hills."

The townsfolk gasped all at once.

"You are making this terrible situation worse with your ridiculous claims, Mr. Smithryn," the mayor accused.

"They are not ridiculous. The sooner you accept we are hunting a werewolf, the sooner we can properly prepare to kill it before it gets anyone else."

"M-maybe he is right?"

"My Pappy told stories of werewolves."

"It is gonna kill us all dead!"

"See what you are doing with your wild fantasies, Mr. Smithryn? You are scaring these people more than they need to be. Can you back up any of these claims? Can you direct the Sheriff and his men to these werewolf tracks you speak of?"

"I can, if we are quick about it. Rain is beginning to fall."

Mayor Fenton cast a hateful glare toward the hunter. "Fine. Lead the Sheriff out there and let him and his men determine what made those tracks."

"I will be outside waiting."

The crowd erupted into panicked conversations while the mayor pulled the sheriff aside. "What do we know about this Mr. Smithryn?"

"Not too much," Sheriff Blake replied. "Keeps to himself mostly and comes into town only rarely."

"And yet he was in town both times when there were murders. Now he is concocting stories of a werewolf, to what end?"

"What are you suggesting, Mayor?"

"I am suggesting he is very suspicious. Perhaps he is attempting to deflect suspicion away from himself. He may have even left false tracks to support his preposterous claims. Watch him closely, Sheriff. Very, very closely."

The sheriff nodded and motioned for two deputies to follow him out. Mayor Fenton remained in the town hall and did his best to reassure the townsfolk that they would be safe and there was no werewolf stalking the residents of Cloverton.

An hour later, Sheriff Blake arrived at the mayor's office and found the light on. Mayor Fenton could find little sleep this night.

"What did you find, Sheriff?"

"Well, the rain picked up before we got out there. Much of the tracks had been washed away but what we did see were peculiar, indeed."

"In what way?"

"No human made those tracks and no animal that I am aware of. It did appear as if it was a cross between the two."

The mayor waved his hands in dismissal. "He must have made those false tracks, don't you see that?"

"Anything is possible, but I have heard tales of werewolves before."

"Oh, good heavens, not you too? We are not living in a fairy-tale world."

"I am just saying."

"I know what you are saying, Sheriff, and you sound just as ridiculous as that hunter. We are obviously dealing with a deranged human here and not some animal. If it were a bear or a pack of wolves you would have found those tracks. And frankly, I find this deeply disturbing that it is a human that is capable of these atrocious acts. We need this man caught, Sheriff, and we need it soon. Do you hear me?"

"Yes, Mayor."

"Good. And pay close attention to that Mr. Smithryn. And I want no more talk of werewolves."

Two uneventful weeks later, Mayor Fenton stepped out of his office to breathe in the fresh morning air, when he noticed a mob gathered around the sheriff's office. He rushed over immediately and pushed his way inside.

"What is this about?"

Sheriff Blake lead the mayor back into the room that housed their cells, which were currently empty.

"There was another murder last night. Heinrich Franz. And like the others, there was not much left of him."

"When did you learn of this?"

"Shortly after midnight."

"Why didn't you wake me?"

"Well, I went by your house last night but you weren't there."

"Oh, right, I slept in my office last night."

"We have a break this time, though."

"Oh? What break?"

"We have a witness this time. Old Man Crumby heard screams and ran over to Heinrich's place with his shotgun. He claims to have seen a giant hairy beast fleeing the scene. A beast that walked on two legs. Crumby got off a shot and said he hit him dead center in the back."

"Well then, nobody could survive that. There must be a body out there to find."

The Sheriff shook his head. "Old Man Crumby said the beast never even slowed. His buckshot had no effect. Me and my men combed that entire area and found nothing, save those peculiar tracks again, which we lost in the river."

"Old Man Crumby is addled. A giant hairy beast? Are we to truly believe that is what he saw?"

The sheriff shrugged.

The mayor gritted his teeth. "I have to go out there and quiet that mob, and I'll be damned if I am going to tell them we are looking for a giant hairy beast. If you ask me, that describes Bart Smithryn. Speaking of which, does anyone know where he was last night?"

"No."

"No? Well maybe you and your men should be out there looking for him. He's probably halfway to Doverport by now, on the run."

Folk found little sleep in the coming days. Many stayed indoors, only peeking at the outside world from drawn curtains. Doors were barricaded. Most windows were boarded. People armed themselves and traveled in groups when it was necessary to be out. Strength in numbers was their mindset. Life in Cloverton was now drastically changed. Who would be next, was on everyone's mind.

One sunny afternoon, Mayor Fenton and Sheriff Blake was scheduled to address nearly the entire town, outside the sheriff's office, with an update. Townsfolk wore weeks-worth of worry and lack of sleep upon their faces. They carried pitchforks, shotguns, pistols, knives, and a variety of other homemade makeshift weapons. They wanted answers and they wanted it now.

"I am afraid to say, that our murderer is still on the loose," the mayor announced. "But rest assured, we are doing everything possible to keep you all safe. There has not been any new attacks as of late. Perhaps, our killer has moved on? We can only hope."

"A full moon is nearly upon on us again and the werewolf will feed," a deep and familiar voice stated from the rear of the gathering.

Folk gasped and the mayor sighed.

"Sheriff Blake, arrest Bart Smithryn, now," Mayor Fenton demanded.

"On what grounds?" the sheriff inquired.

"The man is a suspect!"

"Based on what?"

"Where has been lately? He vanished after the last murder."

"I didn't vanish," Bart replied. "I do not live in town. And you would all do well to heed my warning. Especially before the next full moon which is only days away."

Faces went pale.

Mayor Fenton waved his hands in dismissal. "Not all of the murders were committed during a full moon, Mr. Smithryn, so there goes that theory."

"Werewolves do not only change during the full moon but the full moon is a guaranteed night when it will."

"We are all armed," one person told the hunter, raising his shotgun in the air. "This killer or this werewolf will find no easy prey this time. We are prepared."

Many people nodded in agreement, hoisting their weapons above their heads.

"Let him come," another said, bravely.

Bart only shook his head. "Your weapons are useless against the beast."

"Useless? What do you mean?"

"Only silver can harm a werewolf," the hunter replied.

Mayor Fenton interjected. "We are not going to stand here and discuss werewolves! Have all you people lost your minds? This man is sowing fear among you for some nefarious purpose."

"But we don't have any silver weapons," one man said to Bart, completely ignoring the mayor. "How can we defend ourselves?"

"We need to make silver weapons," Bart answered. "We need to gather every bit of silver in Cloverton in order to melt it down and craft it into weapons. Silver bullets. Silver knives. Silver speartips. Silver arrows. Anything we can think of. And we need to do it soon. Before the next full moon."

"This is utter nonsense!" shouted the mayor.

"If I am wrong, what do you have to lose?"

Mayor Fenton turned to Sheriff Blake. "Are you going to entertain this madness?"

The sheriff shrugged. "It can't hurt. Like he said, what do we have to lose?"

"All your silver for one thing!"

The mayor stormed off as everyone paid him no further heed and gathered around Bart Smithryn.

"What do we need?" several folk asked.

"Gather any silver you own. Coins. Cutlery. Dishware. Anything. Bring it here to the Sheriff's office. We will need to melt it all down and hope there is enough to arm each of you with a silver weapon."

And the citizens of Cloverton did just that, despite the protests of their mayor. Over the next two days, three wagons in front of the Sheriff's Office were filled with various silver items that were generously donated by frightened townsfolk.

The day before the next full moon, armed deputies moved the wagons full of silver to a barn on the outskirts of town. This location would serve as a facility to melt down the silver and craft weapons to combat the werewolf. The barn's whereabouts were kept secret aside from a select few, to protect against any would-be thieves.

When the sun disappeared later that evening, a frustrated Mayor Fenton slipped out the backdoor of his house for some fresh air. He was surprised to find two deputies standing guard.

"What are you both doing here?"

"Orders from Sheriff Blake, Mr. Mayor. We are to keep you safe. Another two men are posted at the front of your house."

"Four men wasting time at my house? Your time could be better spent looking for the real killer, which I might add, is not a werewolf!"

"You are in charge of Cloverton, sir, your safety is paramount."

"Nonsense! You men need to go and watch Bart Smithryn! He is the one that needs watching. I do not trust that man at all."

"But, Sheriff Blake said...,"

"I don't care what Sheriff Blake said. Who did you just say was in charge of Cloverton? Now, go find Bart and keep an eye on his movements if you still want to be employed in the morning."

"Yes, Mr. Mayor, right away, sir."

*　　*　　*　　*

Sheriff Blake paced back and forth within the barn

full of silver, wondering if they were going to have enough time to melt it all down and craft the necessary weapons. He dispatched his other deputies to go and fetch the blacksmiths and bring them back to the barn so they could begin the tedious process.

The sheriff heard someone enter the barn behind him and spoke as he turned. "We have to start unloading these wagons right away."

"That won't be necessary," the newcomer stated.

"What are you doing here? I had men watching you."

"Not anymore. I have come for the silver."

"The blacksmiths are on their way. Help me get these wagons unloaded so they can start their work as soon as they get here."

"There won't be any silver when they get here."

"What are you talking about?"

"I am taking these wagons. I am going to bury all this silver where nobody can ever find it. I cannot have these townsfolk armed with any silver weapons. That would not be good for me."

Sheriff Blake's eyes widened as he realized the killer was standing before him and he drew his pistol. Bart Smithryn growled a most feral growl as the shirt ripped from his body and coarse-brown hair began to sprout from his skin. His fingers elongated into razor-sharp claws and when he growled again, his mouth was full of fangs.

The sheriff fired his weapon and his aim was true, but the bullet was not a silver bullet. The werewolf sprang toward him unharmed. Sheriff Blake screamed.

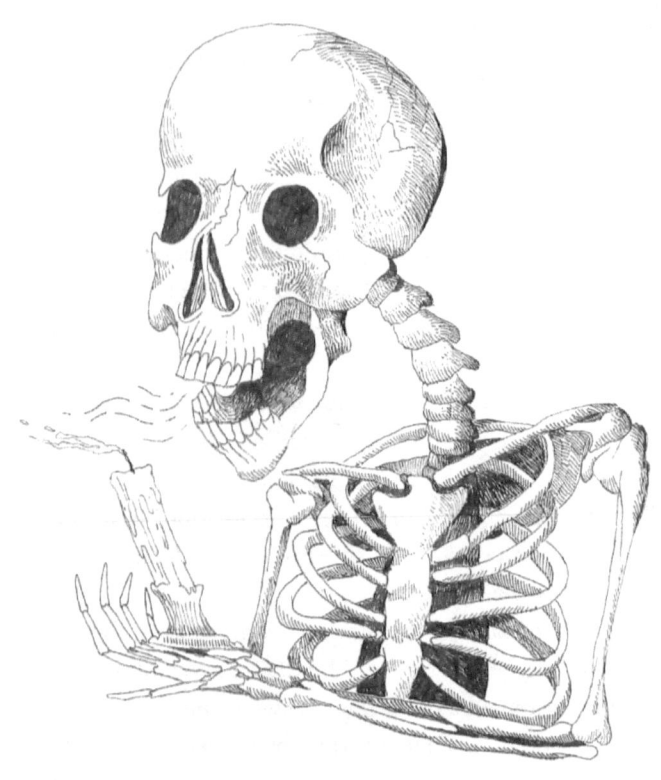

ABOUT THE AUTHOR

Jeremy was born in Scarborough, Ontario, Canada. He started creating his own characters and writing his own stories by the age of 9. He is a boxing fanatic, having been an amateur boxer, and is now a professional boxing judge. In his spare time when not watching boxing, or reruns of Lost in Space and Rocket Robin Hood, Jeremy tries to find time to write some of the many stories floating around in his head.